PARACHUTE KIDS

BETTY C. TANG

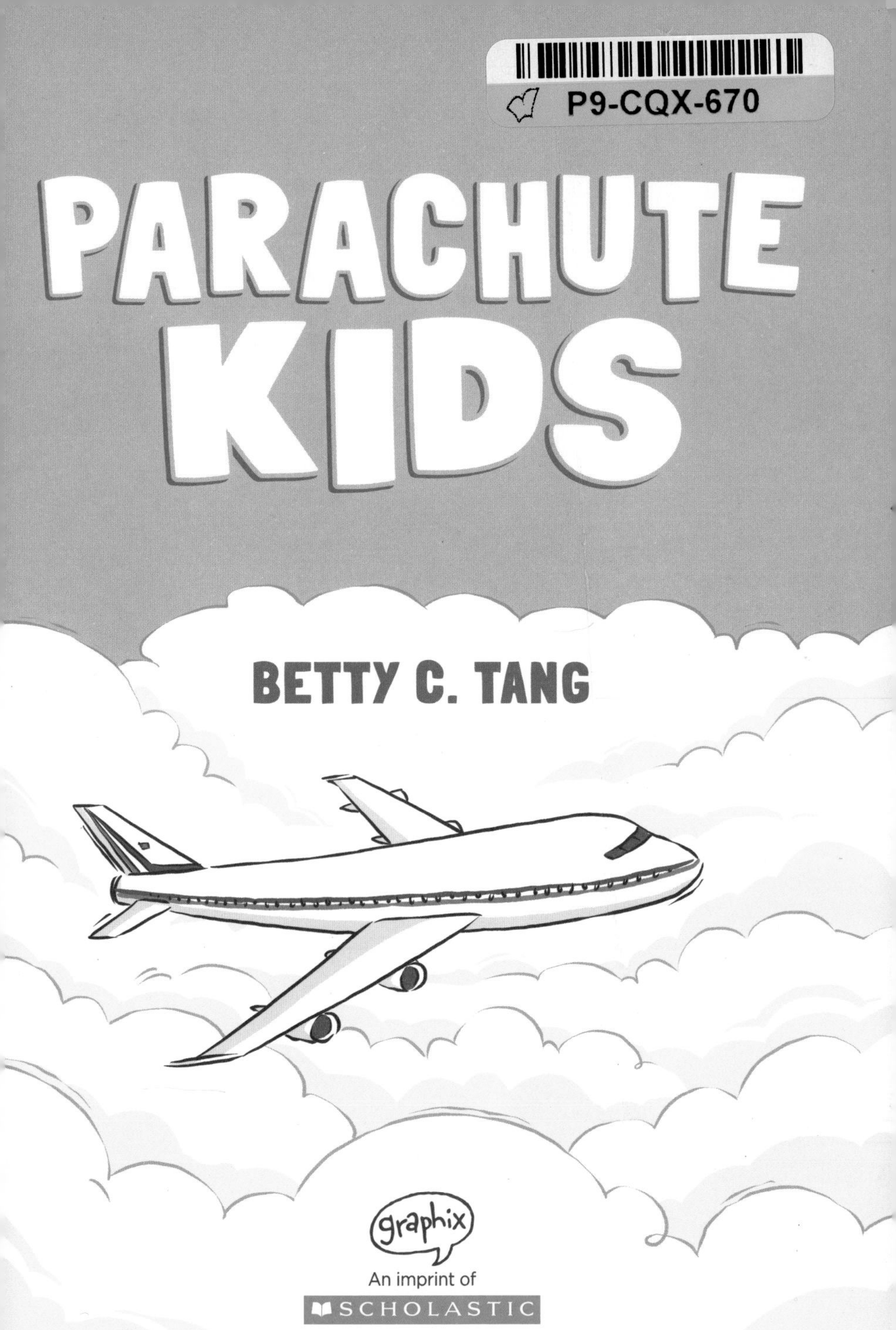

graphix
An imprint of
SCHOLASTIC

All rights reserved. Published by Graphix, an imprint of Scholastic Inc., *Publishers since 1920*. SCHOLASTIC, GRAPHIX, and associated logos are trademarks and/or registered trademarks of Scholastic Inc.

The publisher does not have any control over and does not assume any responsibility for author or third-party websites or their content.

Library of Congress Cataloging-in-Publication Data: 2022004016
ISBN 978-1-338-83269-3 (hardcover) | ISBN 978-1-338-83268-6 (paperback)
10 9 8 7 6 5 4 3 2 1   23 24 25 26 27

Printed in China   62 | First edition, April 2023

Edited by Tracy Mack | Lettering by Betty C. Tang | Book design by Carina Taylor
Creative Director: Phil Falco | Publisher: David Saylor

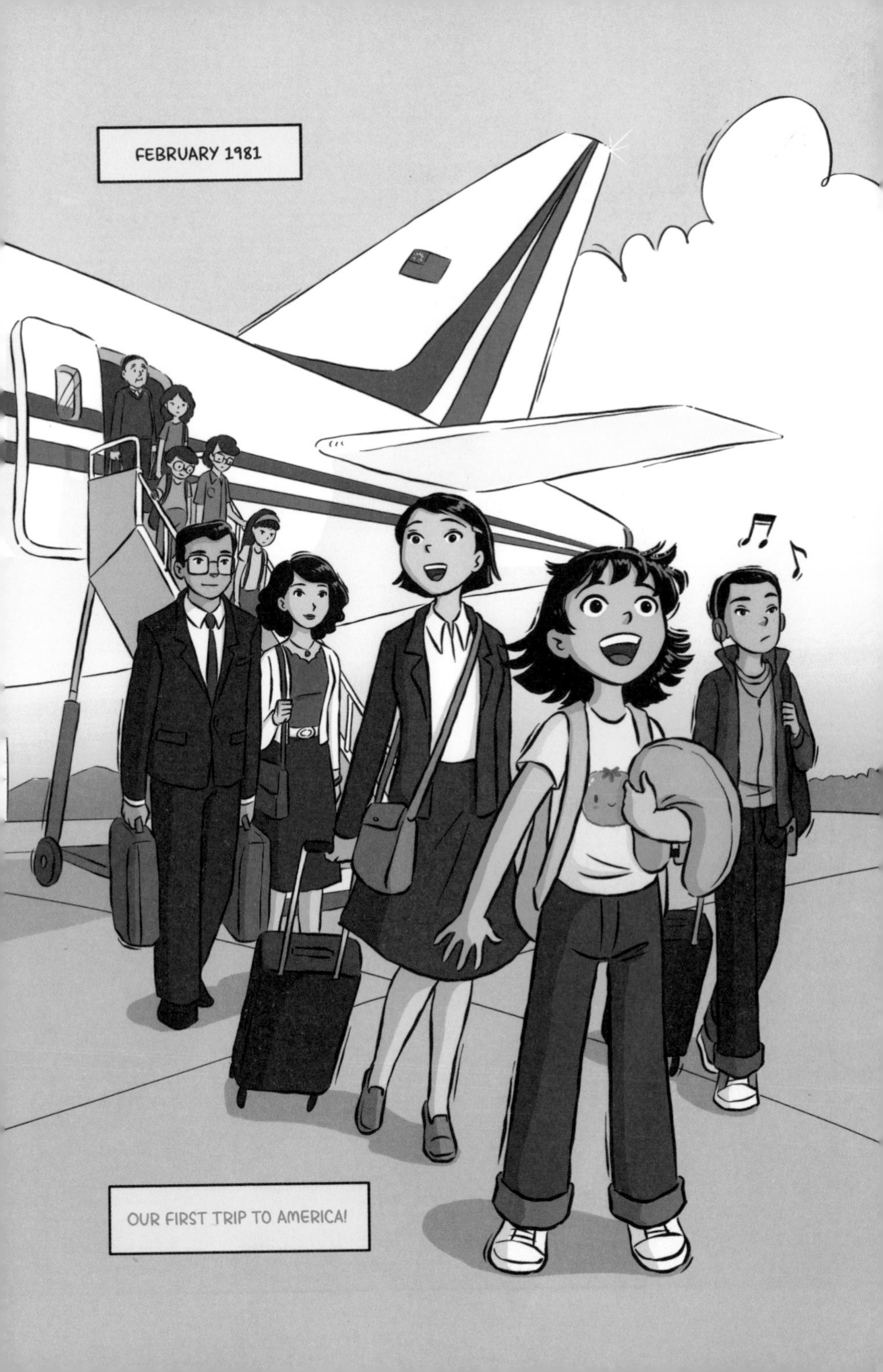
FEBRUARY 1981
OUR FIRST TRIP TO AMERICA!

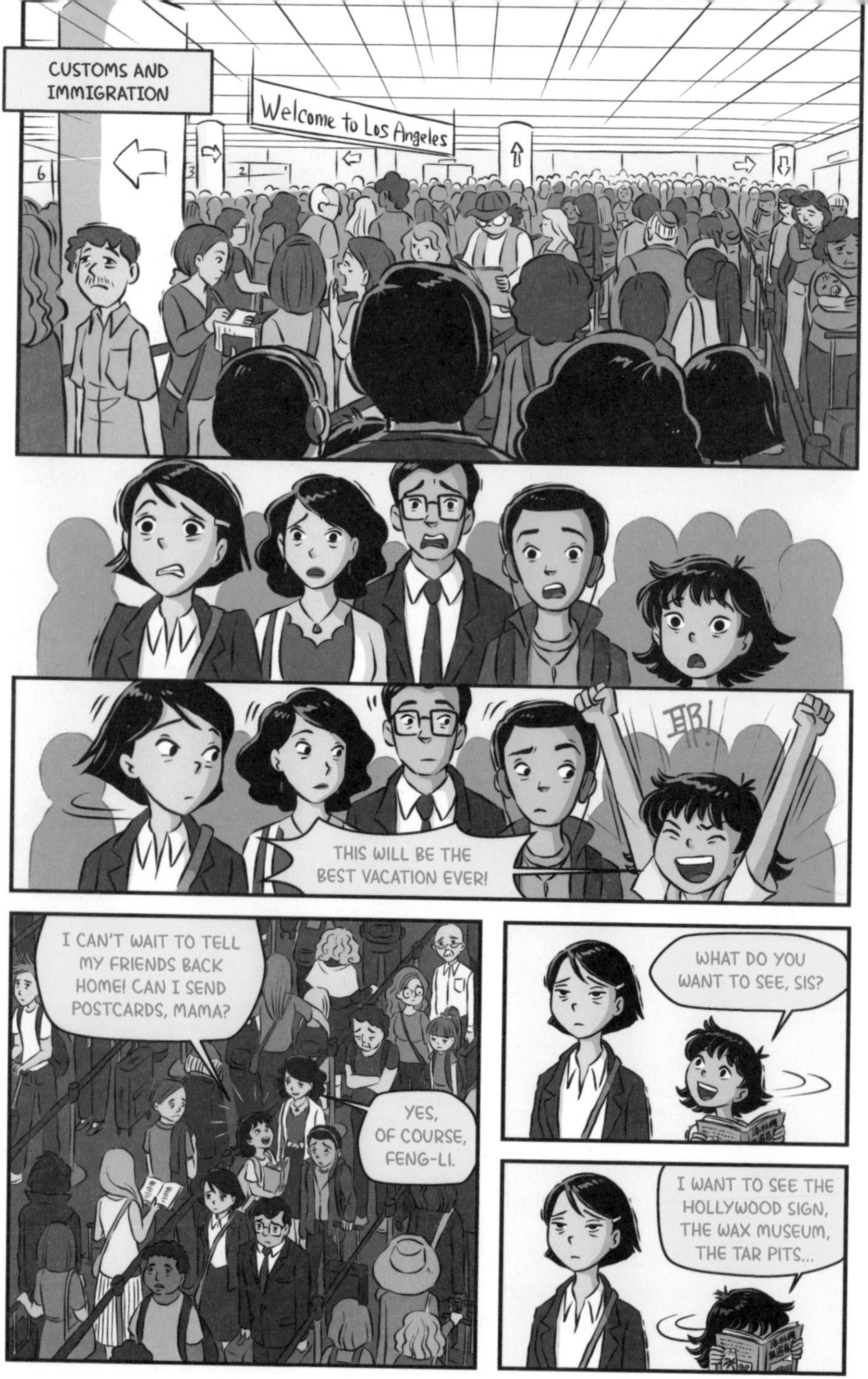
CUSTOMS AND IMMIGRATION
Welcome to Los Angeles
耶!
THIS WILL BE THE BEST VACATION EVER!
I CAN'T WAIT TO TELL MY FRIENDS BACK HOME! CAN I SEND POSTCARDS, MAMA?
YES, OF COURSE, FENG-LI.
WHAT DO YOU WANT TO SEE, SIS?
I WANT TO SEE THE HOLLYWOOD SIGN, THE WAX MUSEUM, THE TAR PITS...

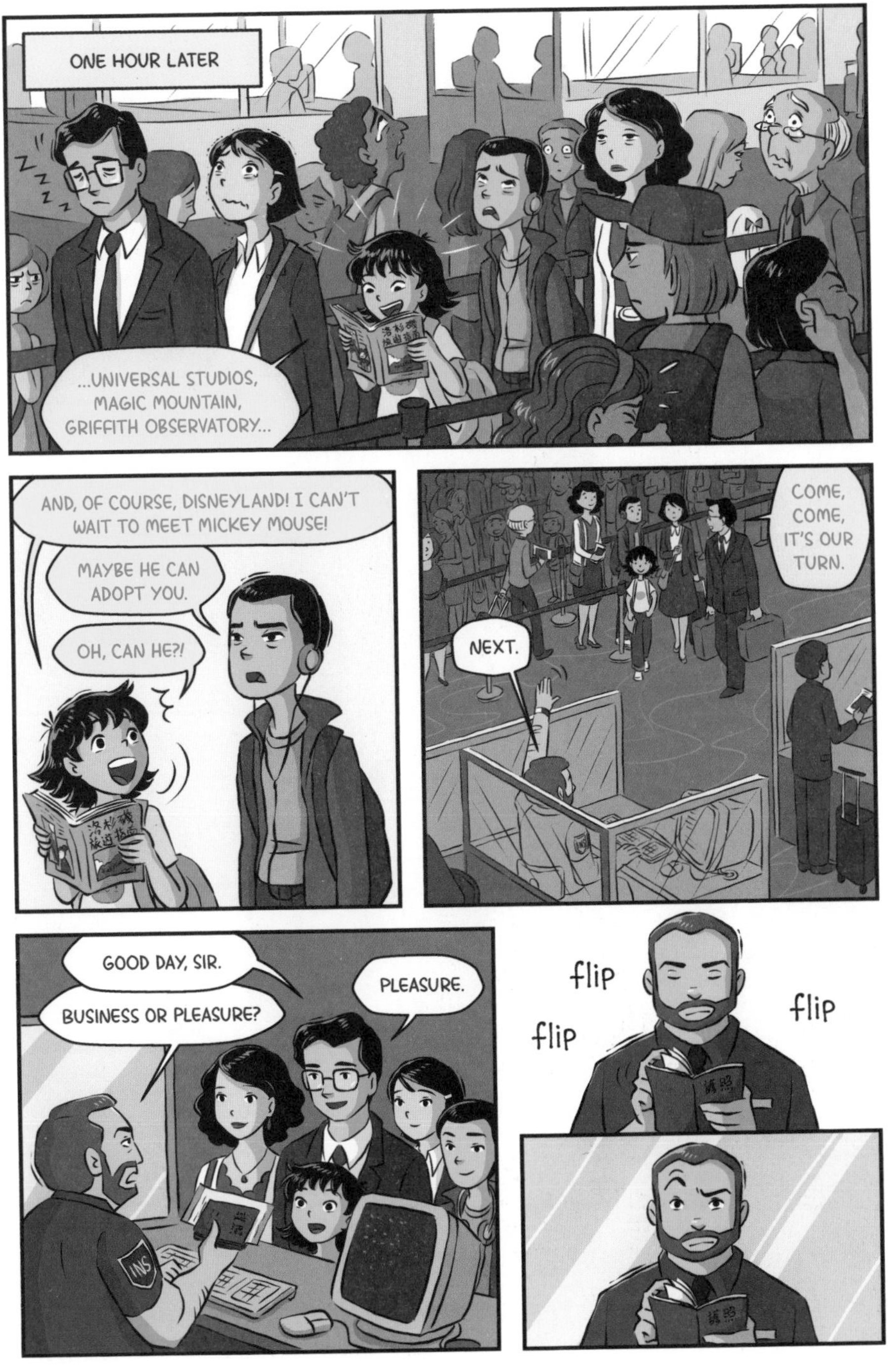
ONE HOUR LATER
...UNIVERSAL STUDIOS, MAGIC MOUNTAIN, GRIFFITH OBSERVATORY...
AND, OF COURSE, DISNEYLAND! I CAN'T WAIT TO MEET MICKEY MOUSE!
MAYBE HE CAN ADOPT YOU.
OH, CAN HE?!
COME, COME, IT'S OUR TURN.
NEXT.
GOOD DAY, SIR.
BUSINESS OR PLEASURE?
PLEASURE.
flip
flip
flip

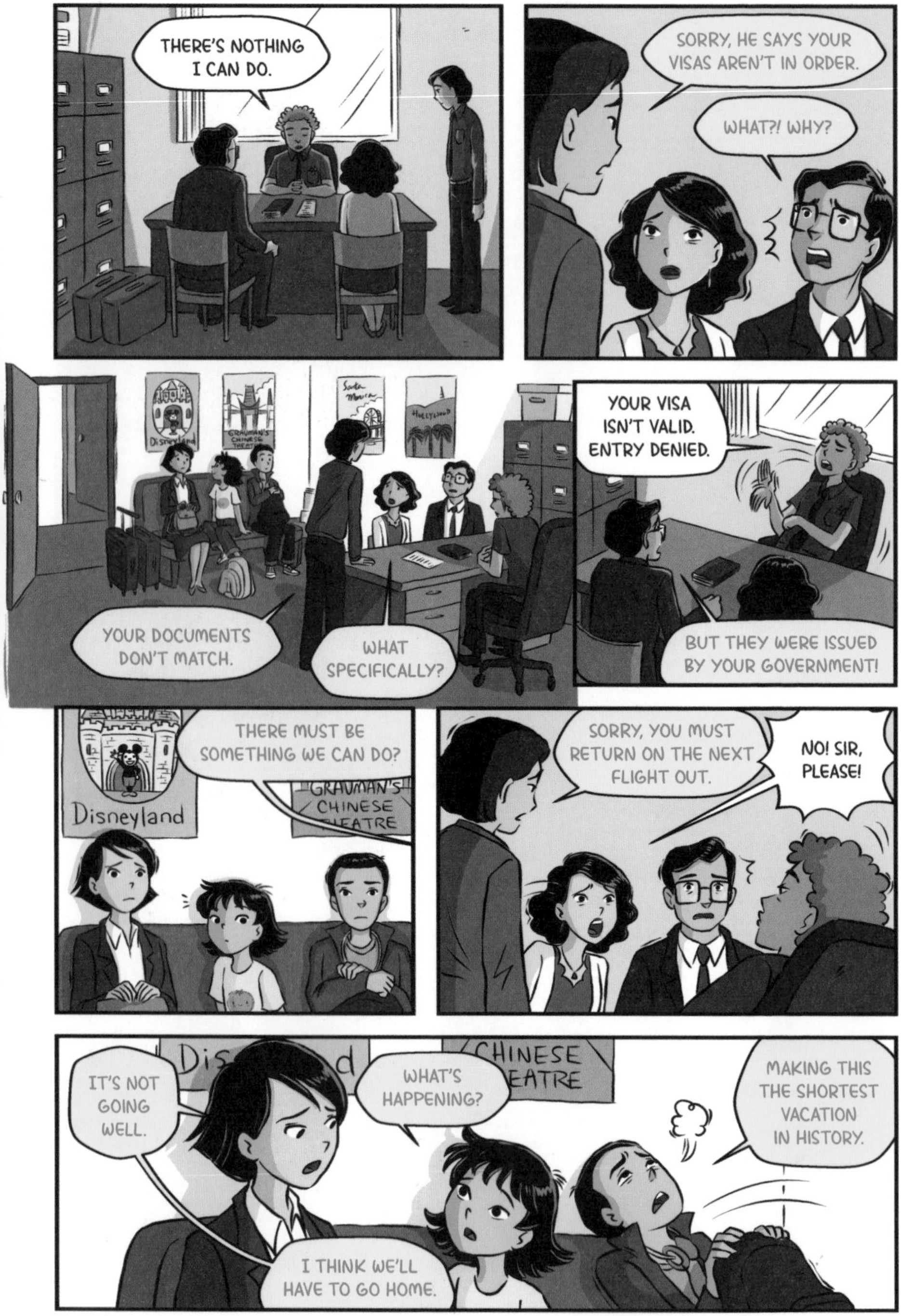
THERE'S NOTHING I CAN DO.
SORRY, HE SAYS YOUR VISAS AREN'T IN ORDER.
WHAT?! WHY?
Disneyland
GRAUMAN'S CHINESE THEATRE
Santa Monica
Hollywood
YOUR DOCUMENTS DON'T MATCH.
WHAT SPECIFICALLY?
YOUR VISA ISN'T VALID. ENTRY DENIED.
BUT THEY WERE ISSUED BY YOUR GOVERNMENT!
Disneyland
GRAUMAN'S CHINESE THEATRE
THERE MUST BE SOMETHING WE CAN DO?
SORRY, YOU MUST RETURN ON THE NEXT FLIGHT OUT.
NO! SIR, PLEASE!
CHINESE
IT'S NOT GOING WELL.
WHAT'S HAPPENING?
MAKING THIS THE SHORTEST VACATION IN HISTORY.
I THINK WE'LL HAVE TO GO HOME.

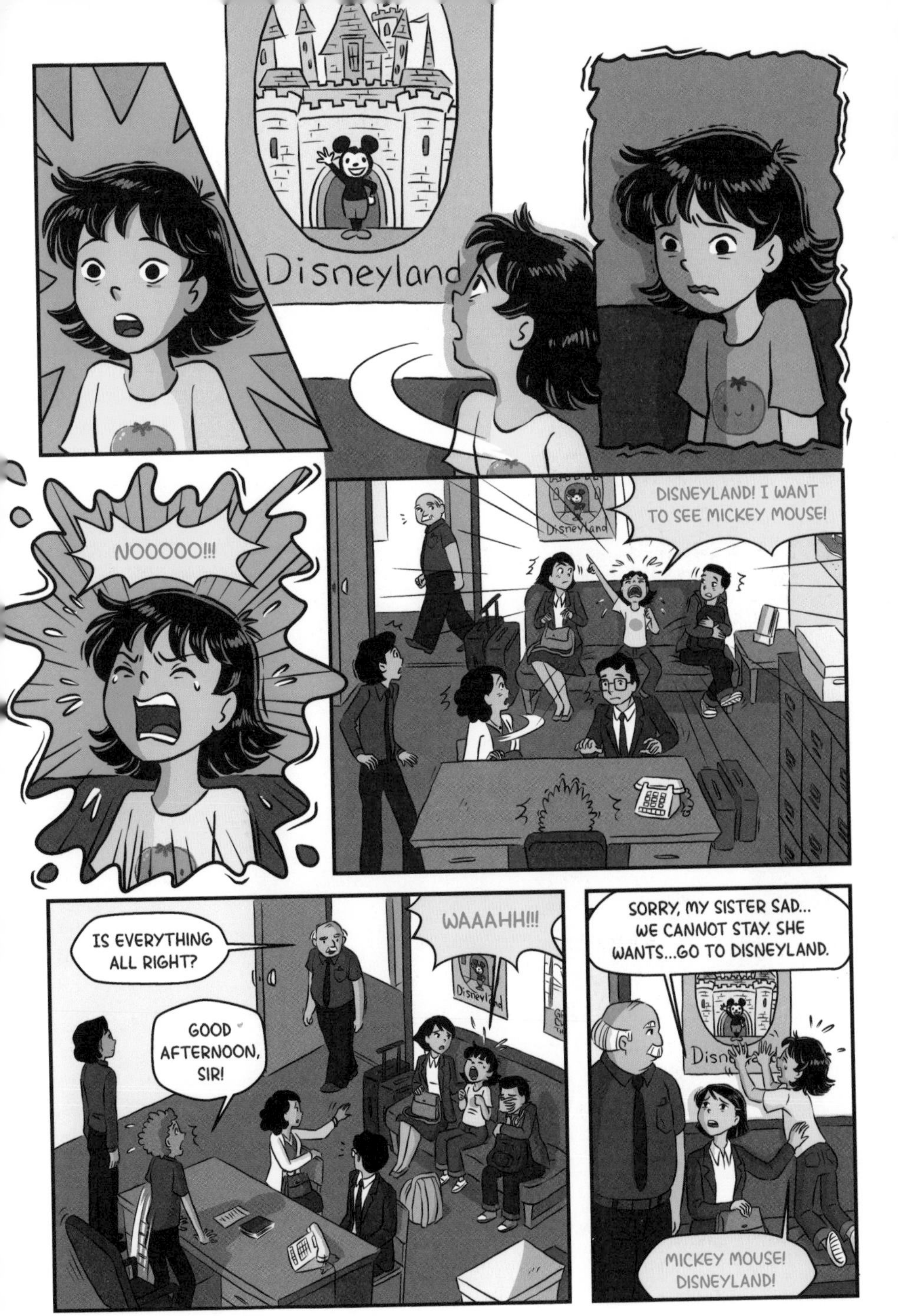

Disneyland
NOOOOO!!!
Disneyland
DISNEYLAND! I WANT TO SEE MICKEY MOUSE!
IS EVERYTHING ALL RIGHT?
WAAAHH!!!
GOOD AFTERNOON, SIR!
Disneyland
SORRY, MY SISTER SAD... WE CANNOT STAY. SHE WANTS...GO TO DISNEYLAND.
MICKEY MOUSE! DISNEYLAND!

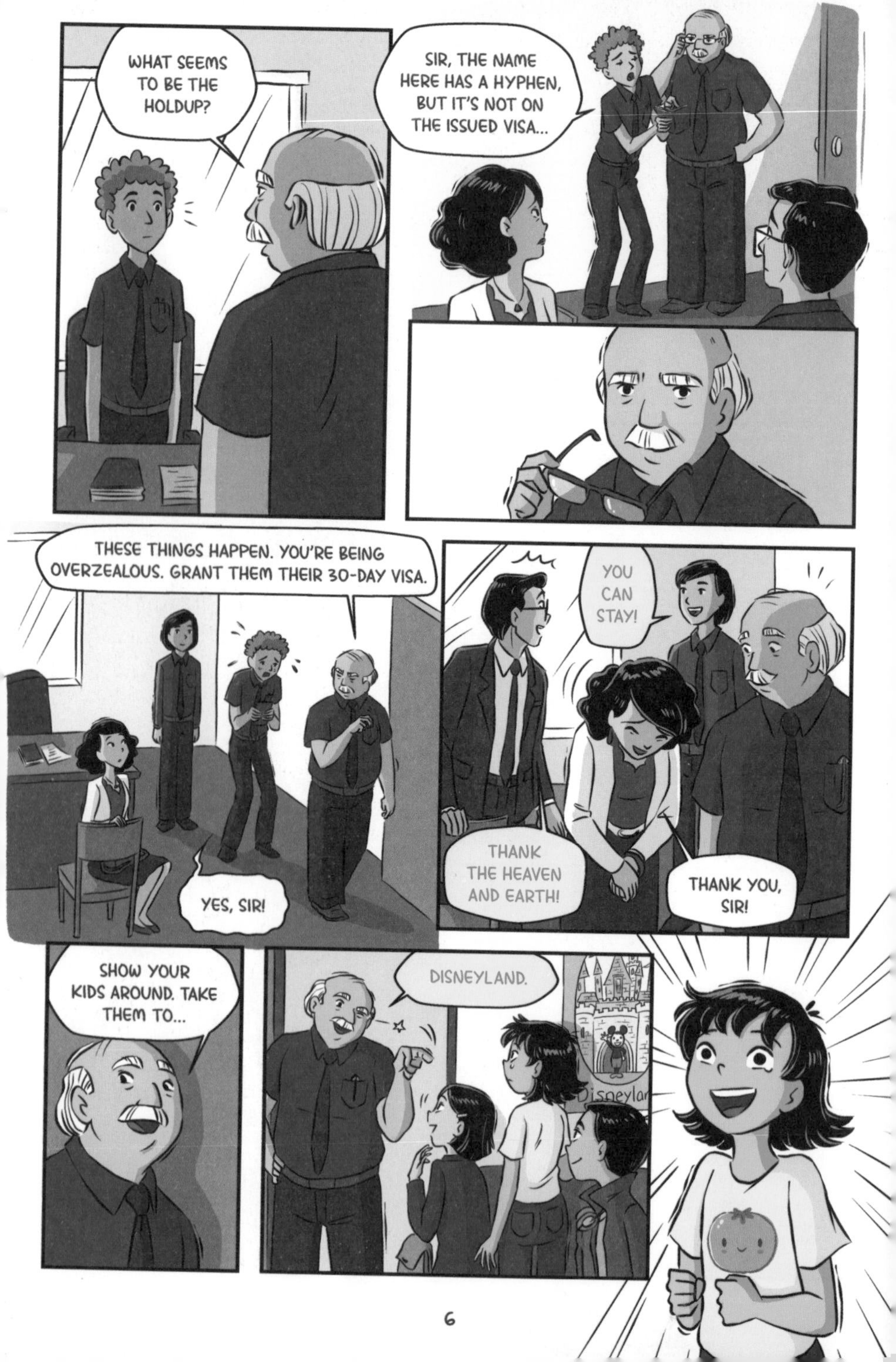
WHAT SEEMS TO BE THE HOLDUP?
SIR, THE NAME HERE HAS A HYPHEN, BUT IT'S NOT ON THE ISSUED VISA...
THESE THINGS HAPPEN. YOU'RE BEING OVERZEALOUS. GRANT THEM THEIR 30-DAY VISA.
YES, SIR!
YOU CAN STAY!
THANK THE HEAVEN AND EARTH!
THANK YOU, SIR!
SHOW YOUR KIDS AROUND. TAKE THEM TO...
DISNEYLAND.
Disneylan

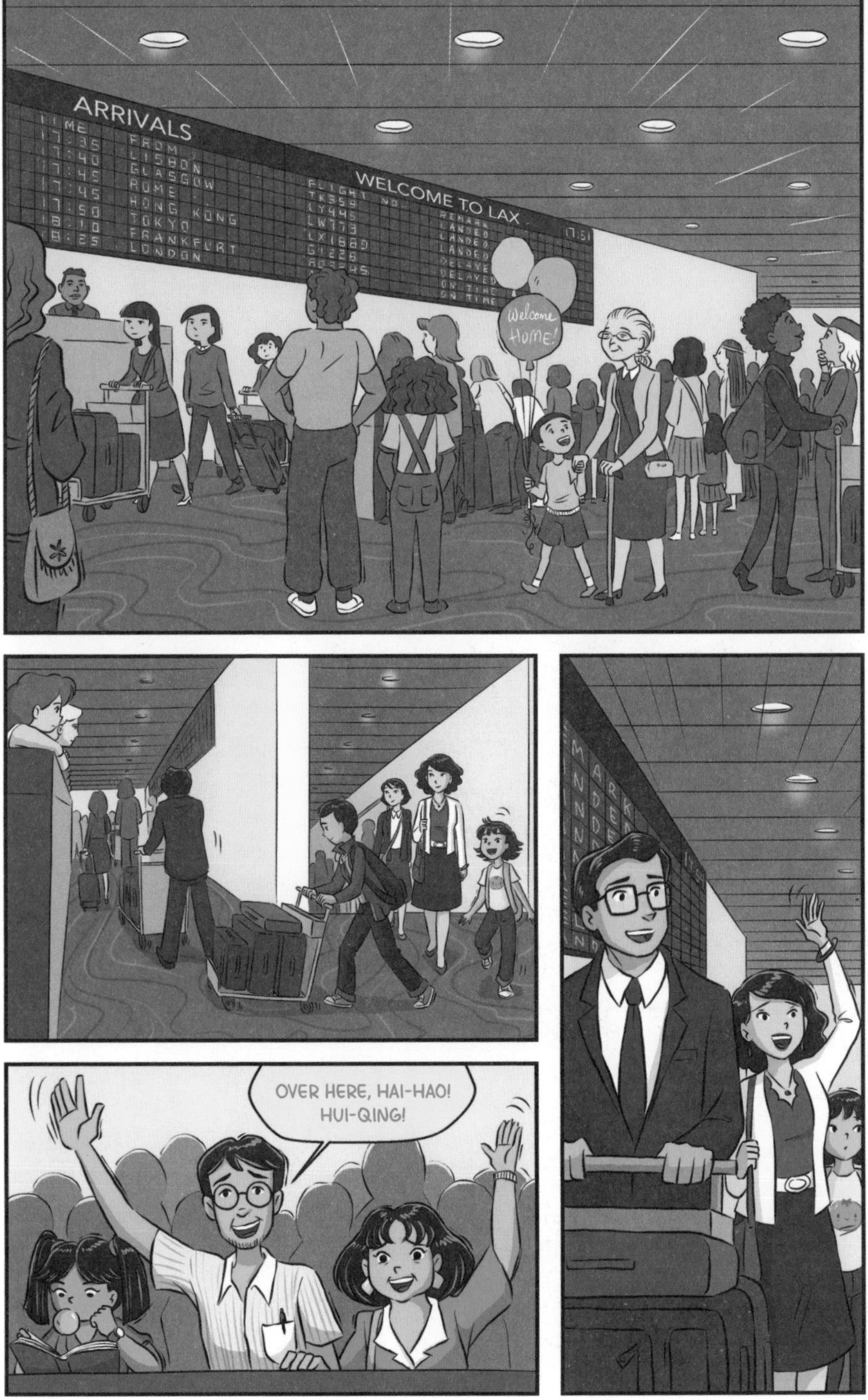
ARRIVALS
TIME FROM
17:35 LISBON
17:40 GLASGOW
17:45 ROME
17:45 HONG KONG
17:50 TOKYO
18:10 FRANKFURT
18:25 LONDON
WELCOME TO LAX
LANDED
LANDED
LANDED
DELAYED
DELAYED
ON TIME
ON TIME
Welcome Home!
OVER HERE, HAI-HAO! HUI-QING!

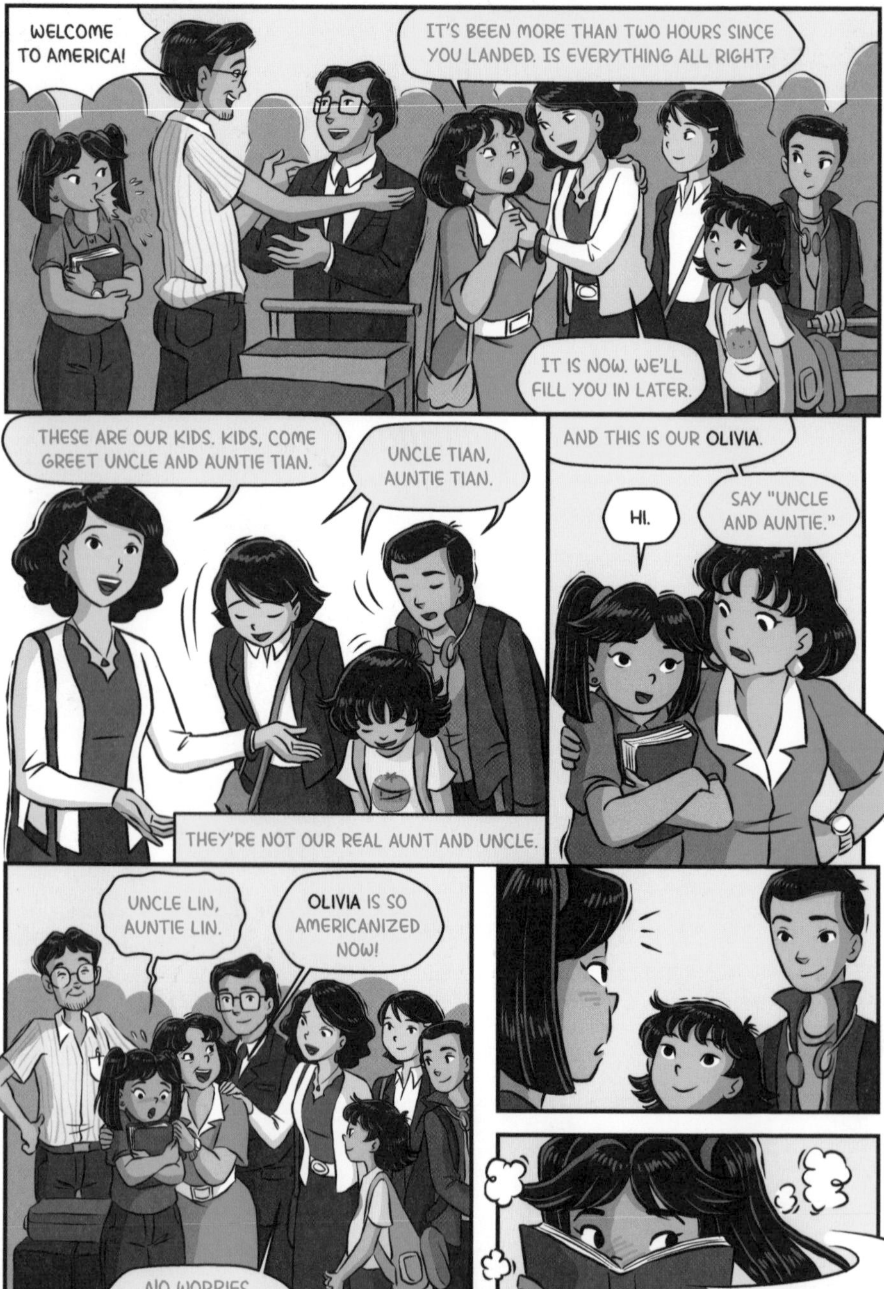
WELCOME TO AMERICA!
IT'S BEEN MORE THAN TWO HOURS SINCE YOU LANDED. IS EVERYTHING ALL RIGHT?
IT IS NOW. WE'LL FILL YOU IN LATER.
THESE ARE OUR KIDS. KIDS, COME GREET UNCLE AND AUNTIE TIAN.
UNCLE TIAN, AUNTIE TIAN.
THEY'RE NOT OUR REAL AUNT AND UNCLE.
AND THIS IS OUR OLIVIA.
HI.
SAY "UNCLE AND AUNTIE."
UNCLE LIN, AUNTIE LIN.
OLIVIA IS SO AMERICANIZED NOW!
NO WORRIES. SHE PRACTICALLY GREW UP HERE!

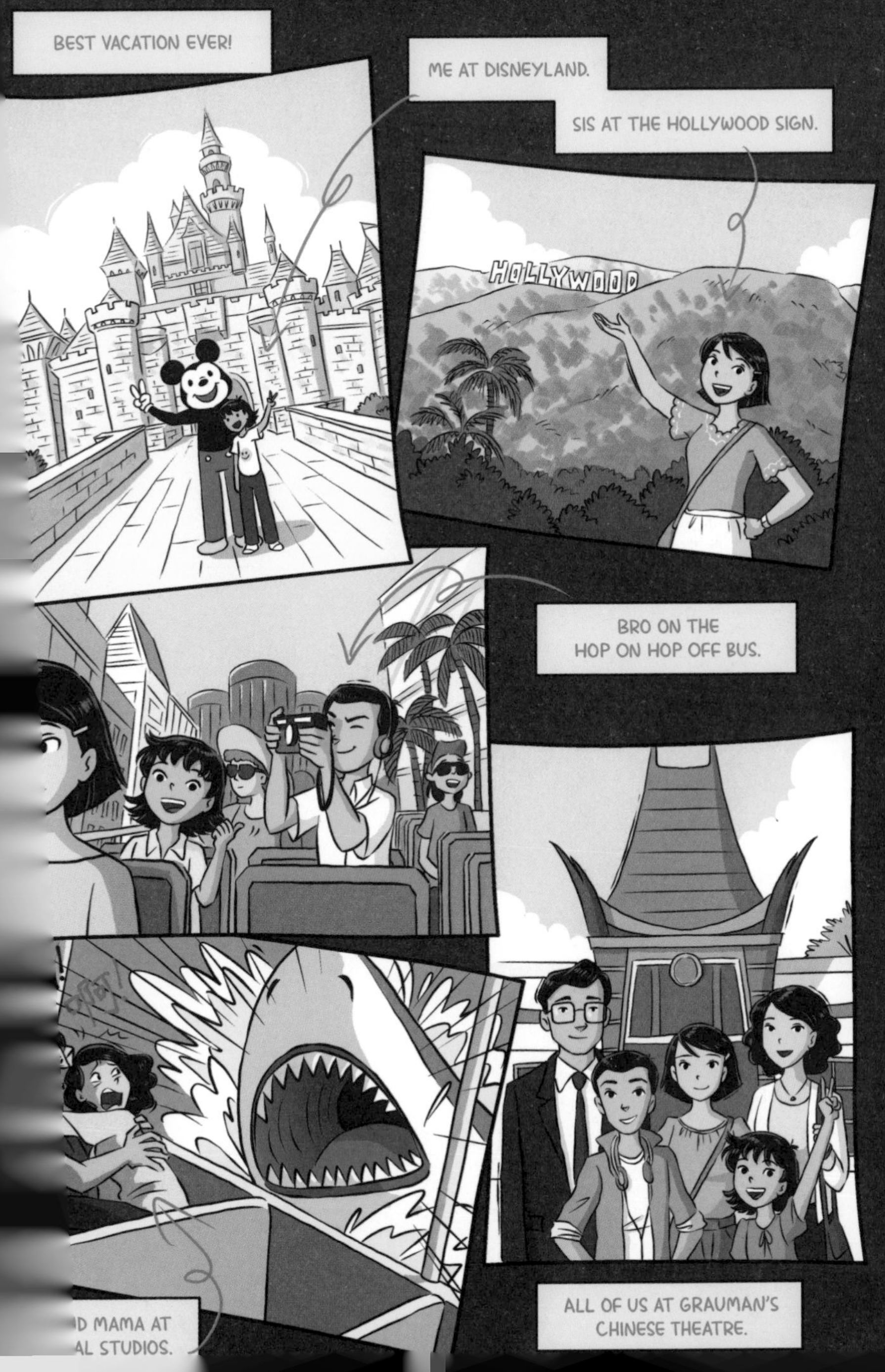
BEST VACATION EVER!
ME AT DISNEYLAND.
SIS AT THE HOLLYWOOD SIGN.
HOLLYWOOD
BRO ON THE
HOP ON HOP OFF BUS.
D MAMA AT
AL STUDIOS.
ALL OF US AT GRAUMAN'S
CHINESE THEATRE.

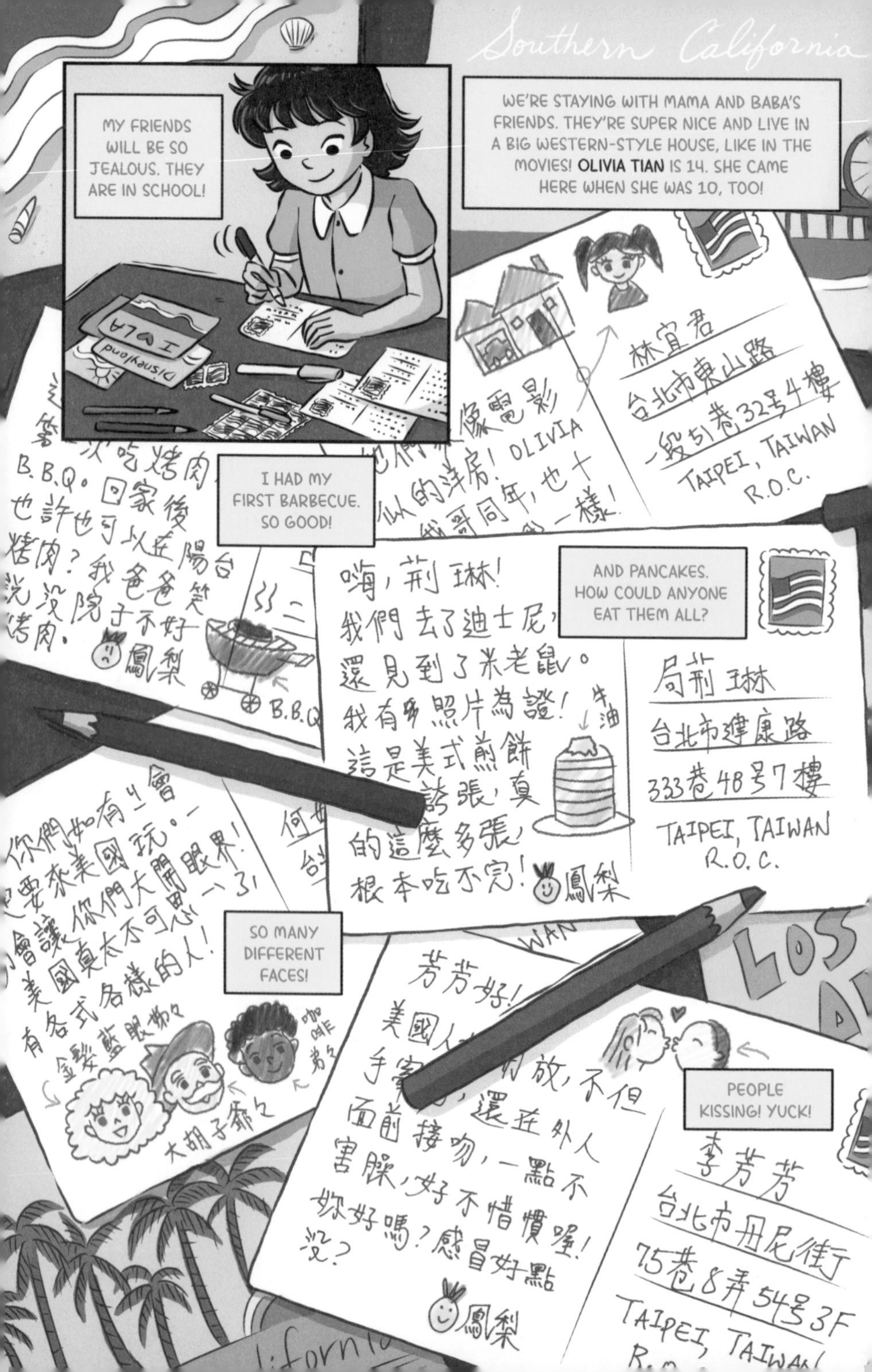
Southern California
MY FRIENDS WILL BE SO JEALOUS. THEY ARE IN SCHOOL!
I ♥ LA
Disneyland
WE'RE STAYING WITH MAMA AND BABA'S FRIENDS. THEY'RE SUPER NICE AND LIVE IN A BIG WESTERN-STYLE HOUSE, LIKE IN THE MOVIES! **OLIVIA TIAN** IS 14. SHE CAME HERE WHEN SHE WAS 10, TOO!
像電影
的洋房! OLIVIA
同年, 也十
一樣!
林宜君
台北市東山路
一段51巷32号4樓
TAIPEI, TAIWAN
R.O.C.
I HAD MY FIRST BARBECUE. SO GOOD!
B.B.Q。回家後
也許也可以在陽台
烤肉? 我爸爸笑
說沒院子不好
烤肉。
鳳梨
B.B.Q
AND PANCAKES. HOW COULD ANYONE EAT THEM ALL?
嗨, 荊琳!
我們去了迪士尼,
還見到了米老鼠。
我有照片為證!
這是美式煎餅
誇張, 真
的這麼多張!
根本吃不完!
鳳梨
牛油
周荊琳
台北市建康路
333巷48号7樓
TAIPEI, TAIWAN
R.O.C.
你們如有機會
要來美國玩。
會讓你們大開眼界!
美國真太不可思議了!
有各式各樣的人!
金髮藍眼珠
咖啡色
大胡子爺爺
SO MANY DIFFERENT FACES!
芳芳好!
美國人
放, 不但
還在外人
面前接吻, 一點不
害羞, 好不習慣喔!
妳好嗎? 感冒好點
沒?
鳳梨
PEOPLE KISSING! YUCK!
李芳芳
台北市丹尼街
75巷8弄54号3F
TAIPEI, TAIWAN
LOS

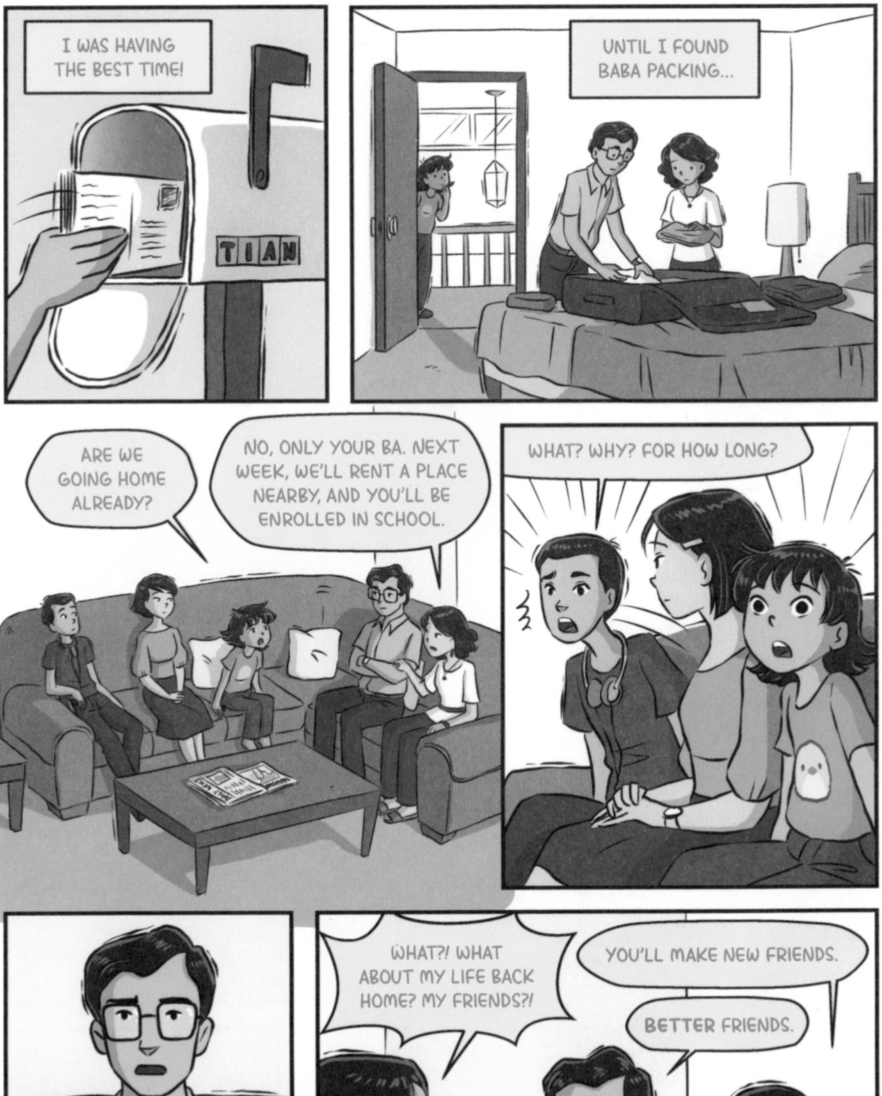
I WAS HAVING THE BEST TIME!
TIAN
UNTIL I FOUND BABA PACKING...
ARE WE GOING HOME ALREADY?
NO, ONLY YOUR BA. NEXT WEEK, WE'LL RENT A PLACE NEARBY, AND YOU'LL BE ENROLLED IN SCHOOL.
WHAT? WHY? FOR HOW LONG?
AMERICA WILL BE YOUR NEW HOME. WE'VE BROUGHT YOU HERE FOR A BETTER LIFE AND OPPORTUNITIES--
WHAT?! WHAT ABOUT MY LIFE BACK HOME? MY FRIENDS?!
YOU'LL MAKE NEW FRIENDS.
BETTER FRIENDS.

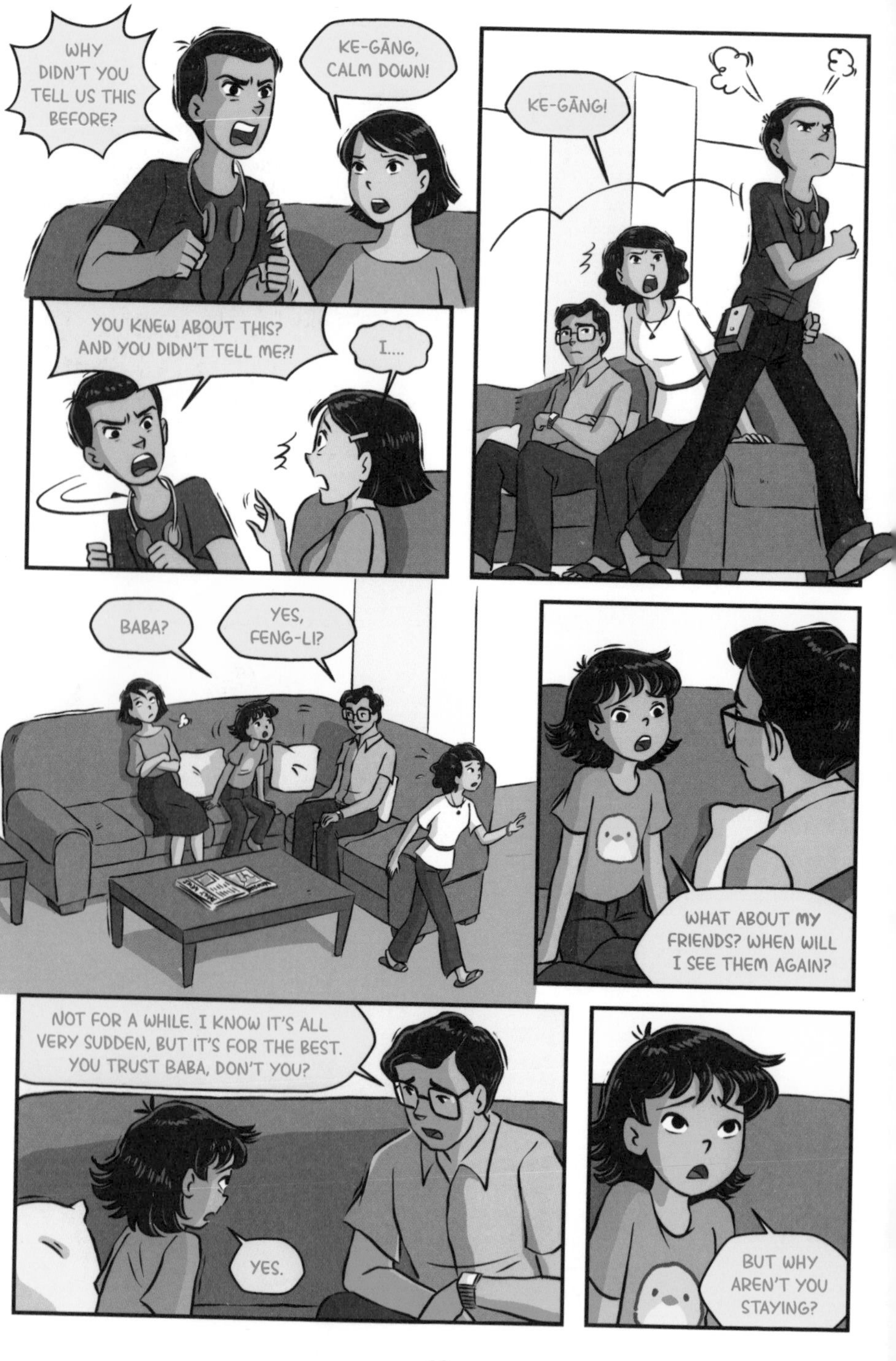
WHY DIDN'T YOU TELL US THIS BEFORE?
KE-GĀNG, CALM DOWN!
KE-GĀNG!
YOU KNEW ABOUT THIS? AND YOU DIDN'T TELL ME?!
I....
BABA?
YES, FENG-LI?
WHAT ABOUT MY FRIENDS? WHEN WILL I SEE THEM AGAIN?
NOT FOR A WHILE. I KNOW IT'S ALL VERY SUDDEN, BUT IT'S FOR THE BEST. YOU TRUST BABA, DON'T YOU?
YES.
BUT WHY AREN'T YOU STAYING?

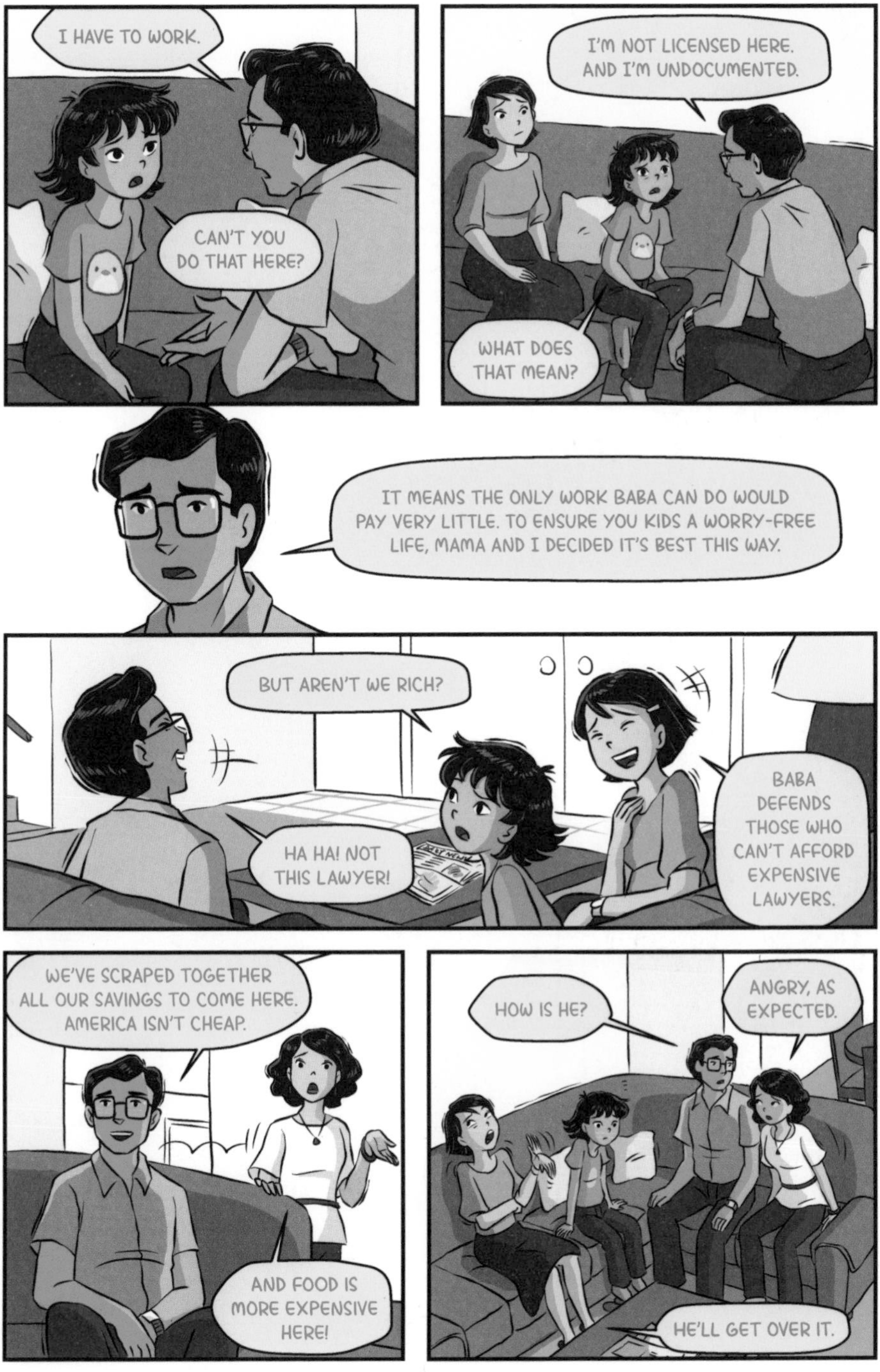
I HAVE TO WORK.
CAN'T YOU DO THAT HERE?
I'M NOT LICENSED HERE. AND I'M UNDOCUMENTED.
WHAT DOES THAT MEAN?
IT MEANS THE ONLY WORK BABA CAN DO WOULD PAY VERY LITTLE. TO ENSURE YOU KIDS A WORRY-FREE LIFE, MAMA AND I DECIDED IT'S BEST THIS WAY.
BUT AREN'T WE RICH?
HA HA! NOT THIS LAWYER!
BABA DEFENDS THOSE WHO CAN'T AFFORD EXPENSIVE LAWYERS.
WE'VE SCRAPED TOGETHER ALL OUR SAVINGS TO COME HERE. AMERICA ISN'T CHEAP.
AND FOOD IS MORE EXPENSIVE HERE!
HOW IS HE?
ANGRY, AS EXPECTED.
HE'LL GET OVER IT.

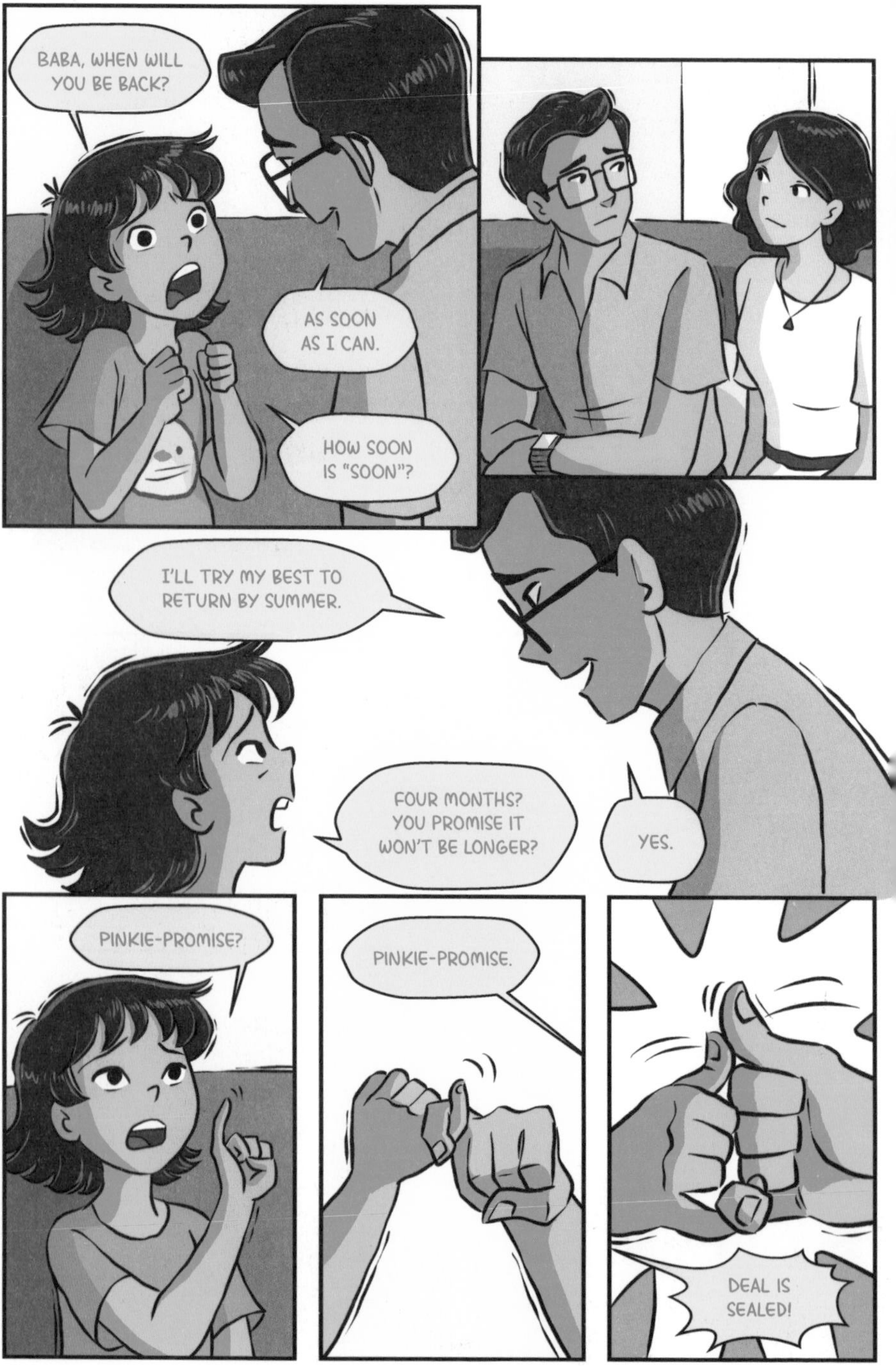
BABA, WHEN WILL YOU BE BACK?
AS SOON AS I CAN.
HOW SOON IS "SOON"?
I'LL TRY MY BEST TO RETURN BY SUMMER.
FOUR MONTHS? YOU PROMISE IT WON'T BE LONGER?
YES.
PINKIE-PROMISE?
PINKIE-PROMISE.
DEAL IS SEALED!

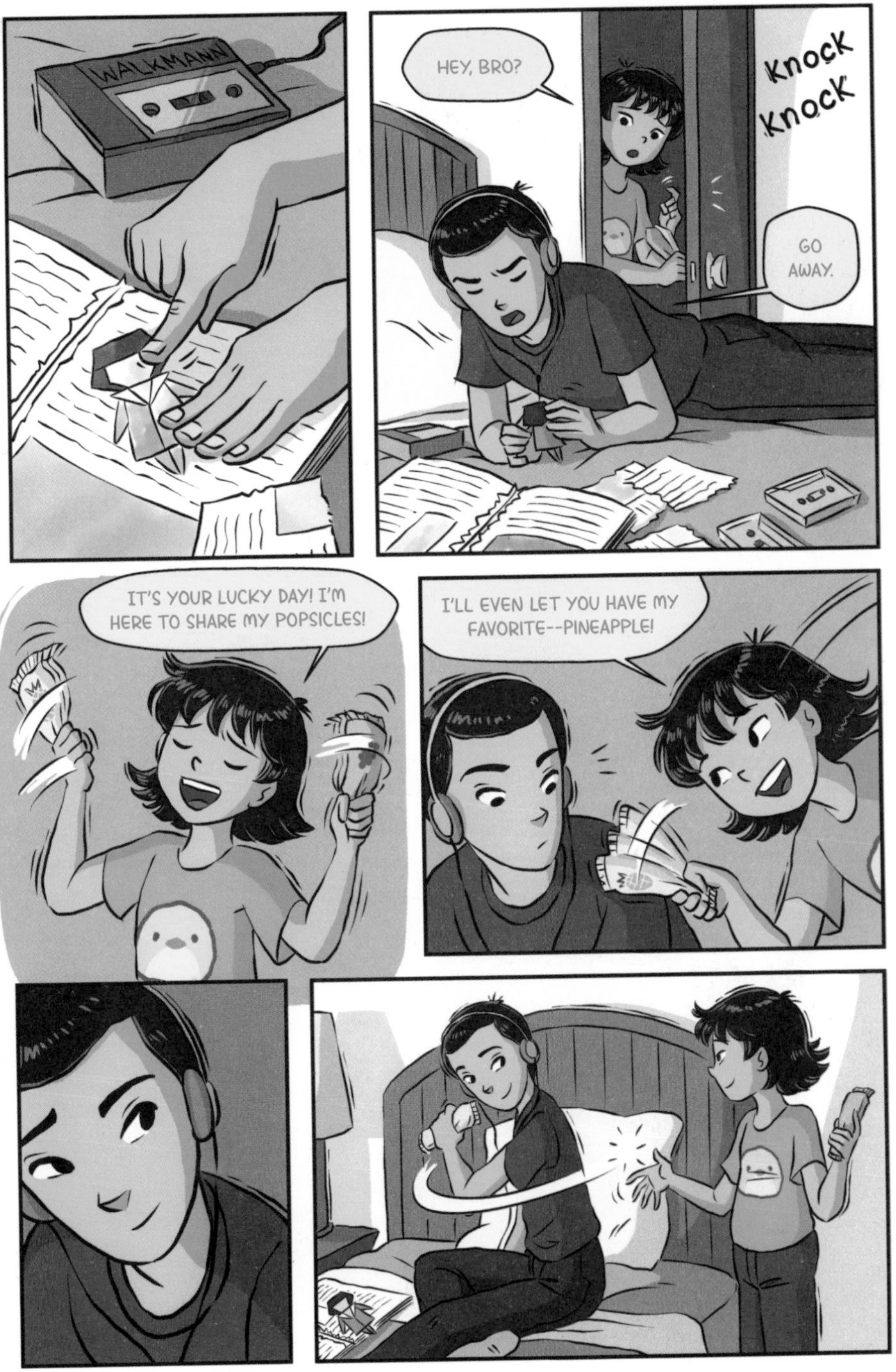
WALKMANN
HEY, BRO?
Knock Knock
GO AWAY.
IT'S YOUR LUCKY DAY! I'M HERE TO SHARE MY POPSICLES!
I'LL EVEN LET YOU HAVE MY FAVORITE--PINEAPPLE!

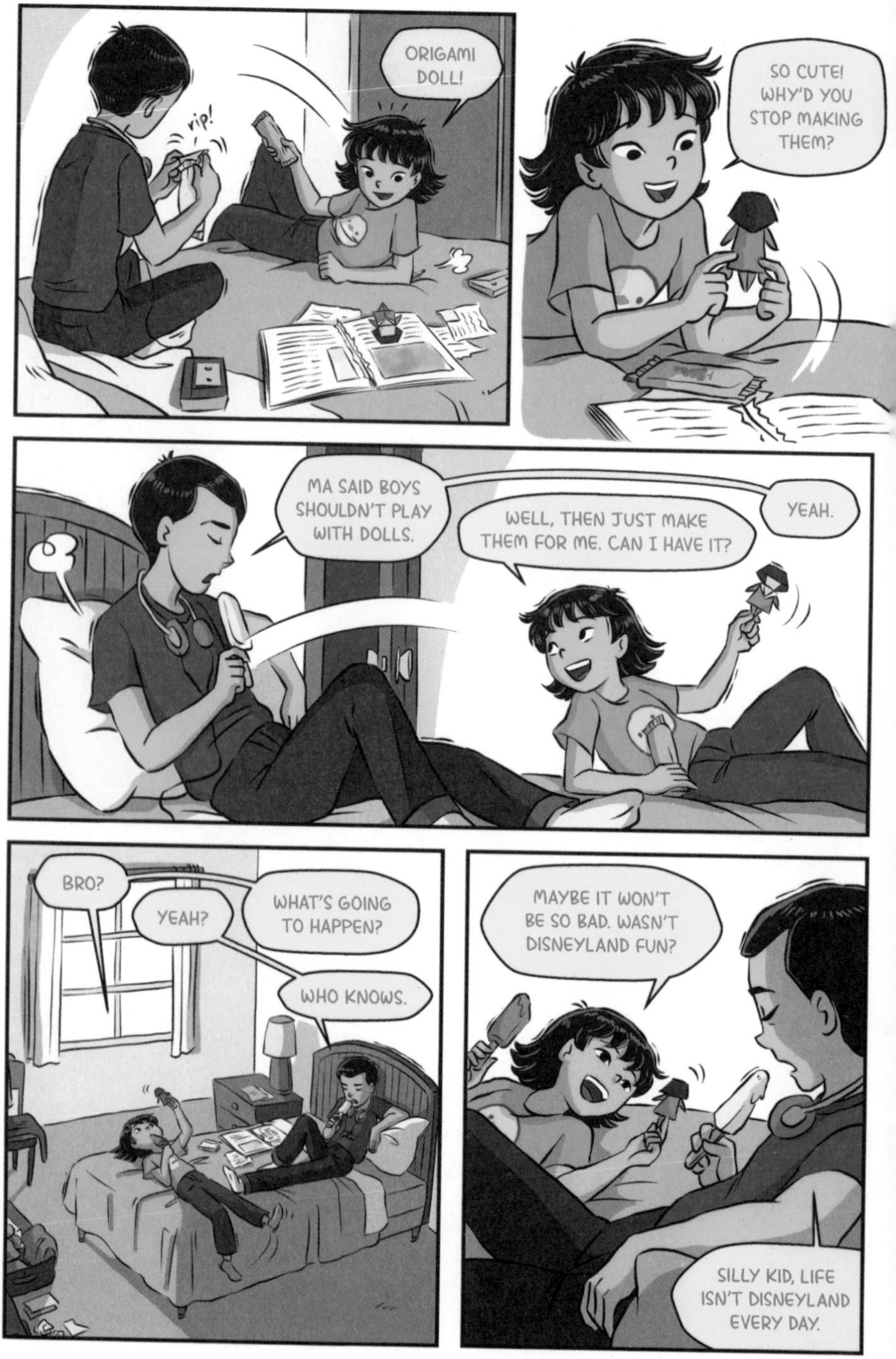
ORIGAMI DOLL!
rip!
SO CUTE! WHY'D YOU STOP MAKING THEM?
MA SAID BOYS SHOULDN'T PLAY WITH DOLLS.
YEAH.
WELL, THEN JUST MAKE THEM FOR ME. CAN I HAVE IT?
BRO?
YEAH?
WHAT'S GOING TO HAPPEN?
WHO KNOWS.
MAYBE IT WON'T BE SO BAD. WASN'T DISNEYLAND FUN?
SILLY KID, LIFE ISN'T DISNEYLAND EVERY DAY.

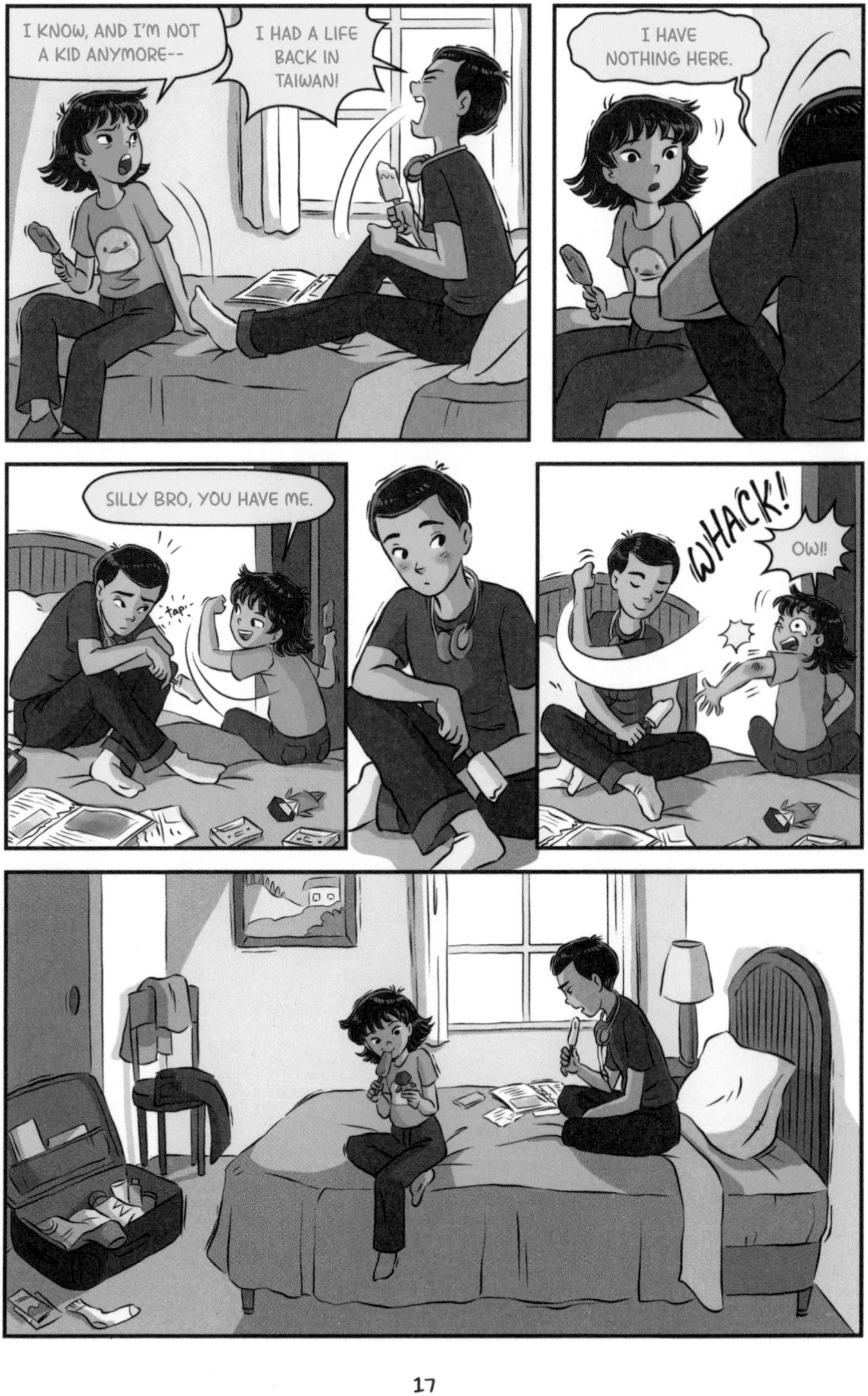
I KNOW, AND I'M NOT A KID ANYMORE--
I HAD A LIFE BACK IN TAIWAN!
I HAVE NOTHING HERE.
SILLY BRO, YOU HAVE ME.
tap
WHACK!
OW!!

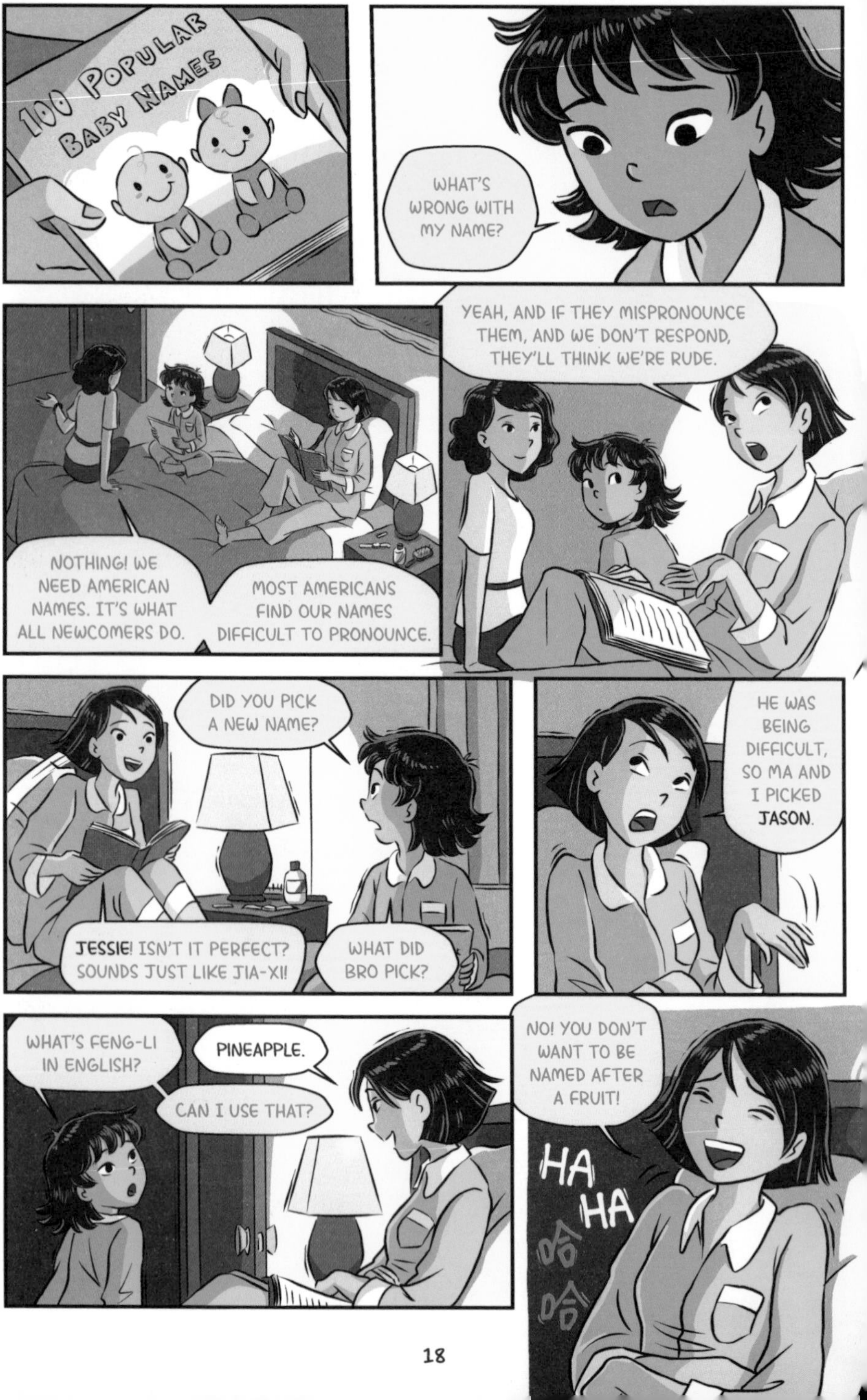
100 POPULAR BABY NAMES
WHAT'S WRONG WITH MY NAME?
NOTHING! WE NEED AMERICAN NAMES. IT'S WHAT ALL NEWCOMERS DO.
MOST AMERICANS FIND OUR NAMES DIFFICULT TO PRONOUNCE.
YEAH, AND IF THEY MISPRONOUNCE THEM, AND WE DON'T RESPOND, THEY'LL THINK WE'RE RUDE.
DID YOU PICK A NEW NAME?
JESSIE! ISN'T IT PERFECT? SOUNDS JUST LIKE JIA-XI!
WHAT DID BRO PICK?
HE WAS BEING DIFFICULT, SO MA AND I PICKED JASON.
WHAT'S FENG-LI IN ENGLISH?
PINEAPPLE.
CAN I USE THAT?
NO! YOU DON'T WANT TO BE NAMED AFTER A FRUIT!
HA HA
哈哈

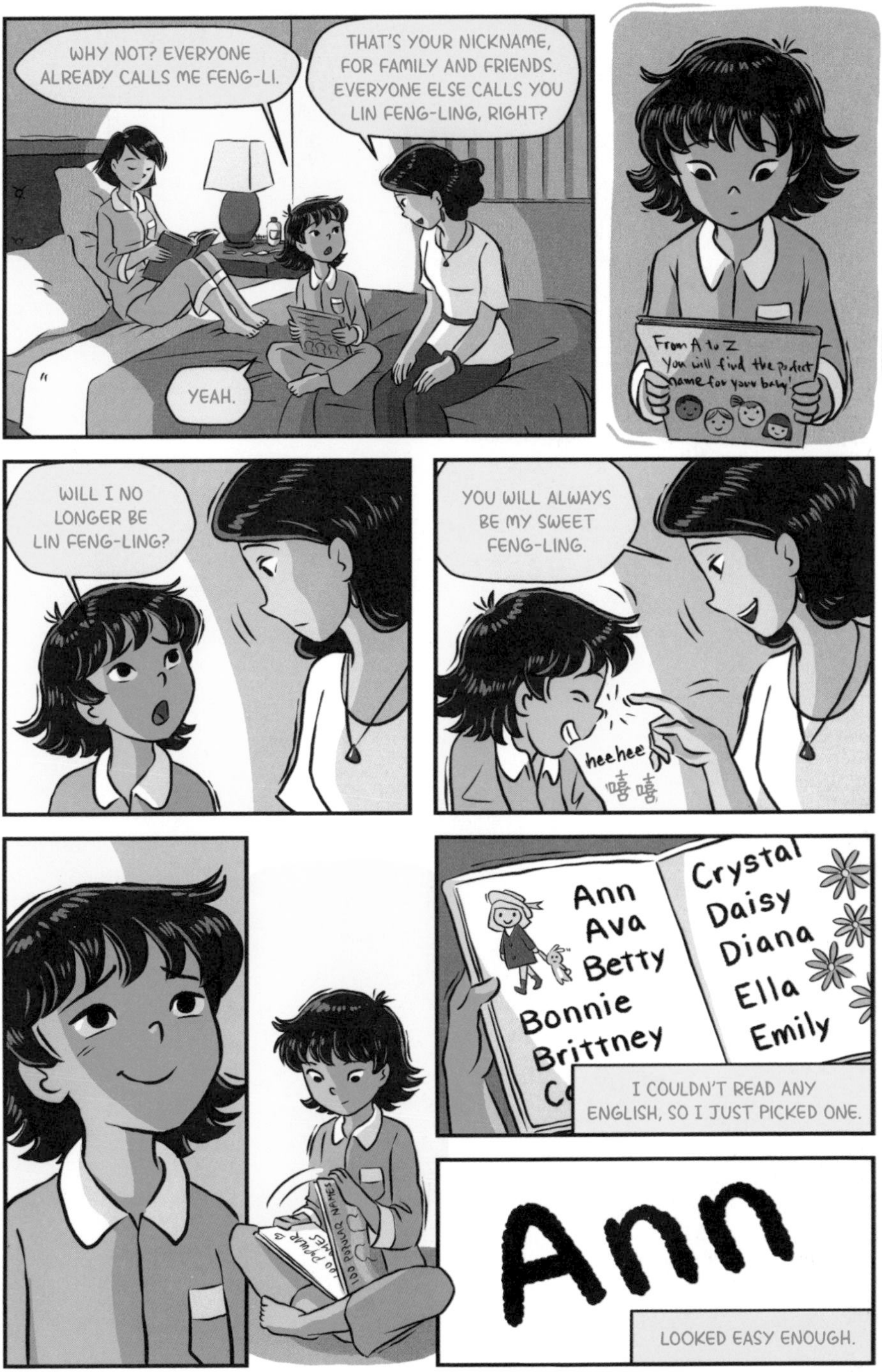
WHY NOT? EVERYONE ALREADY CALLS ME FENG-LI.
THAT'S YOUR NICKNAME, FOR FAMILY AND FRIENDS. EVERYONE ELSE CALLS YOU LIN FENG-LING, RIGHT?
YEAH.
From A to Z You will find the perfect name for your baby!
WILL I NO LONGER BE LIN FENG-LING?
YOU WILL ALWAYS BE MY SWEET FENG-LING.
hee hee
嘻嘻
100 POPULAR NAMES
Ann
Ava
Betty
Bonnie
Brittney
Crystal
Daisy
Diana
Ella
Emily
I COULDN'T READ ANY ENGLISH, SO I JUST PICKED ONE.
Ann
LOOKED EASY ENOUGH.

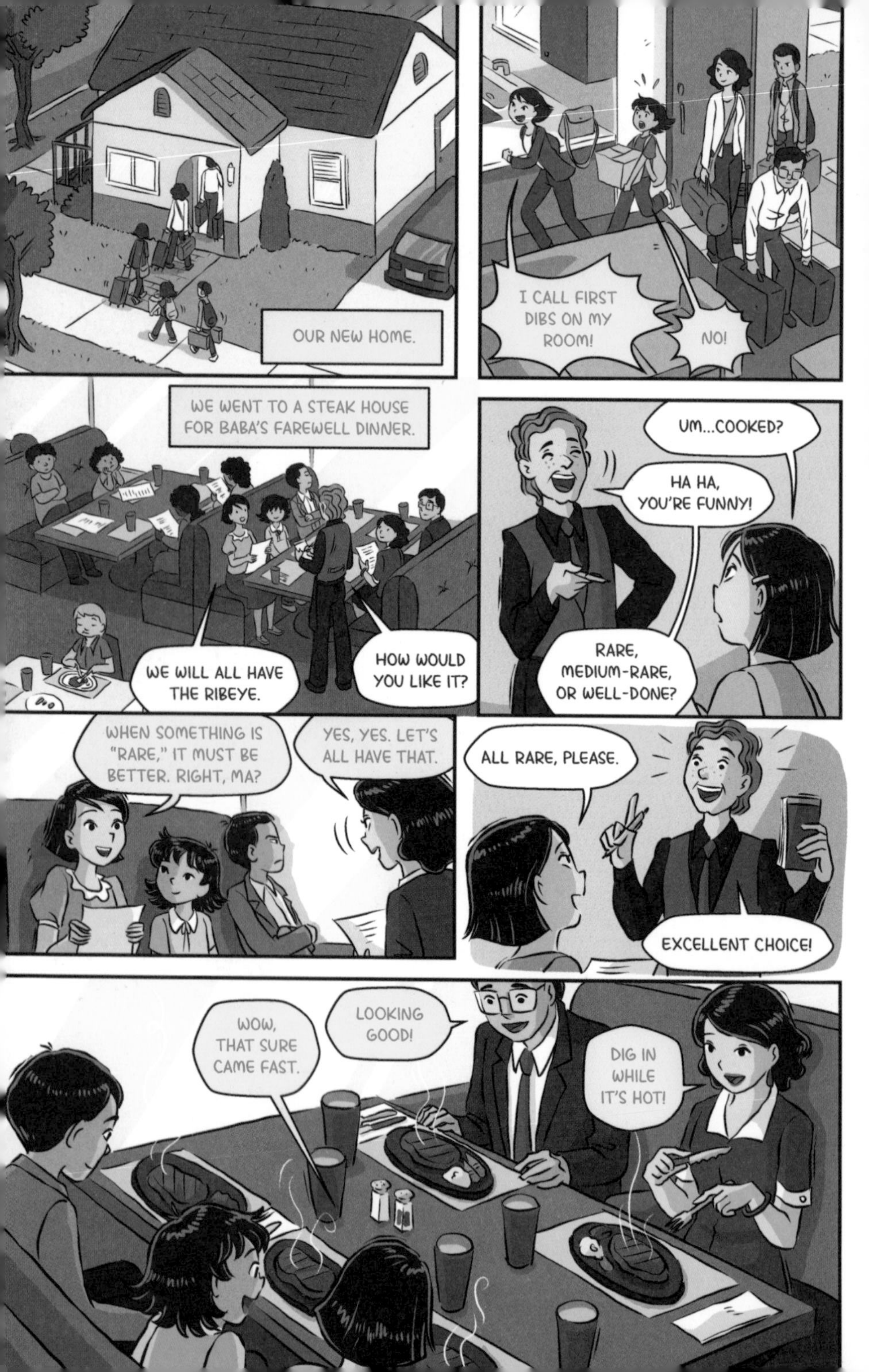

OUR NEW HOME.
I CALL FIRST DIBS ON MY ROOM!
NO!
WE WENT TO A STEAK HOUSE FOR BABA'S FAREWELL DINNER.
WE WILL ALL HAVE THE RIBEYE.
HOW WOULD YOU LIKE IT?
UM...COOKED?
HA HA, YOU'RE FUNNY!
RARE, MEDIUM-RARE, OR WELL-DONE?
WHEN SOMETHING IS "RARE," IT MUST BE BETTER. RIGHT, MA?
YES, YES. LET'S ALL HAVE THAT.
ALL RARE, PLEASE.
EXCELLENT CHOICE!
WOW, THAT SURE CAME FAST.
LOOKING GOOD!
DIG IN WHILE IT'S HOT!

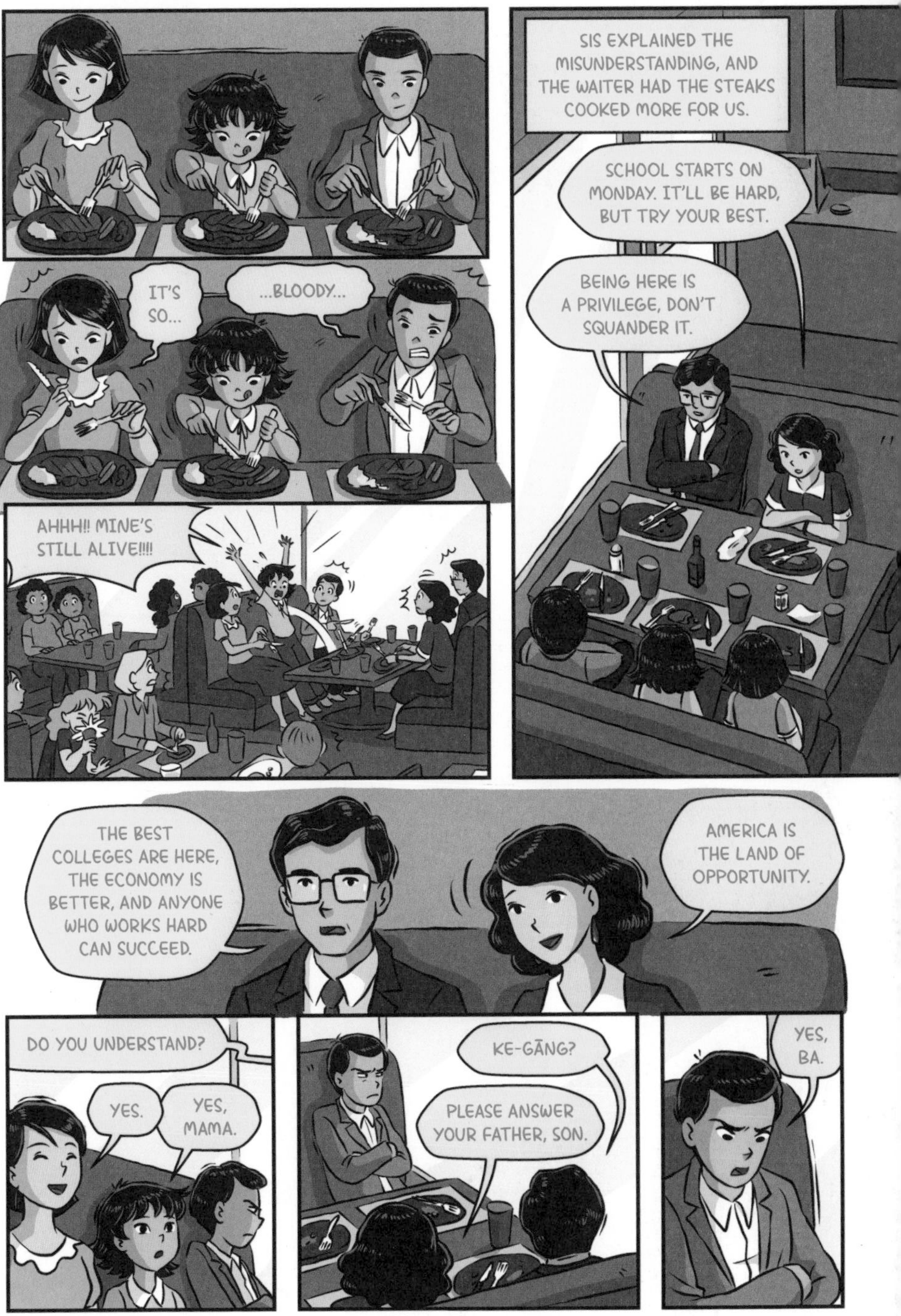
IT'S SO...
...BLOODY...
AHHH!! MINE'S STILL ALIVE!!!!
SIS EXPLAINED THE MISUNDERSTANDING, AND THE WAITER HAD THE STEAKS COOKED MORE FOR US.
SCHOOL STARTS ON MONDAY. IT'LL BE HARD, BUT TRY YOUR BEST.
BEING HERE IS A PRIVILEGE, DON'T SQUANDER IT.
THE BEST COLLEGES ARE HERE, THE ECONOMY IS BETTER, AND ANYONE WHO WORKS HARD CAN SUCCEED.
AMERICA IS THE LAND OF OPPORTUNITY.
DO YOU UNDERSTAND?
YES.
YES, MAMA.
KE-GĀNG?
PLEASE ANSWER YOUR FATHER, SON.
YES, BA.

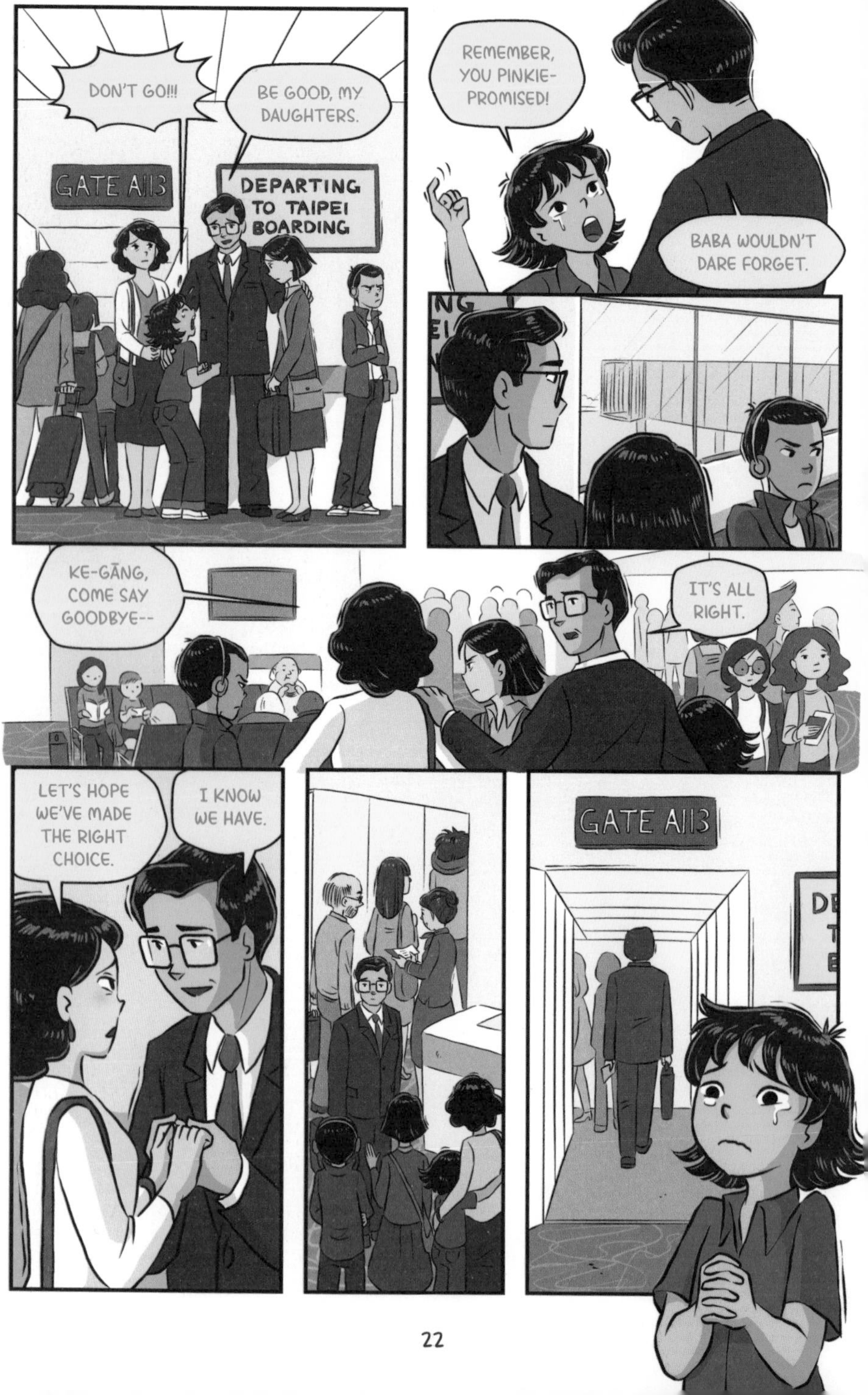
DON'T GO!!!
BE GOOD, MY DAUGHTERS.
GATE A113
DEPARTING TO TAIPEI BOARDING
REMEMBER, YOU PINKIE-PROMISED!
BABA WOULDN'T DARE FORGET.
KE-GĀNG, COME SAY GOODBYE--
IT'S ALL RIGHT.
LET'S HOPE WE'VE MADE THE RIGHT CHOICE.
I KNOW WE HAVE.
GATE A113

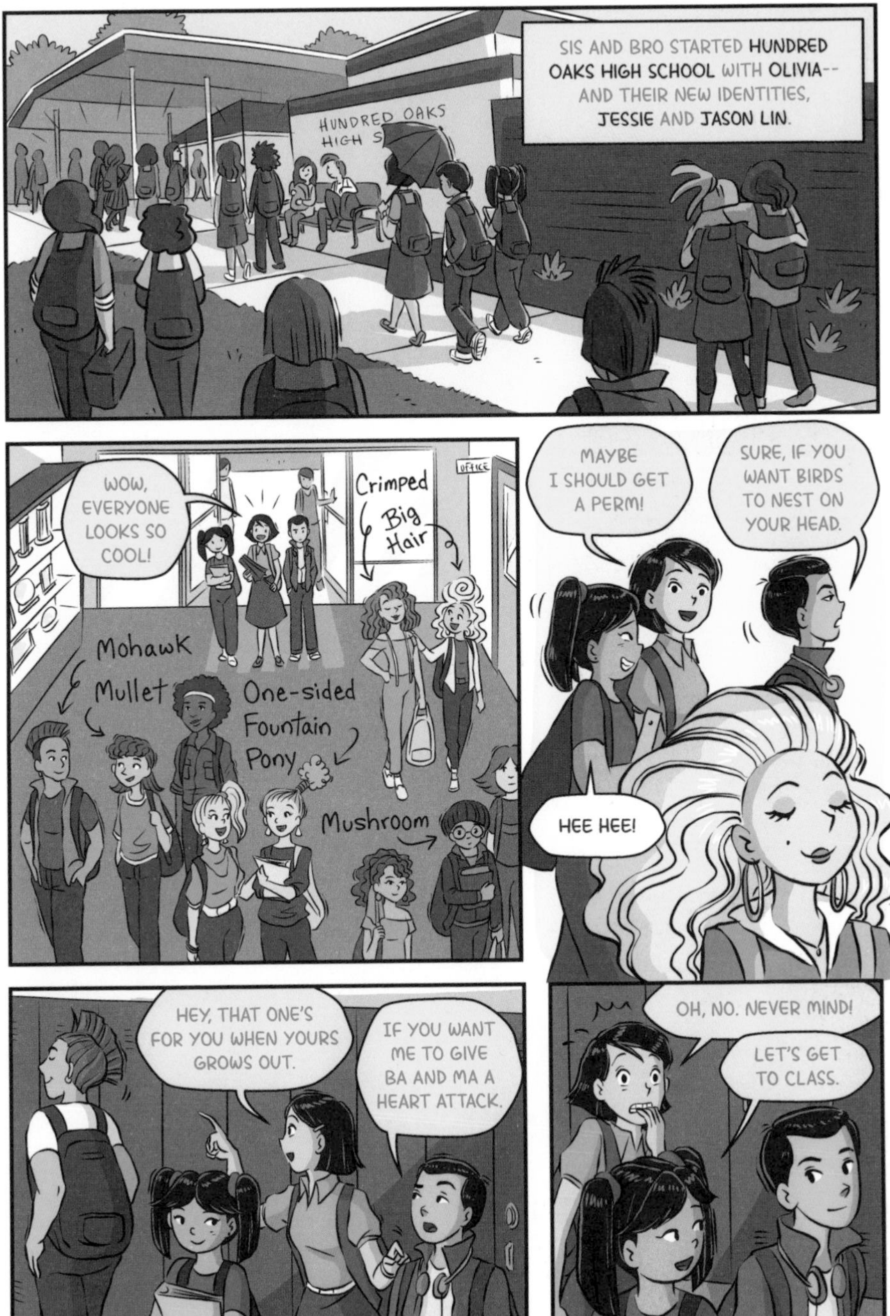
SIS AND BRO STARTED HUNDRED OAKS HIGH SCHOOL WITH OLIVIA-- AND THEIR NEW IDENTITIES, JESSIE AND JASON LIN.
HUNDRED OAKS HIGH S
WOW, EVERYONE LOOKS SO COOL!
OFFICE
Crimped
Big Hair
Mohawk
Mullet
One-sided Fountain Pony
Mushroom
MAYBE I SHOULD GET A PERM!
SURE, IF YOU WANT BIRDS TO NEST ON YOUR HEAD.
HEE HEE!
HEY, THAT ONE'S FOR YOU WHEN YOURS GROWS OUT.
IF YOU WANT ME TO GIVE BA AND MA A HEART ATTACK.
OH, NO. NEVER MIND!
LET'S GET TO CLASS.

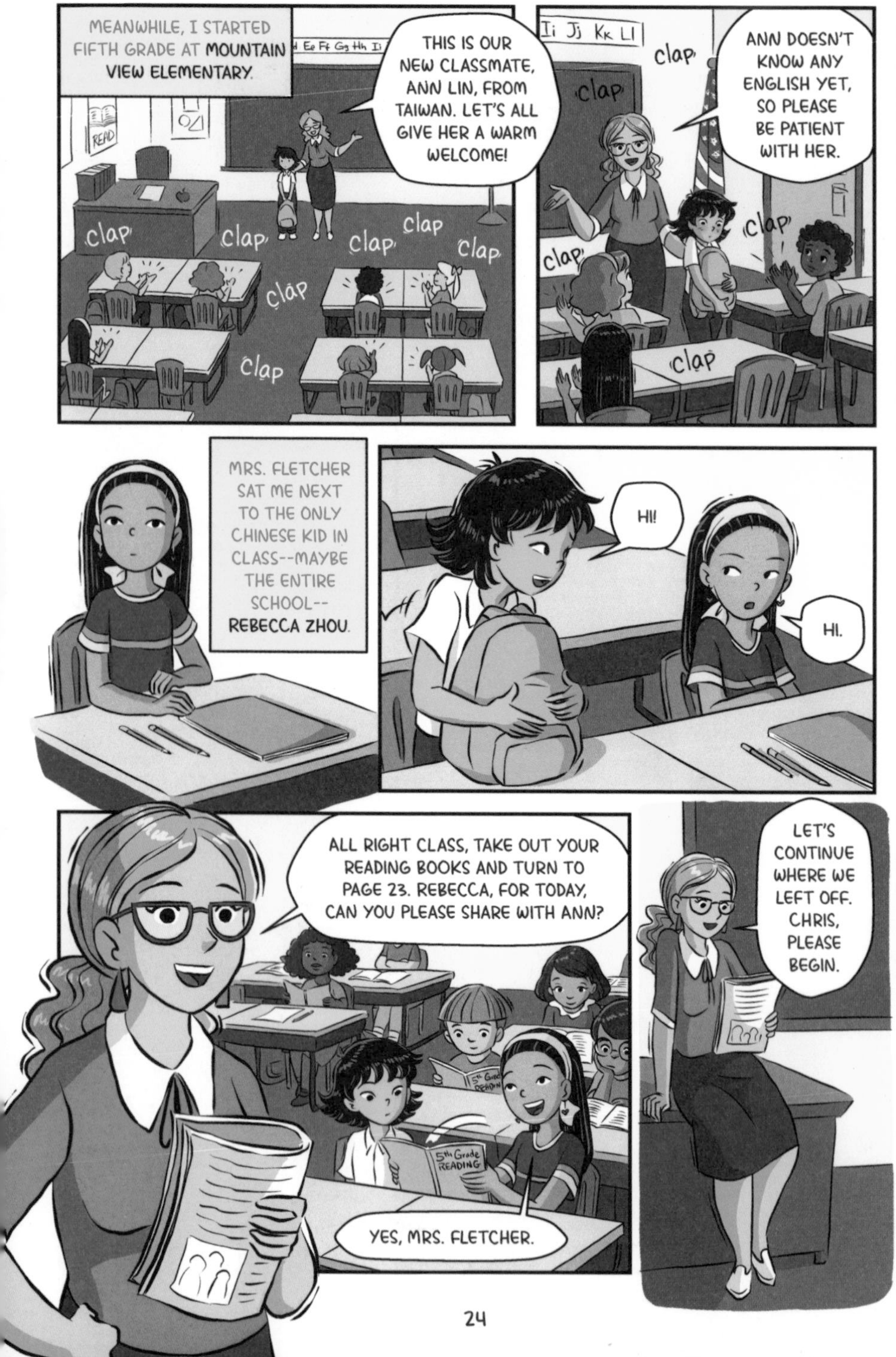
MEANWHILE, I STARTED FIFTH GRADE AT MOUNTAIN VIEW ELEMENTARY.
THIS IS OUR NEW CLASSMATE, ANN LIN, FROM TAIWAN. LET'S ALL GIVE HER A WARM WELCOME!
CLAP CLAP CLAP CLAP CLAP CLAP CLAP
ANN DOESN'T KNOW ANY ENGLISH YET, SO PLEASE BE PATIENT WITH HER.
CLAP CLAP CLAP CLAP CLAP
MRS. FLETCHER SAT ME NEXT TO THE ONLY CHINESE KID IN CLASS--MAYBE THE ENTIRE SCHOOL--REBECCA ZHOU.
HI!
HI.
ALL RIGHT CLASS, TAKE OUT YOUR READING BOOKS AND TURN TO PAGE 23. REBECCA, FOR TODAY, CAN YOU PLEASE SHARE WITH ANN?
5th Grade READING
YES, MRS. FLETCHER.
LET'S CONTINUE WHERE WE LEFT OFF. CHRIS, PLEASE BEGIN.

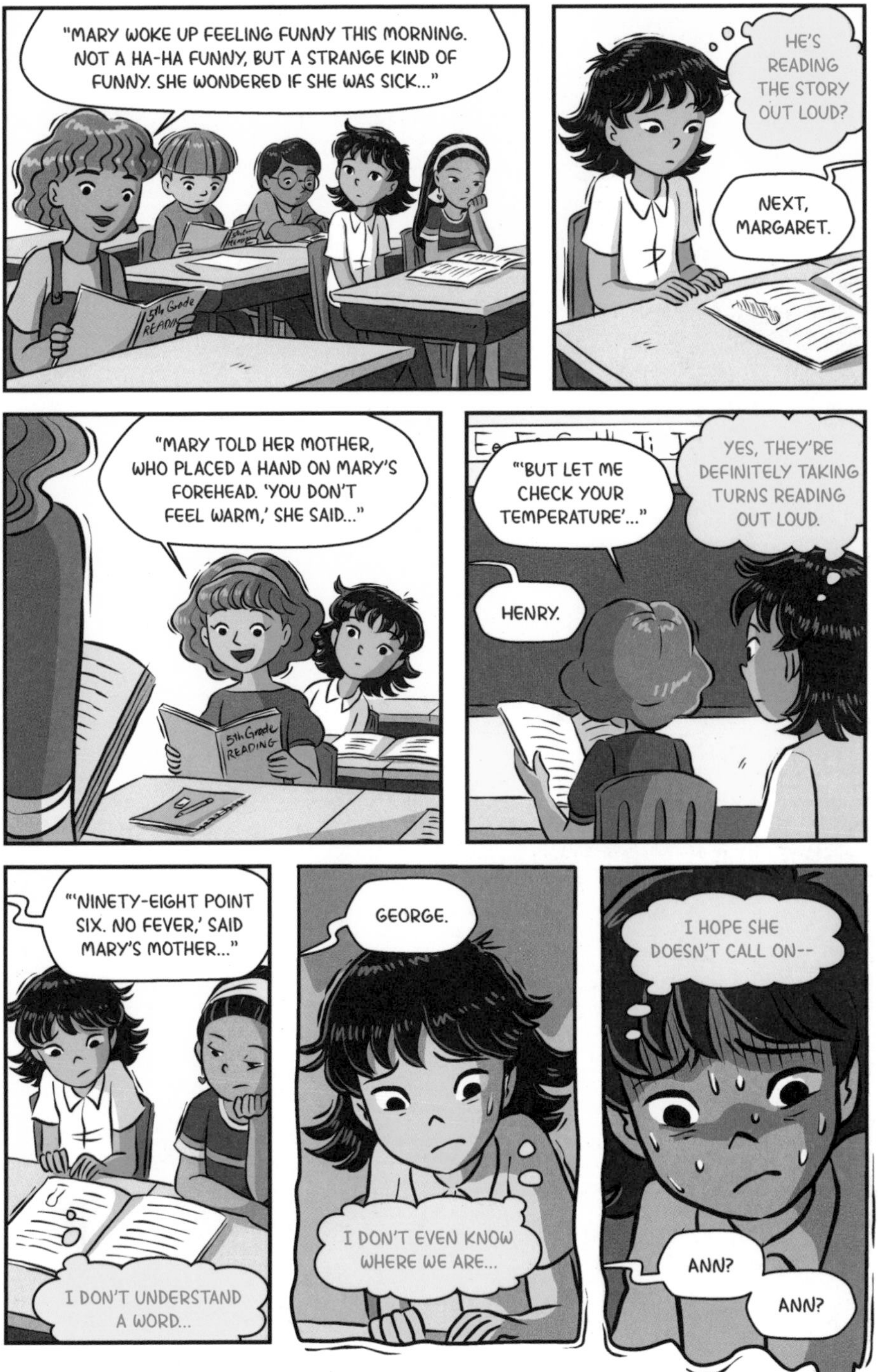
"MARY WOKE UP FEELING FUNNY THIS MORNING. NOT A HA-HA FUNNY, BUT A STRANGE KIND OF FUNNY. SHE WONDERED IF SHE WAS SICK..."
5th Grade READIN
HE'S READING THE STORY OUT LOUD?
NEXT, MARGARET.
"MARY TOLD HER MOTHER, WHO PLACED A HAND ON MARY'S FOREHEAD. 'YOU DON'T FEEL WARM,' SHE SAID..."
5th Grade READING
"'BUT LET ME CHECK YOUR TEMPERATURE'..."
YES, THEY'RE DEFINITELY TAKING TURNS READING OUT LOUD.
HENRY.
"'NINETY-EIGHT POINT SIX. NO FEVER,' SAID MARY'S MOTHER..."
I DON'T UNDERSTAND A WORD...
GEORGE.
I DON'T EVEN KNOW WHERE WE ARE...
I HOPE SHE DOESN'T CALL ON--
ANN?
ANN?

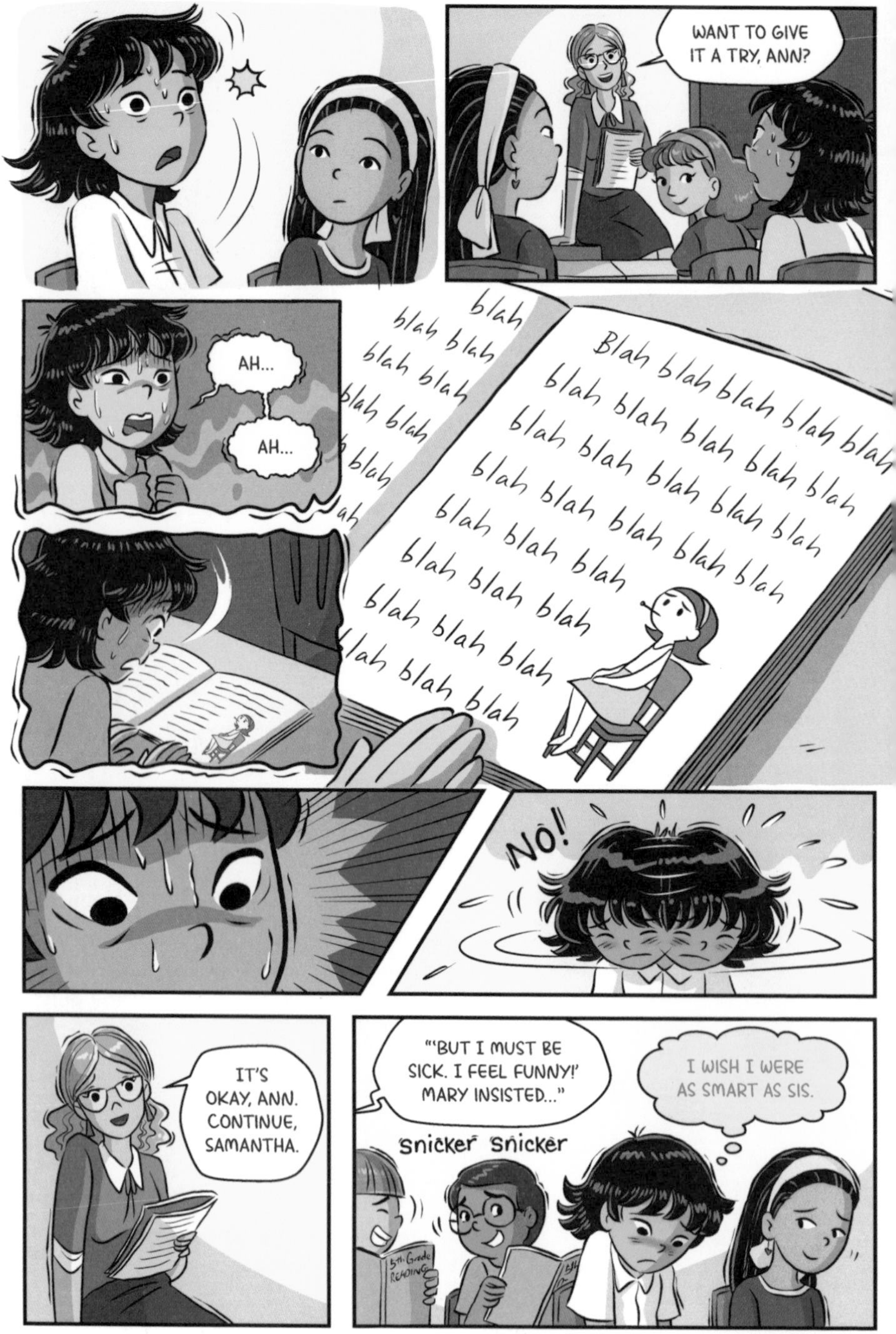
WANT TO GIVE IT A TRY, ANN?
AH...
AH...
Blah blah blah blah blah
blah blah blah blah
blah blah
NO!
IT'S OKAY, ANN. CONTINUE, SAMANTHA.
"'BUT I MUST BE SICK. I FEEL FUNNY!' MARY INSISTED..."
I WISH I WERE AS SMART AS SIS.
snicker snicker
5th Grade READING

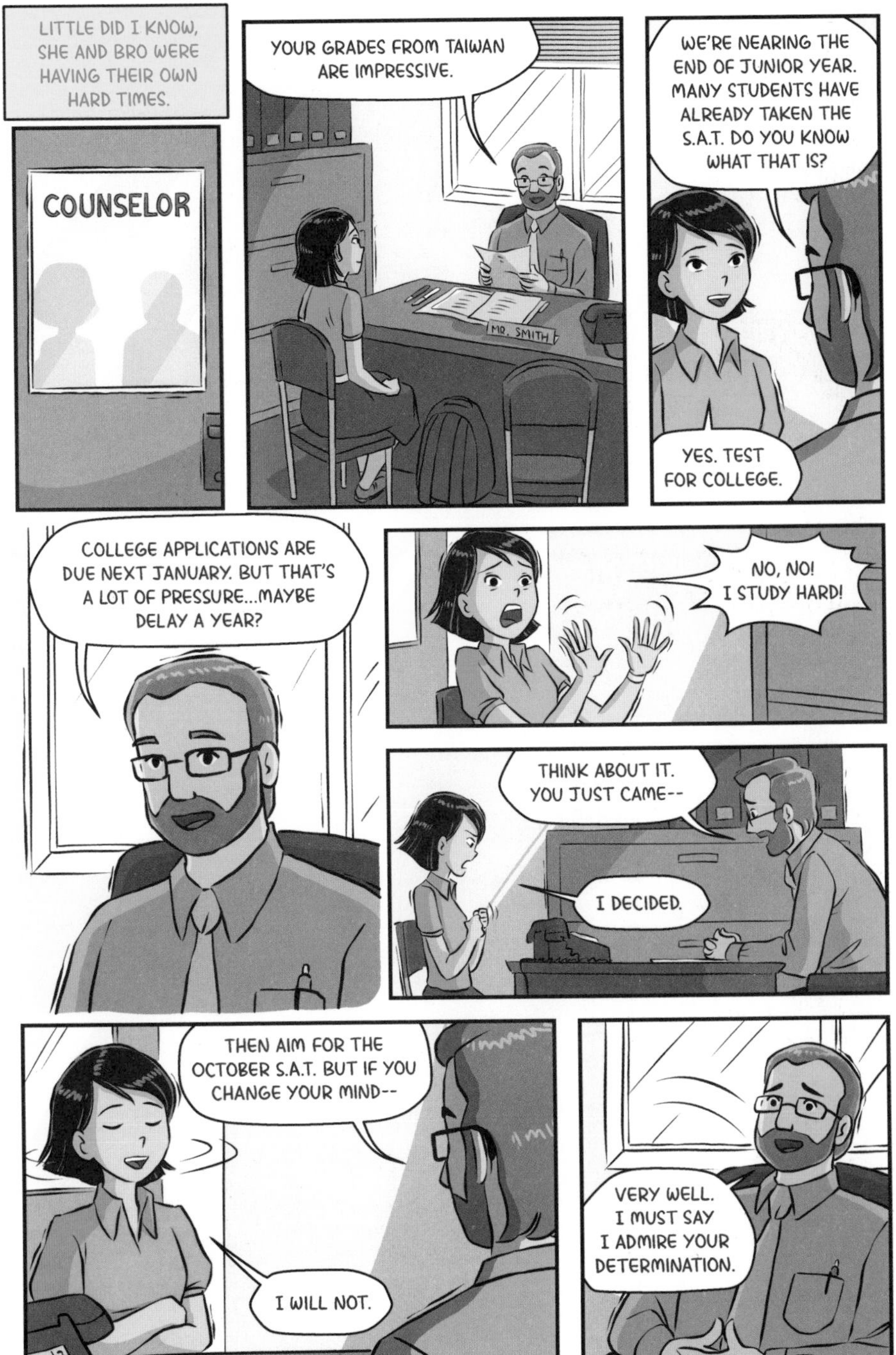
LITTLE DID I KNOW, SHE AND BRO WERE HAVING THEIR OWN HARD TIMES.
COUNSELOR
YOUR GRADES FROM TAIWAN ARE IMPRESSIVE.
MR. SMITH
WE'RE NEARING THE END OF JUNIOR YEAR. MANY STUDENTS HAVE ALREADY TAKEN THE S.A.T. DO YOU KNOW WHAT THAT IS?
YES. TEST FOR COLLEGE.
COLLEGE APPLICATIONS ARE DUE NEXT JANUARY. BUT THAT'S A LOT OF PRESSURE...MAYBE DELAY A YEAR?
NO, NO! I STUDY HARD!
THINK ABOUT IT. YOU JUST CAME--
I DECIDED.
THEN AIM FOR THE OCTOBER S.A.T. BUT IF YOU CHANGE YOUR MIND--
I WILL NOT.
VERY WELL. I MUST SAY I ADMIRE YOUR DETERMINATION.

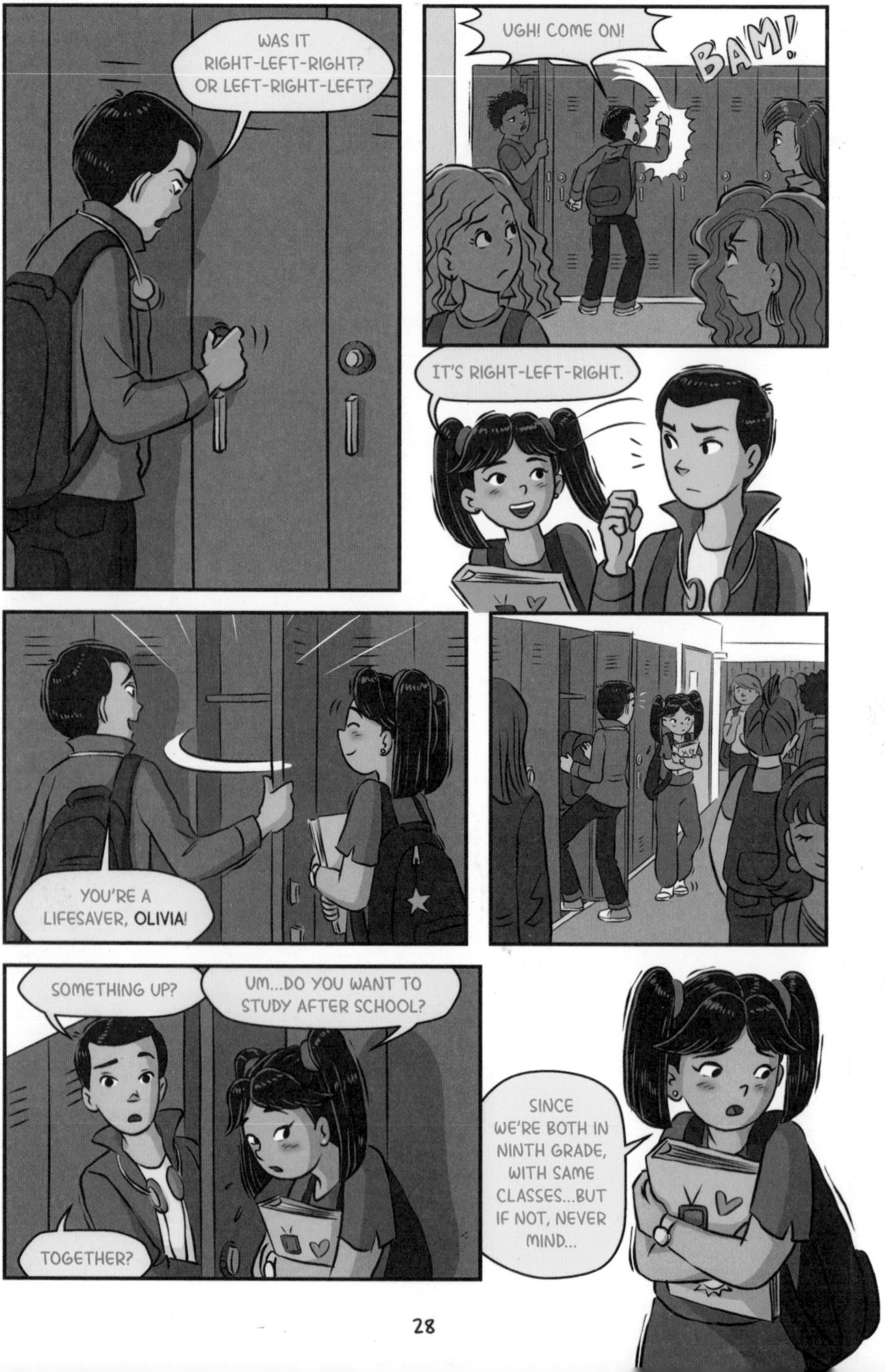
WAS IT RIGHT-LEFT-RIGHT? OR LEFT-RIGHT-LEFT?
UGH! COME ON!
BAM!
IT'S RIGHT-LEFT-RIGHT.
YOU'RE A LIFESAVER, OLIVIA!
SOMETHING UP?
UM...DO YOU WANT TO STUDY AFTER SCHOOL?
TOGETHER?
SINCE WE'RE BOTH IN NINTH GRADE, WITH SAME CLASSES...BUT IF NOT, NEVER MIND...

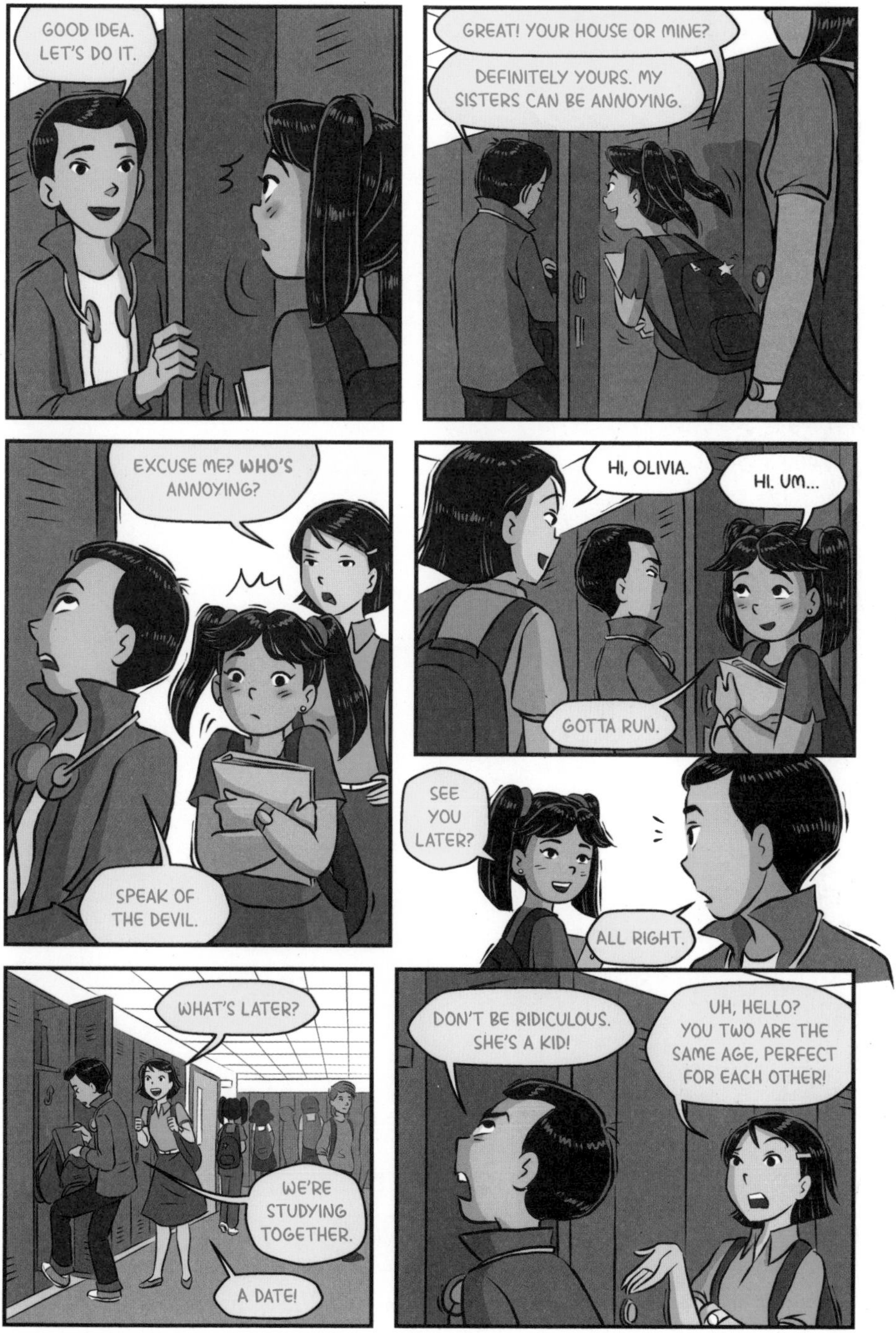
GOOD IDEA. LET'S DO IT.
GREAT! YOUR HOUSE OR MINE?
DEFINITELY YOURS. MY SISTERS CAN BE ANNOYING.
EXCUSE ME? WHO'S ANNOYING?
SPEAK OF THE DEVIL.
HI, OLIVIA.
HI. UM...
GOTTA RUN.
SEE YOU LATER?
ALL RIGHT.
WHAT'S LATER?
WE'RE STUDYING TOGETHER.
A DATE!
DON'T BE RIDICULOUS. SHE'S A KID!
UH, HELLO? YOU TWO ARE THE SAME AGE, PERFECT FOR EACH OTHER!

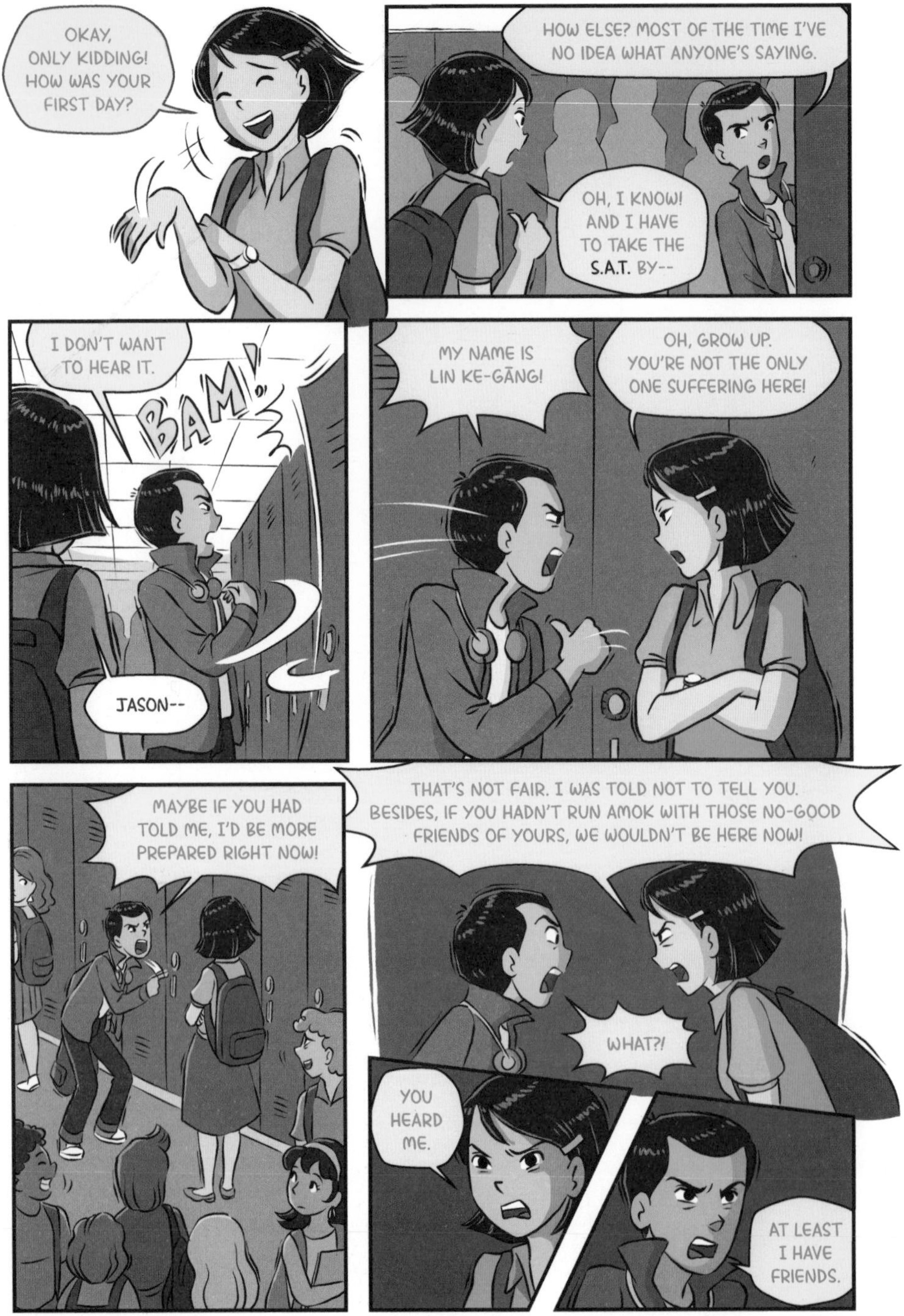
OKAY, ONLY KIDDING! HOW WAS YOUR FIRST DAY?
HOW ELSE? MOST OF THE TIME I'VE NO IDEA WHAT ANYONE'S SAYING.
OH, I KNOW! AND I HAVE TO TAKE THE S.A.T. BY--
I DON'T WANT TO HEAR IT.
BAM!
JASON--
MY NAME IS LIN KE-GĀNG!
OH, GROW UP. YOU'RE NOT THE ONLY ONE SUFFERING HERE!
MAYBE IF YOU HAD TOLD ME, I'D BE MORE PREPARED RIGHT NOW!
THAT'S NOT FAIR. I WAS TOLD NOT TO TELL YOU. BESIDES, IF YOU HADN'T RUN AMOK WITH THOSE NO-GOOD FRIENDS OF YOURS, WE WOULDN'T BE HERE NOW!
WHAT?!
YOU HEARD ME.
AT LEAST I HAVE FRIENDS.

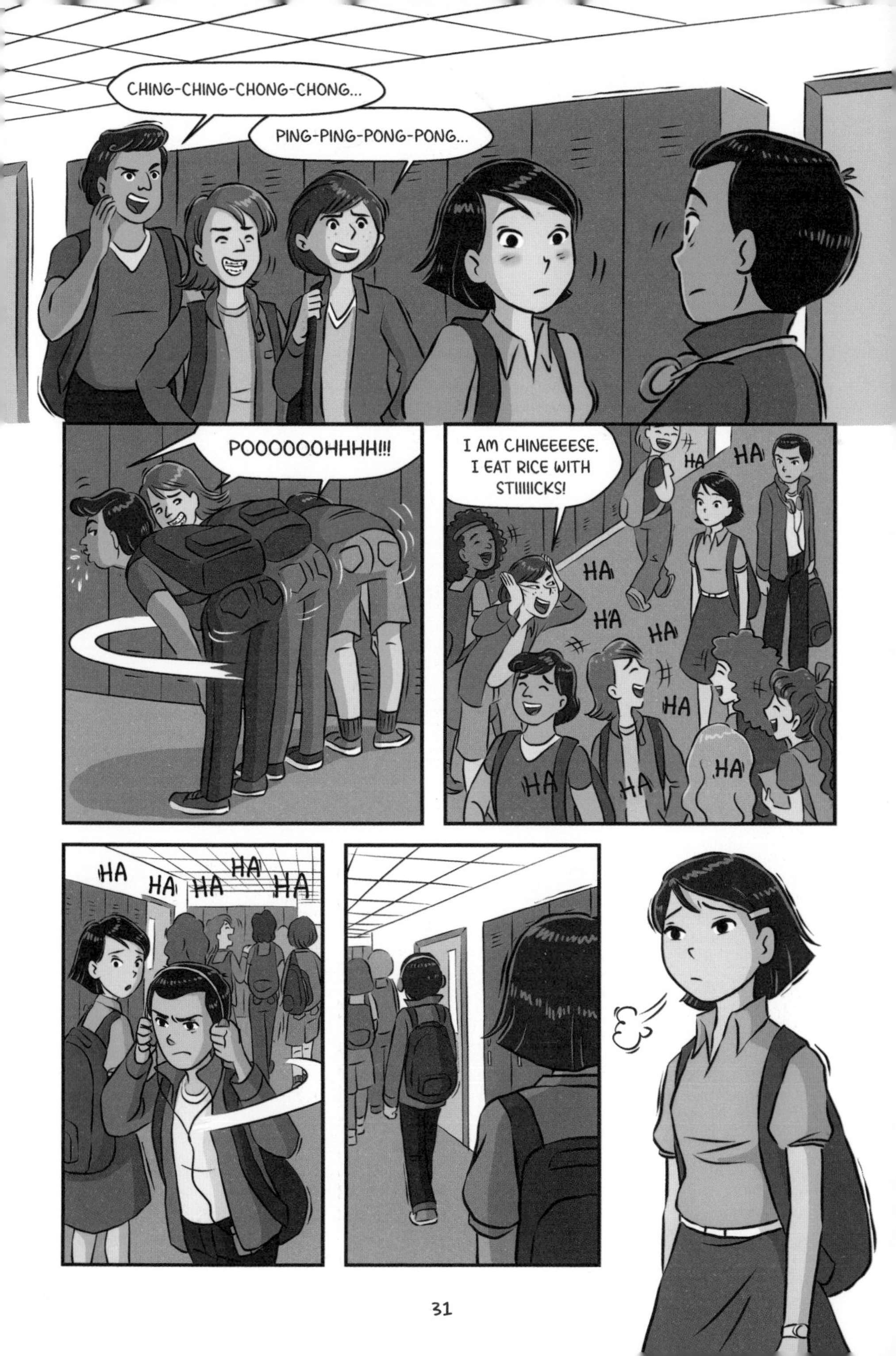
CHING-CHING-CHONG-CHONG...
PING-PING-PONG-PONG...
POOOOOOHHHH!!!
I AM CHINEEEESE. I EAT RICE WITH STIIIIICKS!
HA
HA
HA
HA
HA
HA
HA
HA
HA
HA
HA
HA
HA
HA

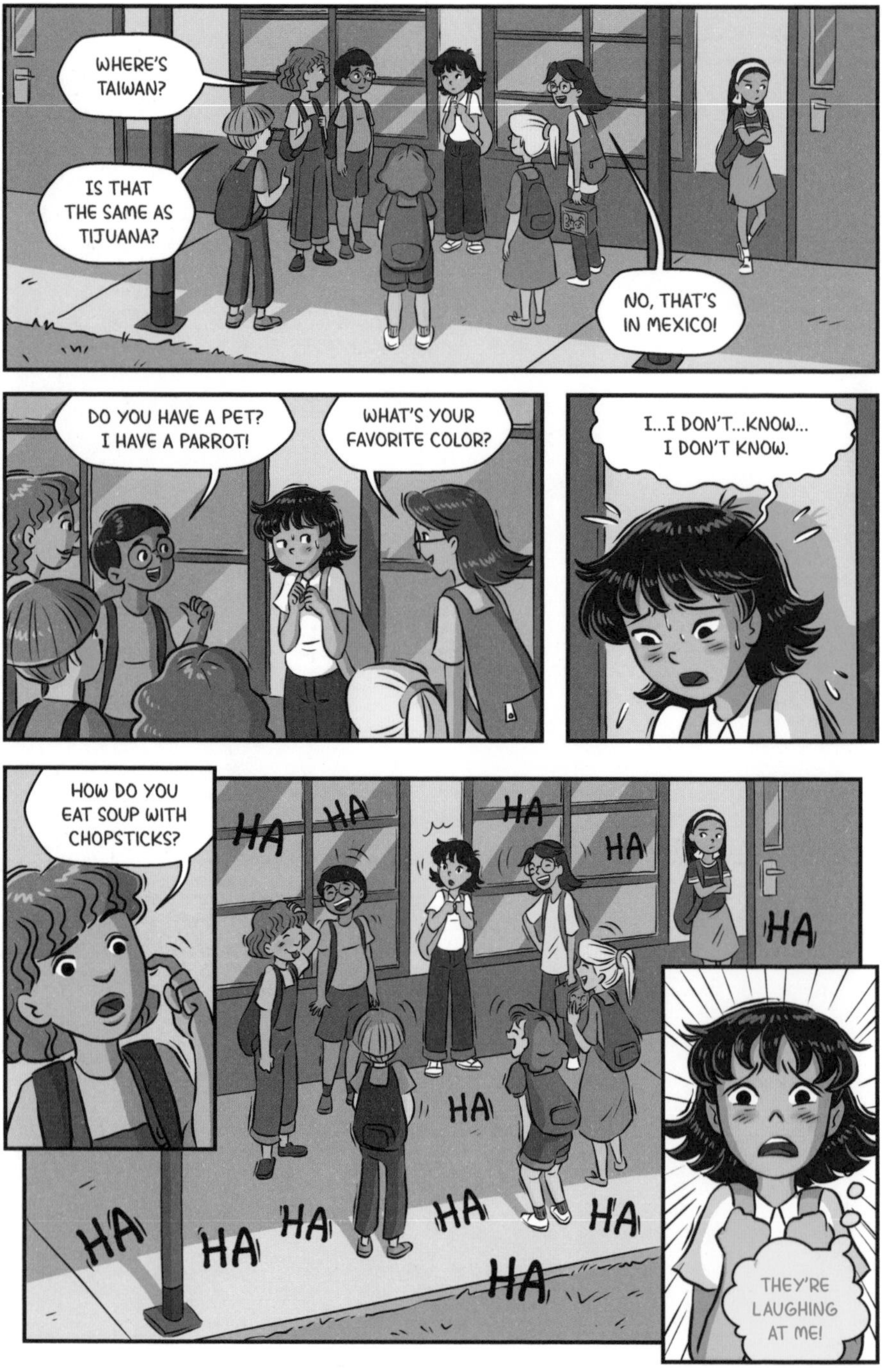
WHERE'S TAIWAN?
IS THAT THE SAME AS TIJUANA?
NO, THAT'S IN MEXICO!
DO YOU HAVE A PET? I HAVE A PARROT!
WHAT'S YOUR FAVORITE COLOR?
I...I DON'T...KNOW... I DON'T KNOW.
HOW DO YOU EAT SOUP WITH CHOPSTICKS?
HA HA HA HA HA
HA HA HA HA HA HA HA
THEY'RE LAUGHING AT ME!

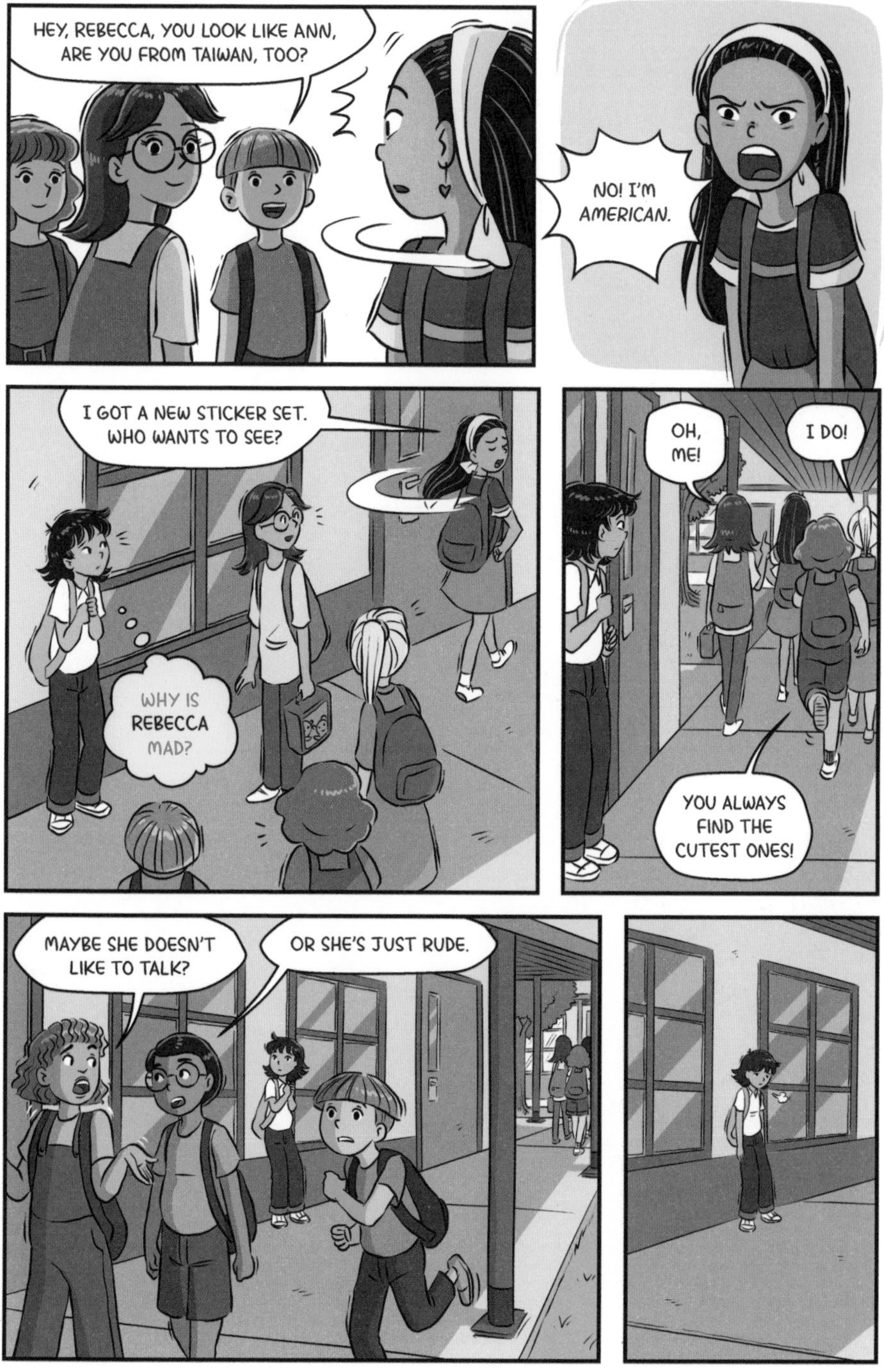
HEY, REBECCA, YOU LOOK LIKE ANN, ARE YOU FROM TAIWAN, TOO?
NO! I'M AMERICAN.
I GOT A NEW STICKER SET. WHO WANTS TO SEE?
WHY IS REBECCA MAD?
OH, ME!
I DO!
YOU ALWAYS FIND THE CUTEST ONES!
MAYBE SHE DOESN'T LIKE TO TALK?
OR SHE'S JUST RUDE.

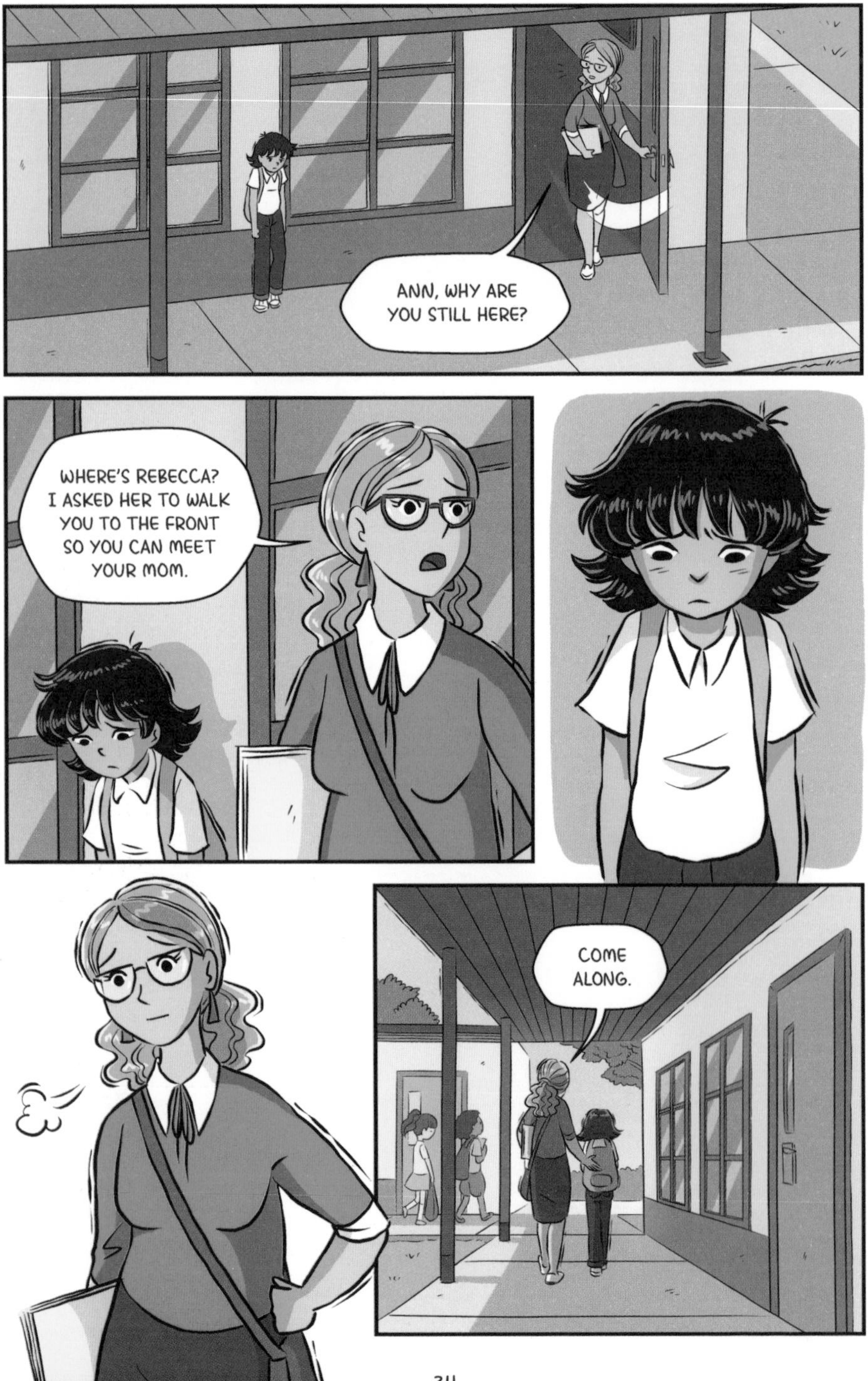
ANN, WHY ARE YOU STILL HERE?
WHERE'S REBECCA? I ASKED HER TO WALK YOU TO THE FRONT SO YOU CAN MEET YOUR MOM.
COME ALONG.

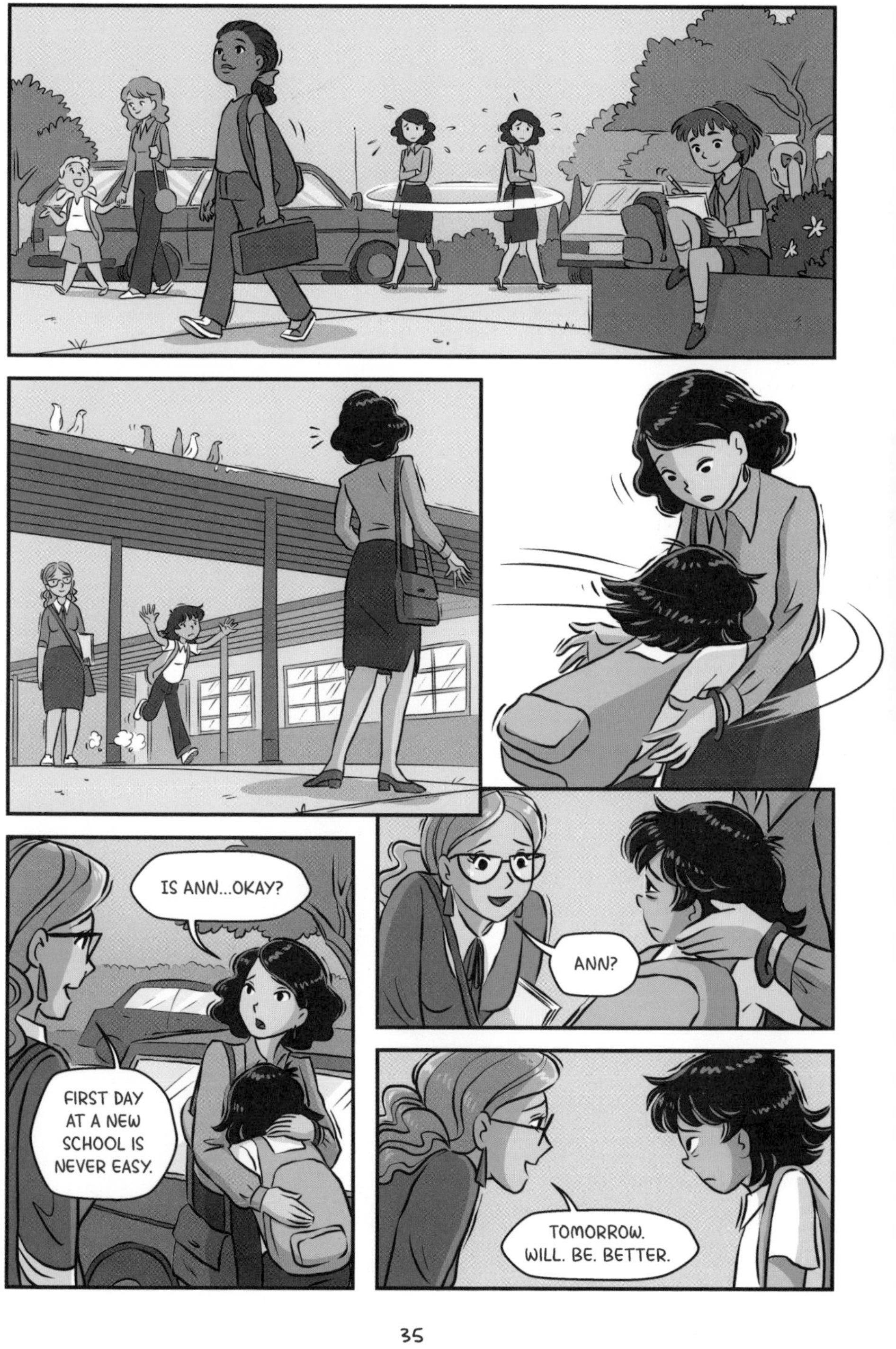

IS ANN...OKAY?
FIRST DAY AT A NEW SCHOOL IS NEVER EASY.
ANN?
TOMORROW. WILL. BE. BETTER.

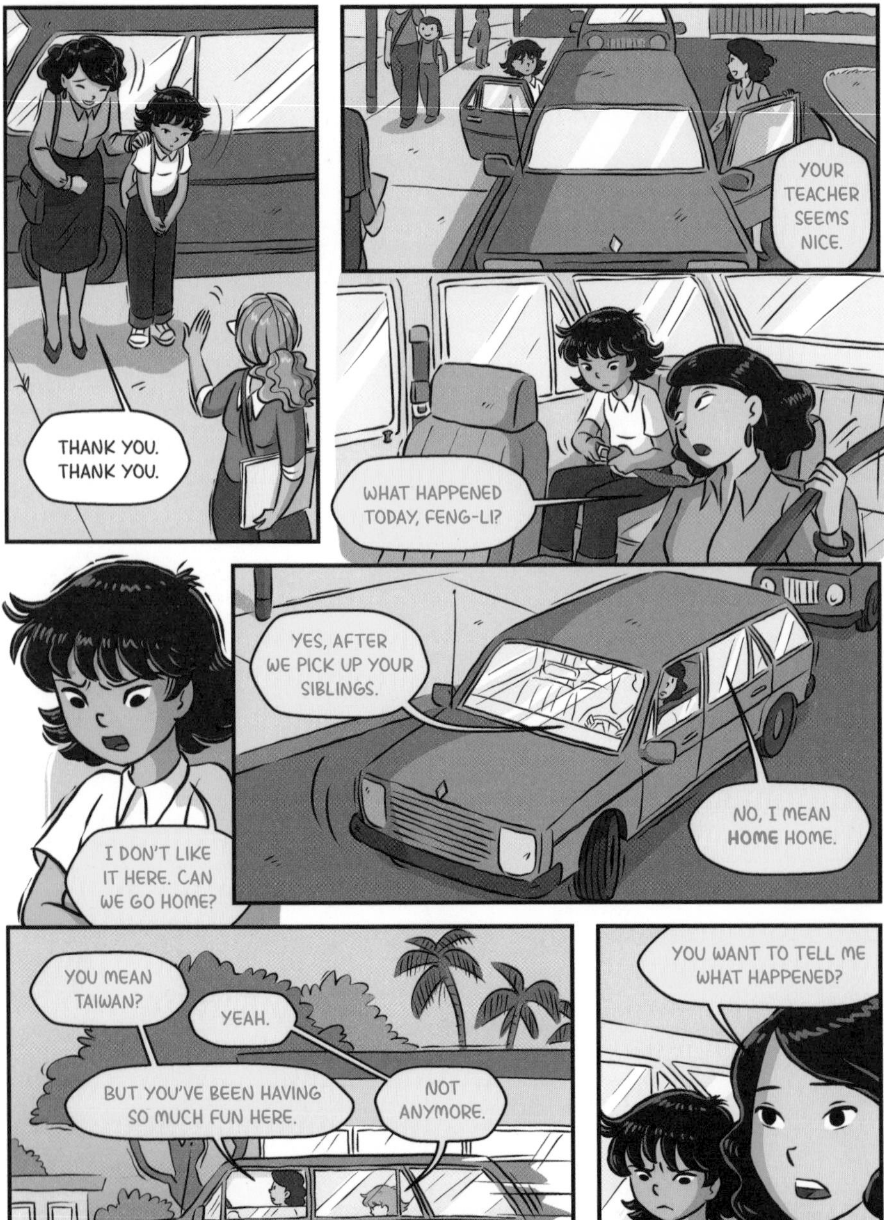
THANK YOU.
THANK YOU.
YOUR TEACHER SEEMS NICE.
WHAT HAPPENED TODAY, FENG-LI?
I DON'T LIKE IT HERE. CAN WE GO HOME?
YES, AFTER WE PICK UP YOUR SIBLINGS.
NO, I MEAN **HOME** HOME.
YOU MEAN TAIWAN?
YEAH.
BUT YOU'VE BEEN HAVING SO MUCH FUN HERE.
NOT ANYMORE.
YOU WANT TO TELL ME WHAT HAPPENED?

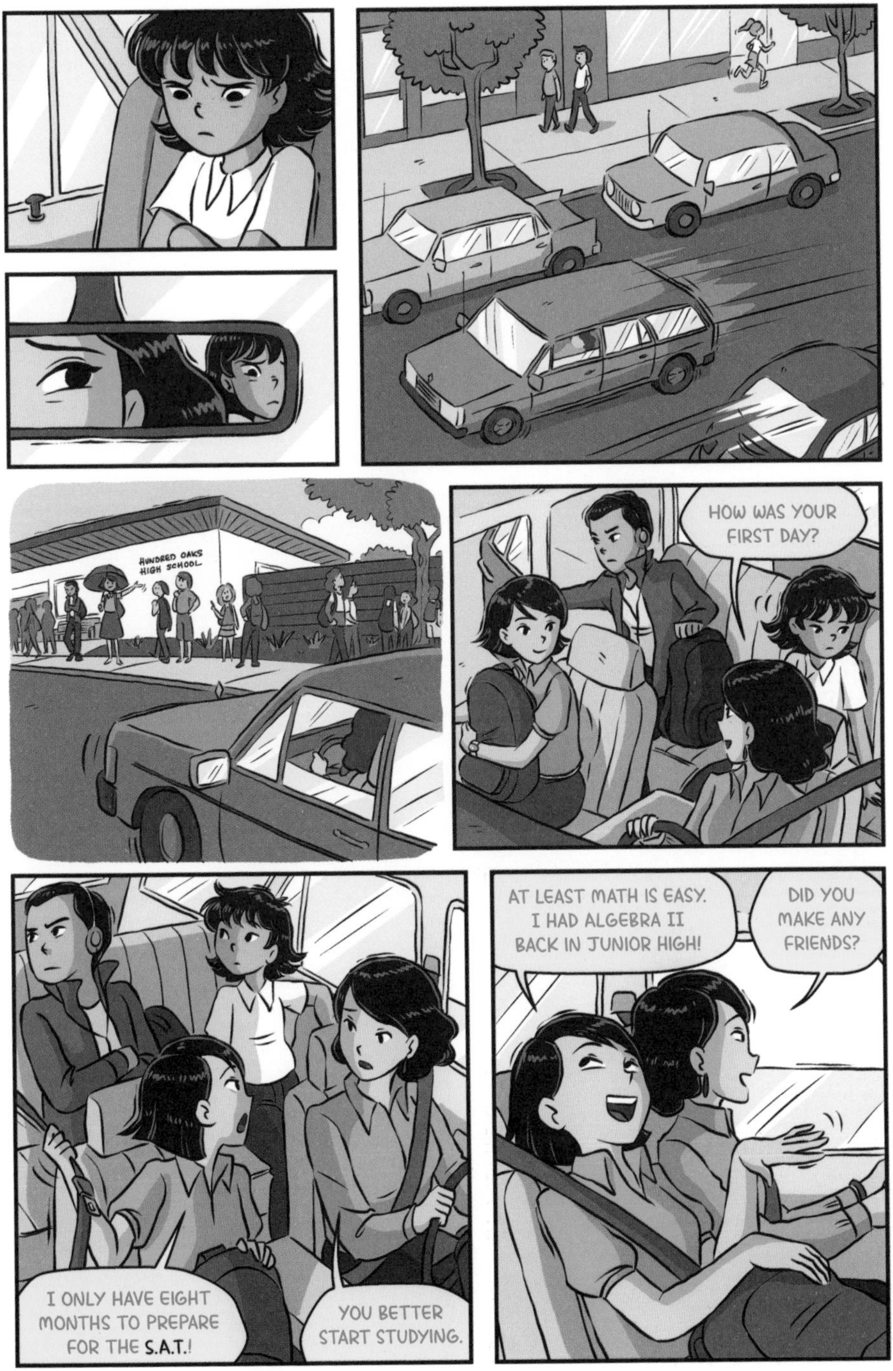
HUNDRED OAKS HIGH SCHOOL
HOW WAS YOUR FIRST DAY?
I ONLY HAVE EIGHT MONTHS TO PREPARE FOR THE S.A.T.!
YOU BETTER START STUDYING.
AT LEAST MATH IS EASY. I HAD ALGEBRA II BACK IN JUNIOR HIGH!
DID YOU MAKE ANY FRIENDS?

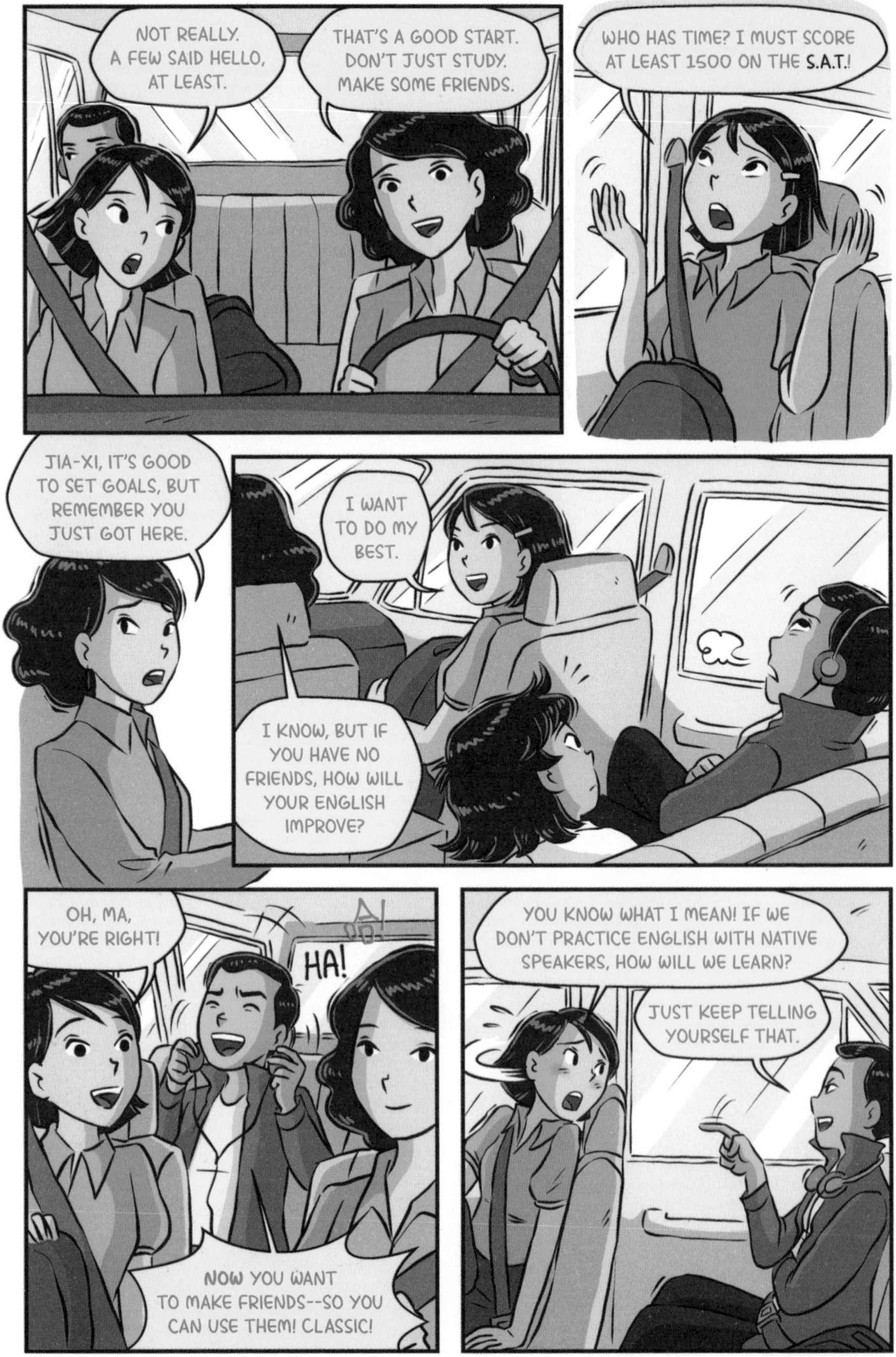
NOT REALLY. A FEW SAID HELLO, AT LEAST.
THAT'S A GOOD START. DON'T JUST STUDY. MAKE SOME FRIENDS.
WHO HAS TIME? I MUST SCORE AT LEAST 1500 ON THE S.A.T.!
JIA-XI, IT'S GOOD TO SET GOALS, BUT REMEMBER YOU JUST GOT HERE.
I WANT TO DO MY BEST.
I KNOW, BUT IF YOU HAVE NO FRIENDS, HOW WILL YOUR ENGLISH IMPROVE?
OH, MA, YOU'RE RIGHT!
HA!
NOW YOU WANT TO MAKE FRIENDS--SO YOU CAN USE THEM! CLASSIC!
YOU KNOW WHAT I MEAN! IF WE DON'T PRACTICE ENGLISH WITH NATIVE SPEAKERS, HOW WILL WE LEARN?
JUST KEEP TELLING YOURSELF THAT.

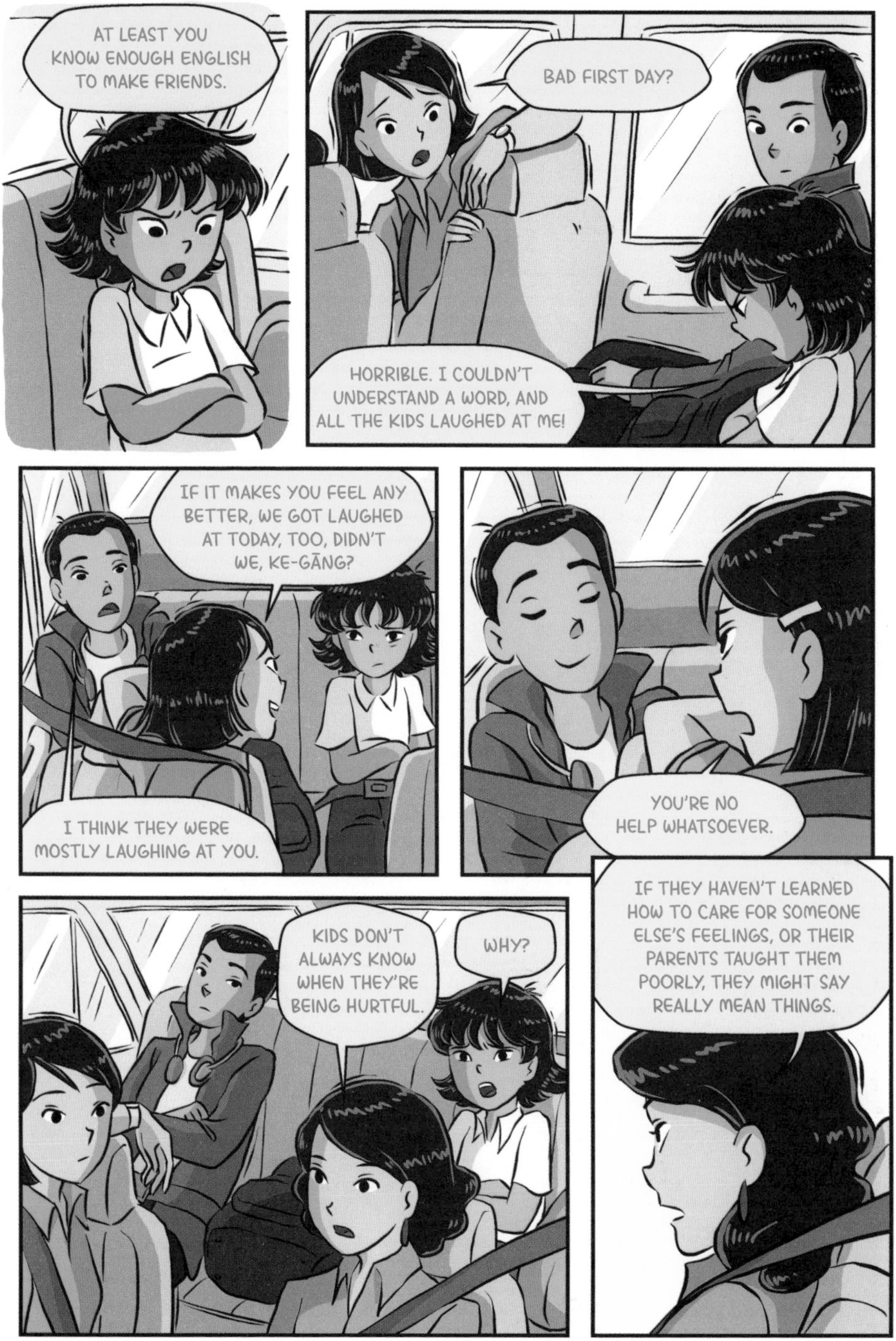
AT LEAST YOU KNOW ENOUGH ENGLISH TO MAKE FRIENDS.
BAD FIRST DAY?
HORRIBLE. I COULDN'T UNDERSTAND A WORD, AND ALL THE KIDS LAUGHED AT ME!
IF IT MAKES YOU FEEL ANY BETTER, WE GOT LAUGHED AT TODAY, TOO, DIDN'T WE, KE-GĀNG?
I THINK THEY WERE MOSTLY LAUGHING AT YOU.
YOU'RE NO HELP WHATSOEVER.
KIDS DON'T ALWAYS KNOW WHEN THEY'RE BEING HURTFUL.
WHY?
IF THEY HAVEN'T LEARNED HOW TO CARE FOR SOMEONE ELSE'S FEELINGS, OR THEIR PARENTS TAUGHT THEM POORLY, THEY MIGHT SAY REALLY MEAN THINGS.

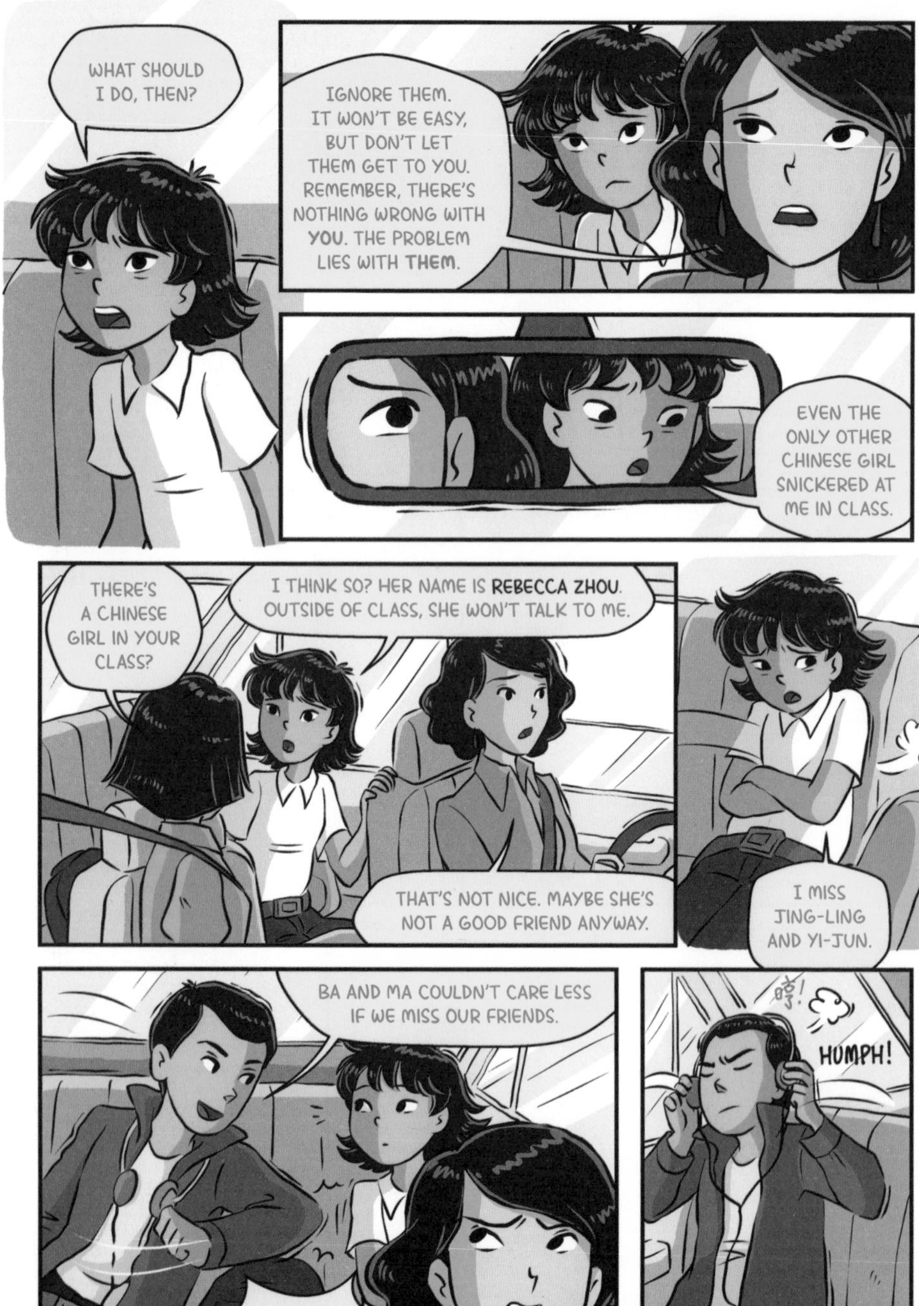
WHAT SHOULD I DO, THEN?
IGNORE THEM. IT WON'T BE EASY, BUT DON'T LET THEM GET TO YOU. REMEMBER, THERE'S NOTHING WRONG WITH **YOU**. THE PROBLEM LIES WITH **THEM**.
EVEN THE ONLY OTHER CHINESE GIRL SNICKERED AT ME IN CLASS.
THERE'S A CHINESE GIRL IN YOUR CLASS?
I THINK SO? HER NAME IS **REBECCA ZHOU**. OUTSIDE OF CLASS, SHE WON'T TALK TO ME.
THAT'S NOT NICE. MAYBE SHE'S NOT A GOOD FRIEND ANYWAY.
I MISS JING-LING AND YI-JUN.
BA AND MA COULDN'T CARE LESS IF WE MISS OUR FRIENDS.
KE-GĀNG, WHAT NONSENSE!
哼!
HUMPH!

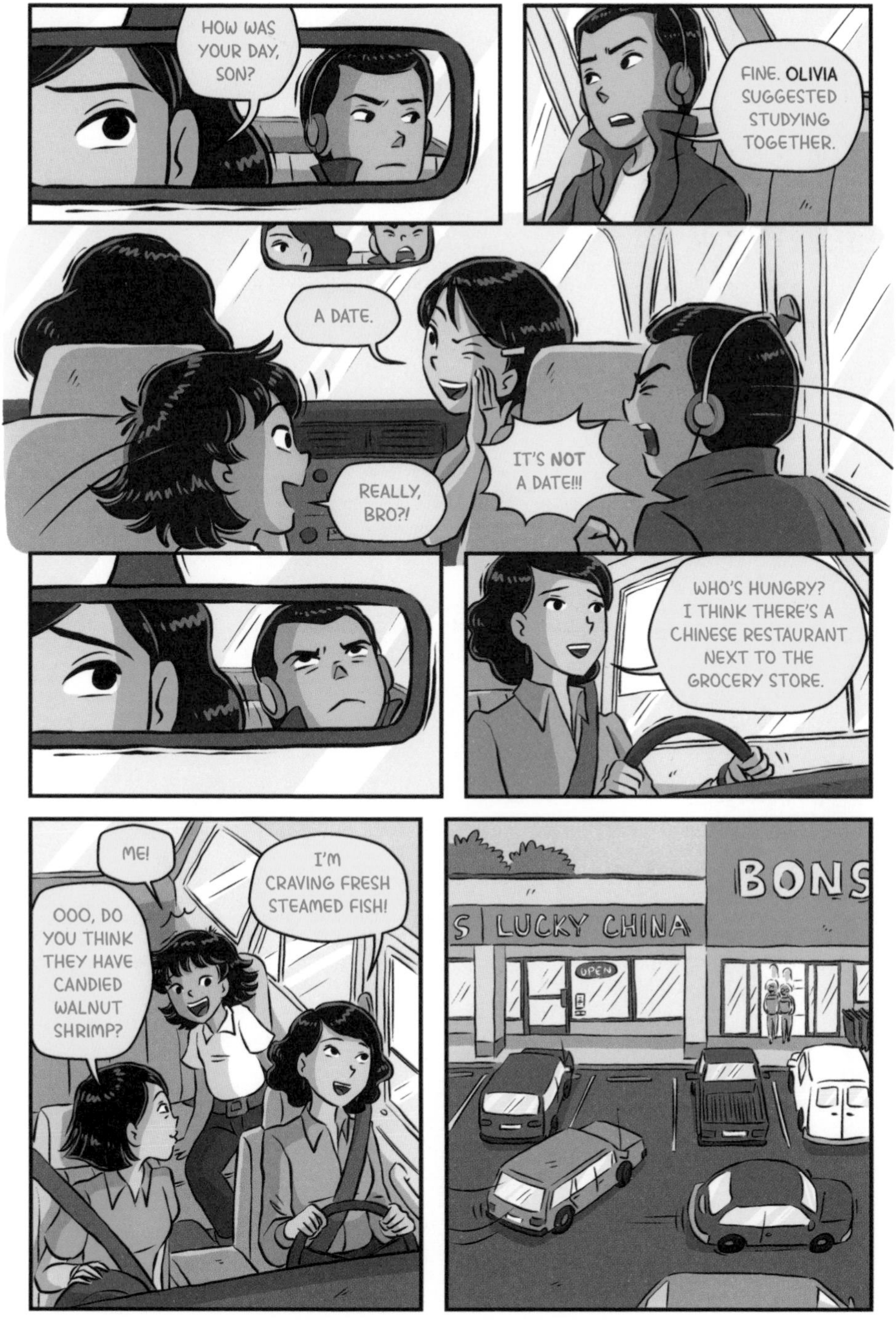
HOW WAS YOUR DAY, SON?
FINE. **OLIVIA** SUGGESTED STUDYING TOGETHER.
A DATE.
REALLY, BRO?!
IT'S **NOT** A DATE!!!
WHO'S HUNGRY? I THINK THERE'S A CHINESE RESTAURANT NEXT TO THE GROCERY STORE.
ME!
I'M CRAVING FRESH STEAMED FISH!
OOO, DO YOU THINK THEY HAVE CANDIED WALNUT SHRIMP?
S LUCKY CHINA
OPEN
BONS

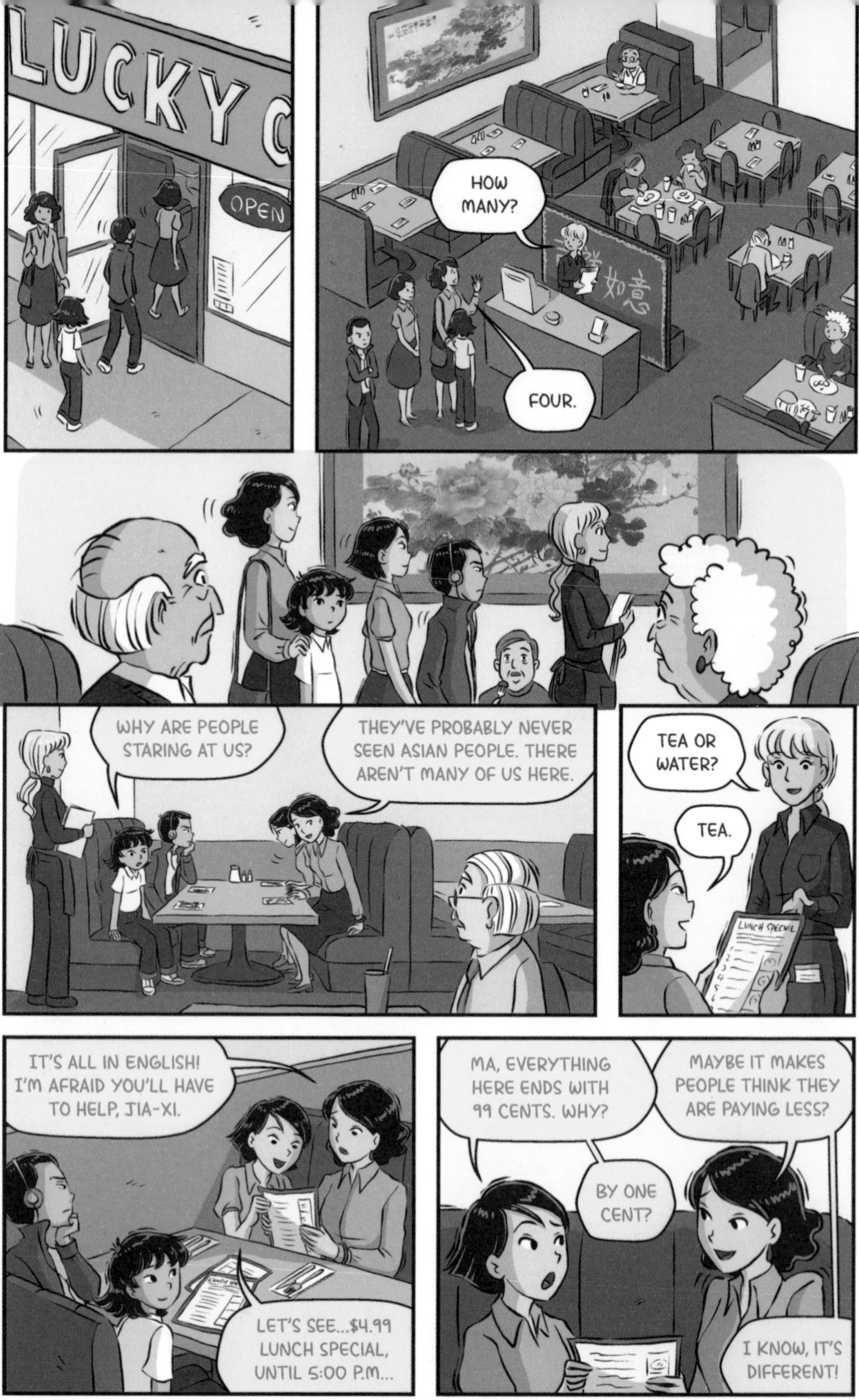
LUCKY
OPEN
HOW MANY?
FOUR.
如意
WHY ARE PEOPLE STARING AT US?
THEY'VE PROBABLY NEVER SEEN ASIAN PEOPLE. THERE AREN'T MANY OF US HERE.
TEA OR WATER?
TEA.
LUNCH SPECIAL
IT'S ALL IN ENGLISH! I'M AFRAID YOU'LL HAVE TO HELP, JIA-XI.
LET'S SEE...$4.99 LUNCH SPECIAL, UNTIL 5:00 P.M...
MA, EVERYTHING HERE ENDS WITH 99 CENTS. WHY?
MAYBE IT MAKES PEOPLE THINK THEY ARE PAYING LESS?
BY ONE CENT?
I KNOW, IT'S DIFFERENT!

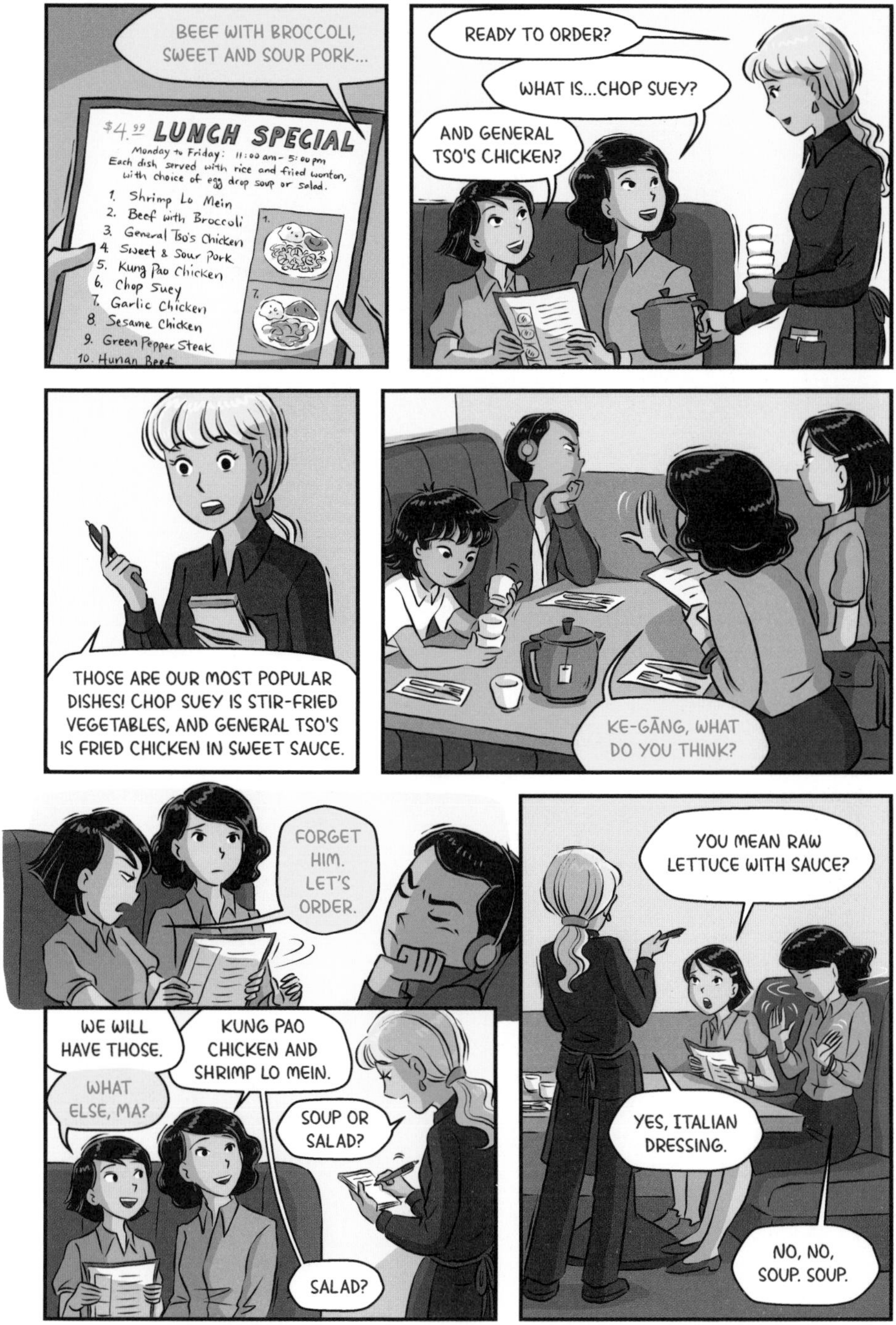
BEEF WITH BROCCOLI, SWEET AND SOUR PORK...
$4.99 LUNCH SPECIAL
Monday to Friday: 11:00 am - 5:00 pm
Each dish served with rice and fried wonton, with choice of egg drop soup or salad.
1. Shrimp Lo Mein
2. Beef with Broccoli
3. General Tso's Chicken
4. Sweet & Sour Pork
5. Kung Pao Chicken
6. Chop Suey
7. Garlic Chicken
8. Sesame Chicken
9. Green Pepper Steak
10. Hunan Beef
READY TO ORDER?
WHAT IS...CHOP SUEY?
AND GENERAL TSO'S CHICKEN?
THOSE ARE OUR MOST POPULAR DISHES! CHOP SUEY IS STIR-FRIED VEGETABLES, AND GENERAL TSO'S IS FRIED CHICKEN IN SWEET SAUCE.
KE-GĀNG, WHAT DO YOU THINK?
FORGET HIM. LET'S ORDER.
WE WILL HAVE THOSE.
WHAT ELSE, MA?
KUNG PAO CHICKEN AND SHRIMP LO MEIN.
SOUP OR SALAD?
SALAD?
YOU MEAN RAW LETTUCE WITH SAUCE?
YES, ITALIAN DRESSING.
NO, NO, SOUP. SOUP.

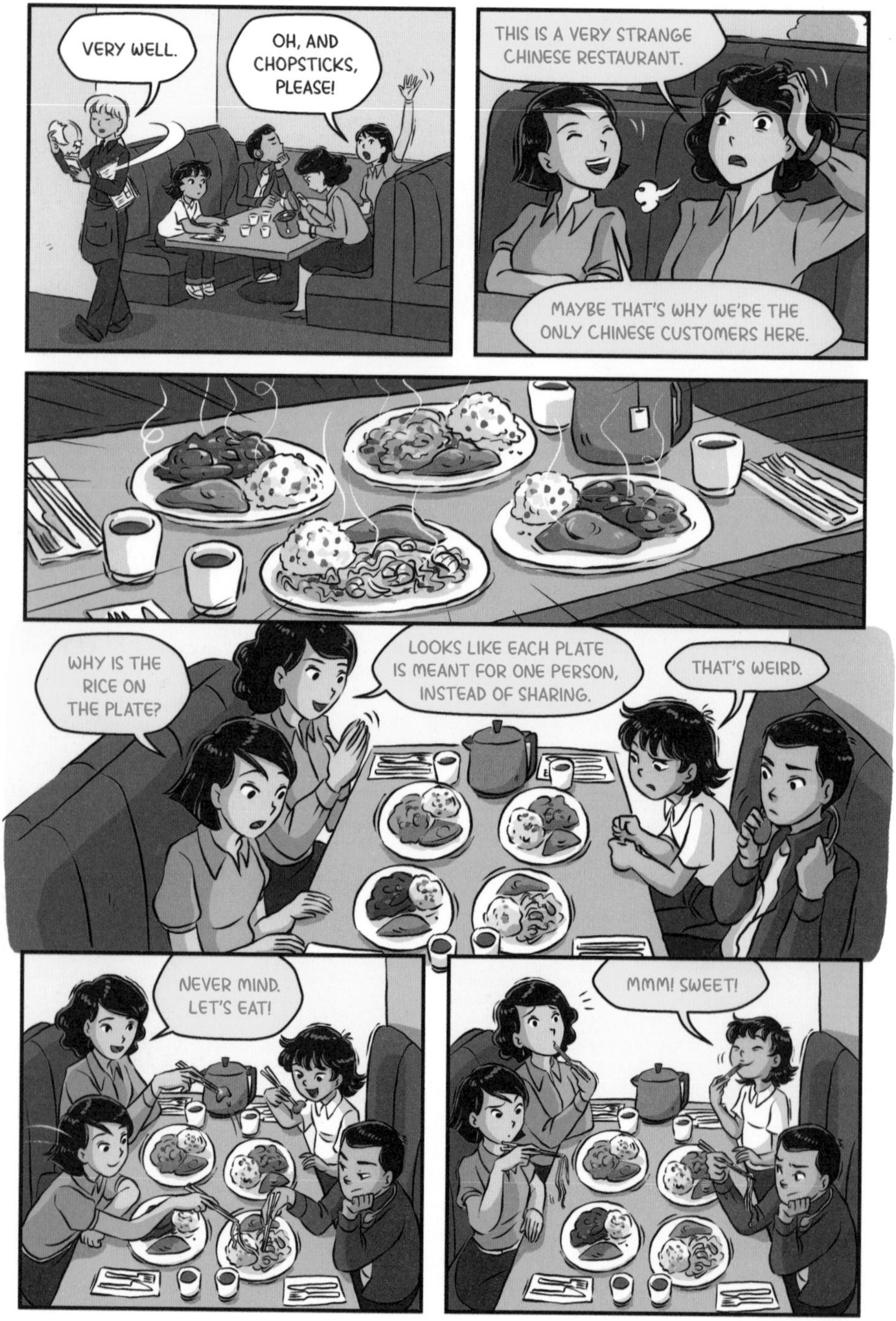
VERY WELL.
OH, AND CHOPSTICKS, PLEASE!
THIS IS A VERY STRANGE CHINESE RESTAURANT.
MAYBE THAT'S WHY WE'RE THE ONLY CHINESE CUSTOMERS HERE.
WHY IS THE RICE ON THE PLATE?
LOOKS LIKE EACH PLATE IS MEANT FOR ONE PERSON, INSTEAD OF SHARING.
THAT'S WEIRD.
NEVER MIND. LET'S EAT!
MMM! SWEET!

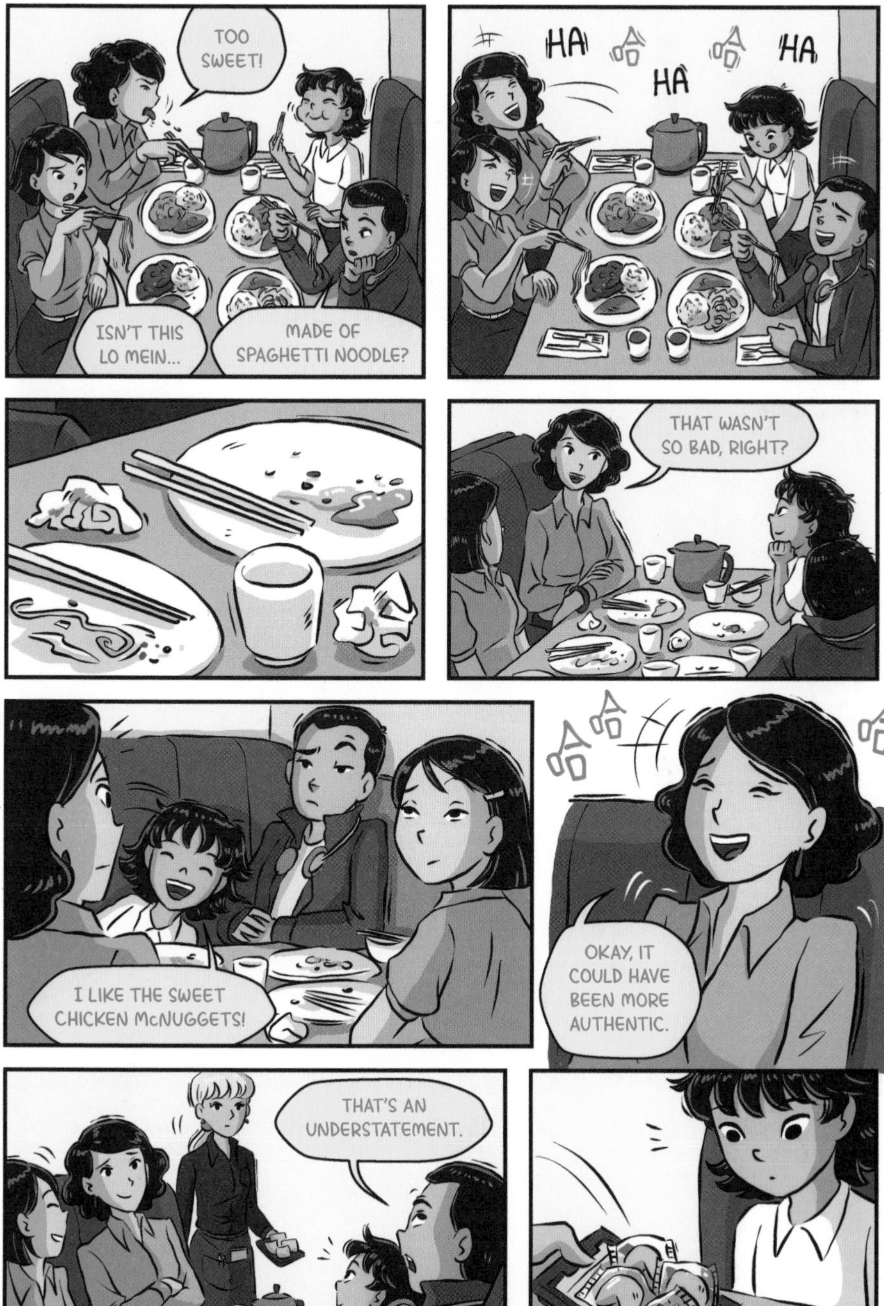
TOO SWEET!
ISN'T THIS LO MEIN...
MADE OF SPAGHETTI NOODLE?
HA
哈
哈
HA
HA
THAT WASN'T SO BAD, RIGHT?
I LIKE THE SWEET CHICKEN McNUGGETS!
哈
哈
哈
OKAY, IT COULD HAVE BEEN MORE AUTHENTIC.
THAT'S AN UNDERSTATEMENT.

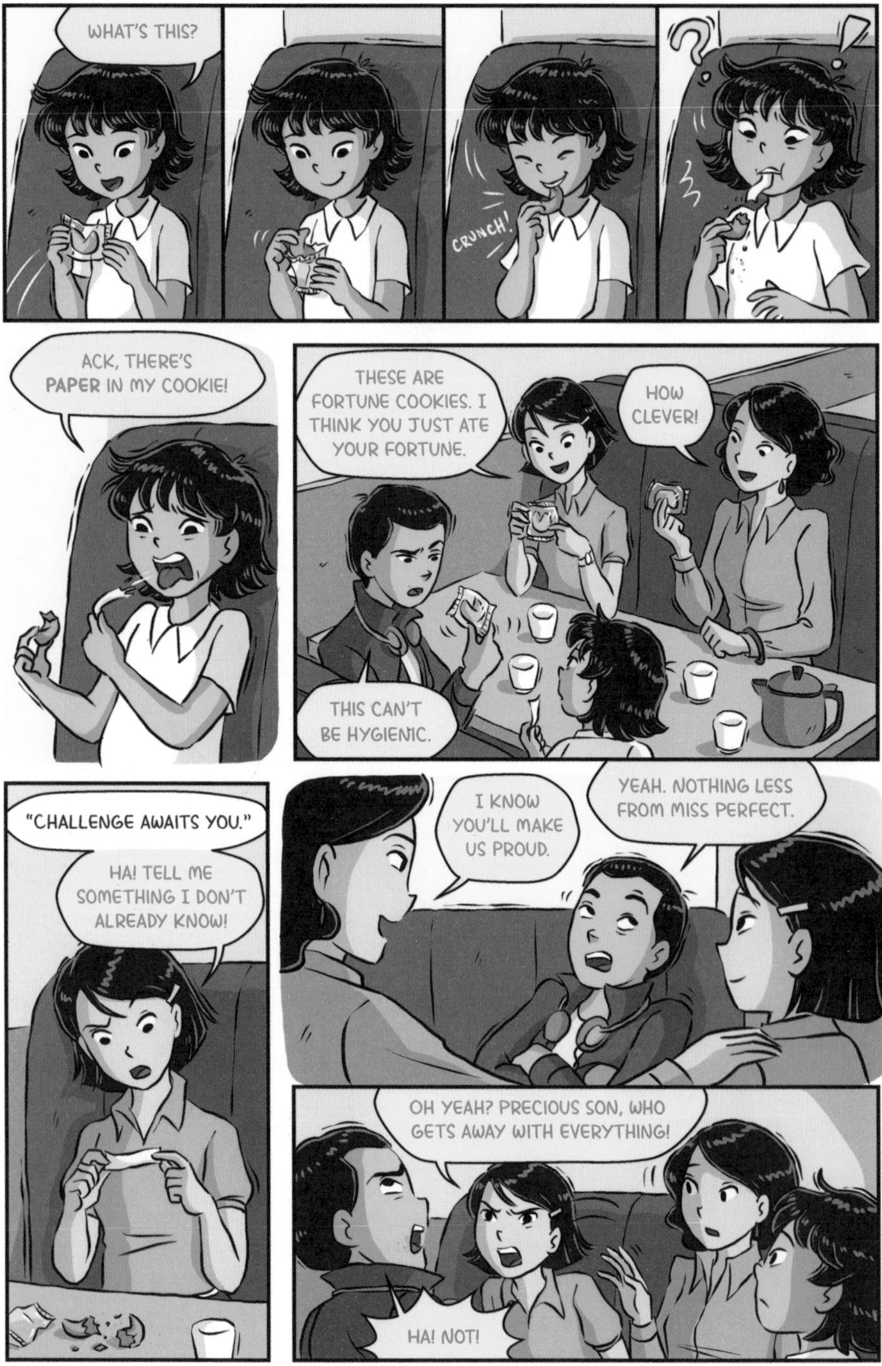
WHAT'S THIS?
CRUNCH!
?
!
ACK, THERE'S **PAPER** IN MY COOKIE!
THESE ARE FORTUNE COOKIES. I THINK YOU JUST ATE YOUR FORTUNE.
HOW CLEVER!
THIS CAN'T BE HYGIENIC.
"CHALLENGE AWAITS YOU."
HA! TELL ME SOMETHING I DON'T ALREADY KNOW!
I KNOW YOU'LL MAKE US PROUD.
YEAH. NOTHING LESS FROM MISS PERFECT.
OH YEAH? PRECIOUS SON, WHO GETS AWAY WITH EVERYTHING!
HA! NOT!

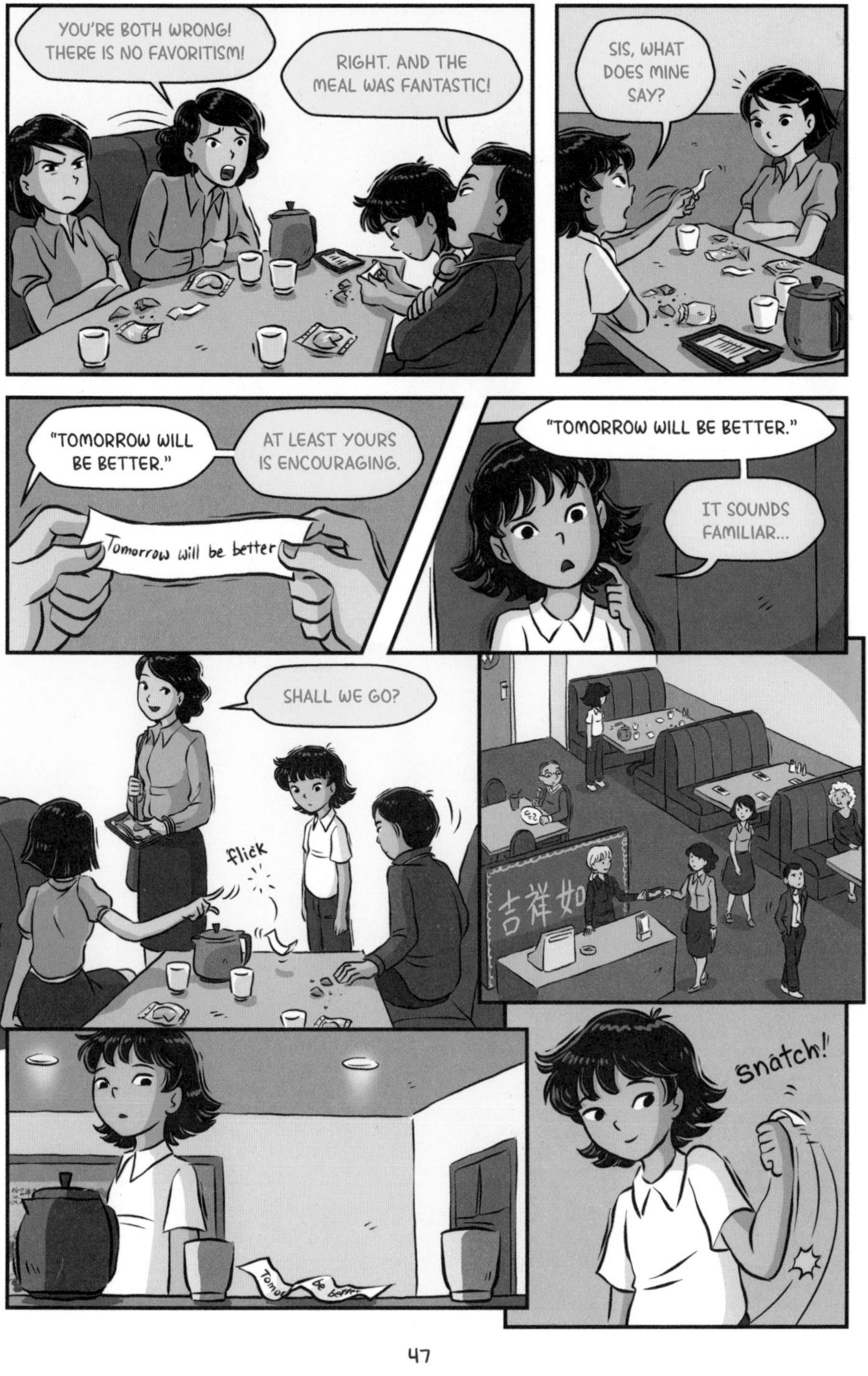
YOU'RE BOTH WRONG! THERE IS NO FAVORITISM!
RIGHT. AND THE MEAL WAS FANTASTIC!
SIS, WHAT DOES MINE SAY?
"TOMORROW WILL BE BETTER."
AT LEAST YOURS IS ENCOURAGING.
Tomorrow will be better
"TOMORROW WILL BE BETTER."
IT SOUNDS FAMILIAR...
SHALL WE GO?
flick
吉祥如
Snatch!

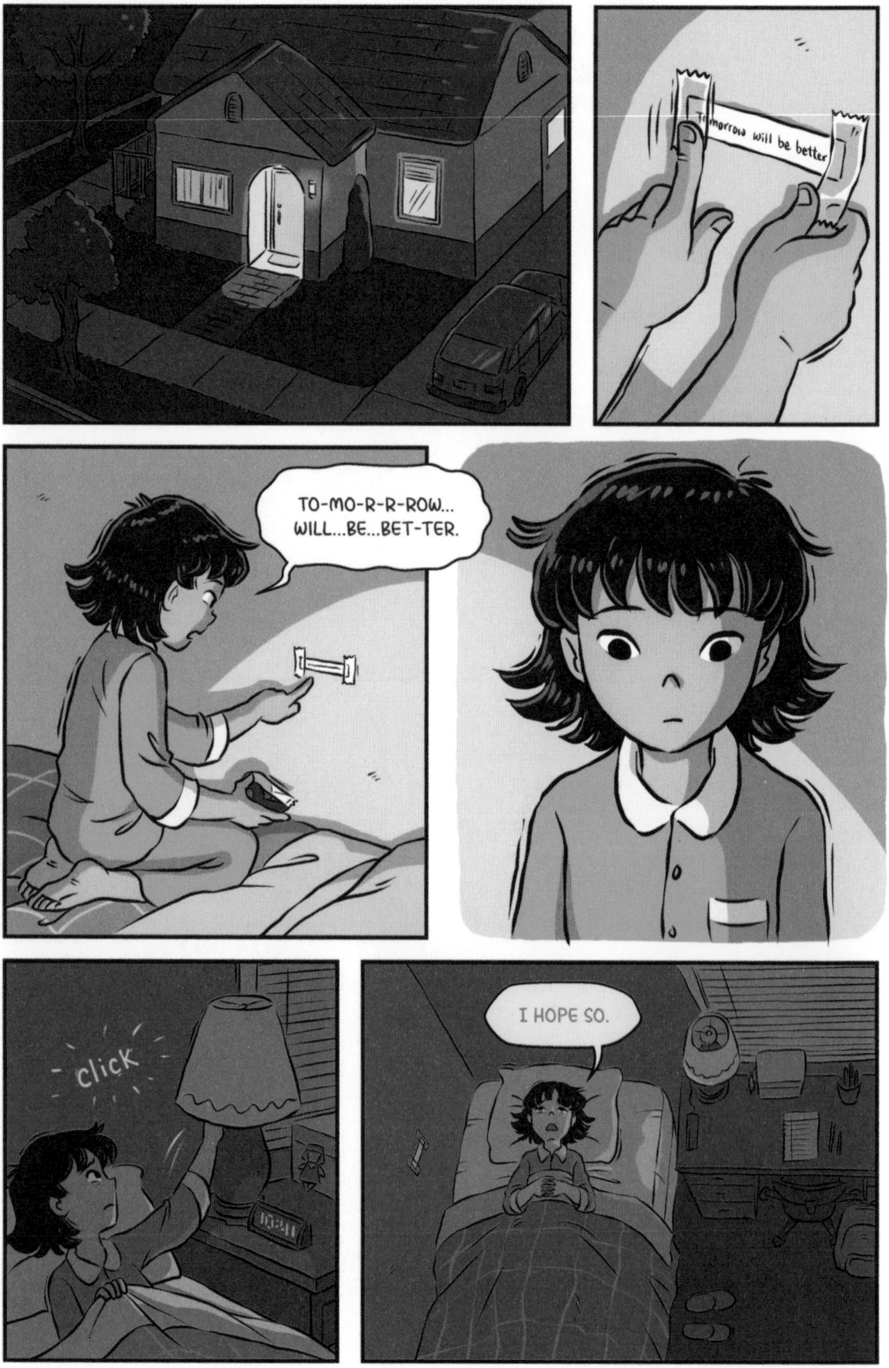
Tomorrow will be better
TO-MO-R-R-ROW... WILL...BE...BET-TER.
click
I HOPE SO.

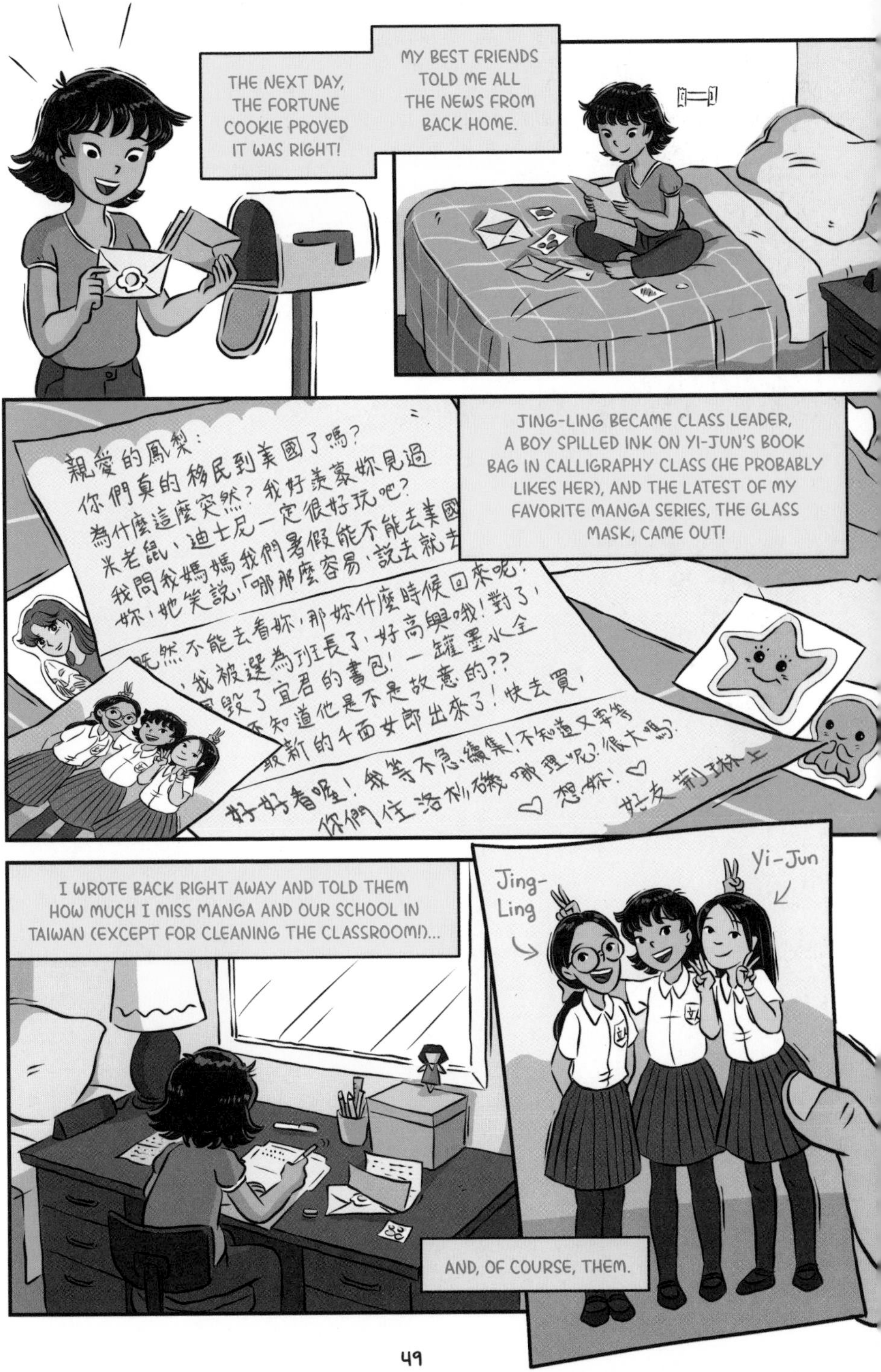
THE NEXT DAY, THE FORTUNE COOKIE PROVED IT WAS RIGHT!
MY BEST FRIENDS TOLD ME ALL THE NEWS FROM BACK HOME.
親愛的鳳梨：
你們真的移民到美國了嗎？
為什麼這麼突然？我好羨慕妳見過
米老鼠、迪士尼一定很好玩吧？
我問我媽媽我們暑假能不能去美國
妳，她笑說，「哪那麼容易，說去就
既然不能去看妳，那妳什麼時候回來呢？
，我被選為班長了，好高興哦！對了，
毀了宜君的書包！一罐墨水全
不知道他是不是故意的？？
新的千面女郎出來了！快去買，
好好看喔！我等不急續集！不知道又要等
你們住洛杉磯哪裡呢？很大嗎？
♡ 想妳！♡
好友 荊玲 上
JING-LING BECAME CLASS LEADER, A BOY SPILLED INK ON YI-JUN'S BOOK BAG IN CALLIGRAPHY CLASS (HE PROBABLY LIKES HER), AND THE LATEST OF MY FAVORITE MANGA SERIES, THE GLASS MASK, CAME OUT!
I WROTE BACK RIGHT AWAY AND TOLD THEM HOW MUCH I MISS MANGA AND OUR SCHOOL IN TAIWAN (EXCEPT FOR CLEANING THE CLASSROOM!)...
Jing-Ling
Yi-Jun
AND, OF COURSE, THEM.

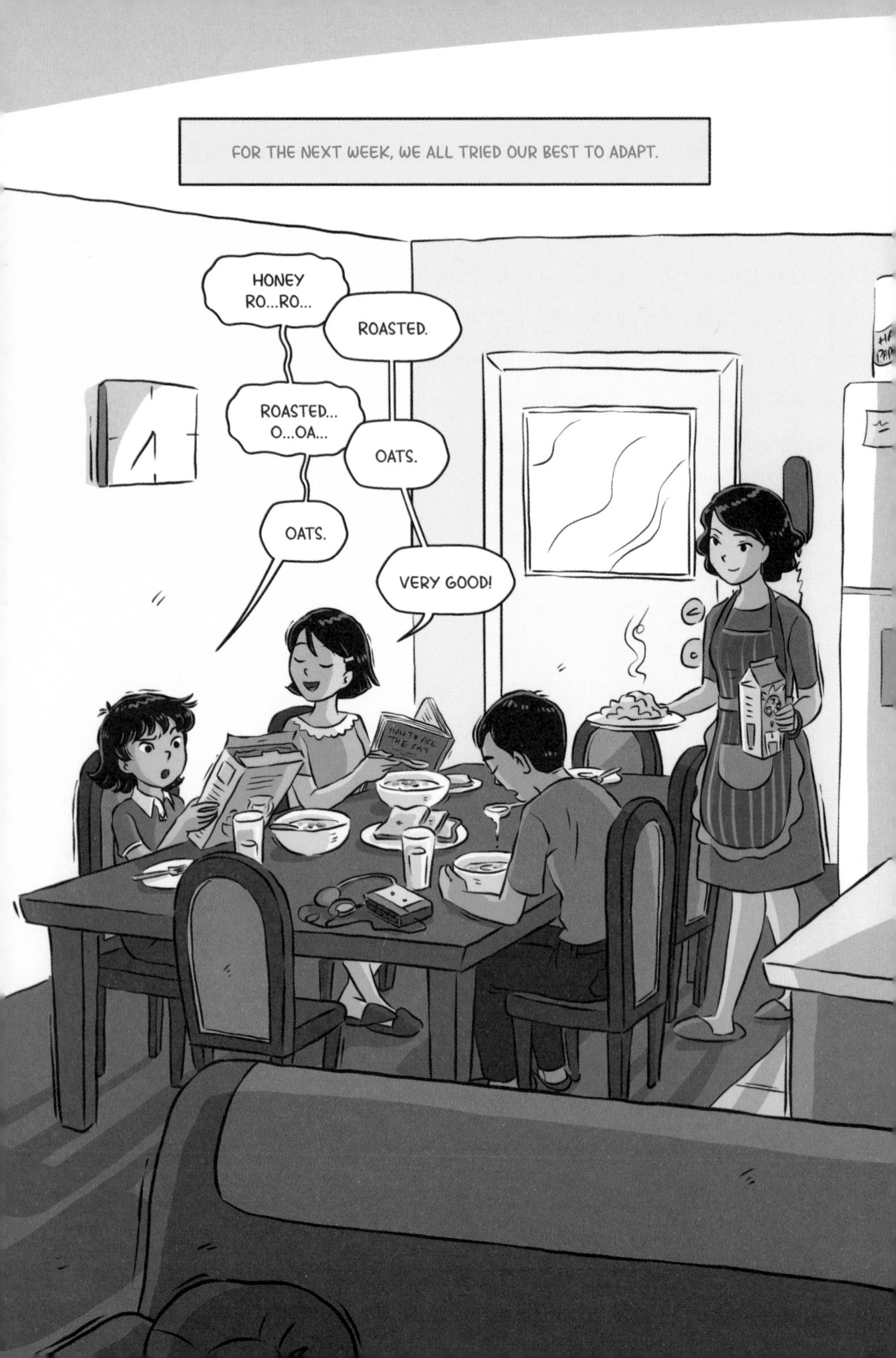
FOR THE NEXT WEEK, WE ALL TRIED OUR BEST TO ADAPT.
HONEY RO...RO...
ROASTED.
ROASTED... O...OA...
OATS.
OATS.
VERY GOOD!
HOW TO ACE THE SAT

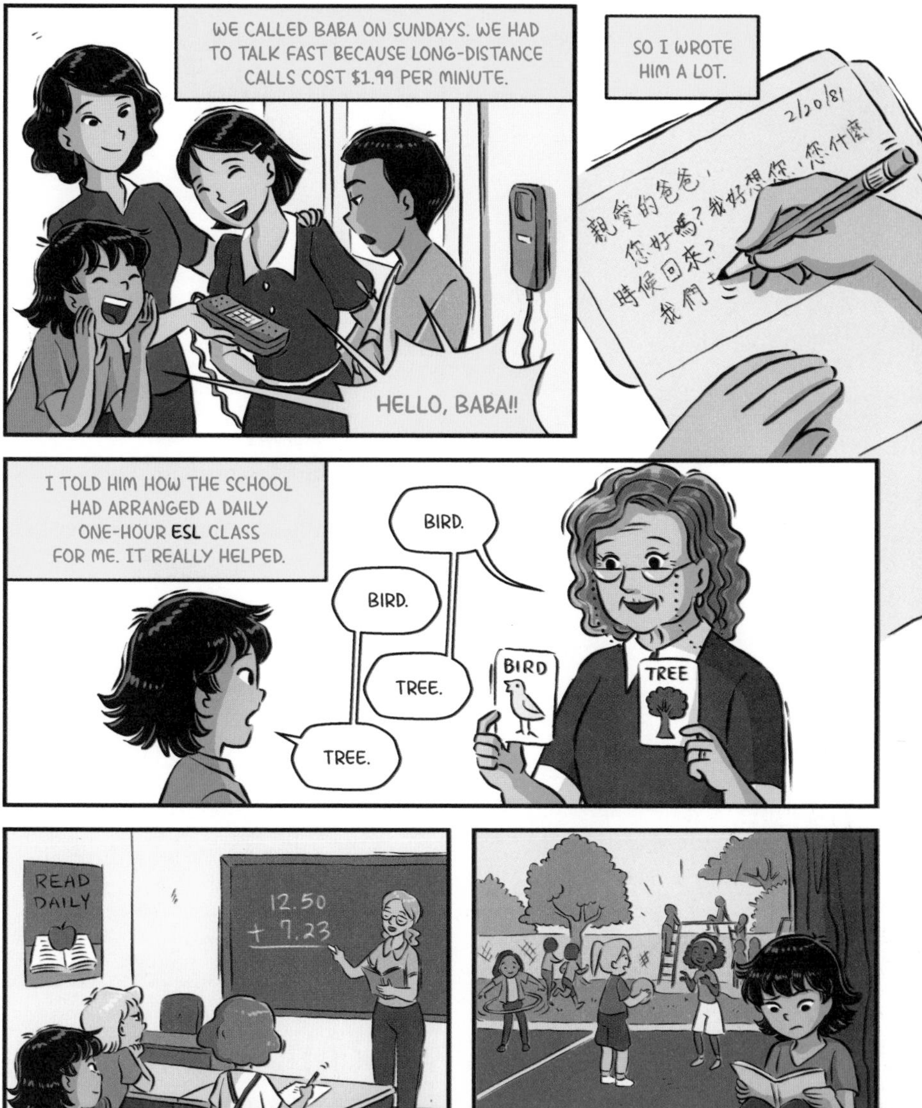

WE CALLED BABA ON SUNDAYS. WE HAD TO TALK FAST BECAUSE LONG-DISTANCE CALLS COST $1.99 PER MINUTE.
HELLO, BABA!!
SO I WROTE HIM A LOT.
2/20/81
親愛的爸爸，
您好嗎？我好想您，您什麼
時候回來？
我們
I TOLD HIM HOW THE SCHOOL HAD ARRANGED A DAILY ONE-HOUR **ESL** CLASS FOR ME. IT REALLY HELPED.
BIRD.
BIRD.
TREE.
TREE.
BIRD
TREE
READ DAILY
12.50
+ 7.23
HOW I STRUGGLED IN EVERYTHING, EXCEPT FOR MATH.
HOW THE OTHER KIDS STILL IGNORED ME, BUT I USED THE TIME TO READ. SIS SAID IT DIDN'T MATTER IF I DIDN'T UNDERSTAND, JUST KEEP ON READING.

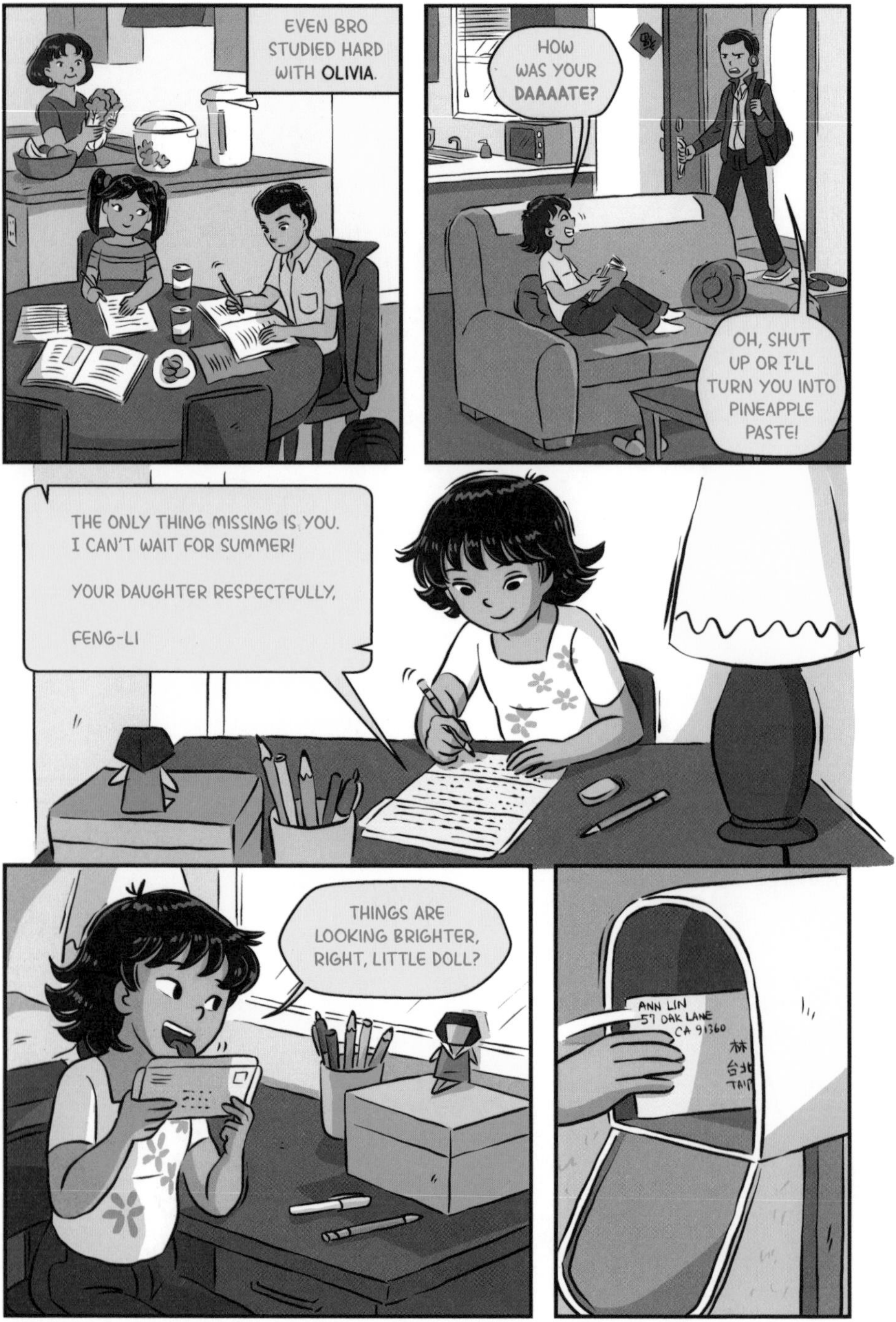
EVEN BRO STUDIED HARD WITH **OLIVIA**.
HOW WAS YOUR **DAAAATE?**
OH, SHUT UP OR I'LL TURN YOU INTO PINEAPPLE PASTE!
THE ONLY THING MISSING IS YOU. I CAN'T WAIT FOR SUMMER!
YOUR DAUGHTER RESPECTFULLY,
FENG-LI
THINGS ARE LOOKING BRIGHTER, RIGHT, LITTLE DOLL?
ANN LIN
57 OAK LANE
CA 91360
林
台北

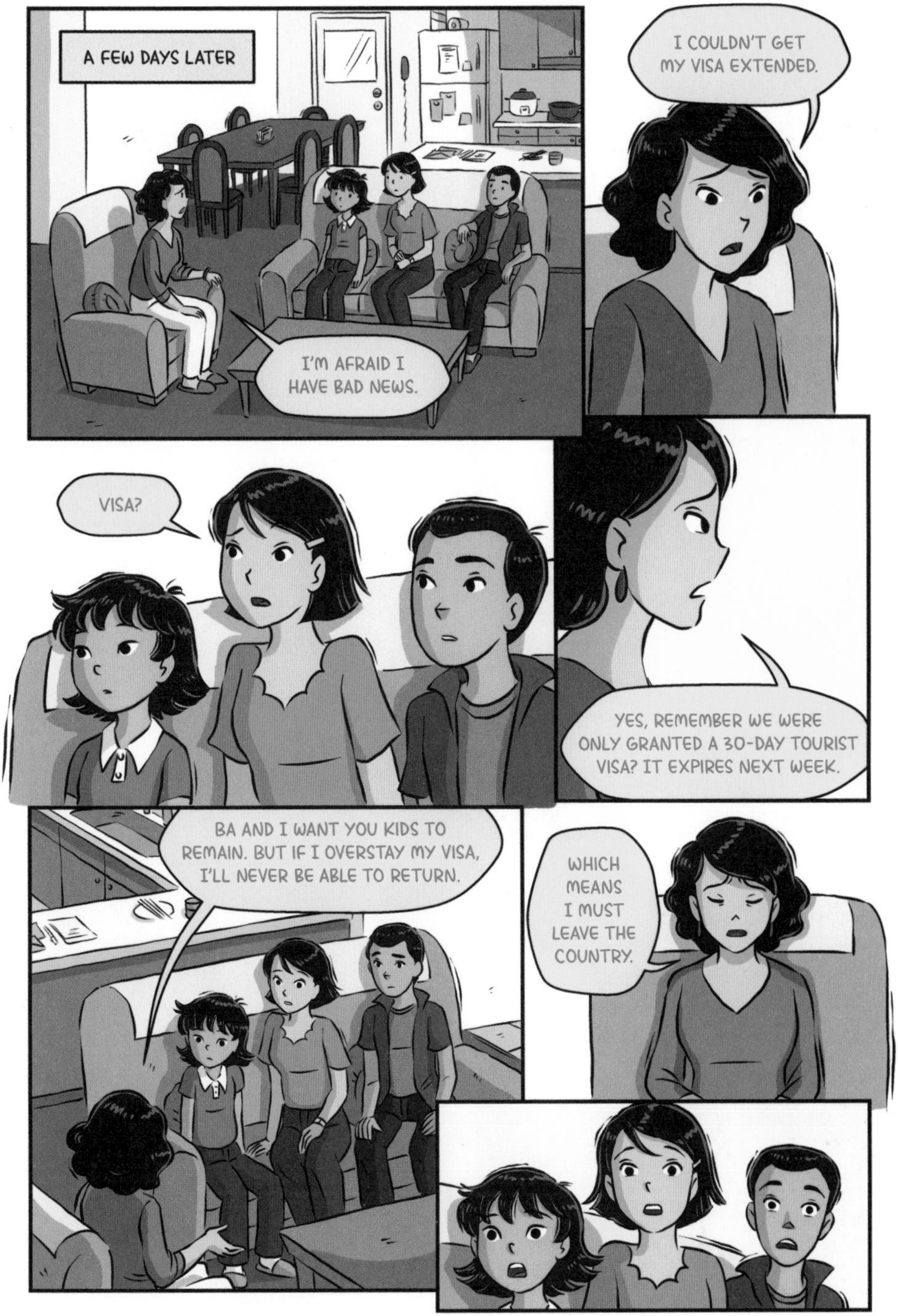
A FEW DAYS LATER
I'M AFRAID I HAVE BAD NEWS.
I COULDN'T GET MY VISA EXTENDED.
VISA?
YES, REMEMBER WE WERE ONLY GRANTED A 30-DAY TOURIST VISA? IT EXPIRES NEXT WEEK.
BA AND I WANT YOU KIDS TO REMAIN. BUT IF I OVERSTAY MY VISA, I'LL NEVER BE ABLE TO RETURN.
WHICH MEANS I MUST LEAVE THE COUNTRY.

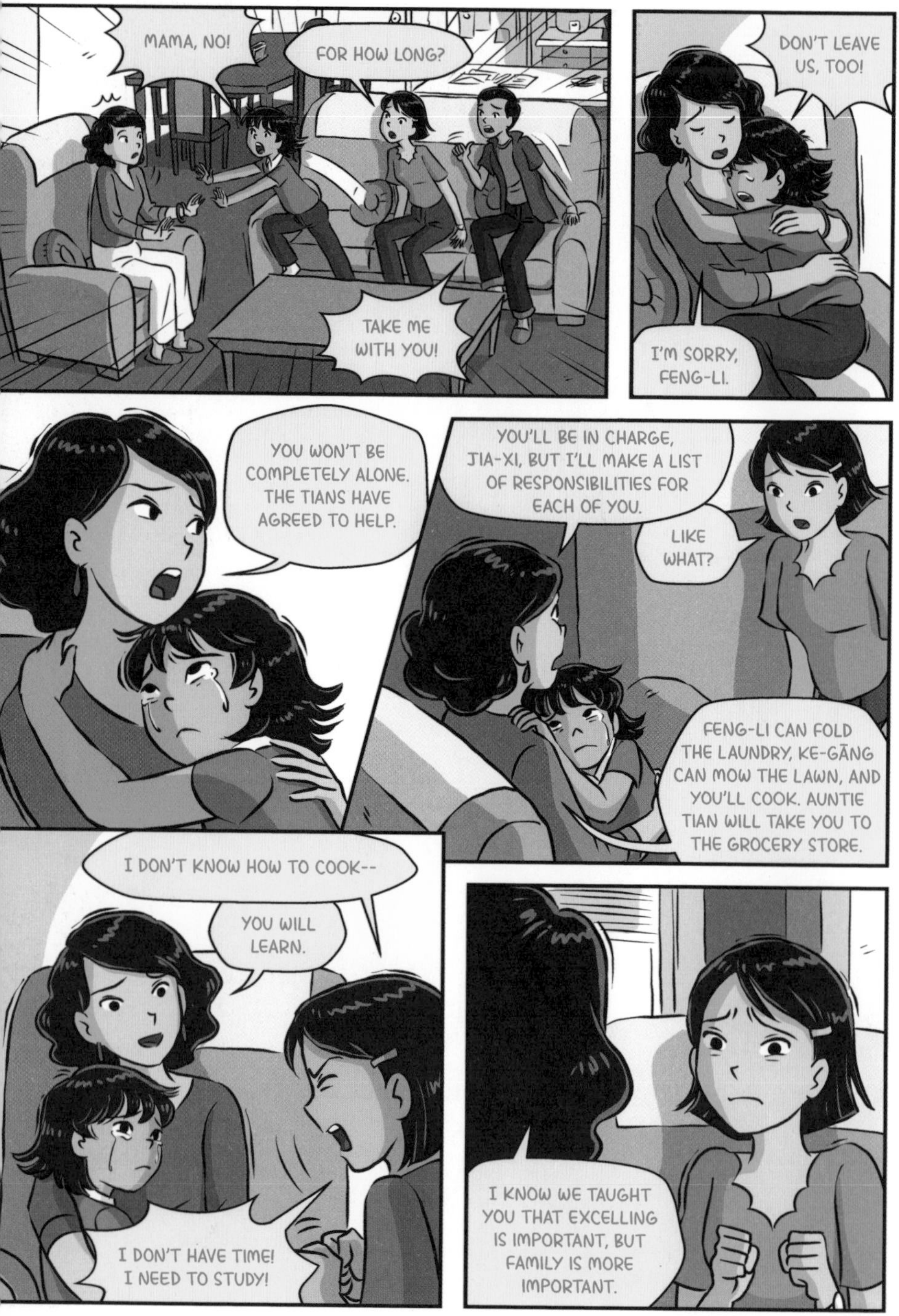
MAMA, NO!
FOR HOW LONG?
TAKE ME WITH YOU!
DON'T LEAVE US, TOO!
I'M SORRY, FENG-LI.
YOU WON'T BE COMPLETELY ALONE. THE TIANS HAVE AGREED TO HELP.
YOU'LL BE IN CHARGE, JIA-XI, BUT I'LL MAKE A LIST OF RESPONSIBILITIES FOR EACH OF YOU.
LIKE WHAT?
FENG-LI CAN FOLD THE LAUNDRY, KE-GĀNG CAN MOW THE LAWN, AND YOU'LL COOK. AUNTIE TIAN WILL TAKE YOU TO THE GROCERY STORE.
I DON'T KNOW HOW TO COOK--
YOU WILL LEARN.
I DON'T HAVE TIME! I NEED TO STUDY!
I KNOW WE TAUGHT YOU THAT EXCELLING IS IMPORTANT, BUT FAMILY IS MORE IMPORTANT.

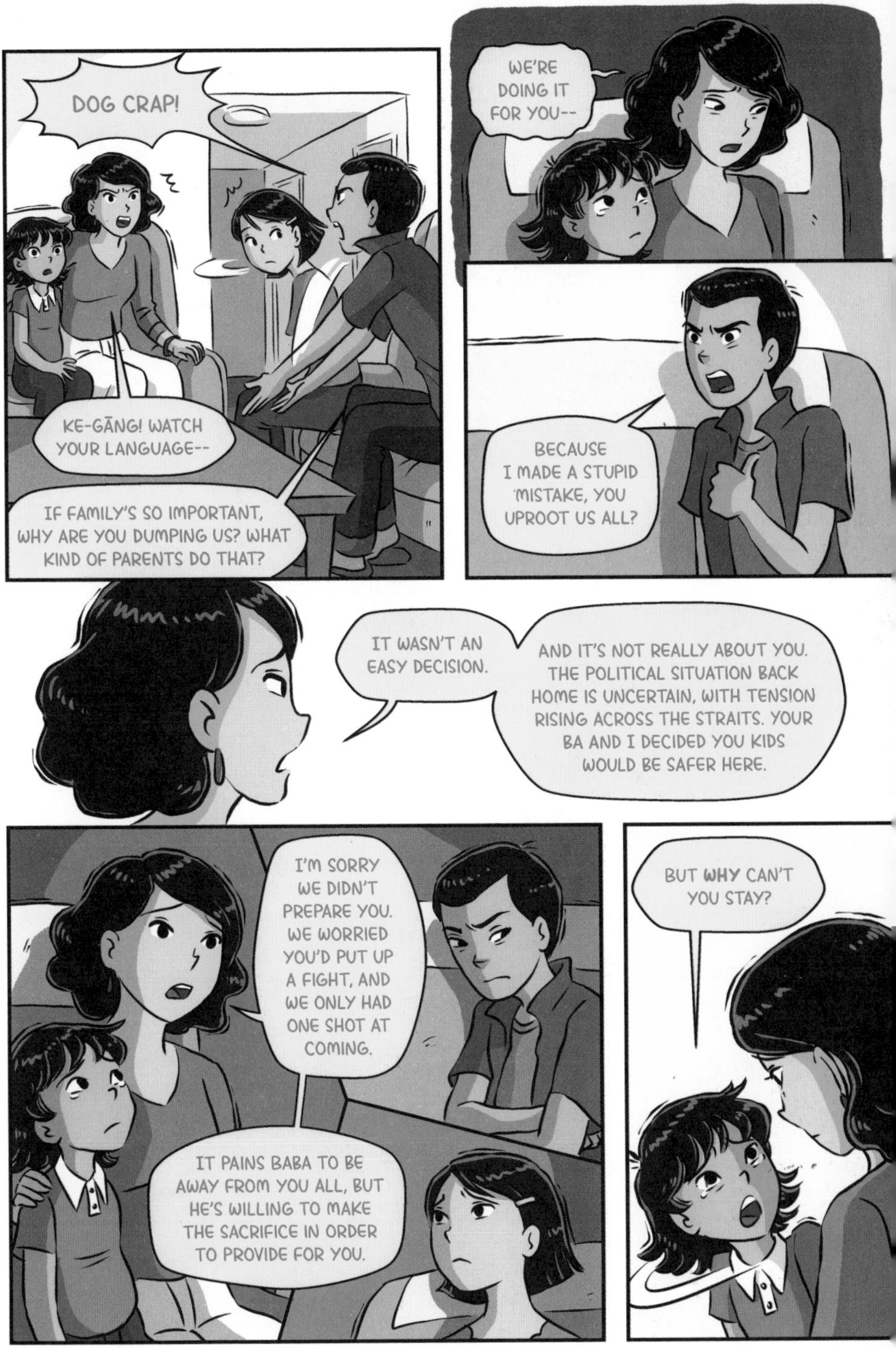
DOG CRAP!
KE-GĀNG! WATCH YOUR LANGUAGE--
IF FAMILY'S SO IMPORTANT, WHY ARE YOU DUMPING US? WHAT KIND OF PARENTS DO THAT?
WE'RE DOING IT FOR YOU--
BECAUSE I MADE A STUPID MISTAKE, YOU UPROOT US ALL?
IT WASN'T AN EASY DECISION.
AND IT'S NOT REALLY ABOUT YOU. THE POLITICAL SITUATION BACK HOME IS UNCERTAIN, WITH TENSION RISING ACROSS THE STRAITS. YOUR BA AND I DECIDED YOU KIDS WOULD BE SAFER HERE.
I'M SORRY WE DIDN'T PREPARE YOU. WE WORRIED YOU'D PUT UP A FIGHT, AND WE ONLY HAD ONE SHOT AT COMING.
IT PAINS BABA TO BE AWAY FROM YOU ALL, BUT HE'S WILLING TO MAKE THE SACRIFICE IN ORDER TO PROVIDE FOR YOU.
BUT **WHY** CAN'T YOU STAY?

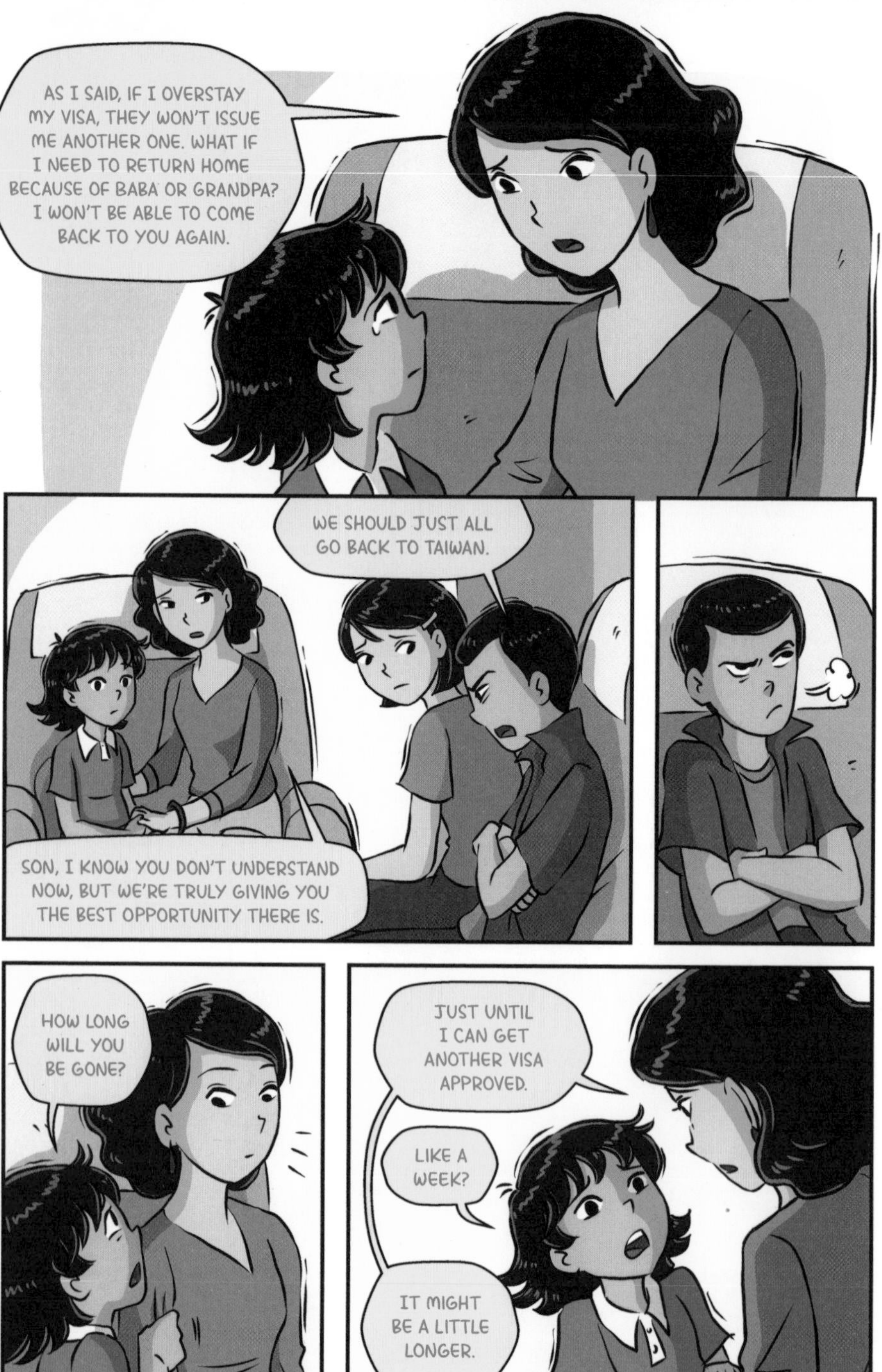
AS I SAID, IF I OVERSTAY MY VISA, THEY WON'T ISSUE ME ANOTHER ONE. WHAT IF I NEED TO RETURN HOME BECAUSE OF BABA OR GRANDPA? I WON'T BE ABLE TO COME BACK TO YOU AGAIN.
WE SHOULD JUST ALL GO BACK TO TAIWAN.
SON, I KNOW YOU DON'T UNDERSTAND NOW, BUT WE'RE TRULY GIVING YOU THE BEST OPPORTUNITY THERE IS.
HOW LONG WILL YOU BE GONE?
JUST UNTIL I CAN GET ANOTHER VISA APPROVED.
LIKE A WEEK?
IT MIGHT BE A LITTLE LONGER.

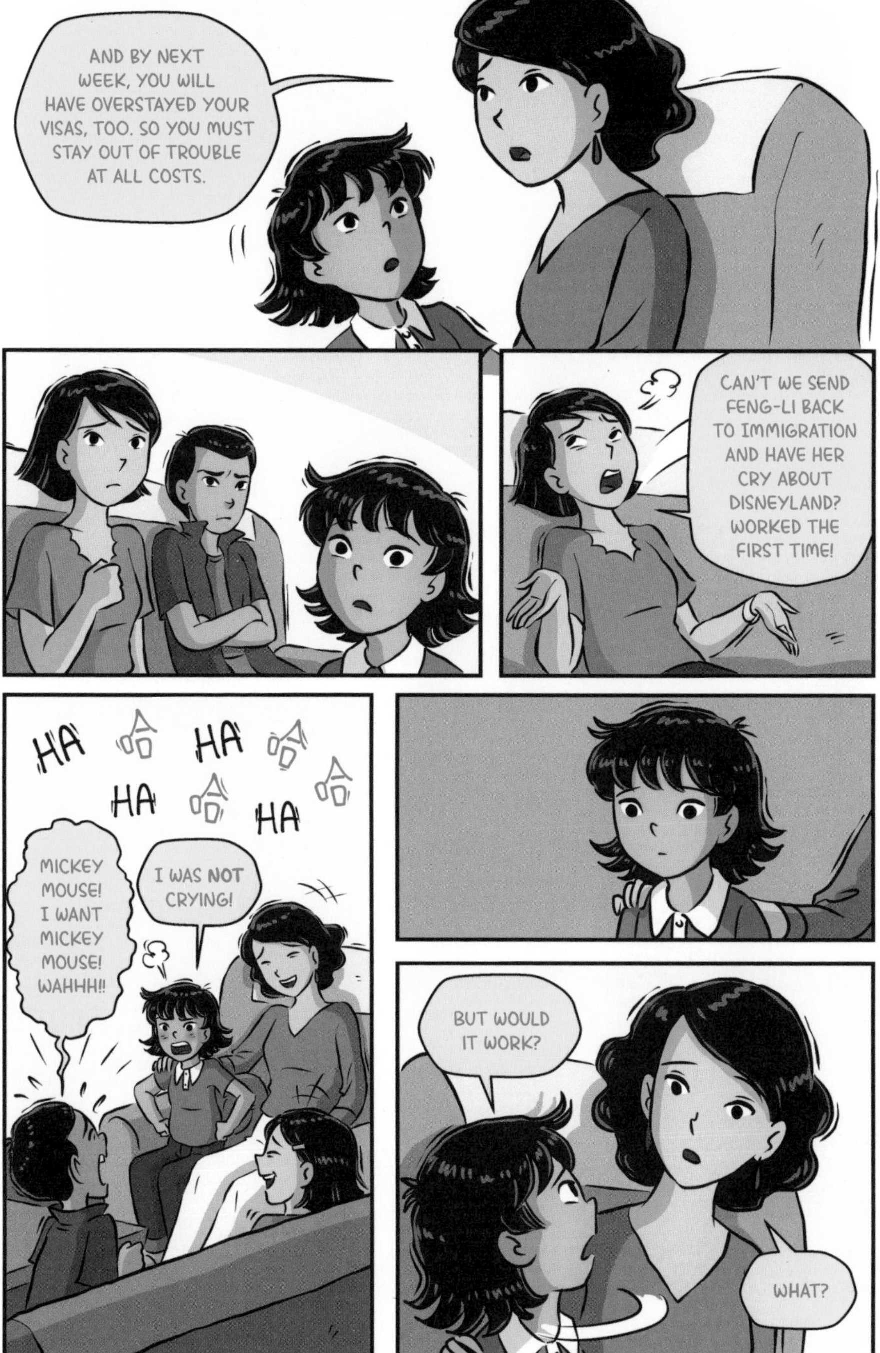
AND BY NEXT WEEK, YOU WILL HAVE OVERSTAYED YOUR VISAS, TOO. SO YOU MUST STAY OUT OF TROUBLE AT ALL COSTS.
CAN'T WE SEND FENG-LI BACK TO IMMIGRATION AND HAVE HER CRY ABOUT DISNEYLAND? WORKED THE FIRST TIME!
HA 哈 HA 哈 HA 哈 哈 HA
MICKEY MOUSE! I WANT MICKEY MOUSE! WAHHH!!
I WAS **NOT** CRYING!
BUT WOULD IT WORK?
WHAT?

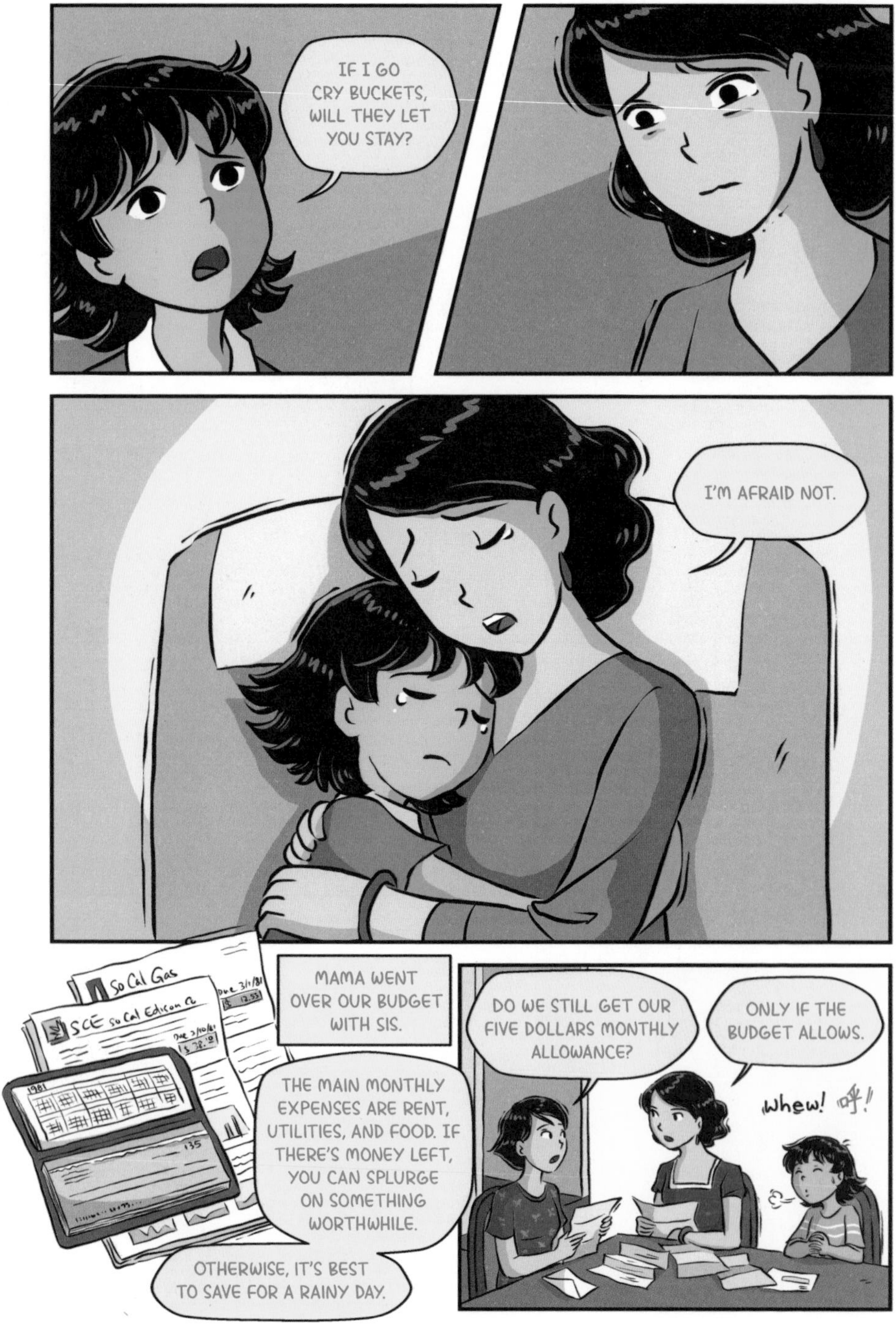
IF I GO CRY BUCKETS, WILL THEY LET YOU STAY?
I'M AFRAID NOT.
So Cal Gas
SCE So Cal Edison Co
MAMA WENT OVER OUR BUDGET WITH SIS.
THE MAIN MONTHLY EXPENSES ARE RENT, UTILITIES, AND FOOD. IF THERE'S MONEY LEFT, YOU CAN SPLURGE ON SOMETHING WORTHWHILE.
OTHERWISE, IT'S BEST TO SAVE FOR A RAINY DAY.
DO WE STILL GET OUR FIVE DOLLARS MONTHLY ALLOWANCE?
ONLY IF THE BUDGET ALLOWS.
whew! 呼!

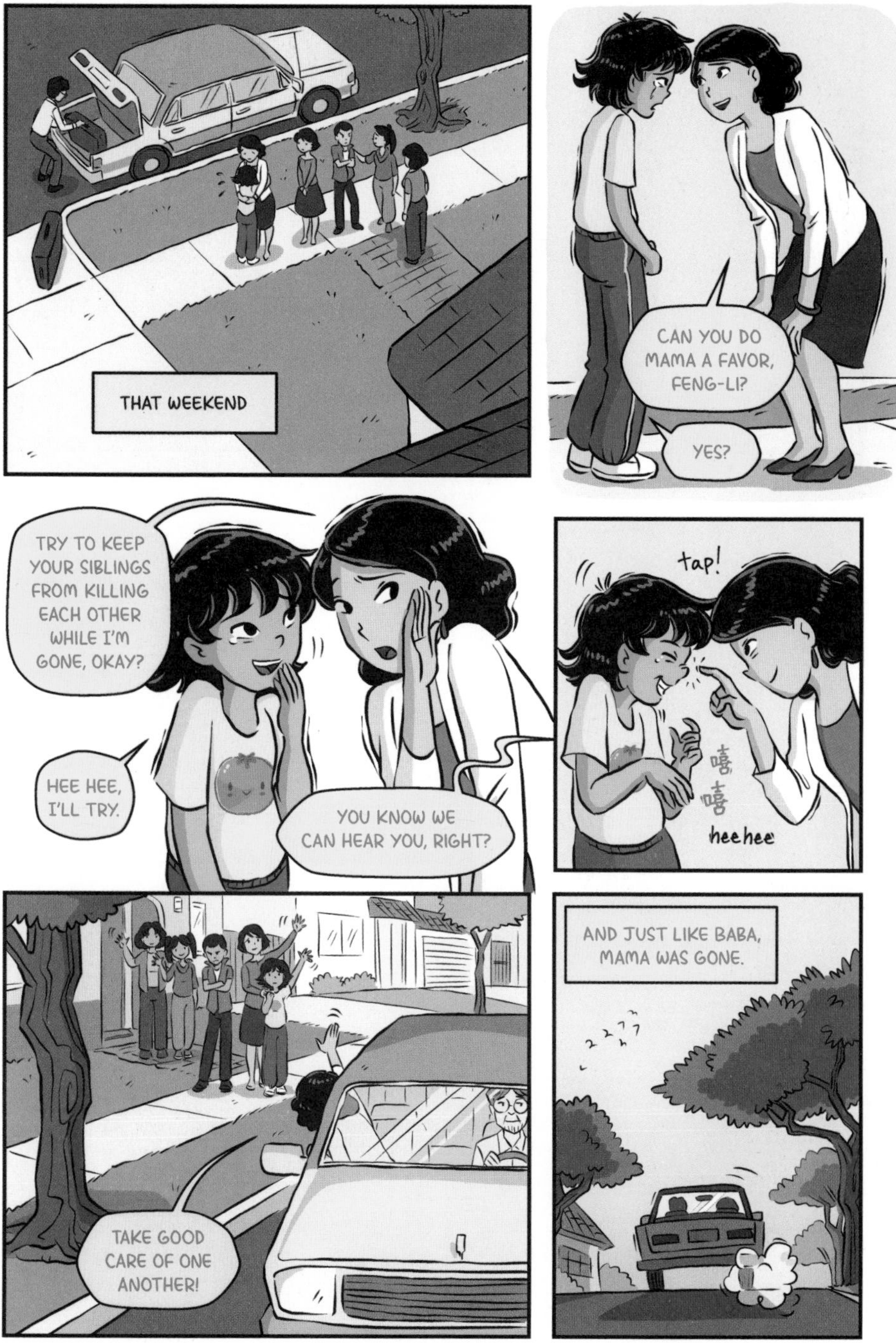
THAT WEEKEND
CAN YOU DO MAMA A FAVOR, FENG-LI?
YES?
TRY TO KEEP YOUR SIBLINGS FROM KILLING EACH OTHER WHILE I'M GONE, OKAY?
HEE HEE, I'LL TRY.
YOU KNOW WE CAN HEAR YOU, RIGHT?
tap!
嘻嘻
heehee
TAKE GOOD CARE OF ONE ANOTHER!
AND JUST LIKE BABA, MAMA WAS GONE.

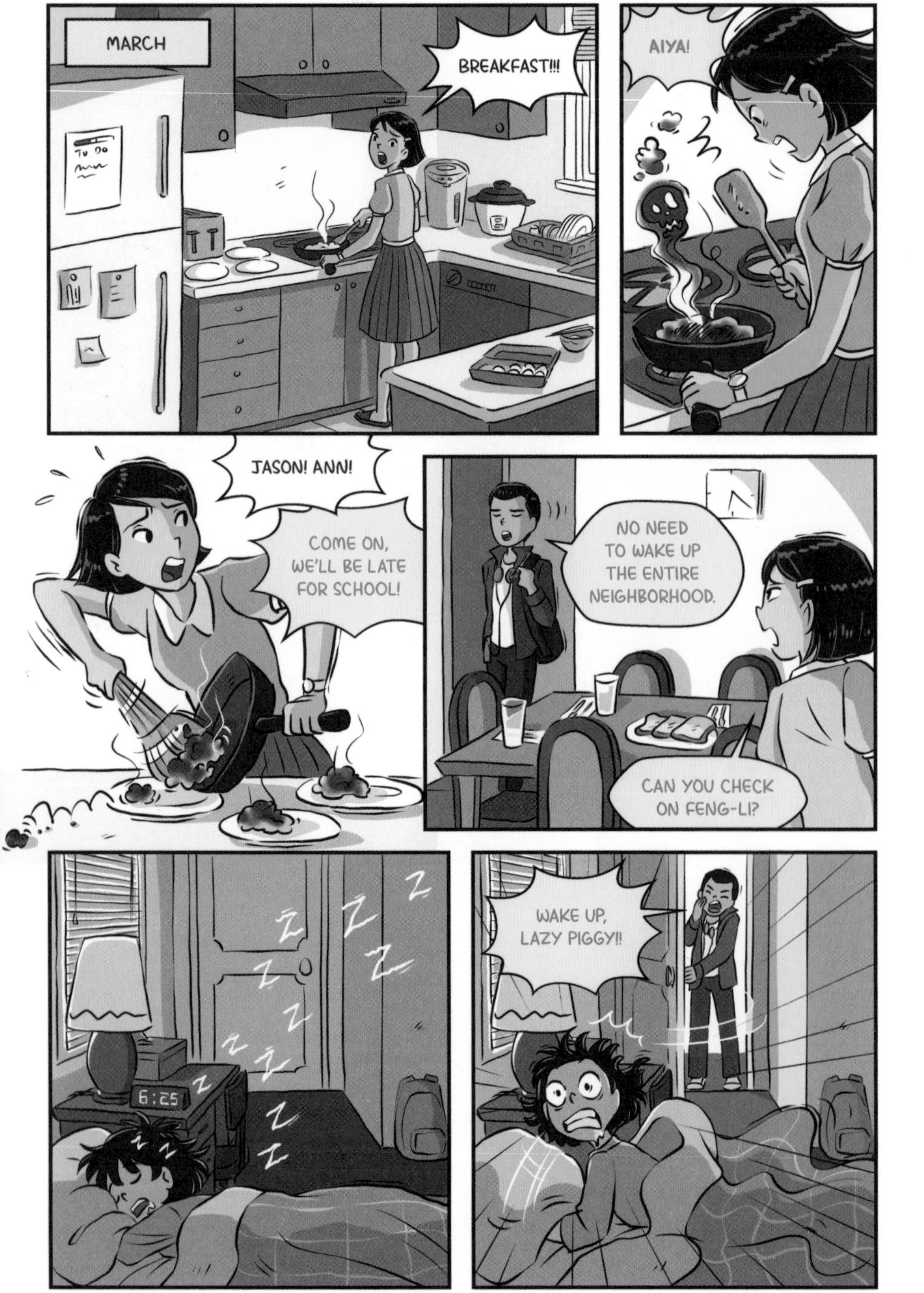

MARCH
BREAKFAST!!!
TO DO
AIYA!
JASON! ANN!
COME ON, WE'LL BE LATE FOR SCHOOL!
NO NEED TO WAKE UP THE ENTIRE NEIGHBORHOOD.
CAN YOU CHECK ON FENG-LI?
6:25
WAKE UP, LAZY PIGGY!!

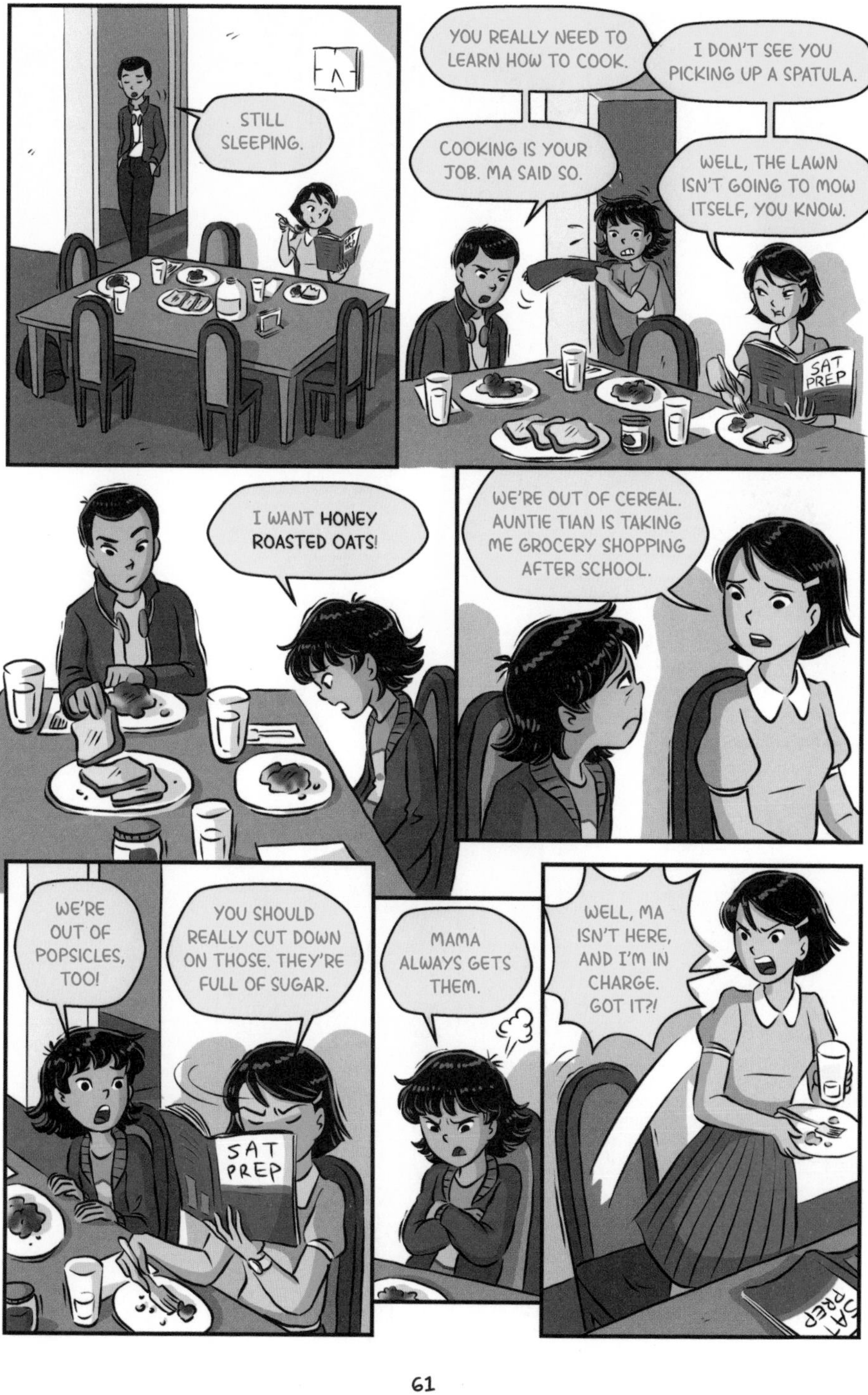
STILL SLEEPING.
YOU REALLY NEED TO LEARN HOW TO COOK.
COOKING IS YOUR JOB. MA SAID SO.
I DON'T SEE YOU PICKING UP A SPATULA.
WELL, THE LAWN ISN'T GOING TO MOW ITSELF, YOU KNOW.
SAT PREP
I WANT HONEY ROASTED OATS!
WE'RE OUT OF CEREAL. AUNTIE TIAN IS TAKING ME GROCERY SHOPPING AFTER SCHOOL.
WE'RE OUT OF POPSICLES, TOO!
YOU SHOULD REALLY CUT DOWN ON THOSE. THEY'RE FULL OF SUGAR.
SAT PREP
MAMA ALWAYS GETS THEM.
WELL, MA ISN'T HERE, AND I'M IN CHARGE. GOT IT?!
SAT PREP

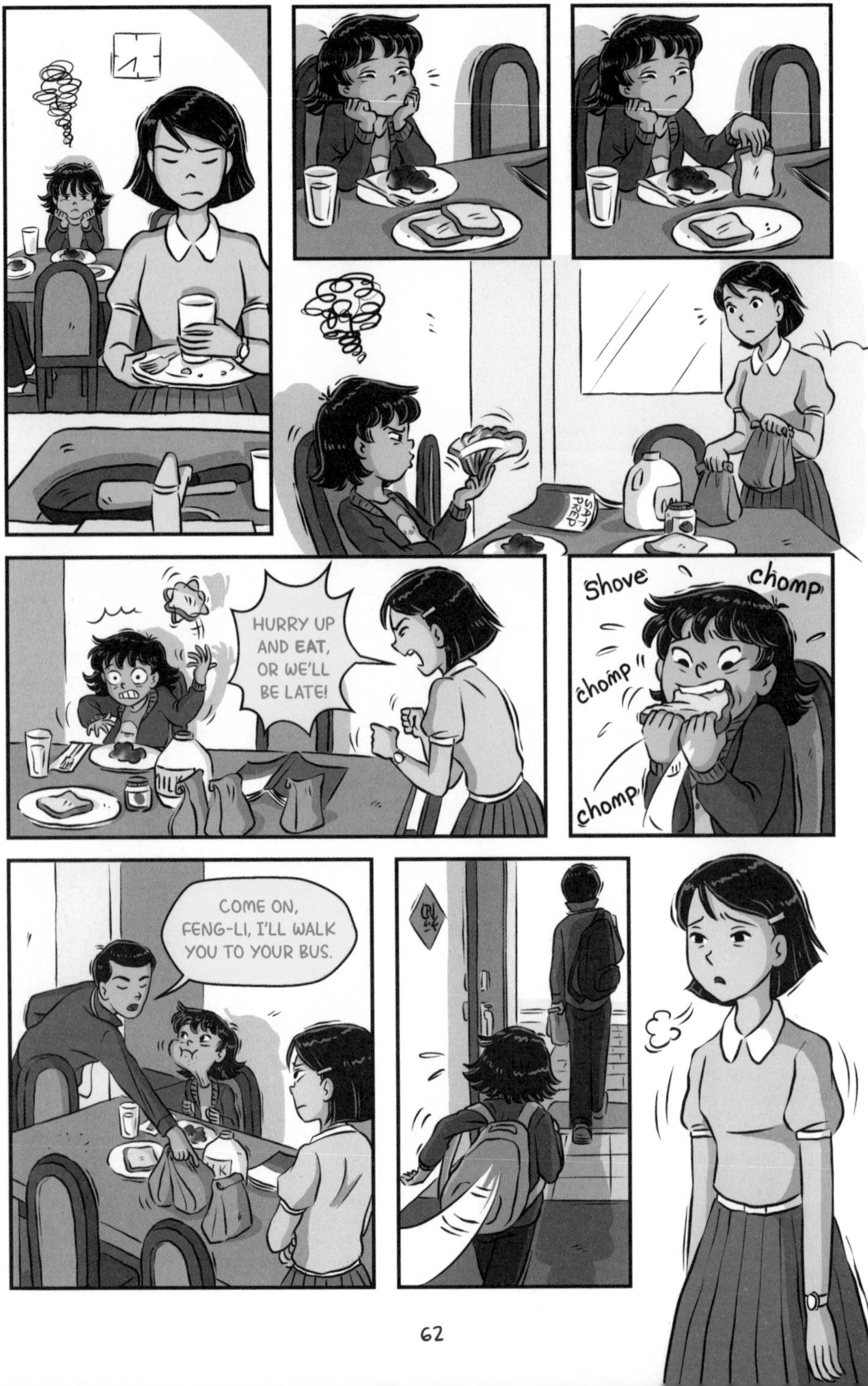
SAT PREP
HURRY UP AND EAT, OR WE'LL BE LATE!
Shove
chomp
chomp
chomp
COME ON, FENG-LI, I'LL WALK YOU TO YOUR BUS.

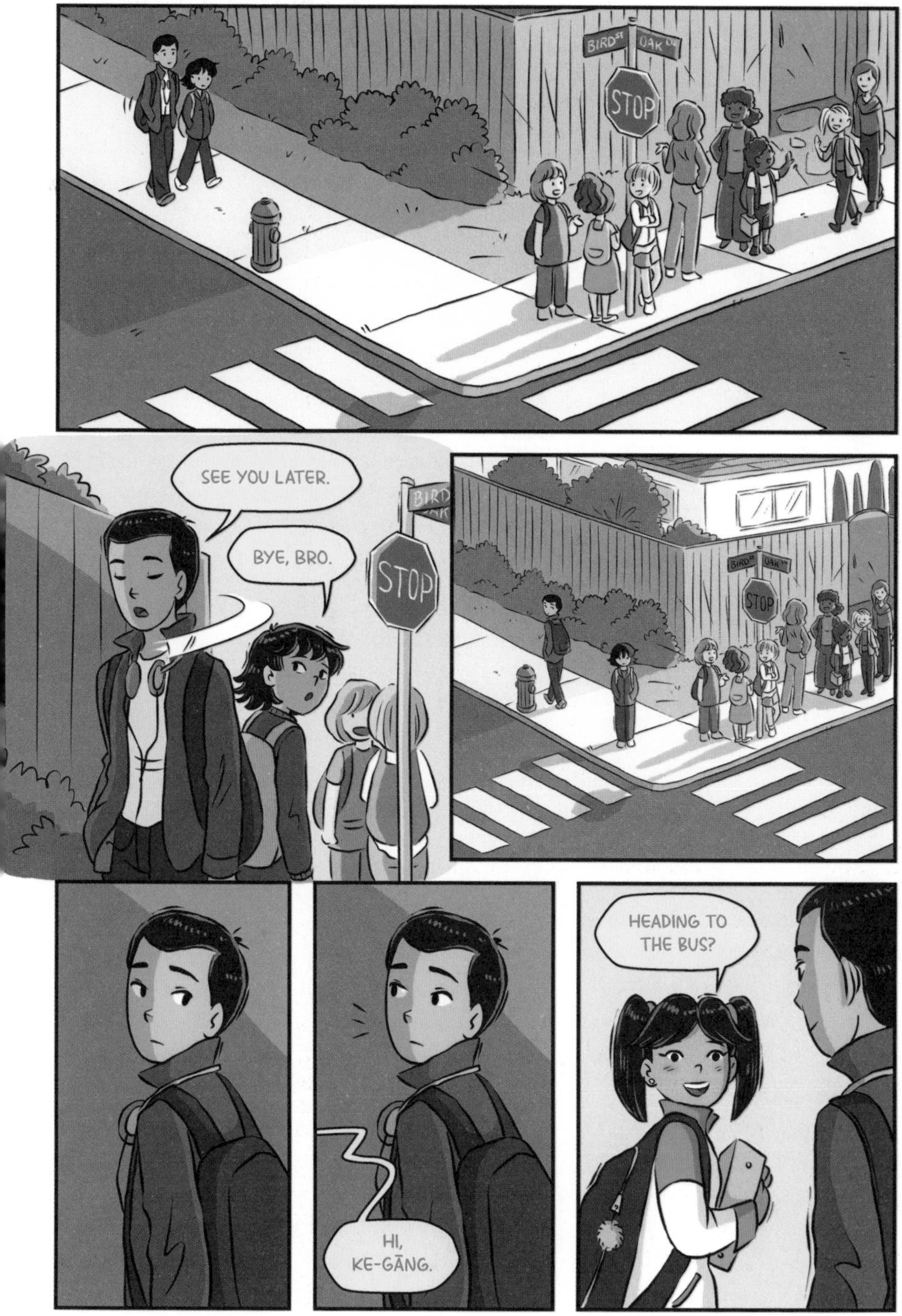
BIRD ST
OAK LN
STOP
SEE YOU LATER.
BYE, BRO.
HI, KE-GĀNG.
HEADING TO THE BUS?

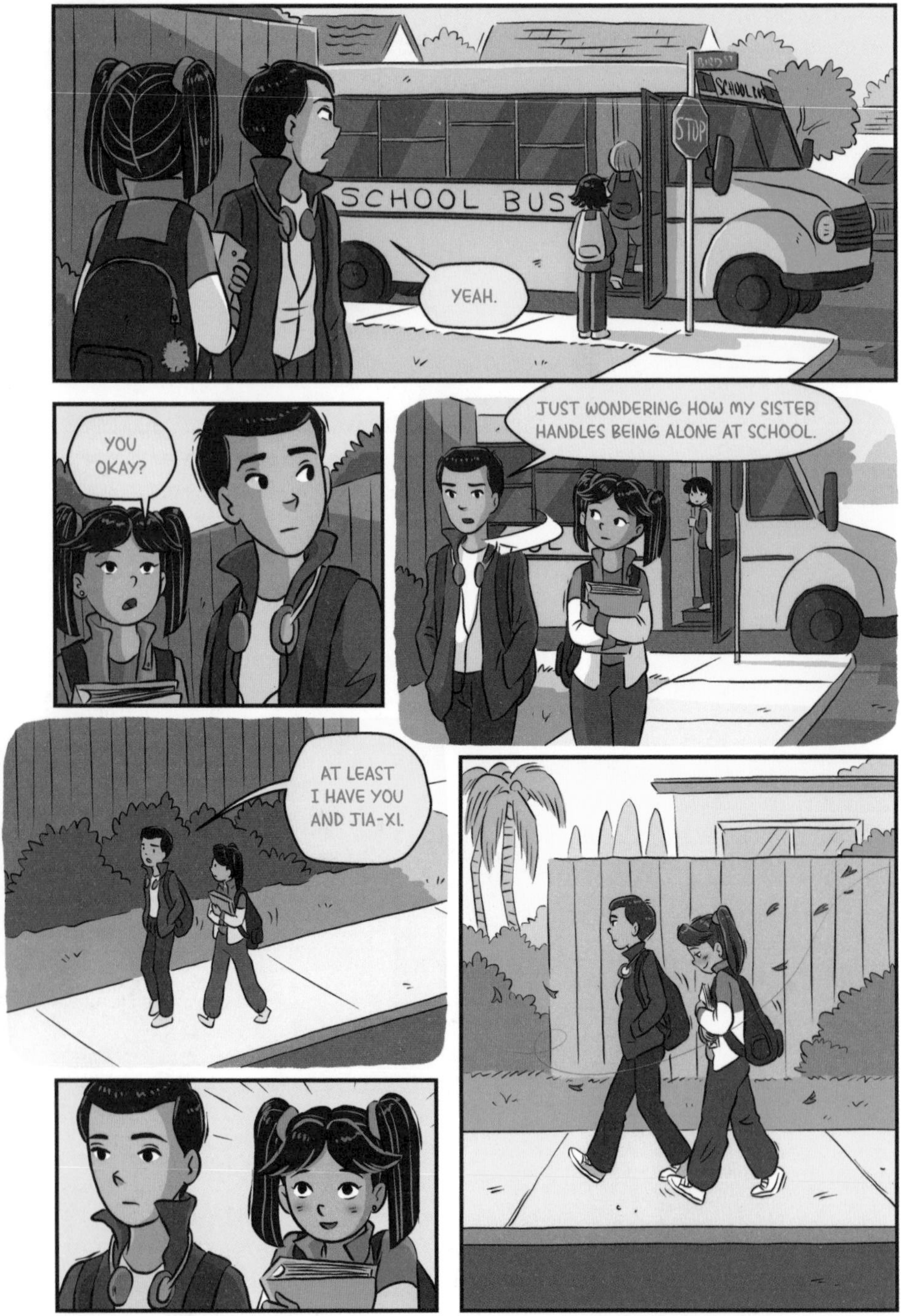
SCHOOL BUS
STOP
YEAH.
YOU OKAY?
JUST WONDERING HOW MY SISTER HANDLES BEING ALONE AT SCHOOL.
AT LEAST I HAVE YOU AND JIA-XI.

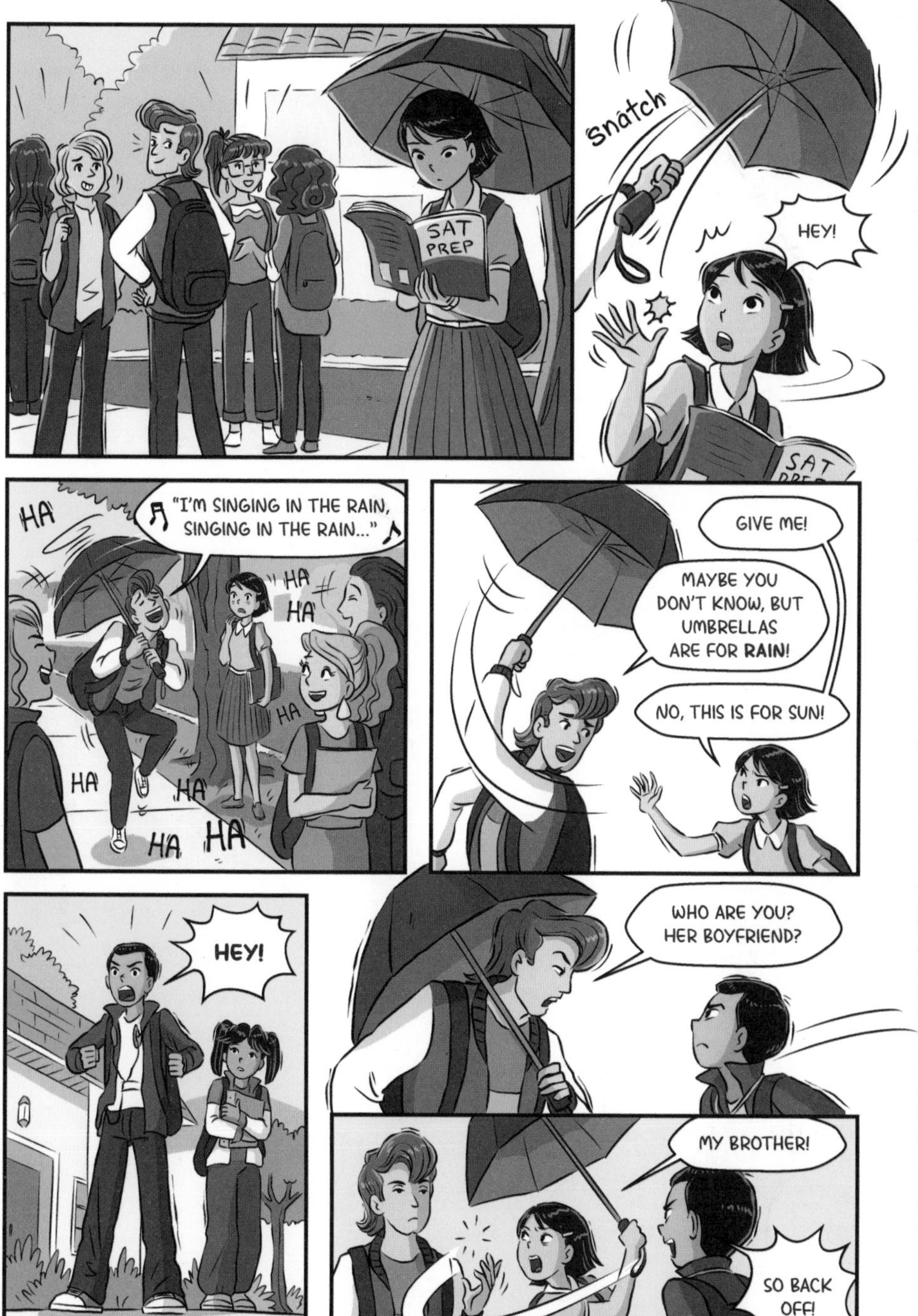
SAT PREP
Snatch
HEY!
SAT
HA
"I'M SINGING IN THE RAIN, SINGING IN THE RAIN..."
HA
HA
HA
HA
HA
HA
HA
GIVE ME!
MAYBE YOU DON'T KNOW, BUT UMBRELLAS ARE FOR **RAIN**!
NO, THIS IS FOR SUN!
HEY!
WHO ARE YOU? HER BOYFRIEND?
MY BROTHER!
SO BACK OFF!

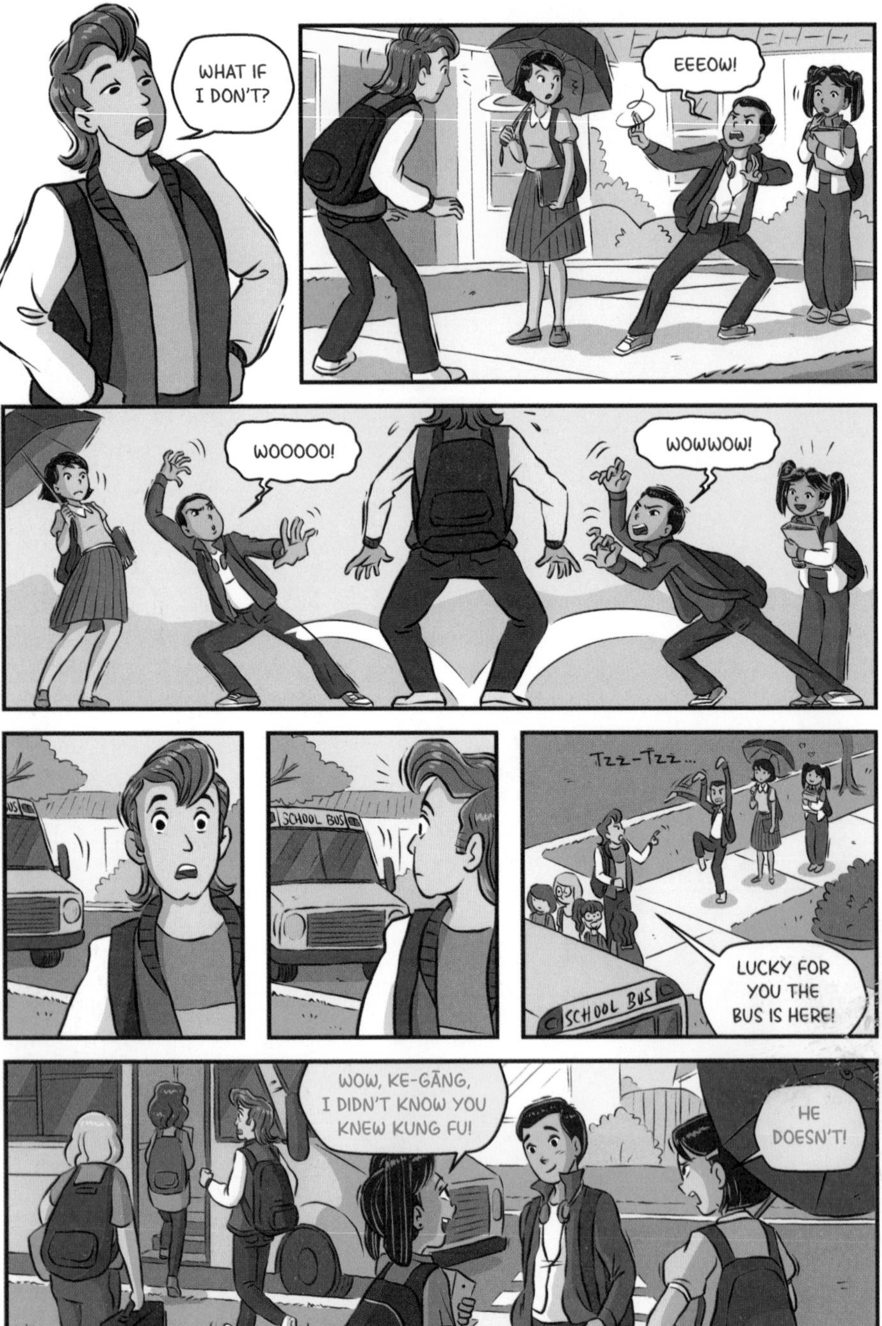
WHAT IF I DON'T?
EEEOW!
WOOOOO!
WOWWOW!
SCHOOL BUS
Tzz-Tzz...
LUCKY FOR YOU THE BUS IS HERE!
SCHOOL BUS
WOW, KE-GĀNG, I DIDN'T KNOW YOU KNEW KUNG FU!
HE DOESN'T!

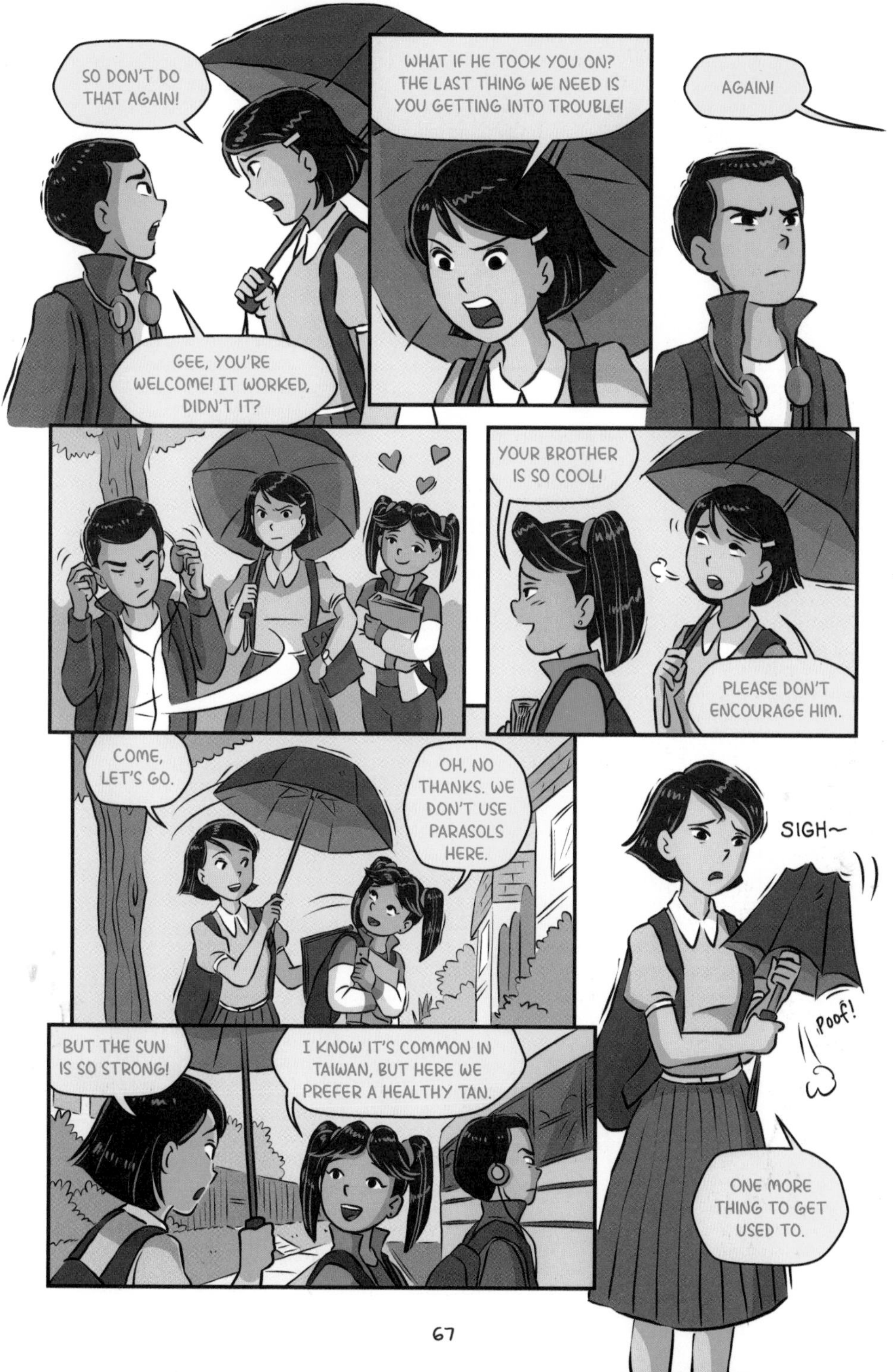
SO DON'T DO THAT AGAIN!
GEE, YOU'RE WELCOME! IT WORKED, DIDN'T IT?
WHAT IF HE TOOK YOU ON? THE LAST THING WE NEED IS YOU GETTING INTO TROUBLE!
AGAIN!
YOUR BROTHER IS SO COOL!
PLEASE DON'T ENCOURAGE HIM.
COME, LET'S GO.
OH, NO THANKS. WE DON'T USE PARASOLS HERE.
BUT THE SUN IS SO STRONG!
I KNOW IT'S COMMON IN TAIWAN, BUT HERE WE PREFER A HEALTHY TAN.
SIGH~
Poof!
ONE MORE THING TO GET USED TO.

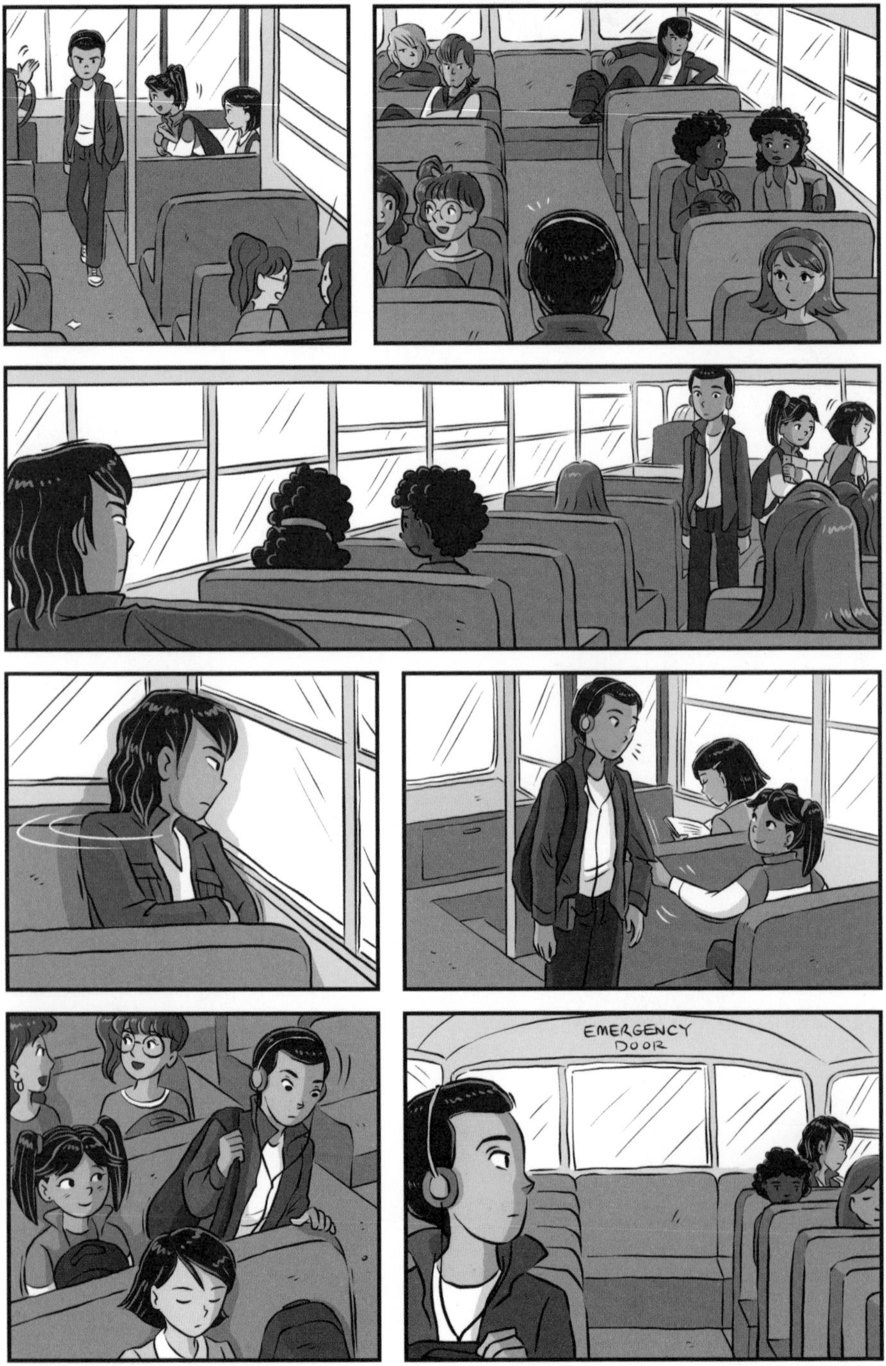
EMERGENCY
DOOR

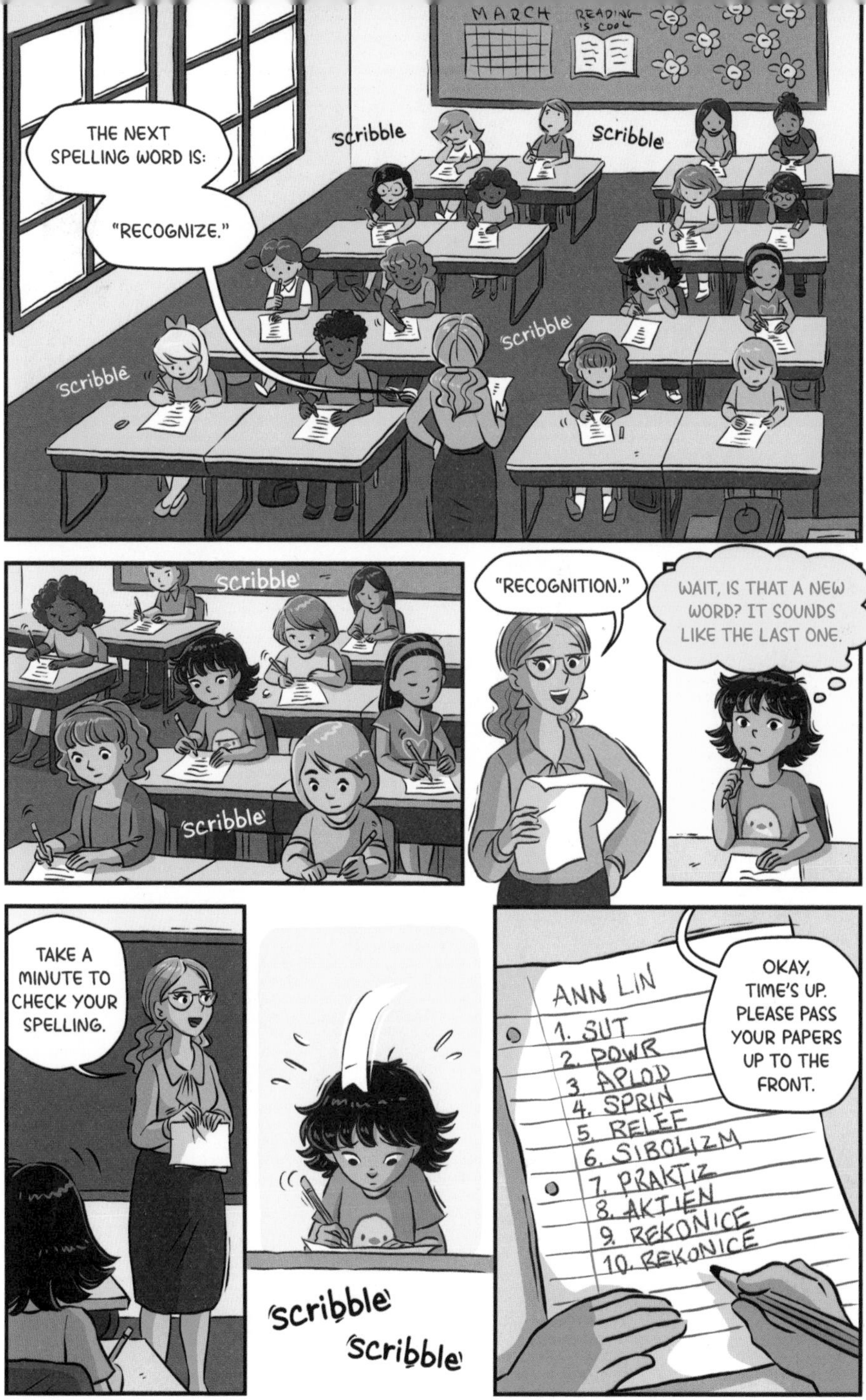
MARCH
READING IS COOL
THE NEXT SPELLING WORD IS:
"RECOGNIZE."
scribble
scribble
scribble
scribble
scribble
scribble
"RECOGNITION."
WAIT, IS THAT A NEW WORD? IT SOUNDS LIKE THE LAST ONE.
TAKE A MINUTE TO CHECK YOUR SPELLING.
scribble
scribble
ANN LIN
1. SUT
2. POWR
3 APLOD
4. SPRIN
5. RELEF
6. SIBOLIZM
7. PRAKTIZ
8. AKTIEN
9. REKONICE
10. REKONICE
OKAY, TIME'S UP. PLEASE PASS YOUR PAPERS UP TO THE FRONT.

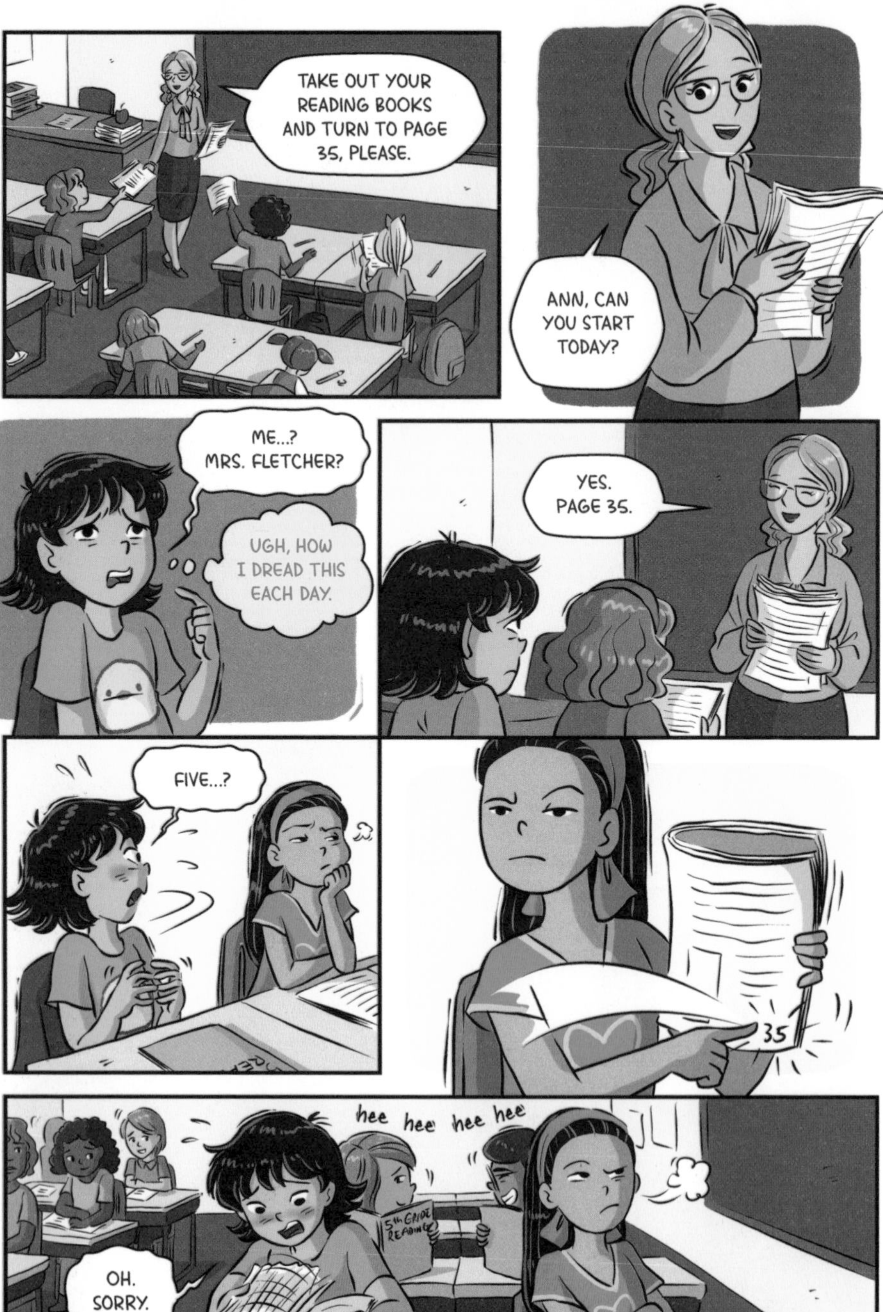
TAKE OUT YOUR READING BOOKS AND TURN TO PAGE 35, PLEASE.
ANN, CAN YOU START TODAY?
ME...? MRS. FLETCHER?
UGH, HOW I DREAD THIS EACH DAY.
YES. PAGE 35.
FIVE...?
35
hee hee hee hee
5th GRADE READING
OH. SORRY.
flip~

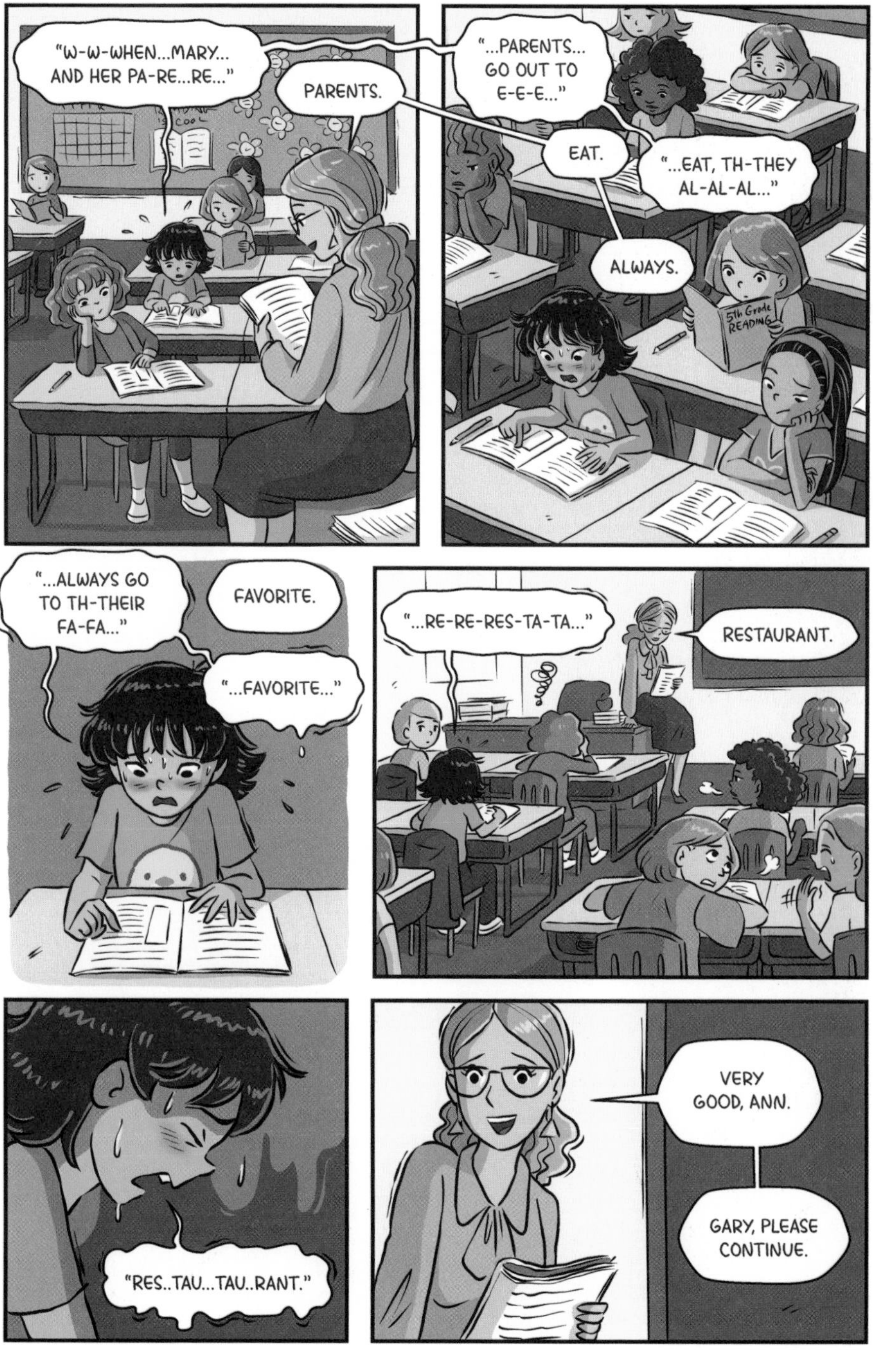

"W-W-WHEN...MARY... AND HER PA-RE...RE..."
PARENTS.
"...PARENTS... GO OUT TO E-E-E..."
EAT.
"...EAT, TH-THEY AL-AL-AL..."
ALWAYS.
5th Grade READING
"...ALWAYS GO TO TH-THEIR FA-FA..."
FAVORITE.
"...FAVORITE..."
"...RE-RE-RES-TA-TA..."
RESTAURANT.
"RES..TAU...TAU..RANT."
VERY GOOD, ANN.
GARY, PLEASE CONTINUE.

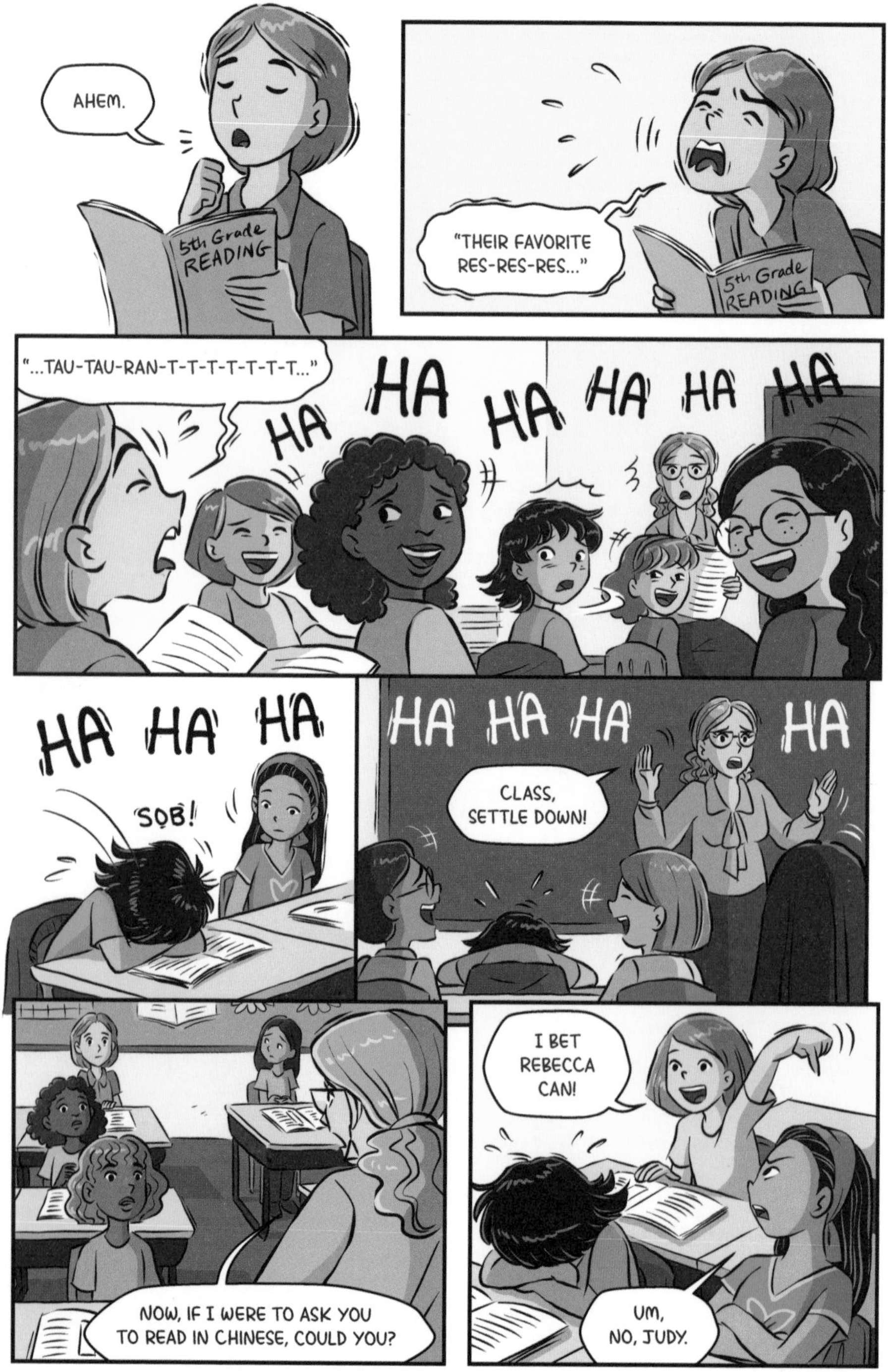
AHEM.
5th Grade READING
"THEIR FAVORITE RES-RES-RES..."
5th Grade READING
"...TAU-TAU-RAN-T-T-T-T-T-T-T..."
HA HA HA HA HA HA
HA HA HA
SOB!
HA HA HA HA
CLASS, SETTLE DOWN!
NOW, IF I WERE TO ASK YOU TO READ IN CHINESE, COULD YOU?
I BET REBECCA CAN!
UM, NO, JUDY.

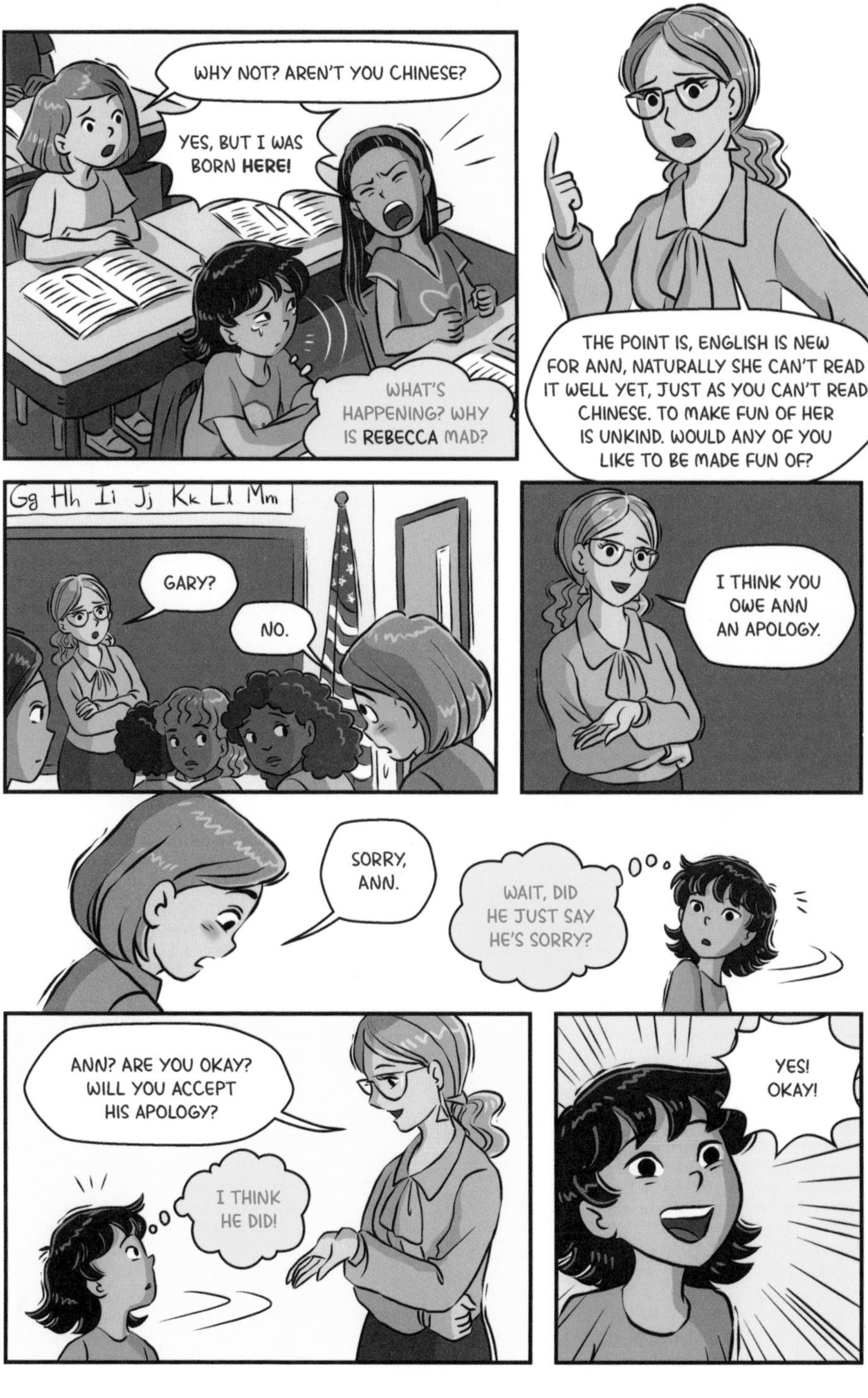
WHY NOT? AREN'T YOU CHINESE?
YES, BUT I WAS BORN **HERE!**
WHAT'S HAPPENING? WHY IS **REBECCA** MAD?
THE POINT IS, ENGLISH IS NEW FOR ANN, NATURALLY SHE CAN'T READ IT WELL YET, JUST AS YOU CAN'T READ CHINESE. TO MAKE FUN OF HER IS UNKIND. WOULD ANY OF YOU LIKE TO BE MADE FUN OF?
Gg Hh Ii Jj Kk Ll Mm
GARY?
NO.
I THINK YOU OWE ANN AN APOLOGY.
SORRY, ANN.
WAIT, DID HE JUST SAY HE'S SORRY?
ANN? ARE YOU OKAY? WILL YOU ACCEPT HIS APOLOGY?
I THINK HE DID!
YES! OKAY!

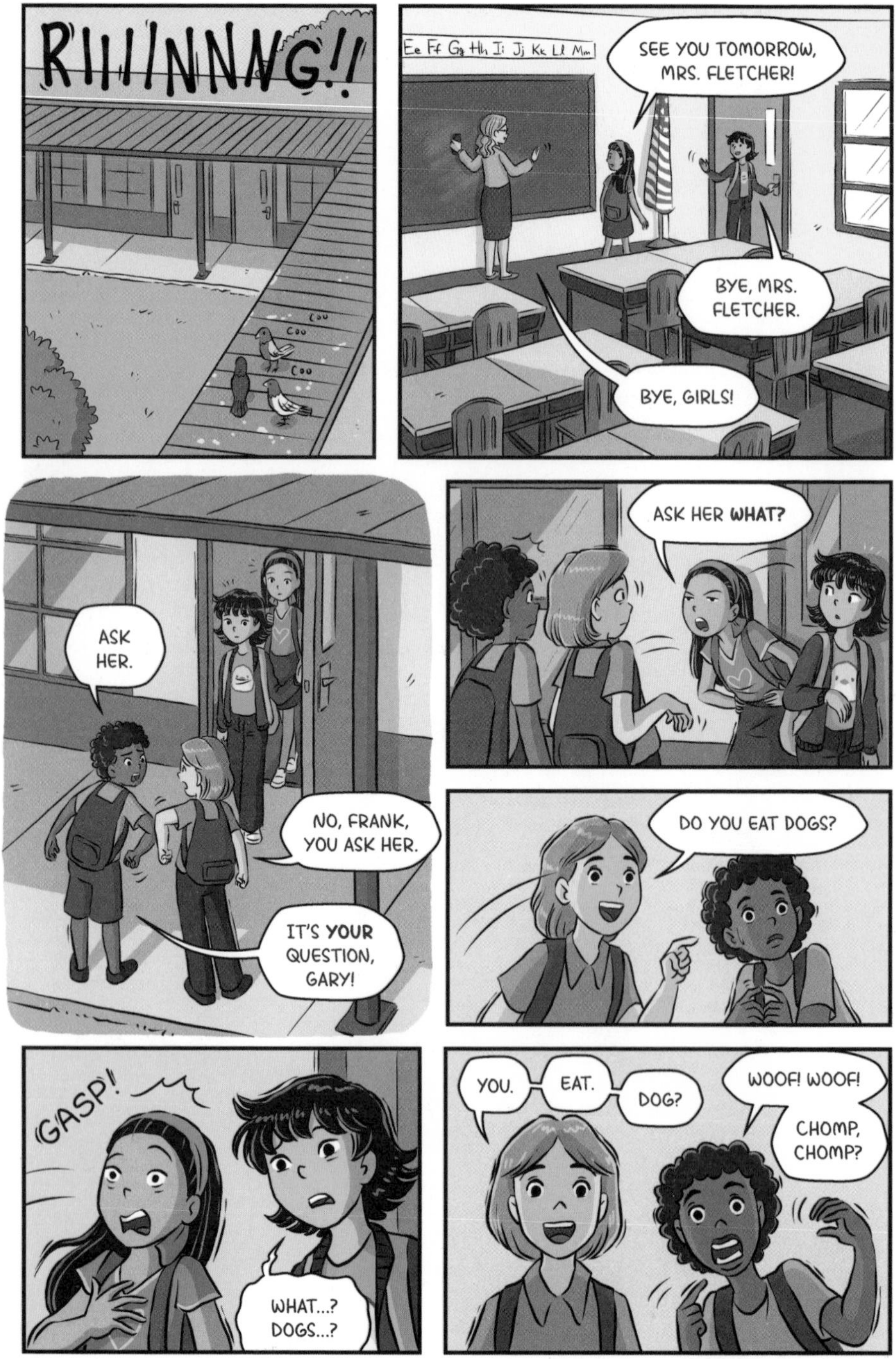
RIIINNNG!!
COO
COO
COO
Ee Ff Gg Hh Ii Jj Kk Ll Mm
SEE YOU TOMORROW, MRS. FLETCHER!
BYE, MRS. FLETCHER.
BYE, GIRLS!
ASK HER.
NO, FRANK, YOU ASK HER.
IT'S **YOUR** QUESTION, GARY!
ASK HER **WHAT?**
DO YOU EAT DOGS?
GASP!
WHAT...? DOGS...?
YOU.
EAT.
DOG?
WOOF! WOOF!
CHOMP, CHOMP?

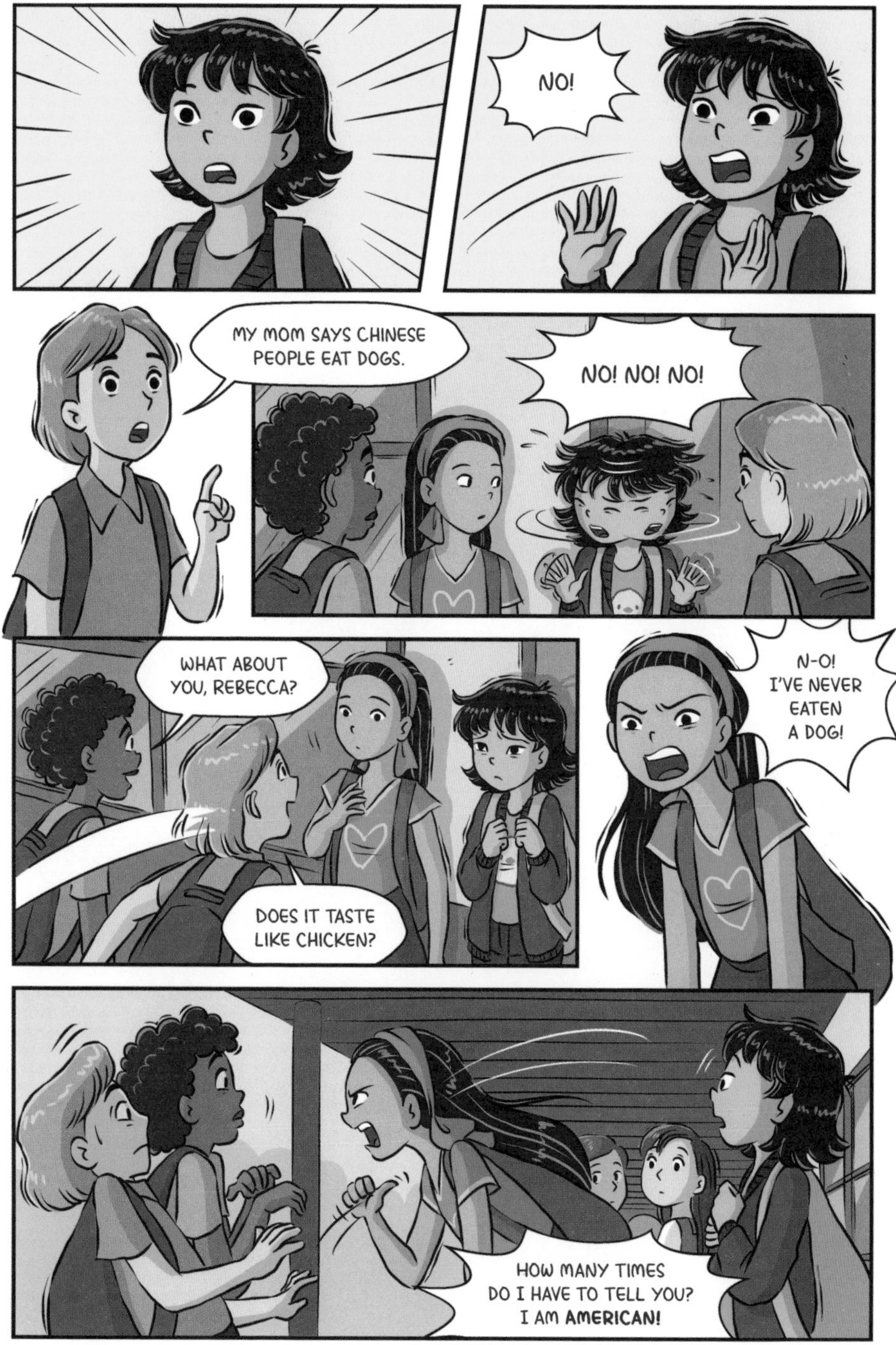
NO!
MY MOM SAYS CHINESE PEOPLE EAT DOGS.
NO! NO! NO!
WHAT ABOUT YOU, REBECCA?
DOES IT TASTE LIKE CHICKEN?
N-O! I'VE NEVER EATEN A DOG!
HOW MANY TIMES DO I HAVE TO TELL YOU? I AM **AMERICAN!**

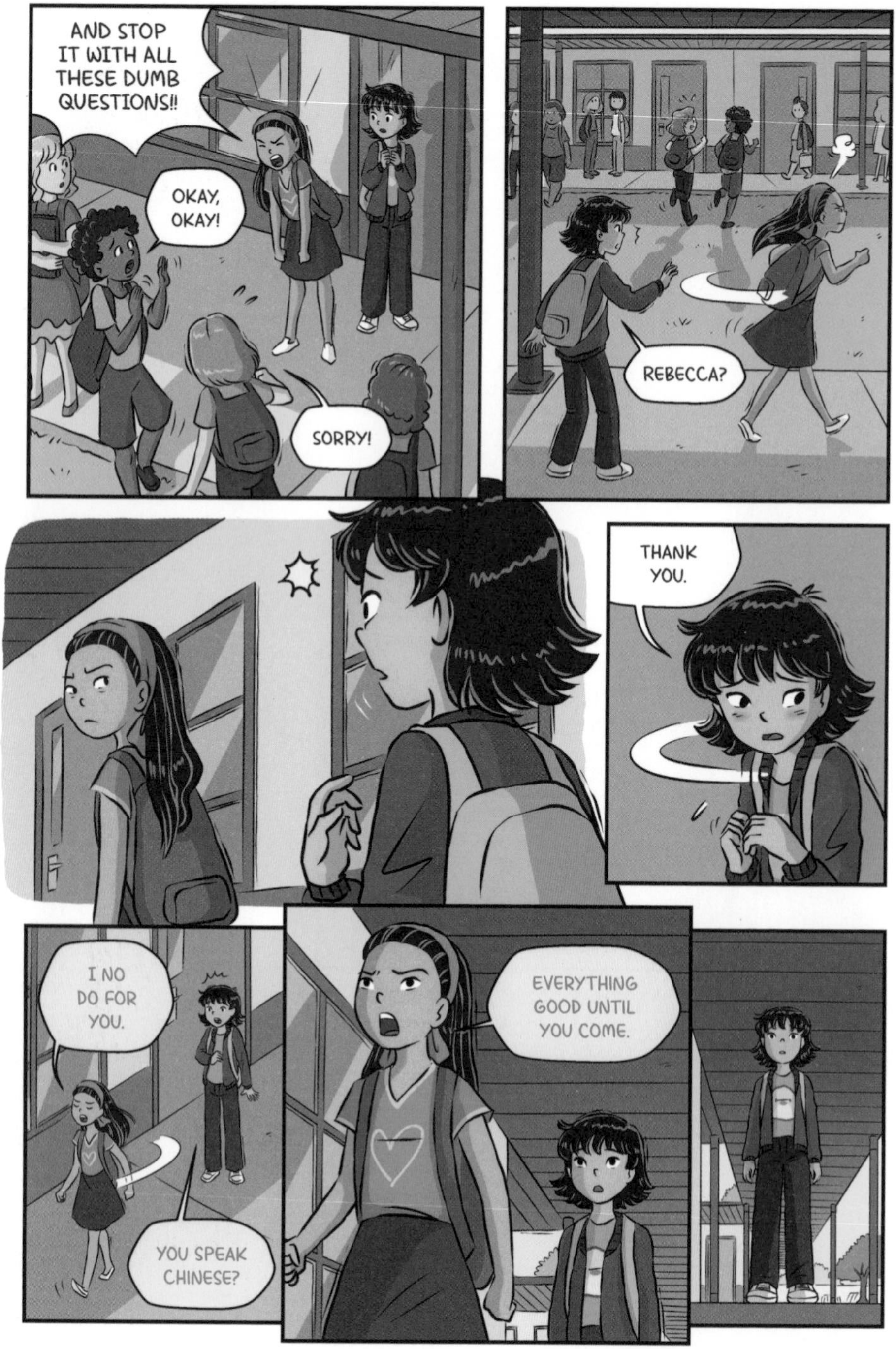
AND STOP IT WITH ALL THESE DUMB QUESTIONS!!
OKAY, OKAY!
SORRY!
REBECCA?
THANK YOU.
I NO DO FOR YOU.
YOU SPEAK CHINESE?
EVERYTHING GOOD UNTIL YOU COME.

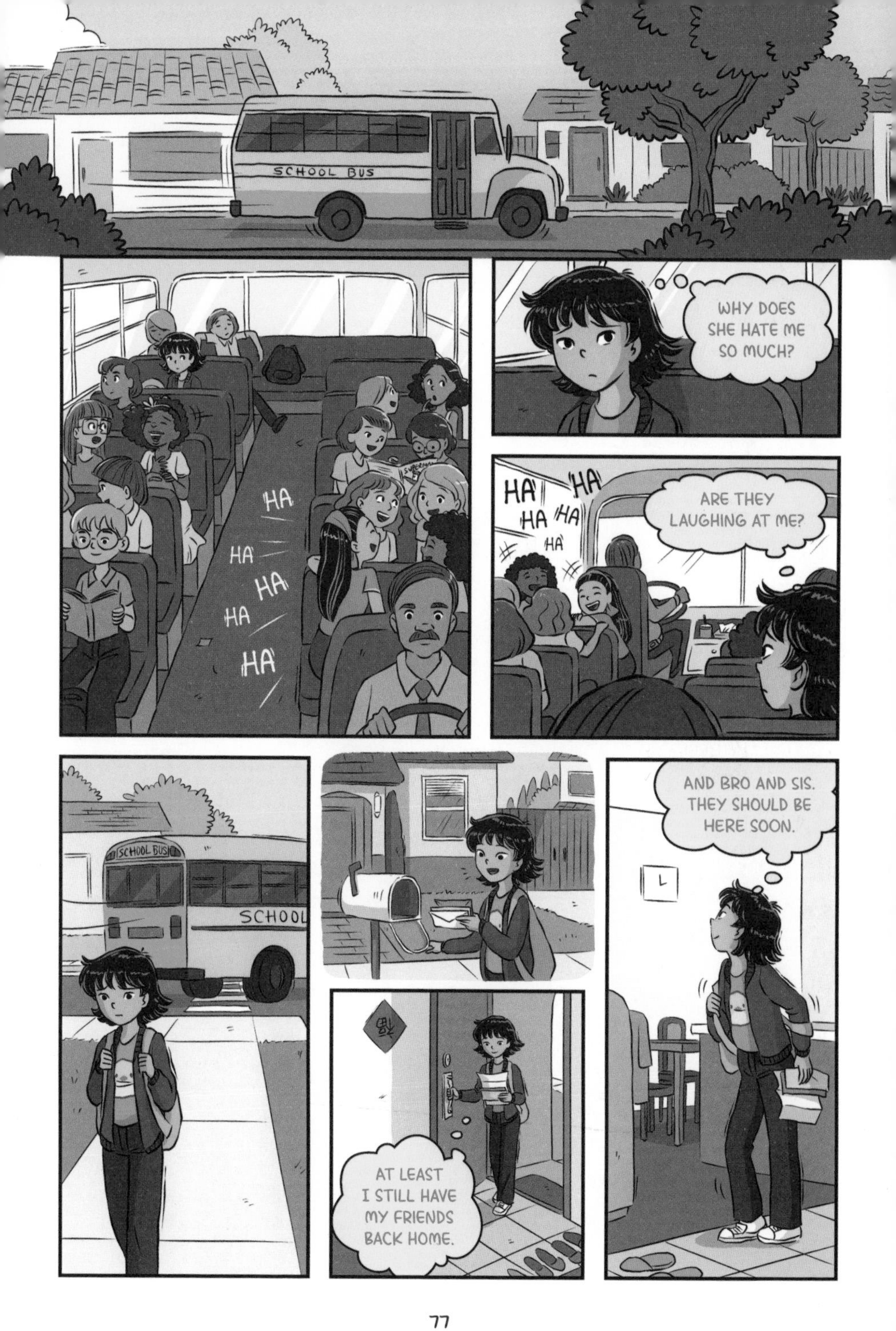
SCHOOL BUS
HA HA HA HA HA
WHY DOES SHE HATE ME SO MUCH?
HA HA HA HA HA
ARE THEY LAUGHING AT ME?
SCHOOL BUS
SCHOOL
AND BRO AND SIS. THEY SHOULD BE HERE SOON.
AT LEAST I STILL HAVE MY FRIENDS BACK HOME.

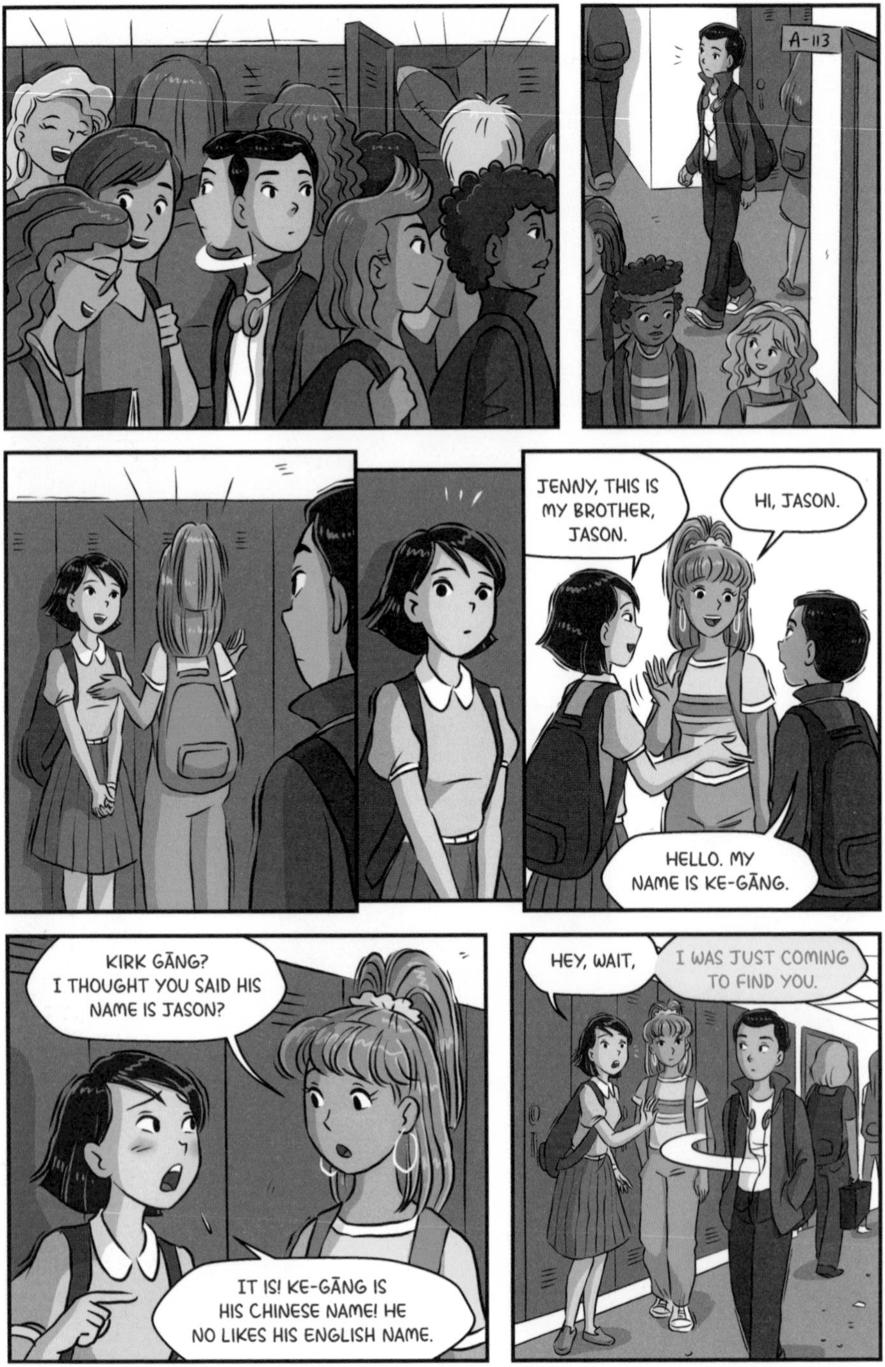
A-113
JENNY, THIS IS MY BROTHER, JASON.
HI, JASON.
HELLO. MY NAME IS KE-GĀNG.
KIRK GĀNG? I THOUGHT YOU SAID HIS NAME IS JASON?
IT IS! KE-GĀNG IS HIS CHINESE NAME! HE NO LIKES HIS ENGLISH NAME.
HEY, WAIT,
I WAS JUST COMING TO FIND YOU.

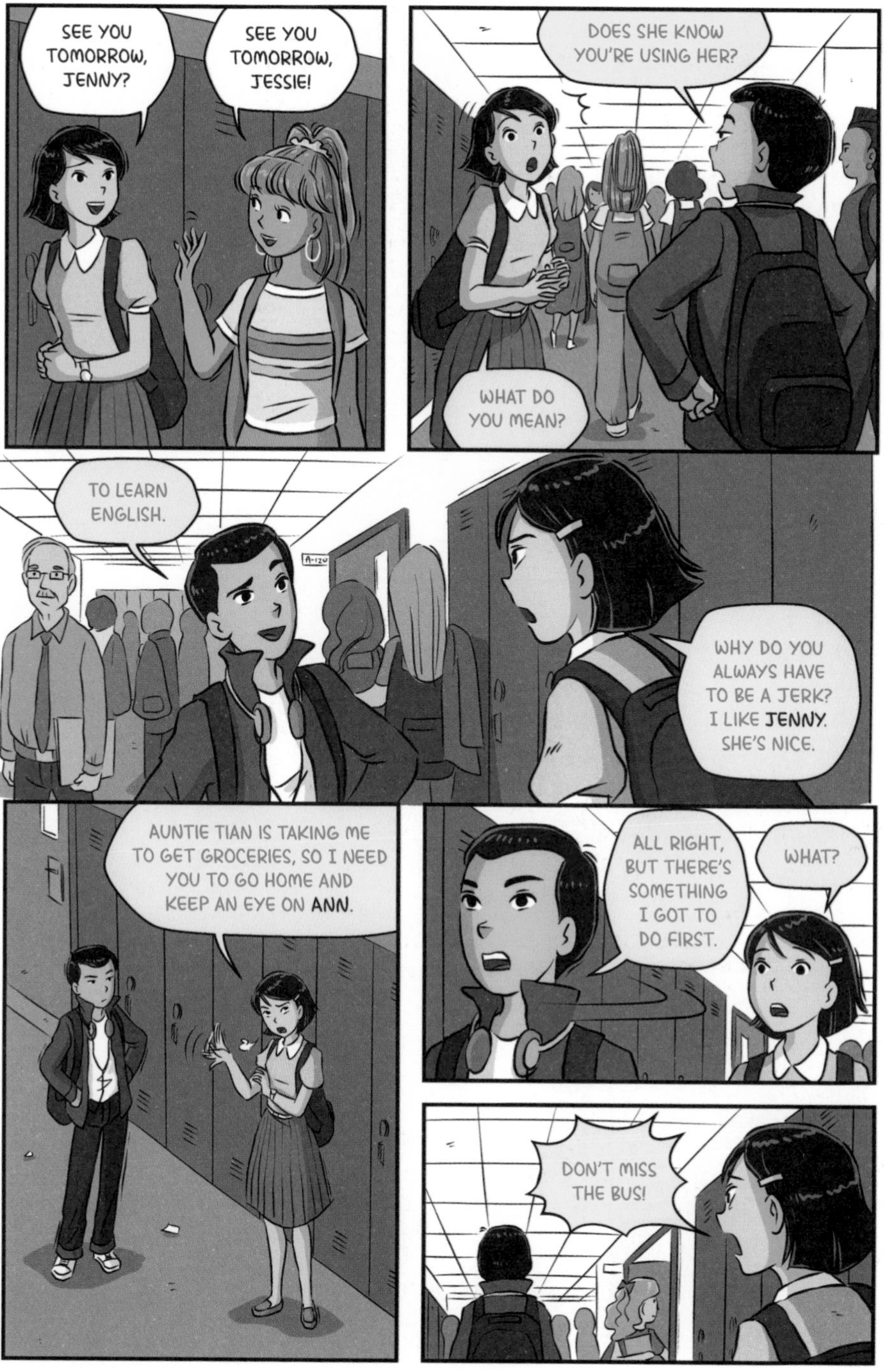
SEE YOU TOMORROW, JENNY?
SEE YOU TOMORROW, JESSIE!
DOES SHE KNOW YOU'RE USING HER?
WHAT DO YOU MEAN?
TO LEARN ENGLISH.
A-120
WHY DO YOU ALWAYS HAVE TO BE A JERK? I LIKE JENNY. SHE'S NICE.
AUNTIE TIAN IS TAKING ME TO GET GROCERIES, SO I NEED YOU TO GO HOME AND KEEP AN EYE ON ANN.
ALL RIGHT, BUT THERE'S SOMETHING I GOT TO DO FIRST.
WHAT?
DON'T MISS THE BUS!

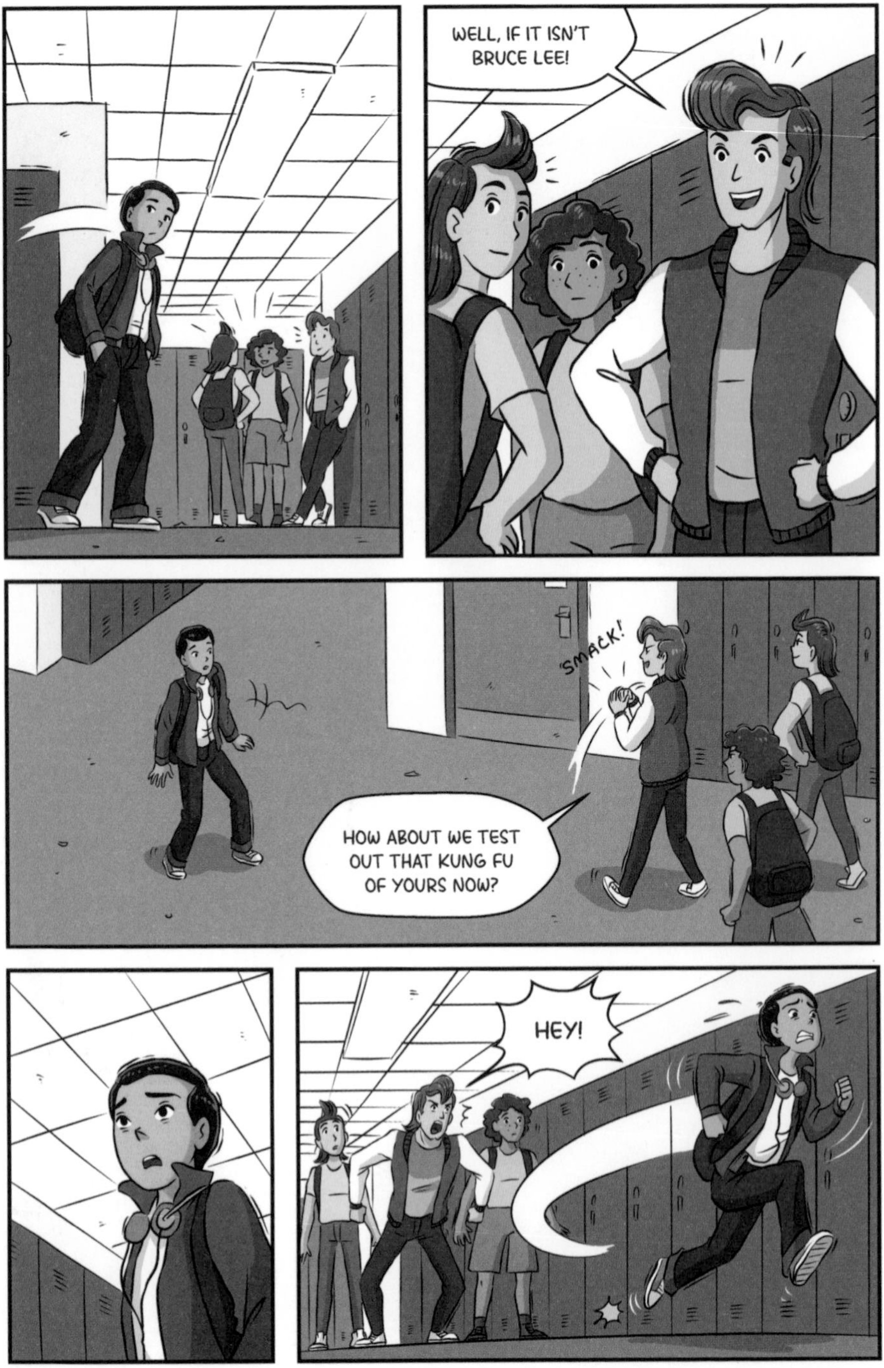
WELL, IF IT ISN'T BRUCE LEE!
SMACK!
HOW ABOUT WE TEST OUT THAT KUNG FU OF YOURS NOW?
HEY!

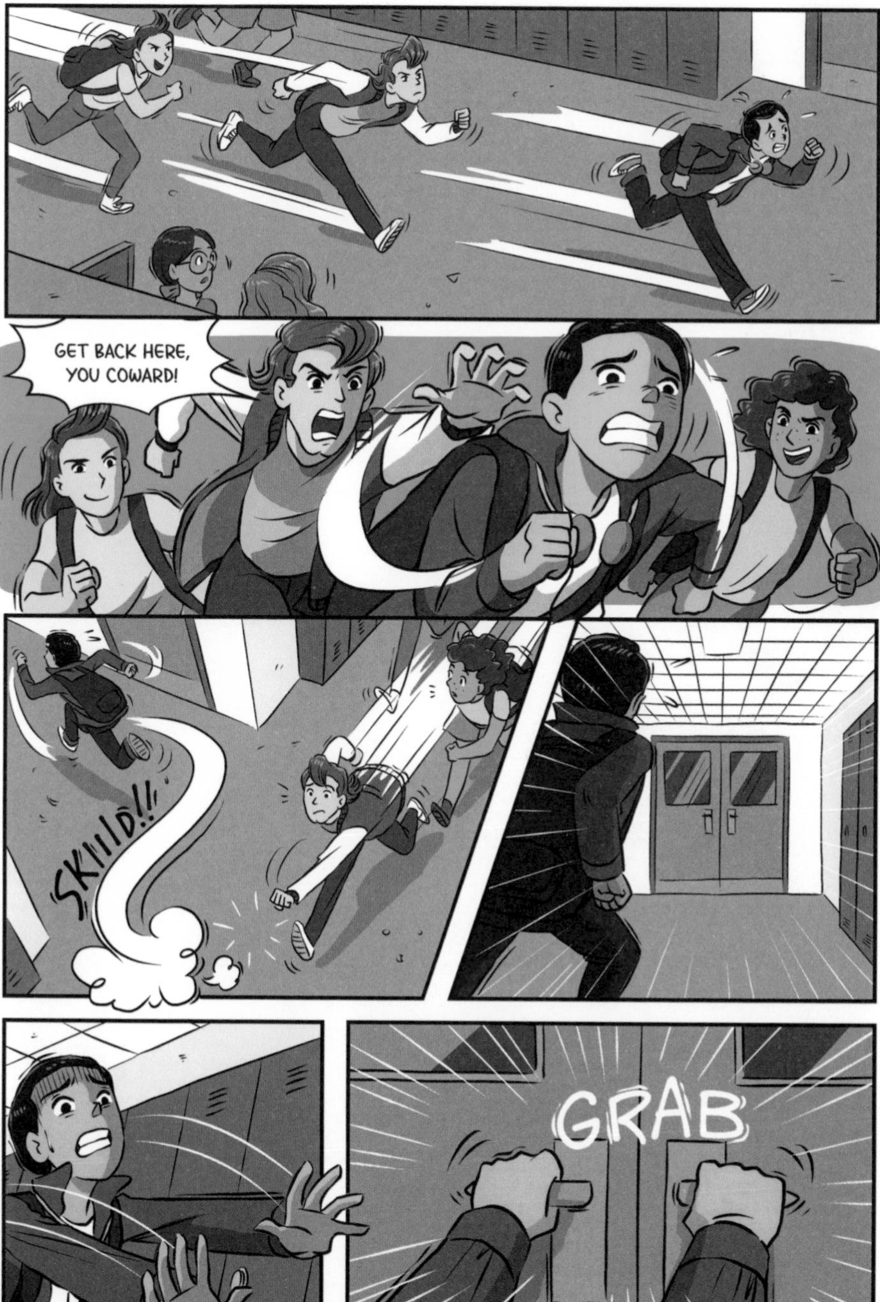
GET BACK HERE,
YOU COWARD!
SKIIID!!
GRAB

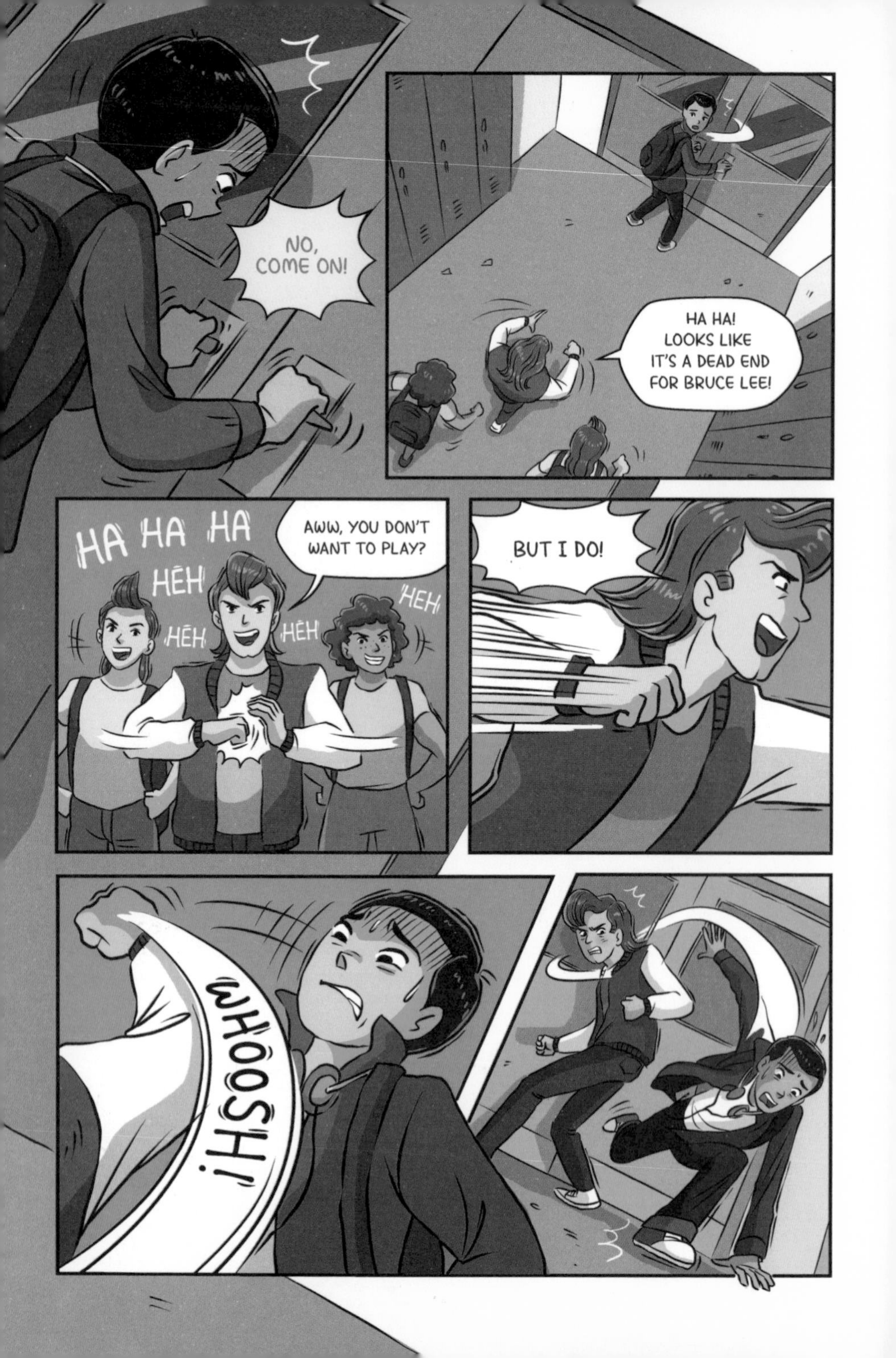
NO, COME ON!
HA HA! LOOKS LIKE IT'S A DEAD END FOR BRUCE LEE!
HA HA HA
HEH
HEH
HEH
HEH
AWW, YOU DON'T WANT TO PLAY?
BUT I DO!
WHOOSH!

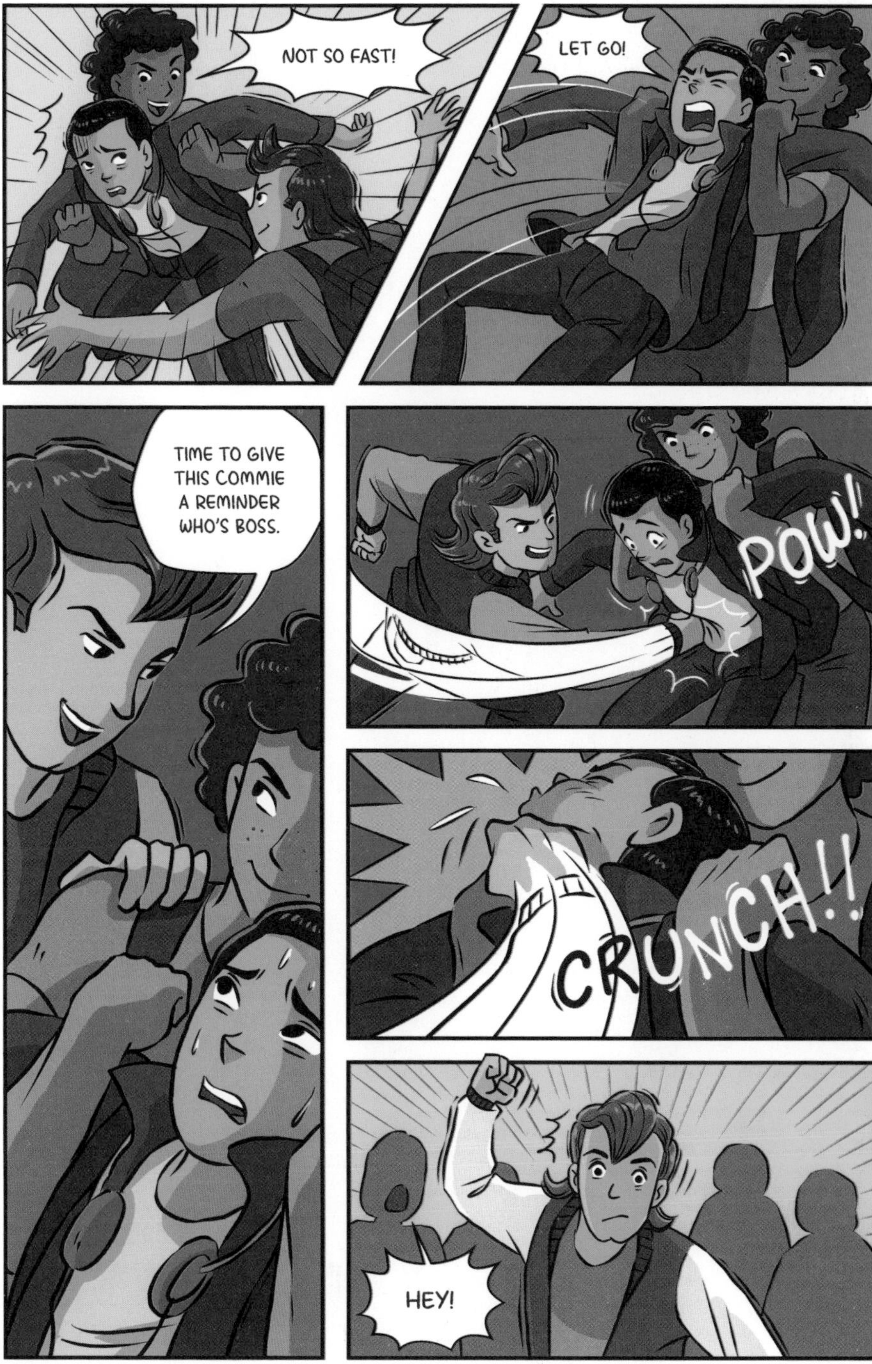
NOT SO FAST!
LET GO!
TIME TO GIVE THIS COMMIE A REMINDER WHO'S BOSS.
POW!!
CRUNCH!!
HEY!

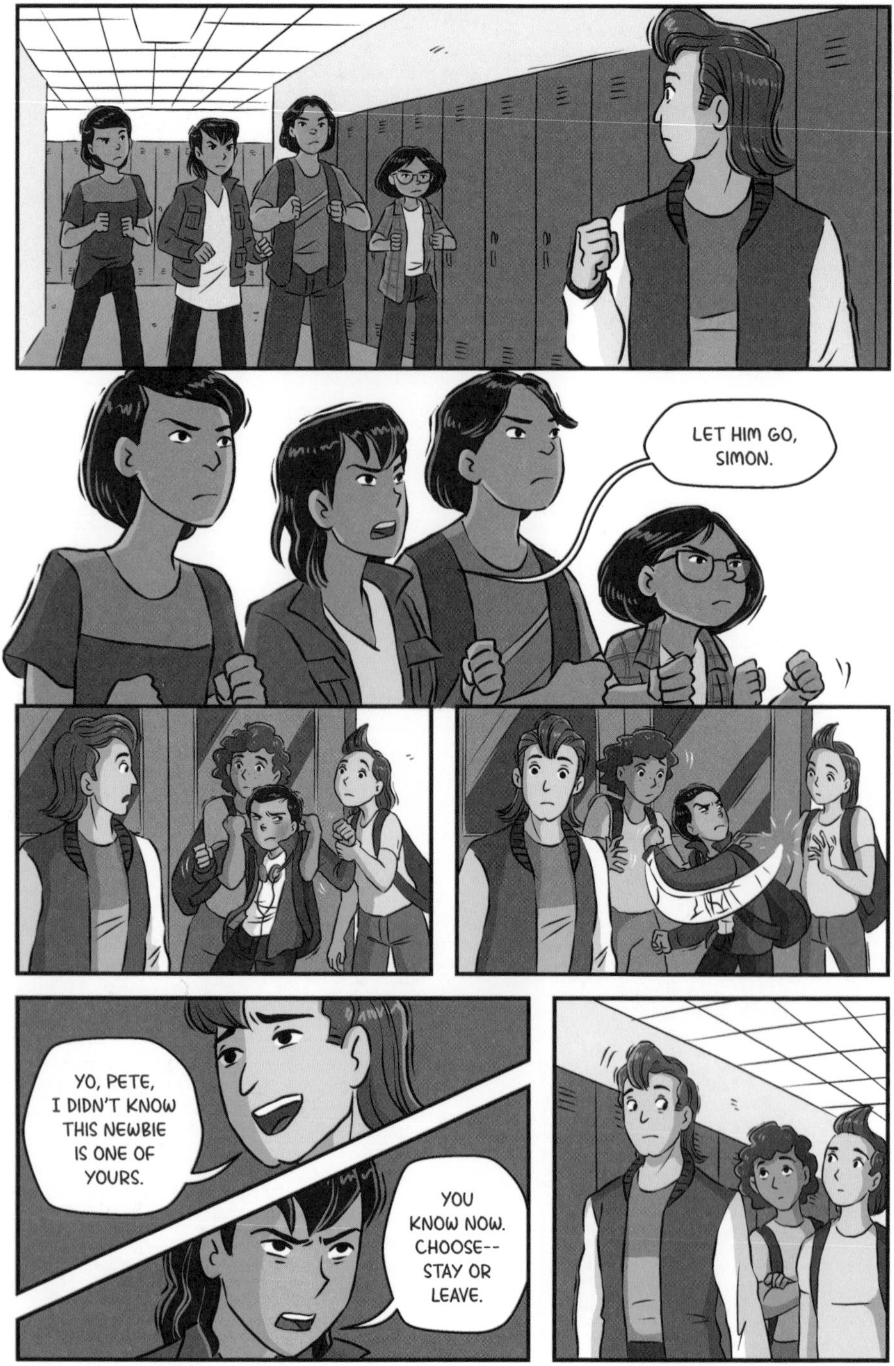

LET HIM GO, SIMON.
YO, PETE, I DIDN'T KNOW THIS NEWBIE IS ONE OF YOURS.
YOU KNOW NOW. CHOOSE-- STAY OR LEAVE.

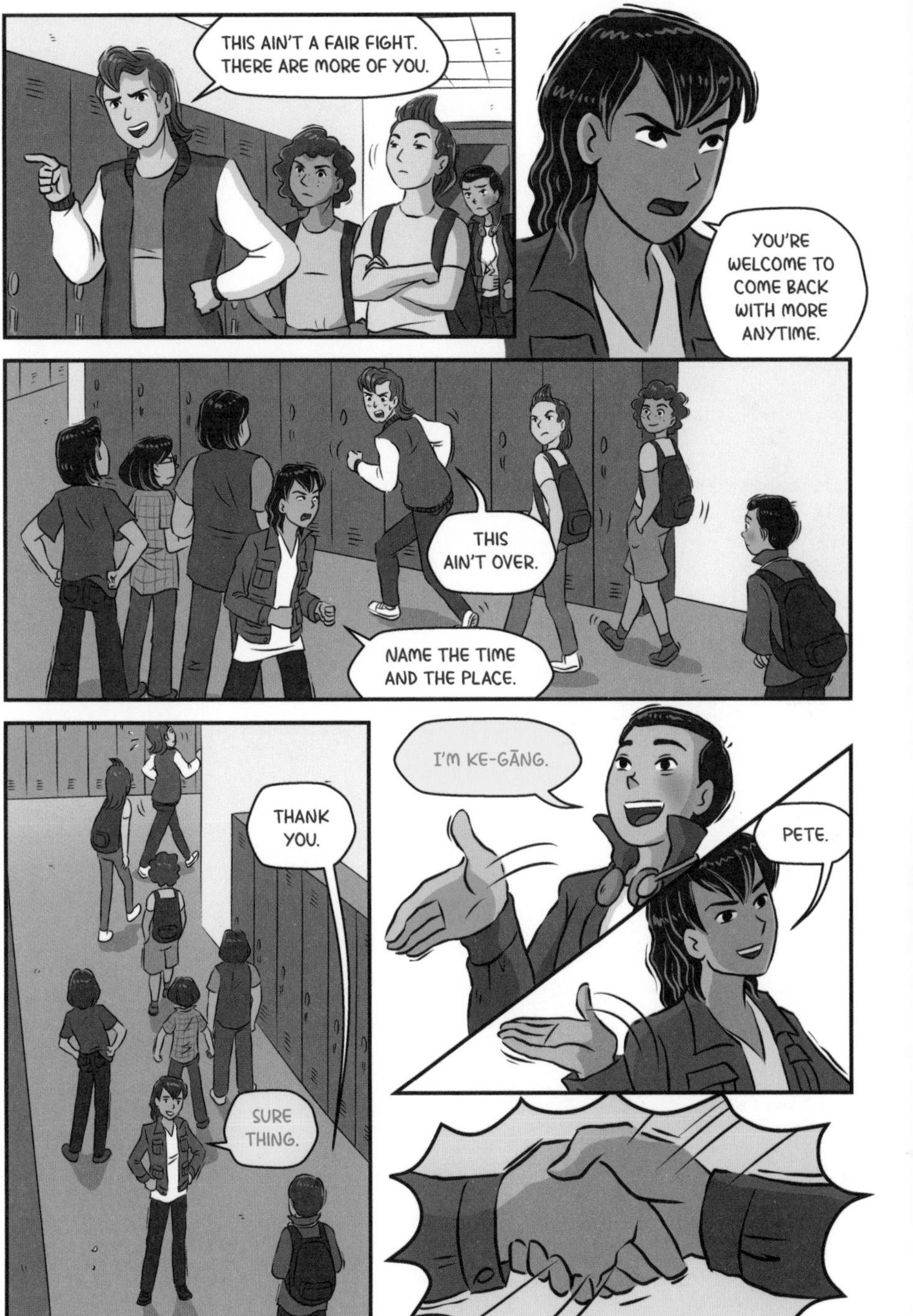
THIS AIN'T A FAIR FIGHT. THERE ARE MORE OF YOU.
YOU'RE WELCOME TO COME BACK WITH MORE ANYTIME.
THIS AIN'T OVER.
NAME THE TIME AND THE PLACE.
THANK YOU.
SURE THING.
I'M KE-GĀNG.
PETE.

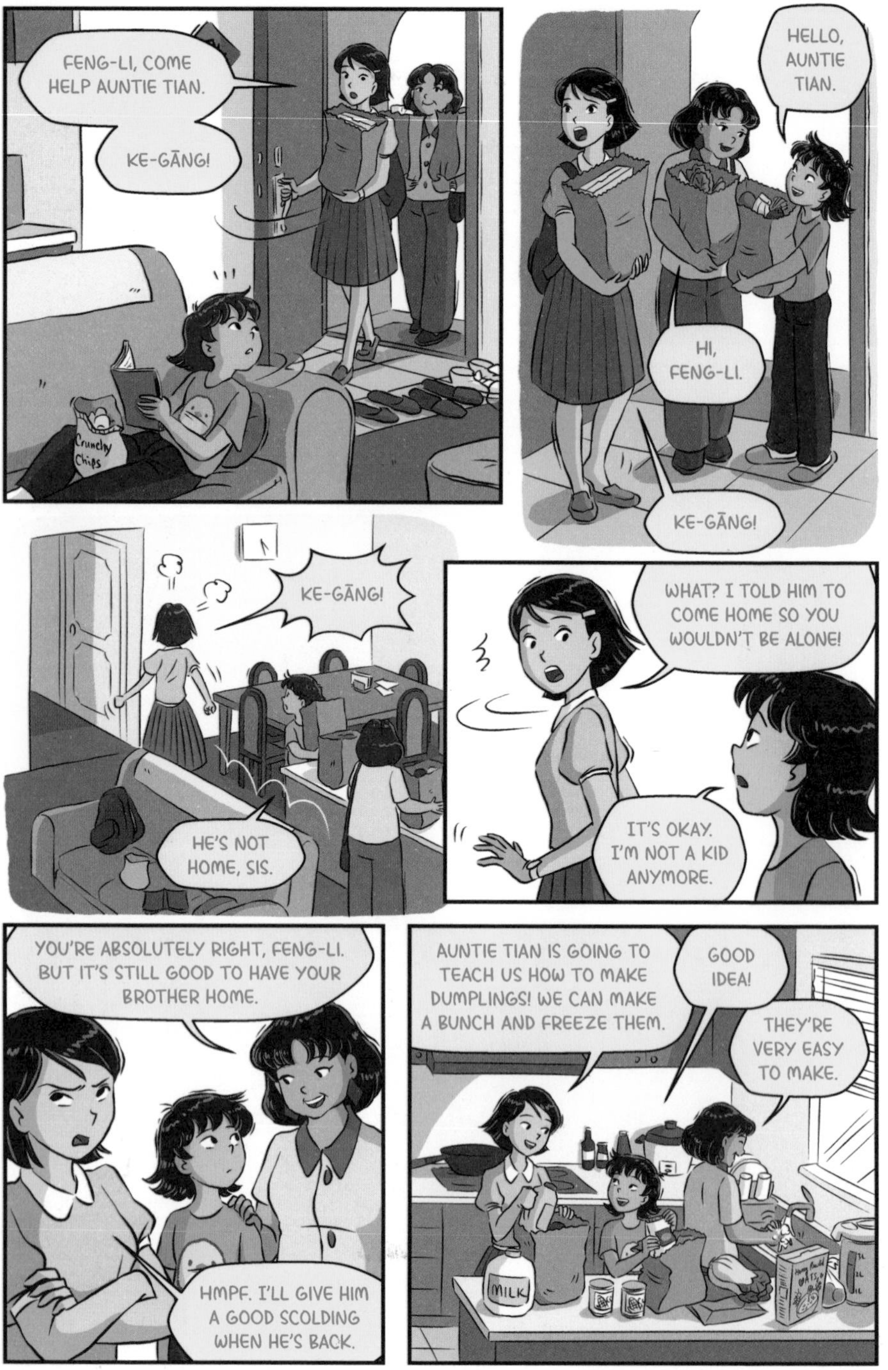
FENG-LI, COME HELP AUNTIE TIAN.
KE-GĀNG!
Crunchy Chips
HELLO, AUNTIE TIAN.
HI, FENG-LI.
KE-GĀNG!
KE-GĀNG!
HE'S NOT HOME, SIS.
WHAT? I TOLD HIM TO COME HOME SO YOU WOULDN'T BE ALONE!
IT'S OKAY. I'M NOT A KID ANYMORE.
YOU'RE ABSOLUTELY RIGHT, FENG-LI. BUT IT'S STILL GOOD TO HAVE YOUR BROTHER HOME.
HMPF. I'LL GIVE HIM A GOOD SCOLDING WHEN HE'S BACK.
AUNTIE TIAN IS GOING TO TEACH US HOW TO MAKE DUMPLINGS! WE CAN MAKE A BUNCH AND FREEZE THEM.
GOOD IDEA!
THEY'RE VERY EASY TO MAKE.
MILK

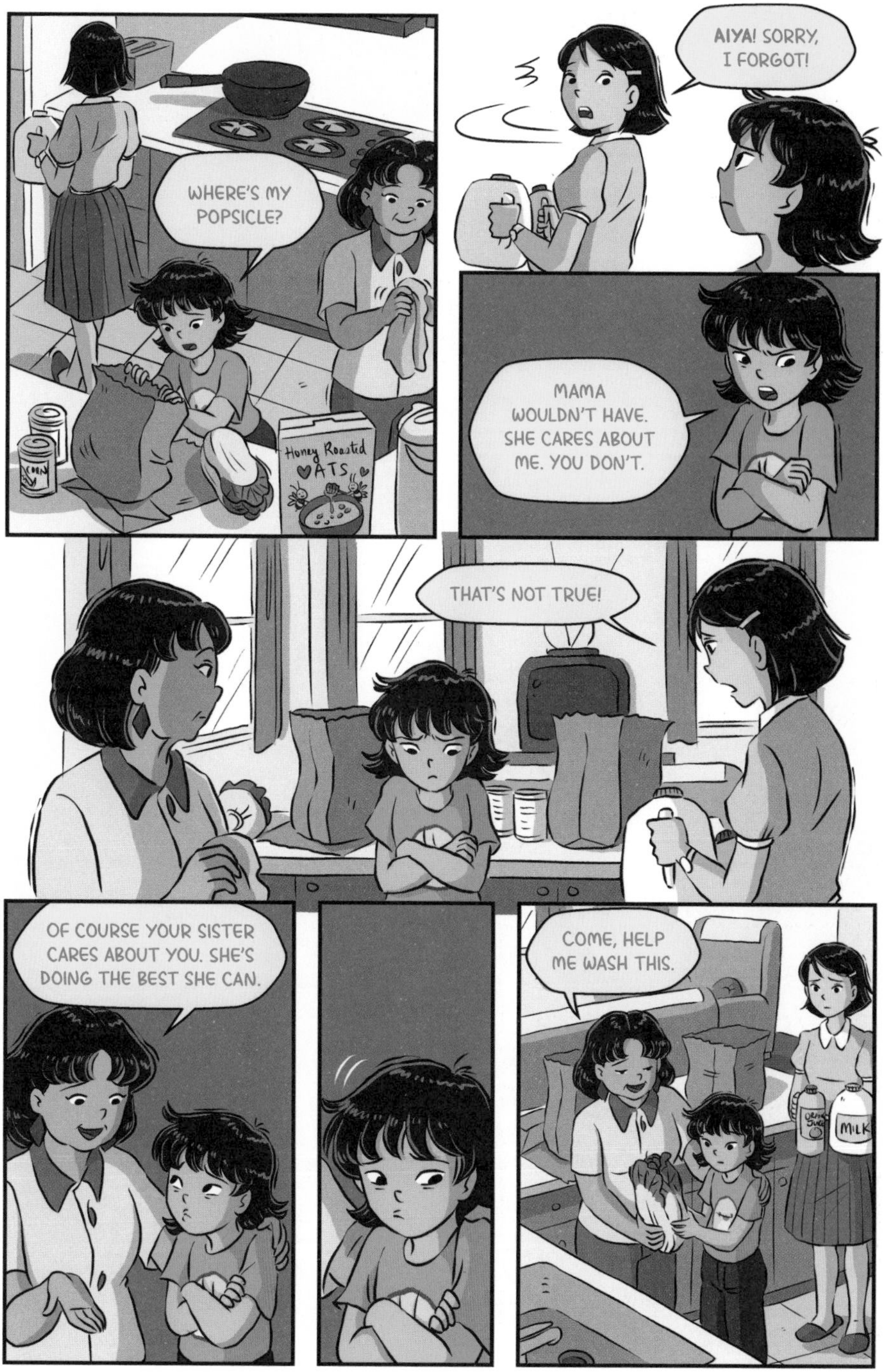
WHERE'S MY POPSICLE?
AIYA! SORRY, I FORGOT!
MAMA WOULDN'T HAVE. SHE CARES ABOUT ME. YOU DON'T.
THAT'S NOT TRUE!
OF COURSE YOUR SISTER CARES ABOUT YOU. SHE'S DOING THE BEST SHE CAN.
COME, HELP ME WASH THIS.
Honey Roasted OATS
MILK

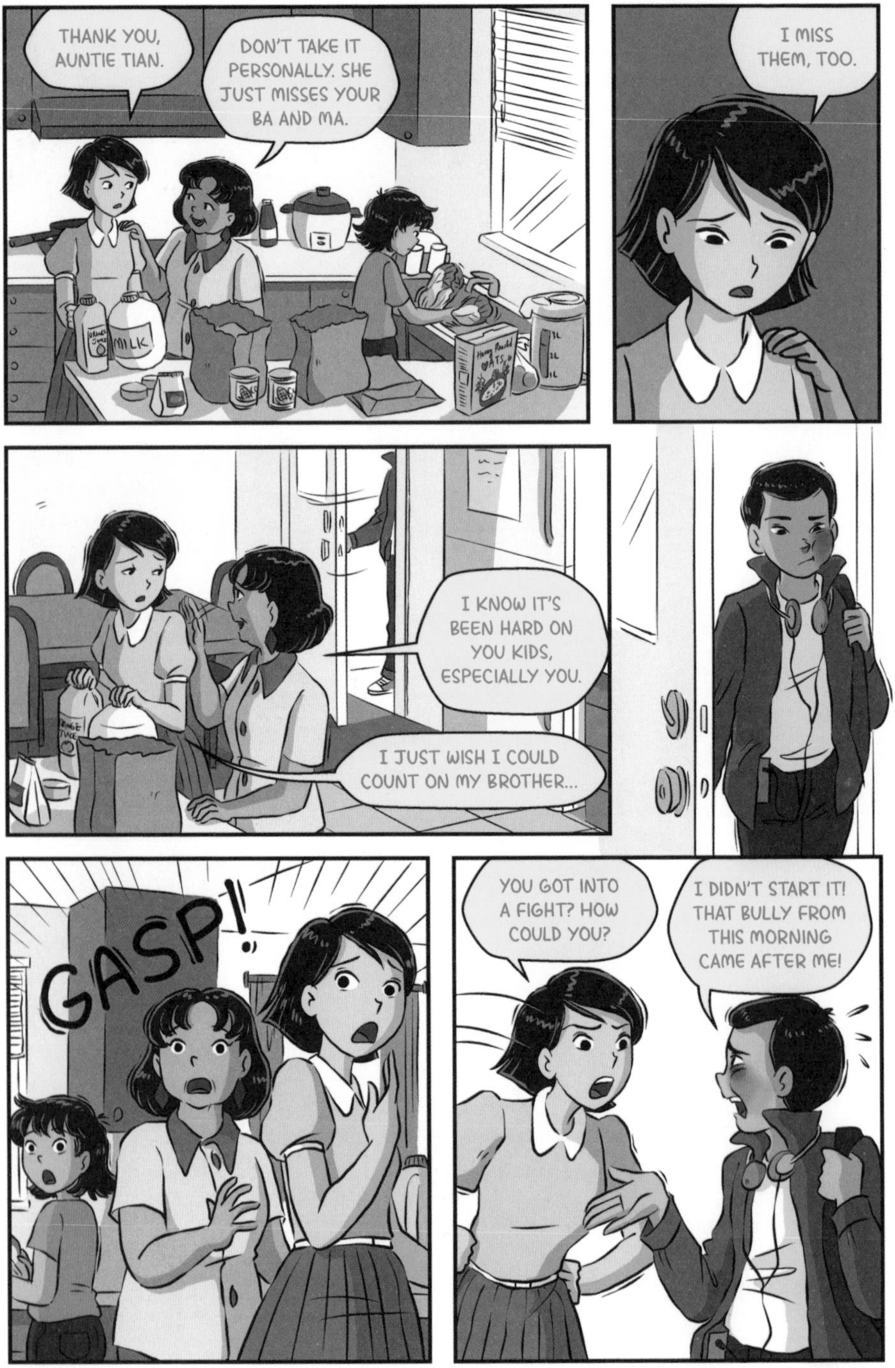
THANK YOU, AUNTIE TIAN.
DON'T TAKE IT PERSONALLY. SHE JUST MISSES YOUR BA AND MA.
I MISS THEM, TOO.
I KNOW IT'S BEEN HARD ON YOU KIDS, ESPECIALLY YOU.
I JUST WISH I COULD COUNT ON MY BROTHER...
GASP!
YOU GOT INTO A FIGHT? HOW COULD YOU?
I DIDN'T START IT! THAT BULLY FROM THIS MORNING CAME AFTER ME!

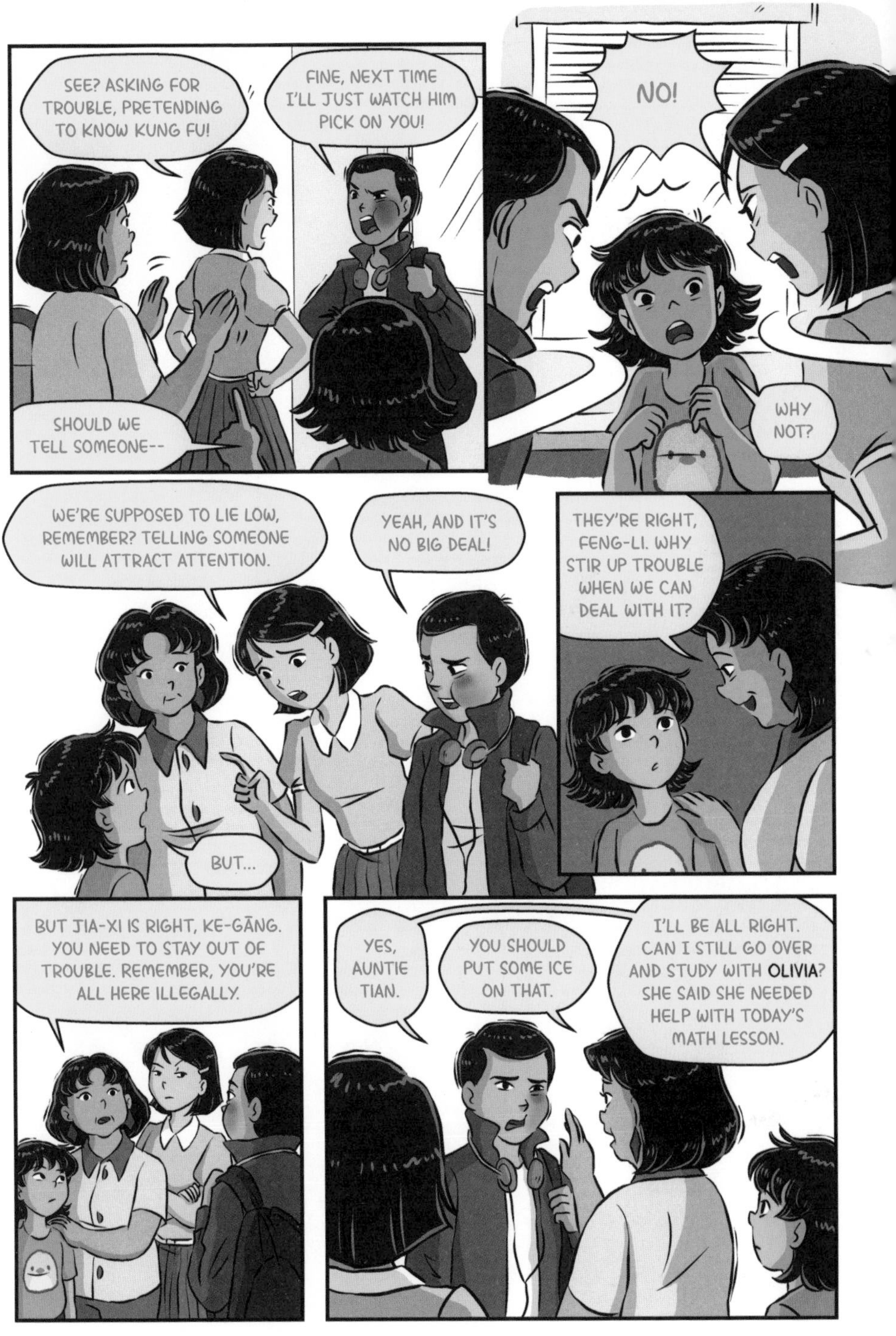
SEE? ASKING FOR TROUBLE, PRETENDING TO KNOW KUNG FU!
FINE, NEXT TIME I'LL JUST WATCH HIM PICK ON YOU!
SHOULD WE TELL SOMEONE--
NO!
WHY NOT?
WE'RE SUPPOSED TO LIE LOW, REMEMBER? TELLING SOMEONE WILL ATTRACT ATTENTION.
YEAH, AND IT'S NO BIG DEAL!
BUT...
THEY'RE RIGHT, FENG-LI. WHY STIR UP TROUBLE WHEN WE CAN DEAL WITH IT?
BUT JIA-XI IS RIGHT, KE-GĀNG. YOU NEED TO STAY OUT OF TROUBLE. REMEMBER, YOU'RE ALL HERE ILLEGALLY.
YES, AUNTIE TIAN.
YOU SHOULD PUT SOME ICE ON THAT.
I'LL BE ALL RIGHT. CAN I STILL GO OVER AND STUDY WITH OLIVIA? SHE SAID SHE NEEDED HELP WITH TODAY'S MATH LESSON.

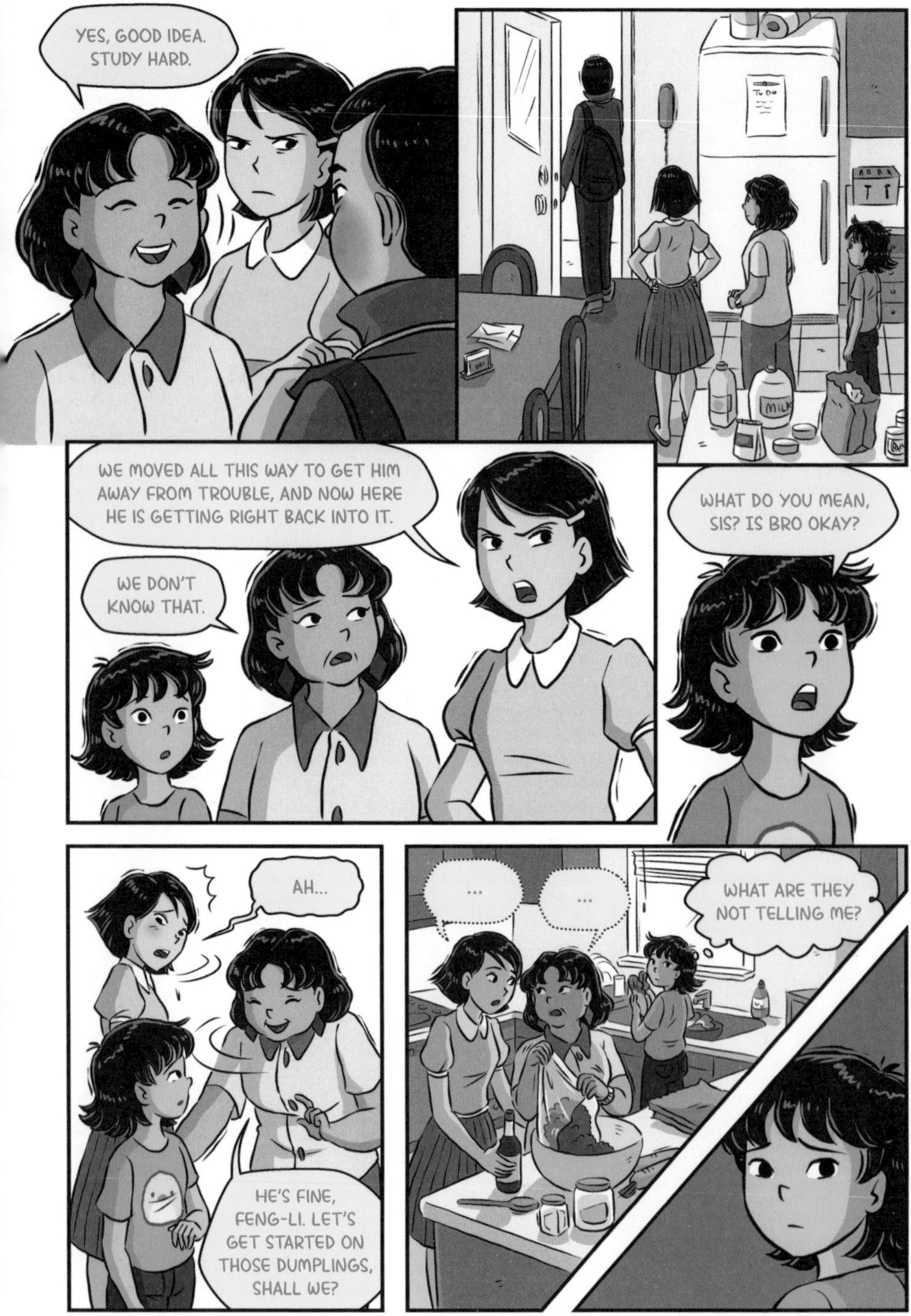
YES, GOOD IDEA. STUDY HARD.
WE MOVED ALL THIS WAY TO GET HIM AWAY FROM TROUBLE, AND NOW HERE HE IS GETTING RIGHT BACK INTO IT.
WE DON'T KNOW THAT.
WHAT DO YOU MEAN, SIS? IS BRO OKAY?
AH...
HE'S FINE, FENG-LI. LET'S GET STARTED ON THOSE DUMPLINGS, SHALL WE?
...
...
WHAT ARE THEY NOT TELLING ME?

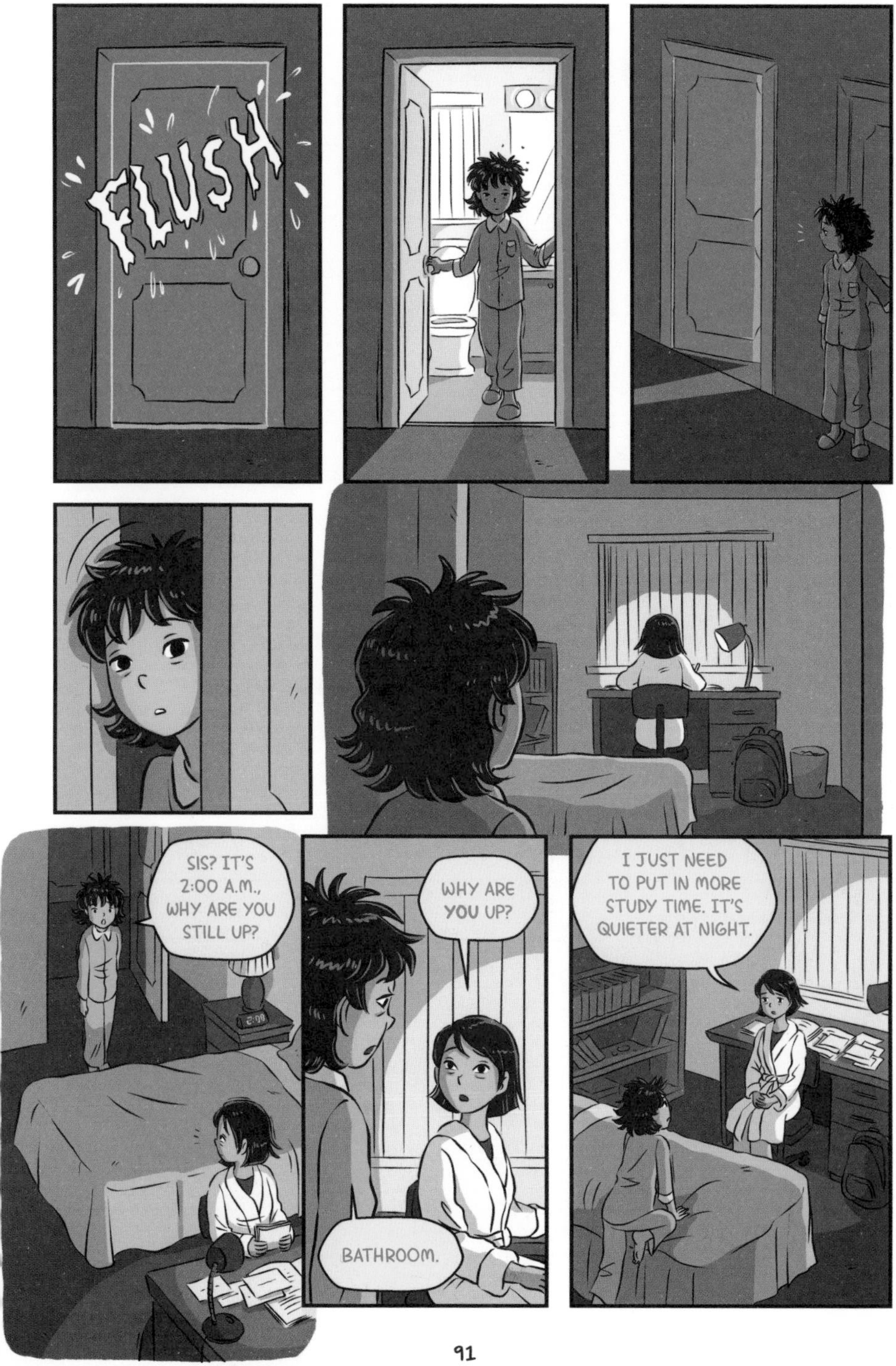
FLUSH
SIS? IT'S 2:00 A.M., WHY ARE YOU STILL UP?
2:08
WHY ARE YOU UP?
BATHROOM.
I JUST NEED TO PUT IN MORE STUDY TIME. IT'S QUIETER AT NIGHT.

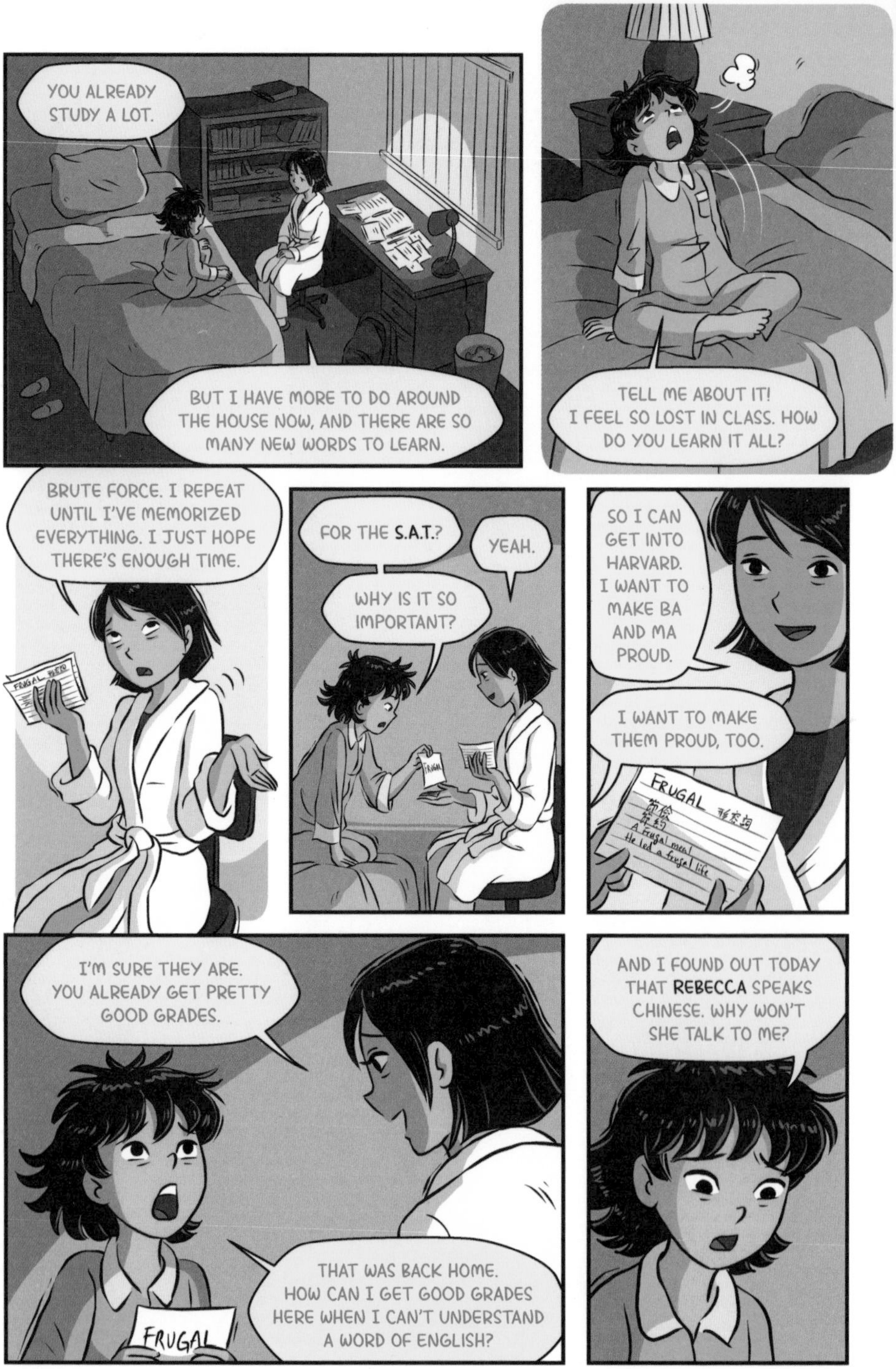
YOU ALREADY STUDY A LOT.
BUT I HAVE MORE TO DO AROUND THE HOUSE NOW, AND THERE ARE SO MANY NEW WORDS TO LEARN.
TELL ME ABOUT IT! I FEEL SO LOST IN CLASS. HOW DO YOU LEARN IT ALL?
BRUTE FORCE. I REPEAT UNTIL I'VE MEMORIZED EVERYTHING. I JUST HOPE THERE'S ENOUGH TIME.
FOR THE **S.A.T.**?
YEAH.
WHY IS IT SO IMPORTANT?
SO I CAN GET INTO HARVARD. I WANT TO MAKE BA AND MA PROUD.
I WANT TO MAKE THEM PROUD, TOO.
FRUGAL
A frugal meal
He led a frugal life
I'M SURE THEY ARE. YOU ALREADY GET PRETTY GOOD GRADES.
THAT WAS BACK HOME. HOW CAN I GET GOOD GRADES HERE WHEN I CAN'T UNDERSTAND A WORD OF ENGLISH?
FRUGAL
AND I FOUND OUT TODAY THAT **REBECCA** SPEAKS CHINESE. WHY WON'T SHE TALK TO ME?

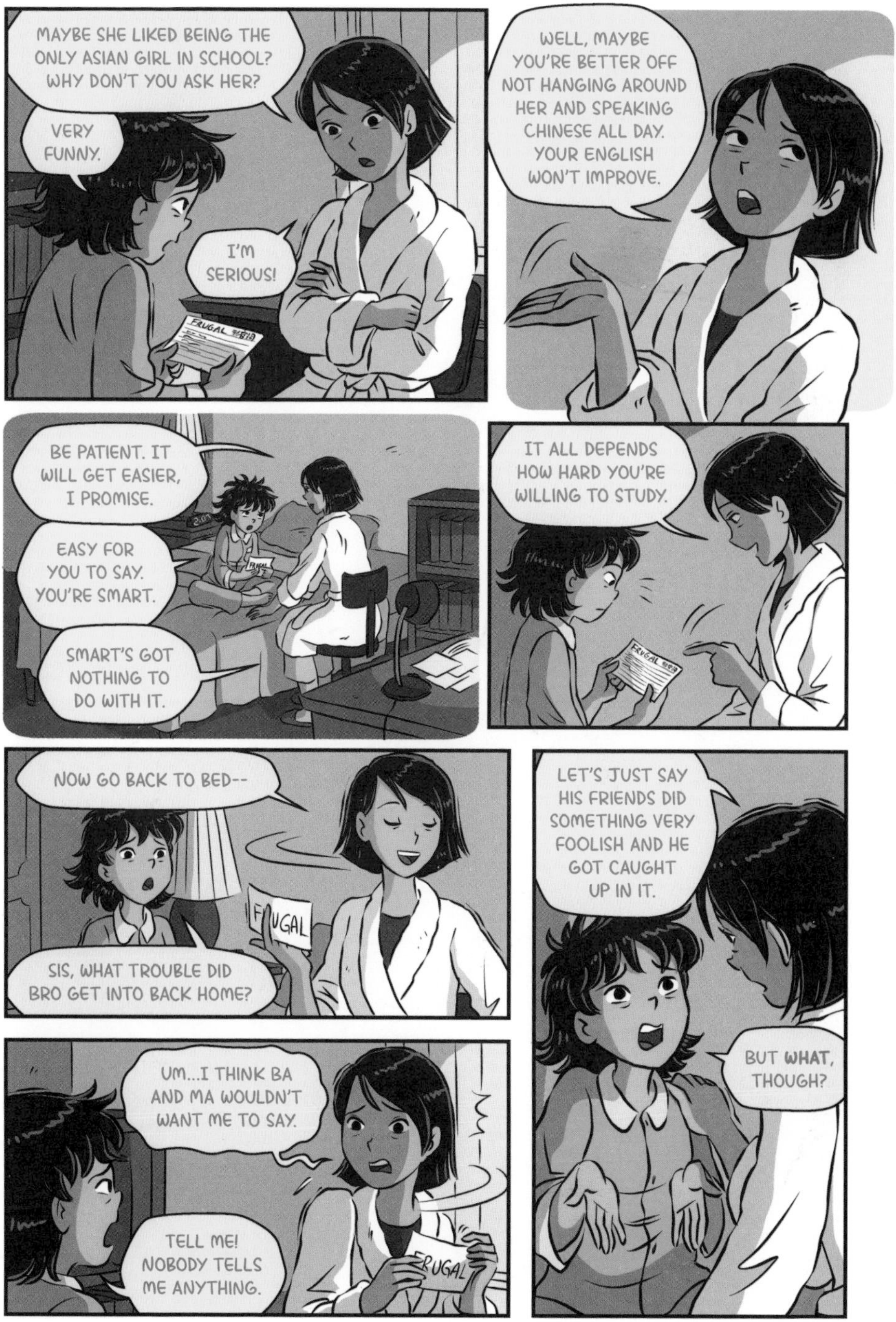
MAYBE SHE LIKED BEING THE ONLY ASIAN GIRL IN SCHOOL? WHY DON'T YOU ASK HER?
VERY FUNNY.
I'M SERIOUS!
FRUGAL
WELL, MAYBE YOU'RE BETTER OFF NOT HANGING AROUND HER AND SPEAKING CHINESE ALL DAY. YOUR ENGLISH WON'T IMPROVE.
BE PATIENT. IT WILL GET EASIER, I PROMISE.
EASY FOR YOU TO SAY. YOU'RE SMART.
SMART'S GOT NOTHING TO DO WITH IT.
IT ALL DEPENDS HOW HARD YOU'RE WILLING TO STUDY.
FRUGAL
NOW GO BACK TO BED--
FRUGAL
SIS, WHAT TROUBLE DID BRO GET INTO BACK HOME?
UM...I THINK BA AND MA WOULDN'T WANT ME TO SAY.
TELL ME! NOBODY TELLS ME ANYTHING.
FRUGAL
LET'S JUST SAY HIS FRIENDS DID SOMETHING VERY FOOLISH AND HE GOT CAUGHT UP IN IT.
BUT WHAT, THOUGH?

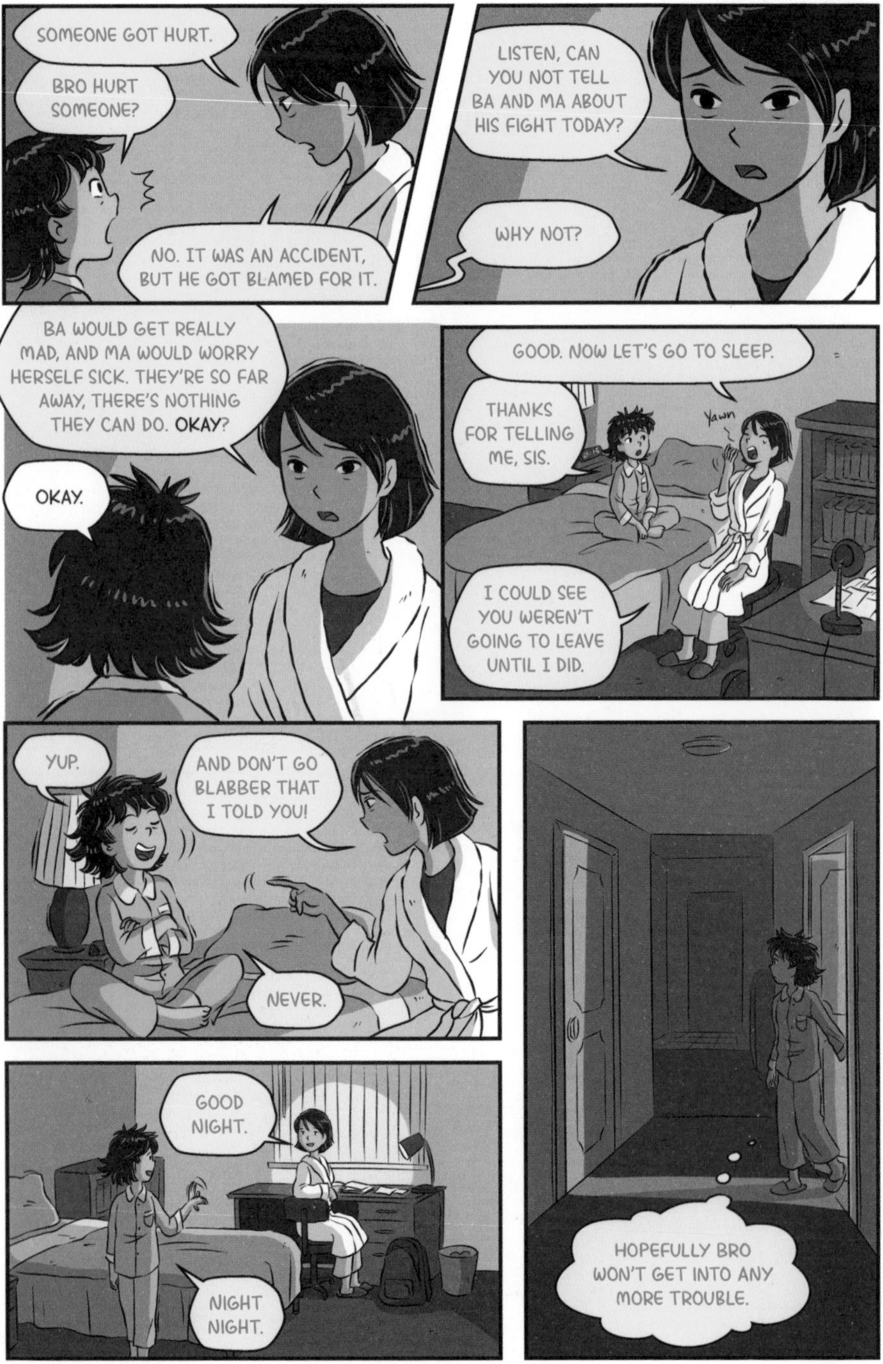
SOMEONE GOT HURT.
BRO HURT SOMEONE?
NO. IT WAS AN ACCIDENT, BUT HE GOT BLAMED FOR IT.
LISTEN, CAN YOU NOT TELL BA AND MA ABOUT HIS FIGHT TODAY?
WHY NOT?
BA WOULD GET REALLY MAD, AND MA WOULD WORRY HERSELF SICK. THEY'RE SO FAR AWAY, THERE'S NOTHING THEY CAN DO. **OKAY**?
OKAY.
GOOD. NOW LET'S GO TO SLEEP.
THANKS FOR TELLING ME, SIS.
Yawn
I COULD SEE YOU WEREN'T GOING TO LEAVE UNTIL I DID.
YUP.
AND DON'T GO BLABBER THAT I TOLD YOU!
NEVER.
GOOD NIGHT.
NIGHT NIGHT.
HOPEFULLY BRO WON'T GET INTO ANY MORE TROUBLE.

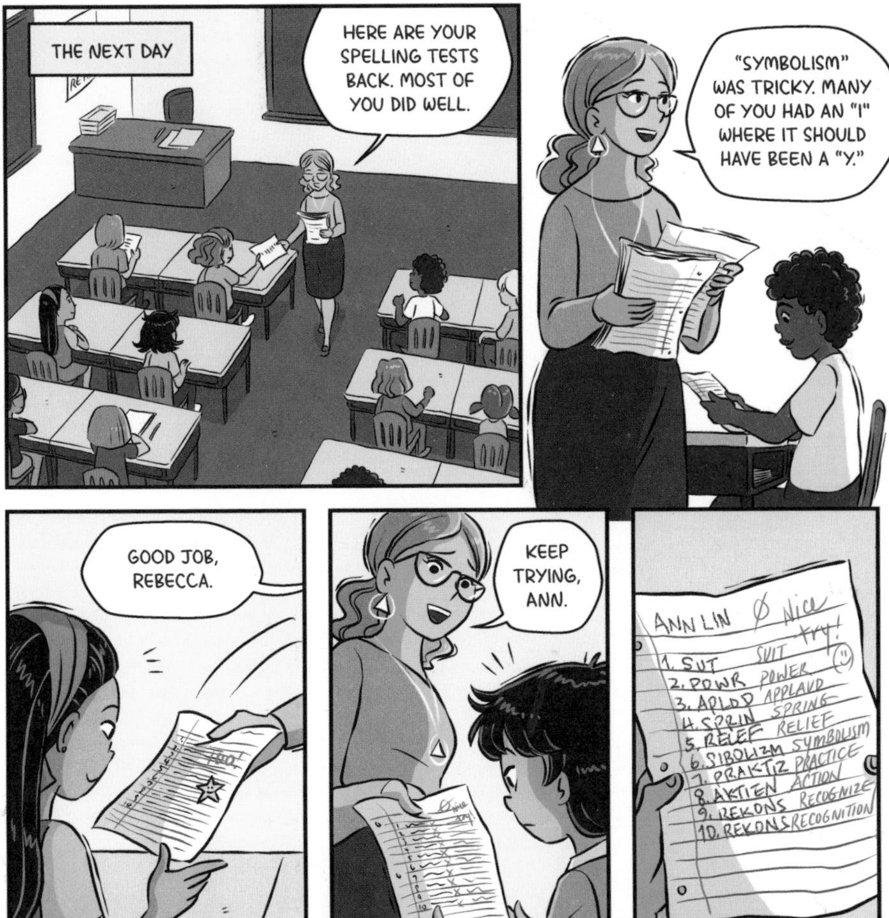
THE NEXT DAY
HERE ARE YOUR SPELLING TESTS BACK. MOST OF YOU DID WELL.
"SYMBOLISM" WAS TRICKY. MANY OF YOU HAD AN "I" WHERE IT SHOULD HAVE BEEN A "Y."
GOOD JOB, REBECCA.
KEEP TRYING, ANN.
ANN LIN Ø Nice try!
1. SUT SUIT
2. POWR POWER
3. APLOD APPLAUD
4. SPRIN SPRING
5. RELEF RELIEF
6. SIBOLIZM SYMBOLISM
7. PRAKTIZ PRACTICE
8. AKTIEN ACTION
9. REKONS RECOGNIZE
10. REKONS RECOGNITION
ANOTHER "DUCK EGG" ZERO!
零鴨蛋

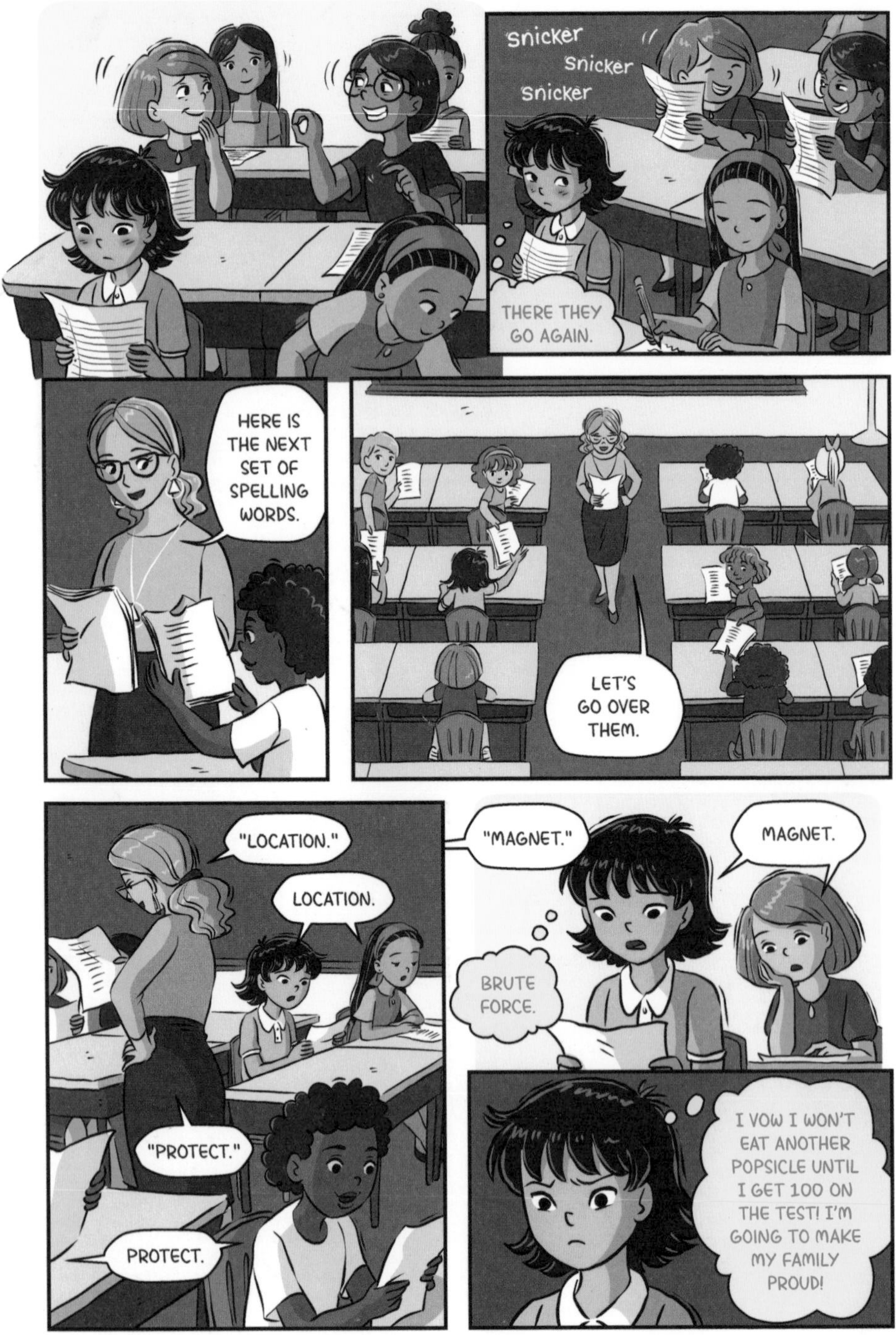
snicker
snicker
snicker
THERE THEY GO AGAIN.
HERE IS THE NEXT SET OF SPELLING WORDS.
LET'S GO OVER THEM.
"LOCATION."
LOCATION.
"PROTECT."
PROTECT.
"MAGNET."
MAGNET.
BRUTE FORCE.
I VOW I WON'T EAT ANOTHER POPSICLE UNTIL I GET 100 ON THE TEST! I'M GOING TO MAKE MY FAMILY PROUD!

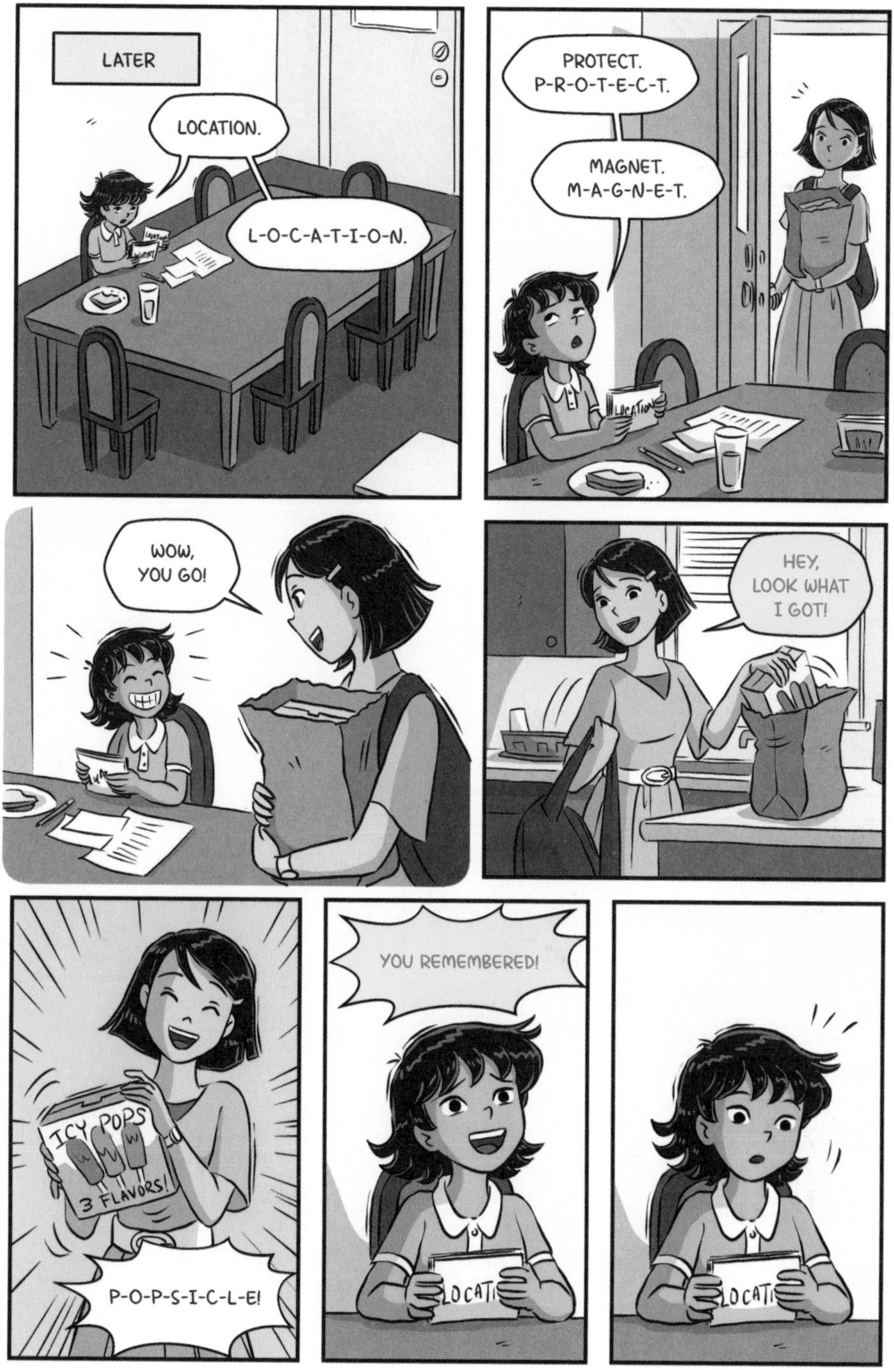
LATER
LOCATION.
L-O-C-A-T-I-O-N.
PROTECT.
P-R-O-T-E-C-T.
MAGNET.
M-A-G-N-E-T.
WOW,
YOU GO!
HEY,
LOOK WHAT
I GOT!
ICY POPS
3 FLAVORS!
P-O-P-S-I-C-L-E!
YOU REMEMBERED!

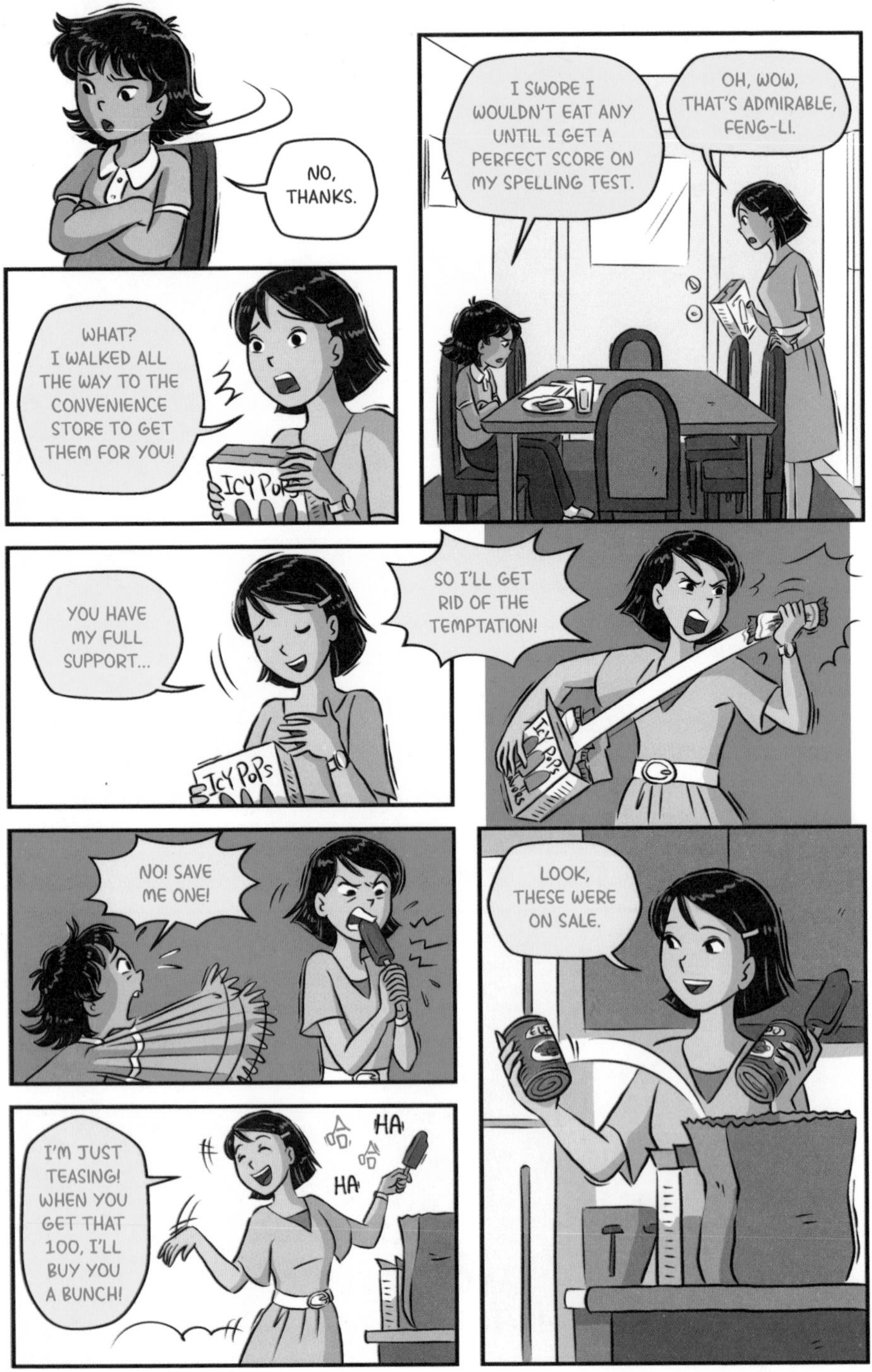
NO, THANKS.
I SWORE I WOULDN'T EAT ANY UNTIL I GET A PERFECT SCORE ON MY SPELLING TEST.
OH, WOW, THAT'S ADMIRABLE, FENG-LI.
WHAT? I WALKED ALL THE WAY TO THE CONVENIENCE STORE TO GET THEM FOR YOU!
ICY POPS
YOU HAVE MY FULL SUPPORT...
ICY POPS
SO I'LL GET RID OF THE TEMPTATION!
ICY POPS
NO! SAVE ME ONE!
I'M JUST TEASING! WHEN YOU GET THAT 100, I'LL BUY YOU A BUNCH!
哈 HA 哈 HA
LOOK, THESE WERE ON SALE.

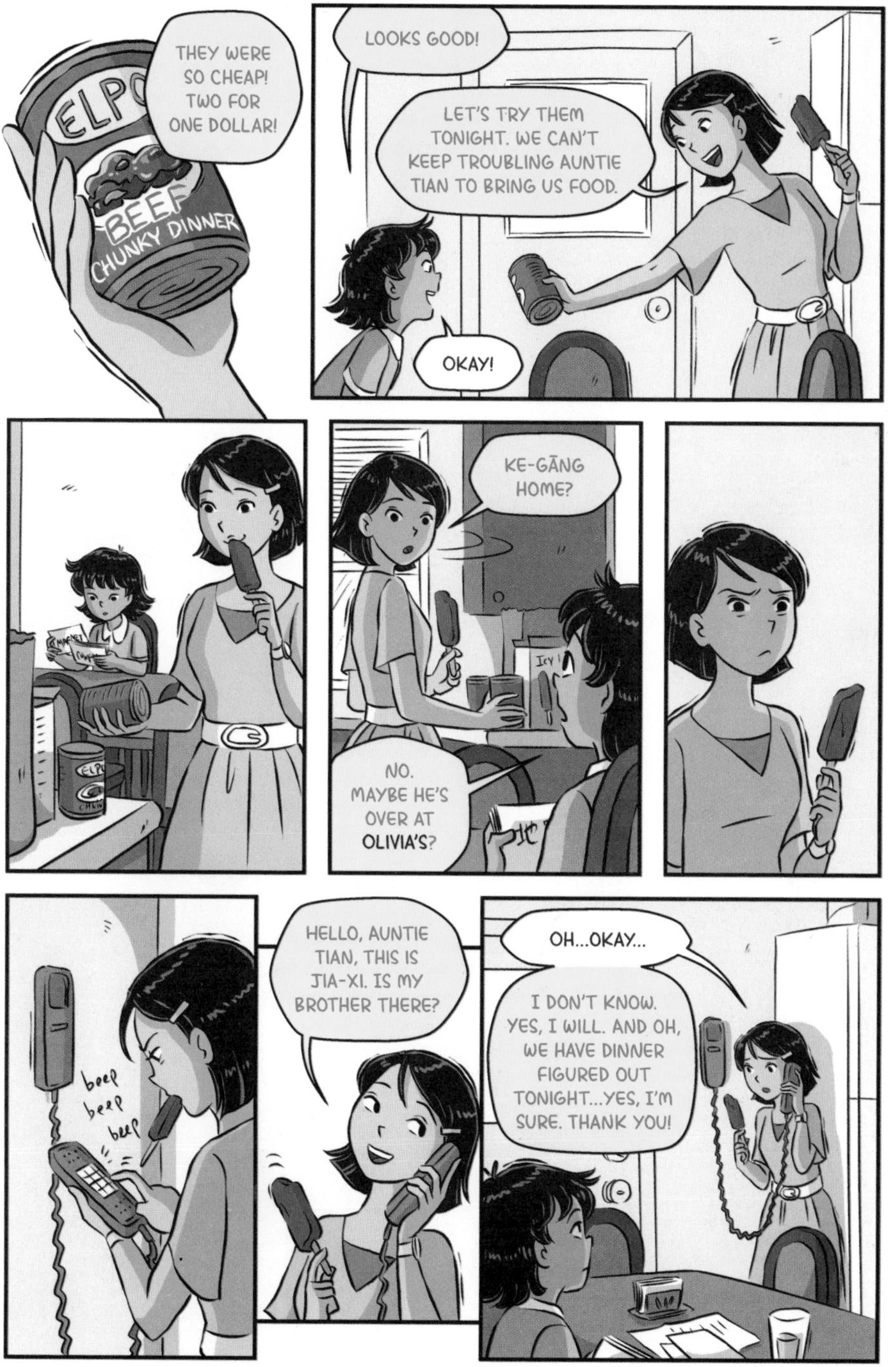
ELPO
BEEF CHUNKY DINNER
THEY WERE SO CHEAP! TWO FOR ONE DOLLAR!
LOOKS GOOD!
LET'S TRY THEM TONIGHT. WE CAN'T KEEP TROUBLING AUNTIE TIAN TO BRING US FOOD.
OKAY!
KE-GĀNG HOME?
NO. MAYBE HE'S OVER AT OLIVIA'S?
beep beep beep
HELLO, AUNTIE TIAN, THIS IS JIA-XI. IS MY BROTHER THERE?
OH...OKAY...
I DON'T KNOW. YES, I WILL. AND OH, WE HAVE DINNER FIGURED OUT TONIGHT...YES, I'M SURE. THANK YOU!

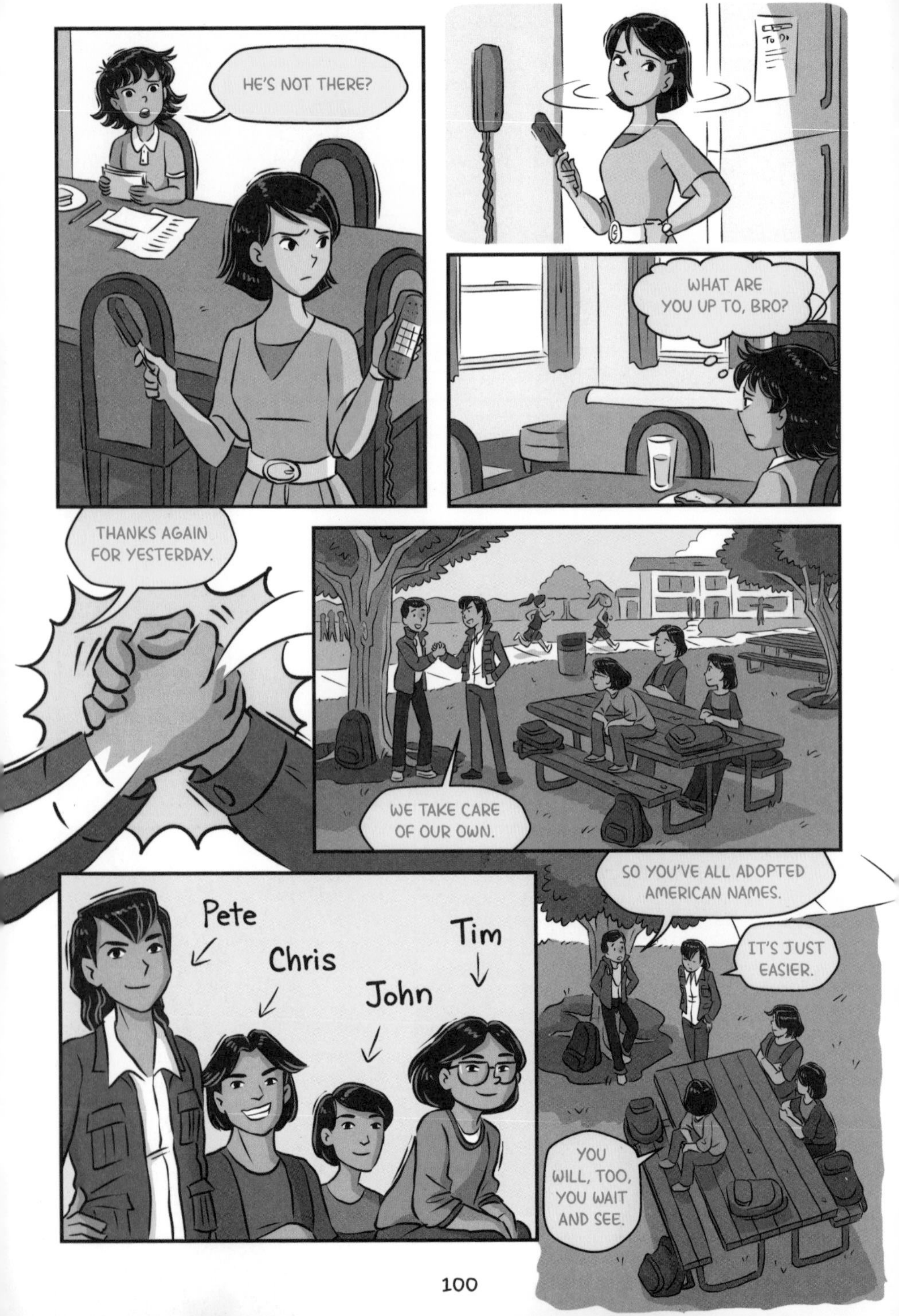
HE'S NOT THERE?
WHAT ARE YOU UP TO, BRO?
THANKS AGAIN FOR YESTERDAY.
WE TAKE CARE OF OUR OWN.
Pete
Chris
John
Tim
SO YOU'VE ALL ADOPTED AMERICAN NAMES.
IT'S JUST EASIER.
YOU WILL, TOO, YOU WAIT AND SEE.

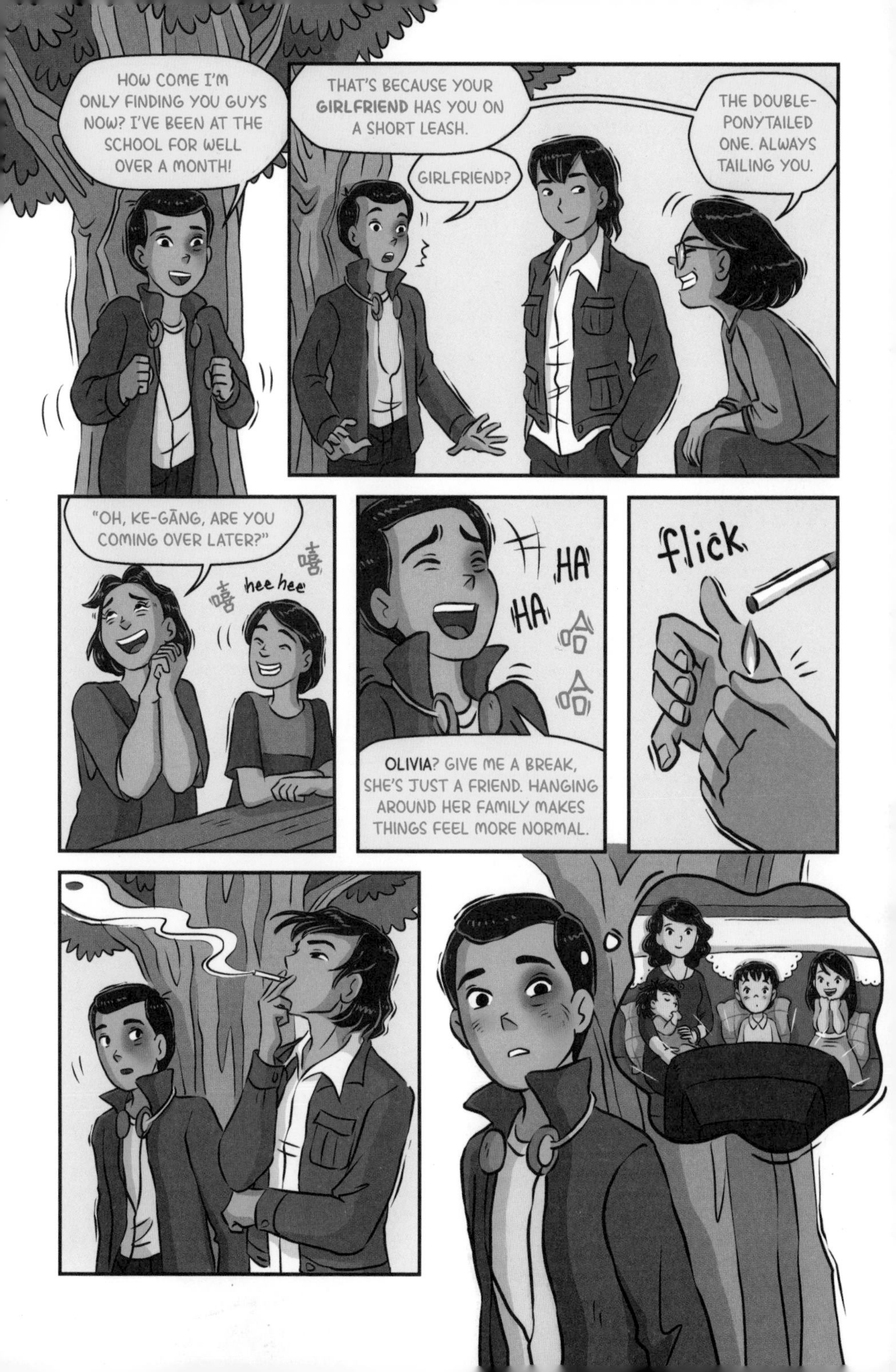

HOW COME I'M ONLY FINDING YOU GUYS NOW? I'VE BEEN AT THE SCHOOL FOR WELL OVER A MONTH!
THAT'S BECAUSE YOUR **GIRLFRIEND** HAS YOU ON A SHORT LEASH.
GIRLFRIEND?
THE DOUBLE-PONYTAILED ONE. ALWAYS TAILING YOU.
"OH, KE-GĀNG, ARE YOU COMING OVER LATER?"
嘻
嘻
hee hee
HA
HA
哈
哈
OLIVIA? GIVE ME A BREAK, SHE'S JUST A FRIEND. HANGING AROUND HER FAMILY MAKES THINGS FEEL MORE NORMAL.
flick

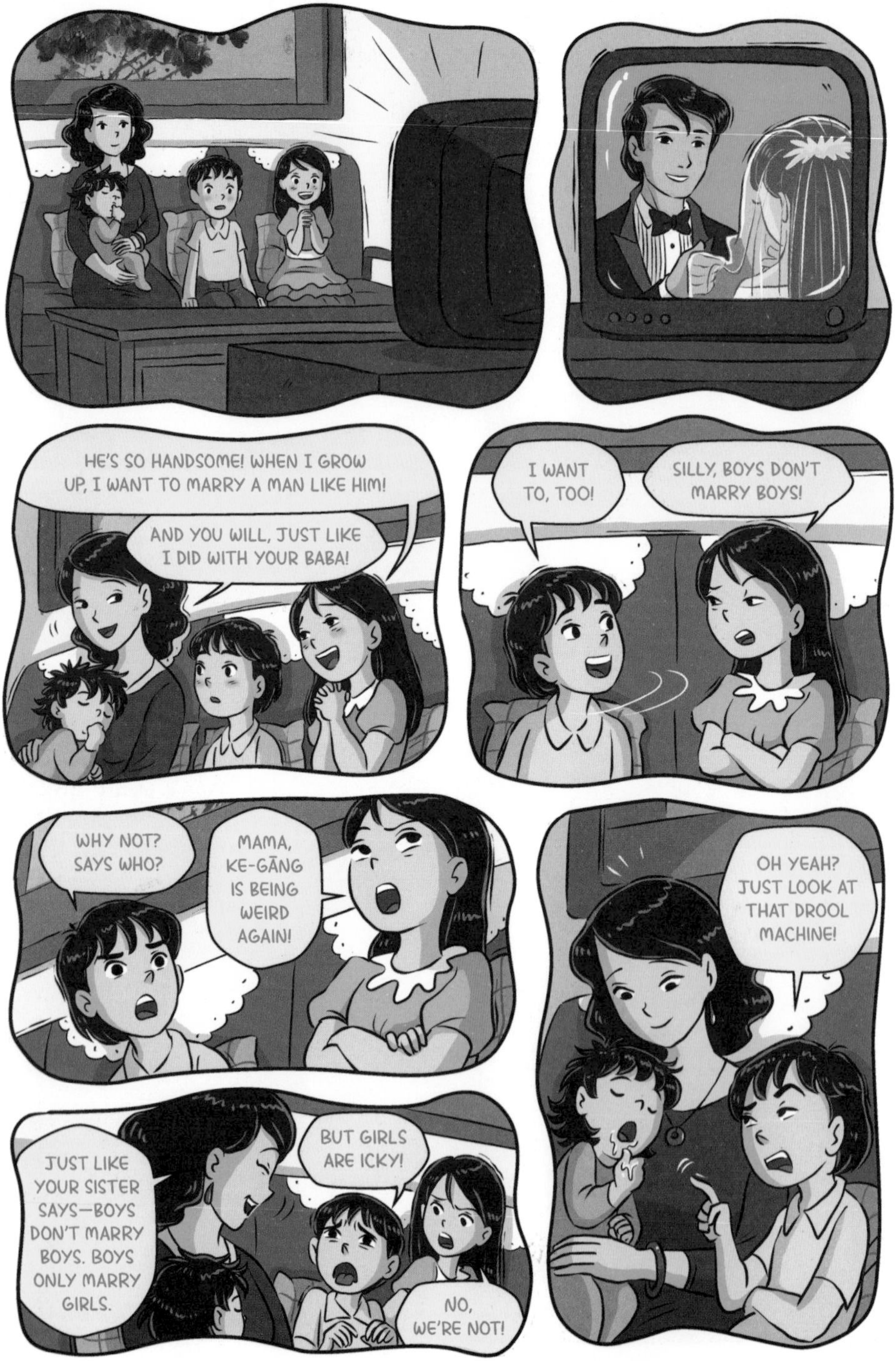
HE'S SO HANDSOME! WHEN I GROW UP, I WANT TO MARRY A MAN LIKE HIM!
AND YOU WILL, JUST LIKE I DID WITH YOUR BABA!
I WANT TO, TOO!
SILLY, BOYS DON'T MARRY BOYS!
WHY NOT? SAYS WHO?
MAMA, KE-GĀNG IS BEING WEIRD AGAIN!
JUST LIKE YOUR SISTER SAYS—BOYS DON'T MARRY BOYS. BOYS ONLY MARRY GIRLS.
BUT GIRLS ARE ICKY!
NO, WE'RE NOT!
OH YEAH? JUST LOOK AT THAT DROOL MACHINE!

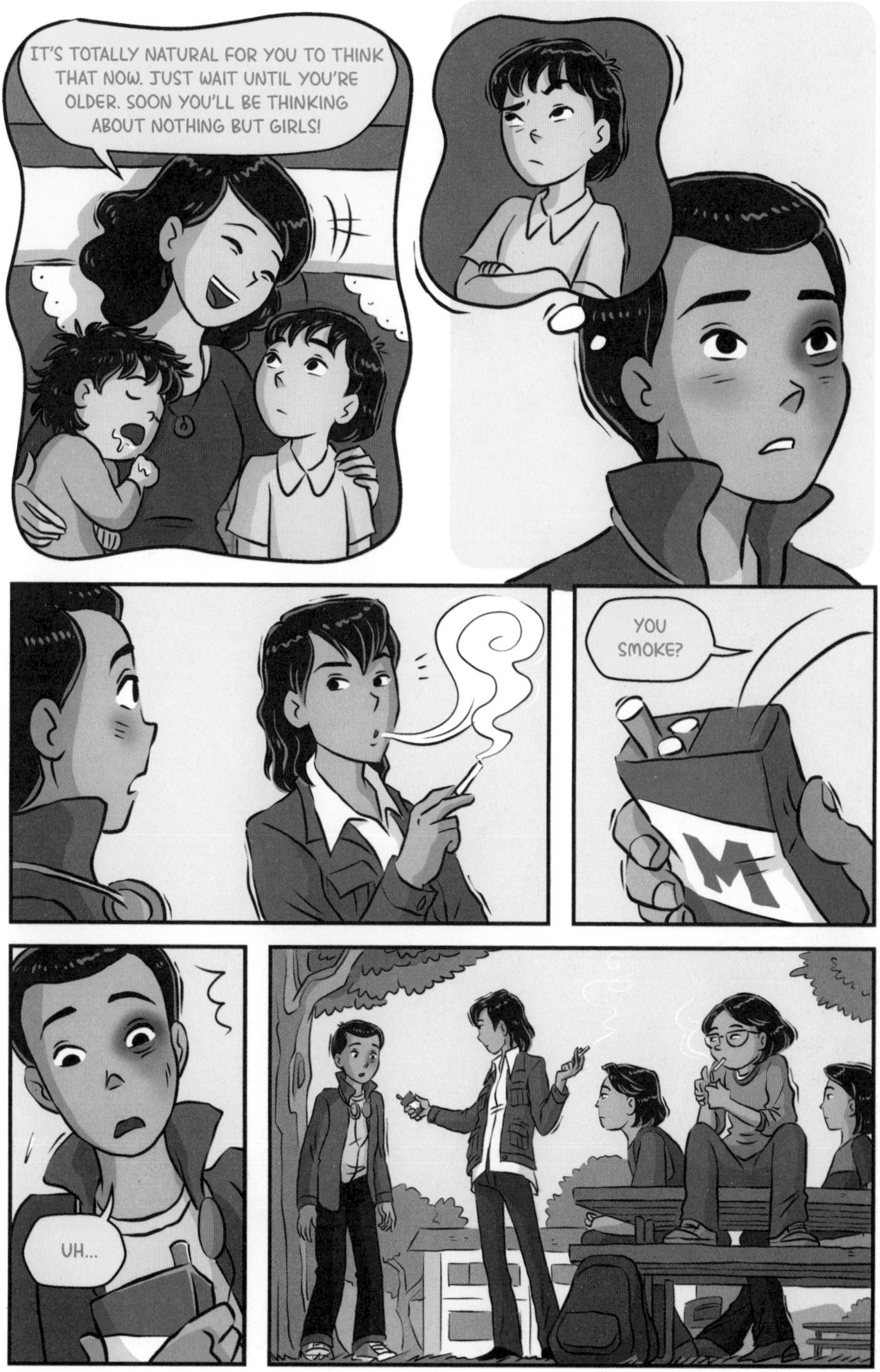
IT'S TOTALLY NATURAL FOR YOU TO THINK THAT NOW. JUST WAIT UNTIL YOU'RE OLDER. SOON YOU'LL BE THINKING ABOUT NOTHING BUT GIRLS!
YOU SMOKE?
M
UH...

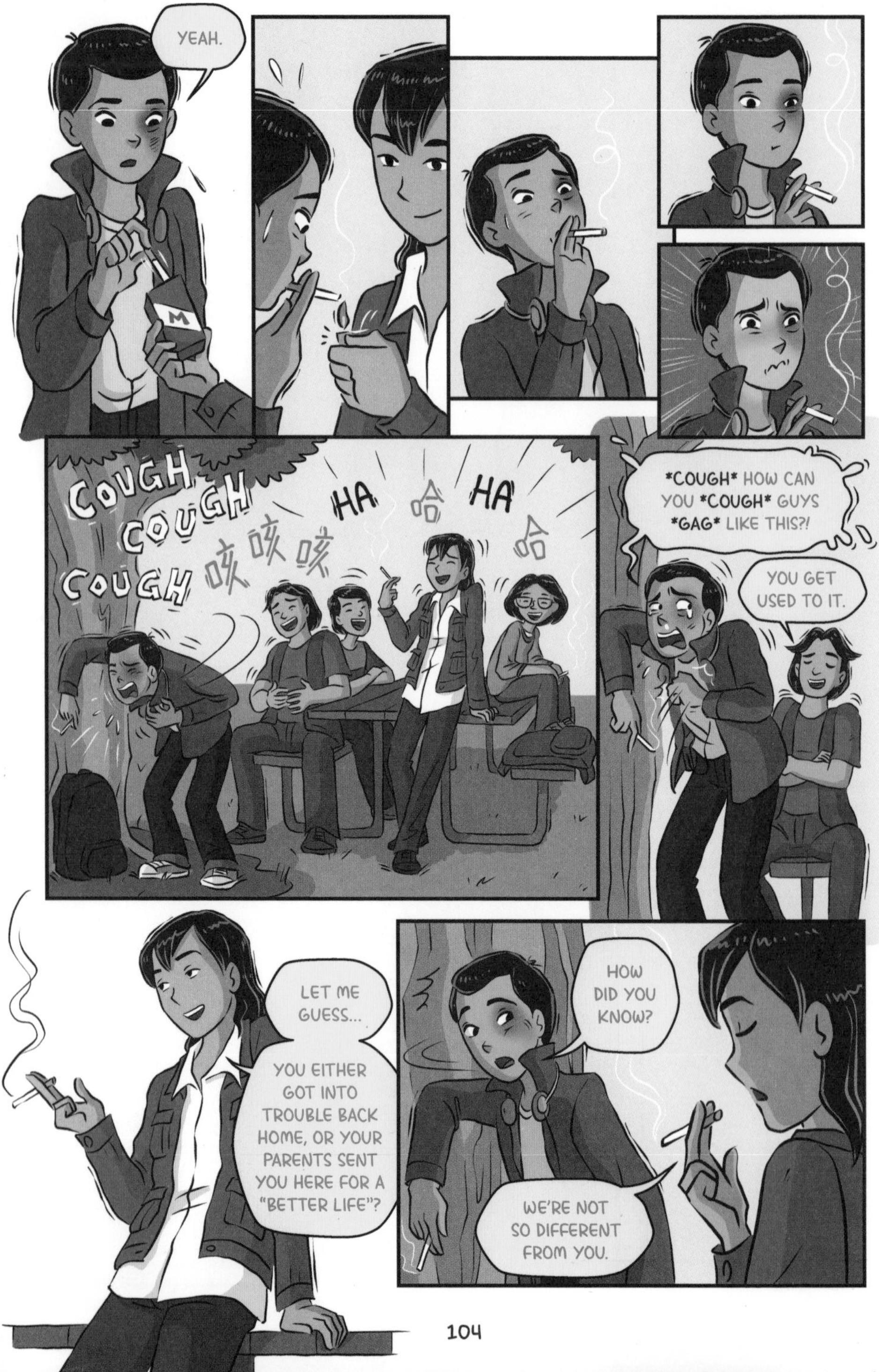
YEAH.
COUGH
COUGH
COUGH
咳咳咳
HA
哈
HA
哈
COUGH HOW CAN YOU *COUGH* GUYS *GAG* LIKE THIS?!
YOU GET USED TO IT.
LET ME GUESS...
YOU EITHER GOT INTO TROUBLE BACK HOME, OR YOUR PARENTS SENT YOU HERE FOR A "BETTER LIFE"?
HOW DID YOU KNOW?
WE'RE NOT SO DIFFERENT FROM YOU.

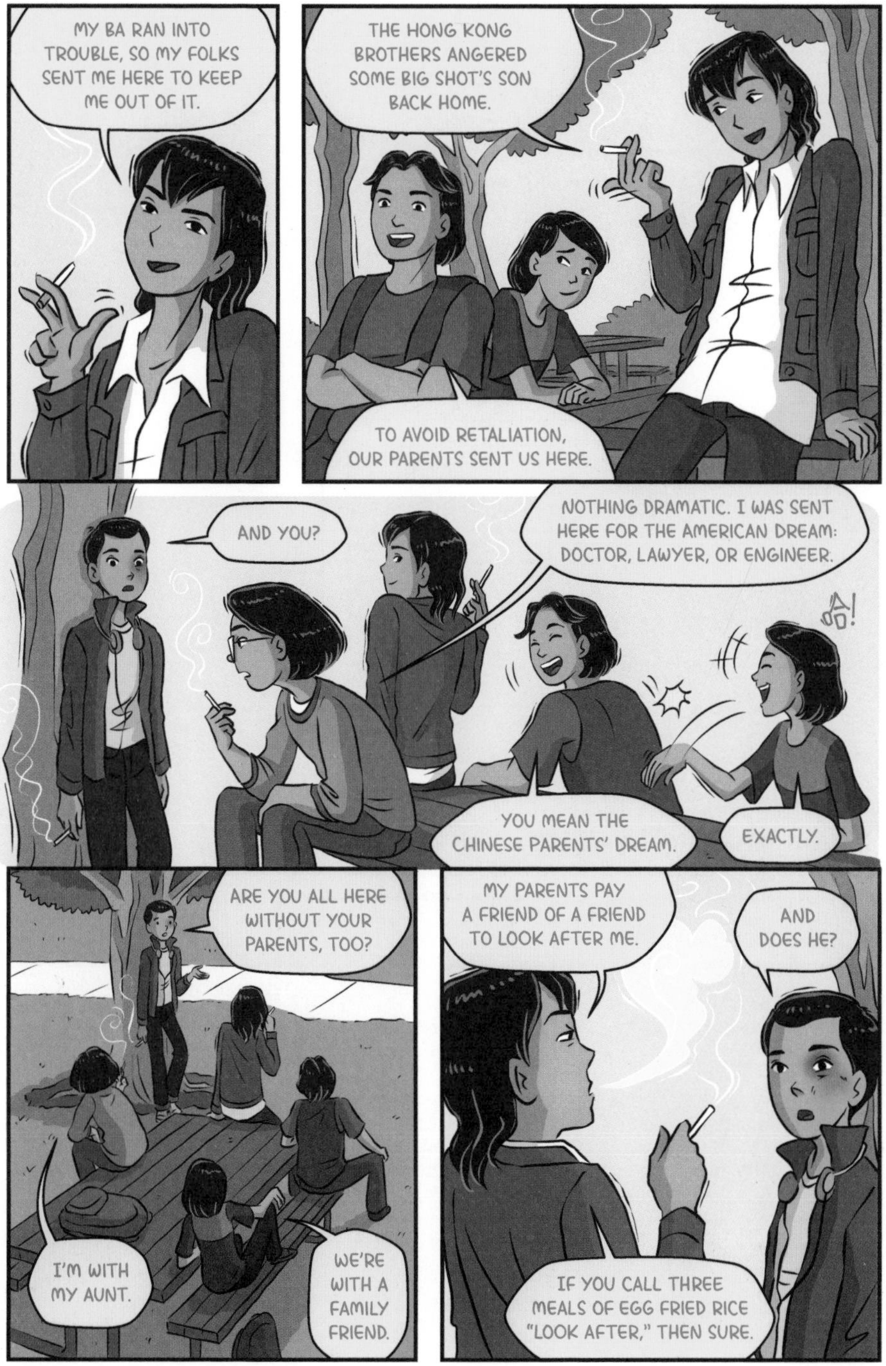

MY BA RAN INTO TROUBLE, SO MY FOLKS SENT ME HERE TO KEEP ME OUT OF IT.
THE HONG KONG BROTHERS ANGERED SOME BIG SHOT'S SON BACK HOME.
TO AVOID RETALIATION, OUR PARENTS SENT US HERE.
AND YOU?
NOTHING DRAMATIC. I WAS SENT HERE FOR THE AMERICAN DREAM: DOCTOR, LAWYER, OR ENGINEER.
哈!
YOU MEAN THE CHINESE PARENTS' DREAM.
EXACTLY.
ARE YOU ALL HERE WITHOUT YOUR PARENTS, TOO?
I'M WITH MY AUNT.
WE'RE WITH A FAMILY FRIEND.
MY PARENTS PAY A FRIEND OF A FRIEND TO LOOK AFTER ME.
AND DOES HE?
IF YOU CALL THREE MEALS OF EGG FRIED RICE "LOOK AFTER," THEN SURE.

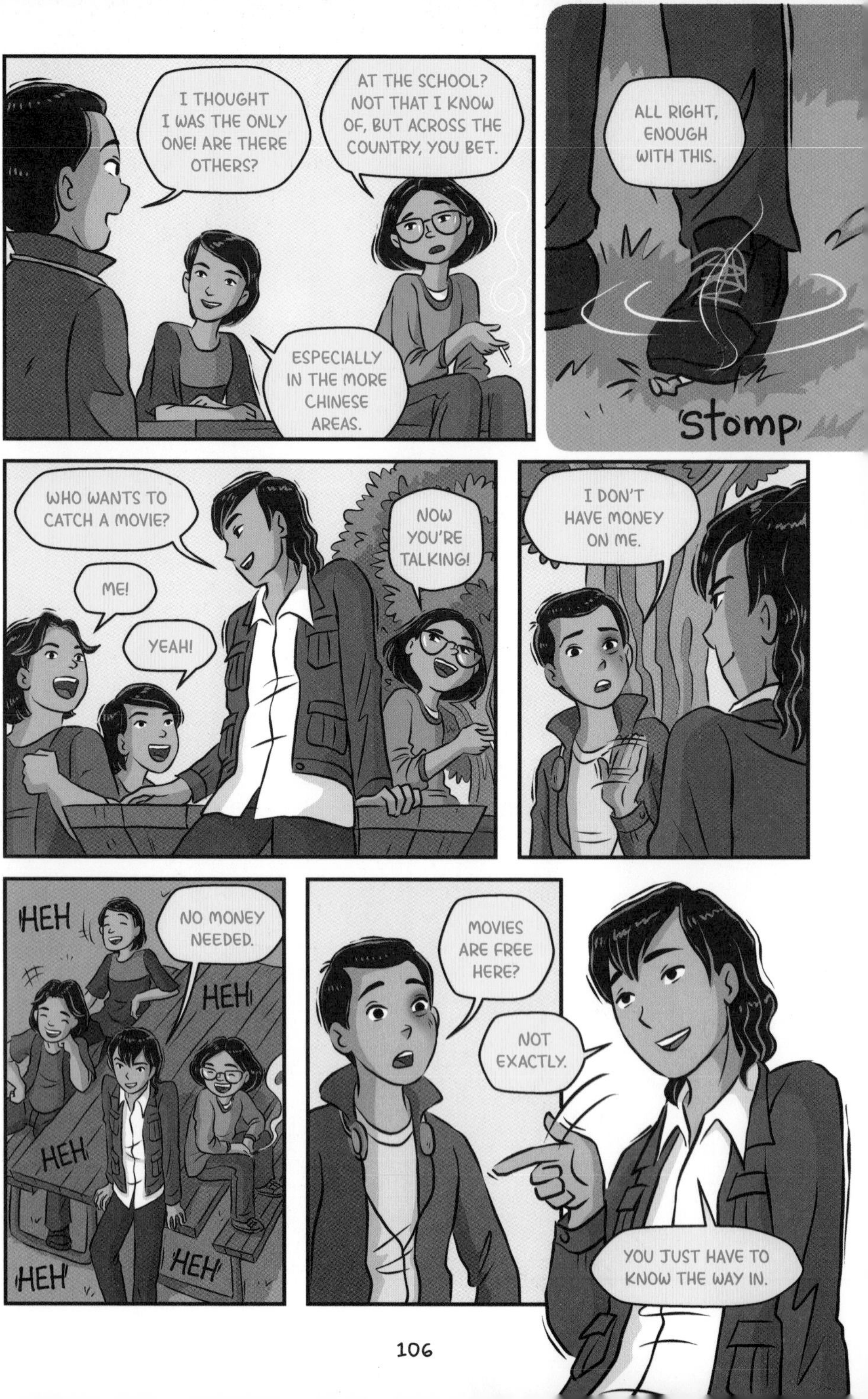

I THOUGHT I WAS THE ONLY ONE! ARE THERE OTHERS?
AT THE SCHOOL? NOT THAT I KNOW OF, BUT ACROSS THE COUNTRY, YOU BET.
ESPECIALLY IN THE MORE CHINESE AREAS.
ALL RIGHT, ENOUGH WITH THIS.
STOMP
WHO WANTS TO CATCH A MOVIE?
ME!
YEAH!
NOW YOU'RE TALKING!
I DON'T HAVE MONEY ON ME.
HEH
NO MONEY NEEDED.
HEH
HEH
HEH
HEH
MOVIES ARE FREE HERE?
NOT EXACTLY.
YOU JUST HAVE TO KNOW THE WAY IN.

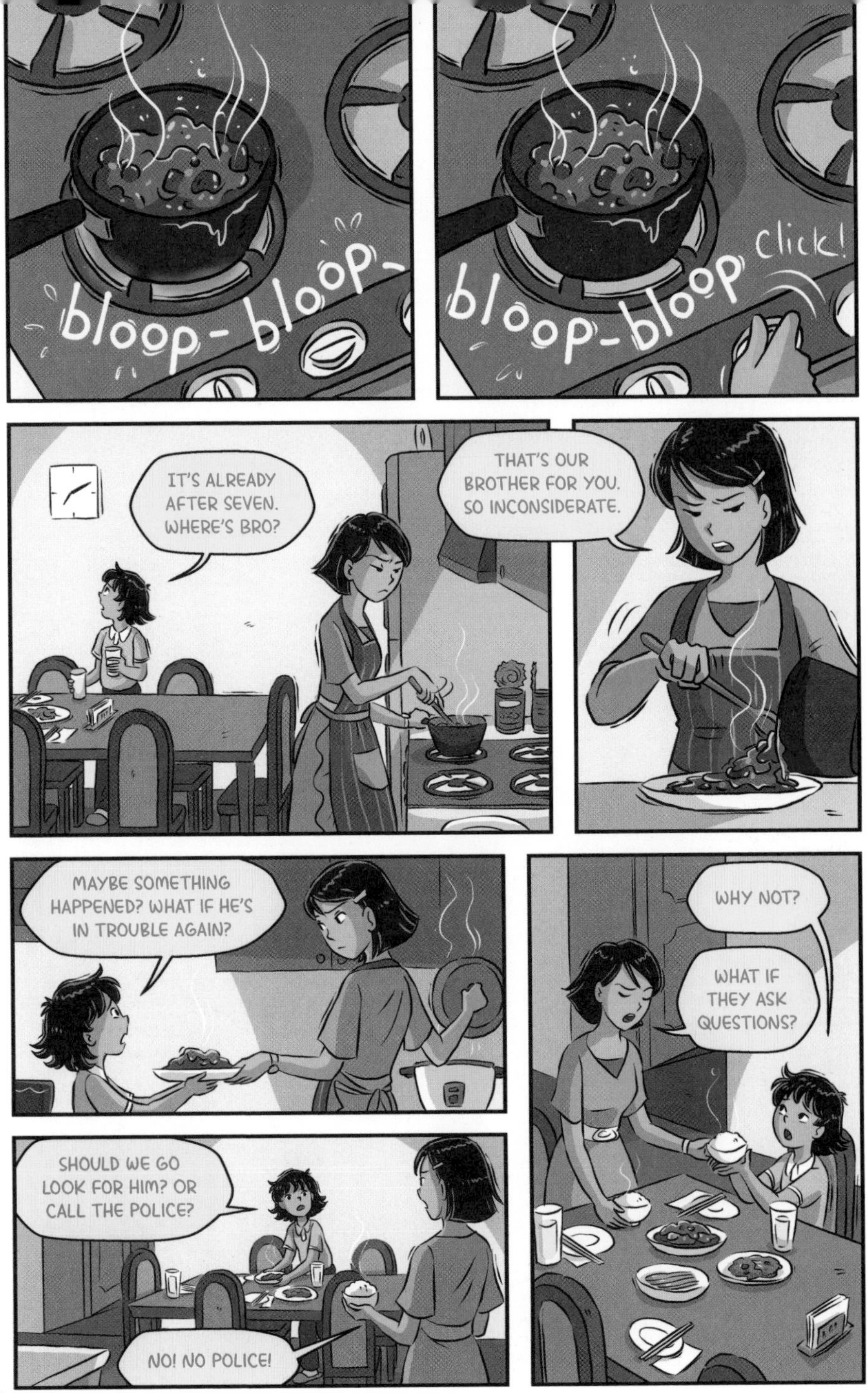
bloop-bloop-
bloop-bloop
click!
IT'S ALREADY AFTER SEVEN. WHERE'S BRO?
THAT'S OUR BROTHER FOR YOU. SO INCONSIDERATE.
MAYBE SOMETHING HAPPENED? WHAT IF HE'S IN TROUBLE AGAIN?
SHOULD WE GO LOOK FOR HIM? OR CALL THE POLICE?
NO! NO POLICE!
WHY NOT?
WHAT IF THEY ASK QUESTIONS?

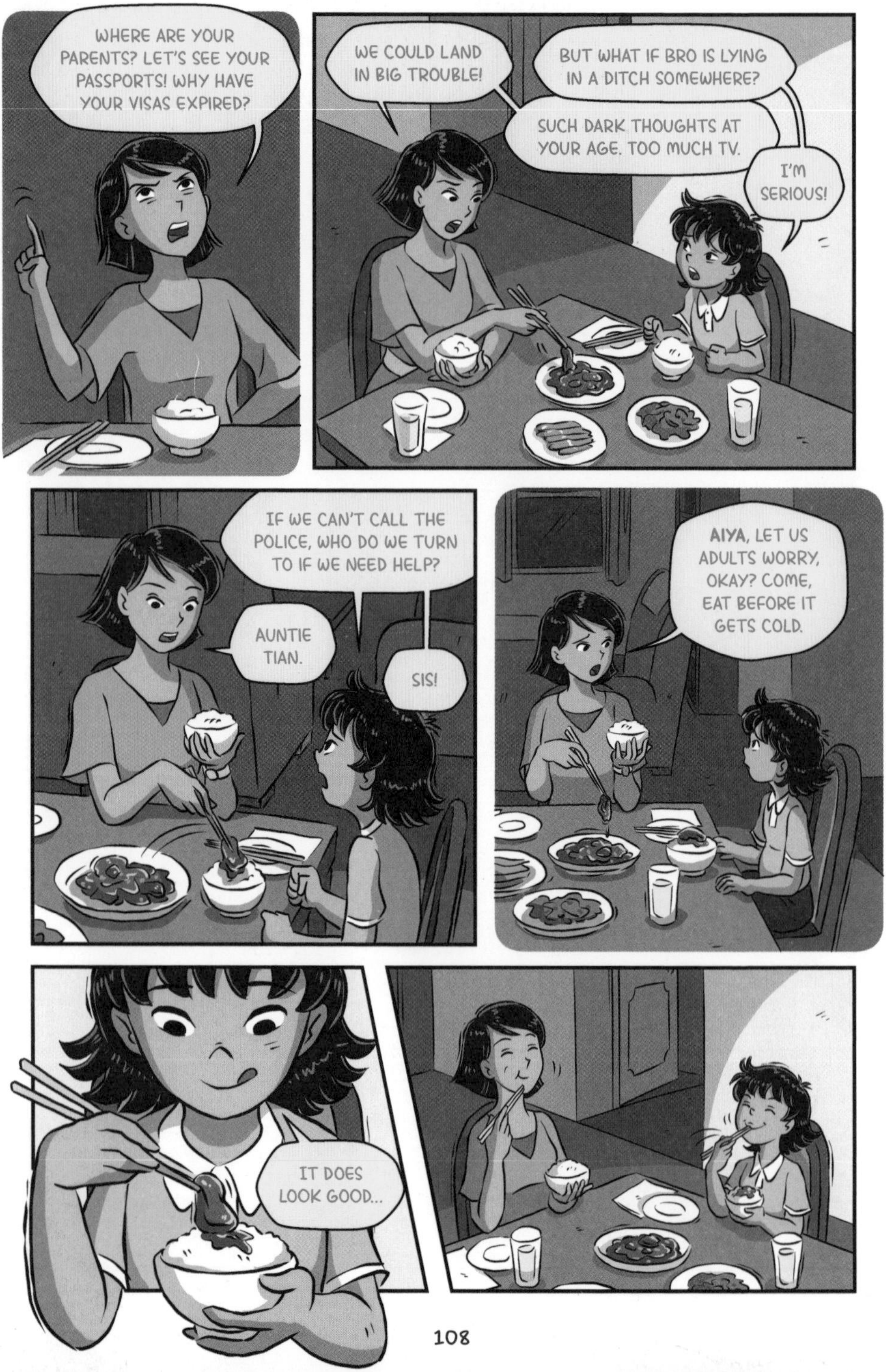
WHERE ARE YOUR PARENTS? LET'S SEE YOUR PASSPORTS! WHY HAVE YOUR VISAS EXPIRED?
WE COULD LAND IN BIG TROUBLE!
BUT WHAT IF BRO IS LYING IN A DITCH SOMEWHERE?
SUCH DARK THOUGHTS AT YOUR AGE. TOO MUCH TV.
I'M SERIOUS!
IF WE CAN'T CALL THE POLICE, WHO DO WE TURN TO IF WE NEED HELP?
AUNTIE TIAN.
SIS!
AIYA, LET US ADULTS WORRY, OKAY? COME, EAT BEFORE IT GETS COLD.
IT DOES LOOK GOOD...

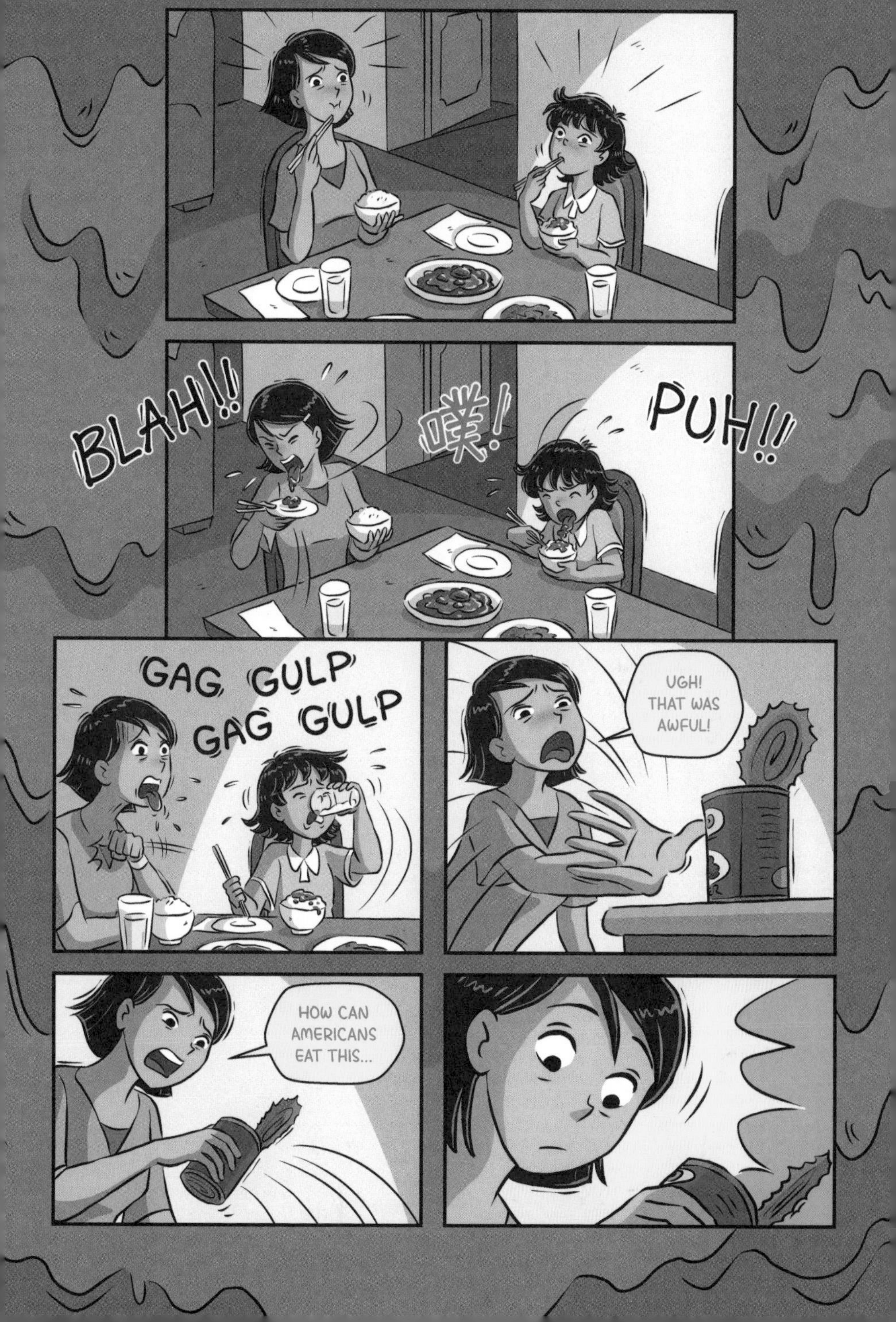
BLAH!!
噗!
PUH!!
GAG GULP
GAG GULP
UGH! THAT WAS AWFUL!
HOW CAN AMERICANS EAT THIS...

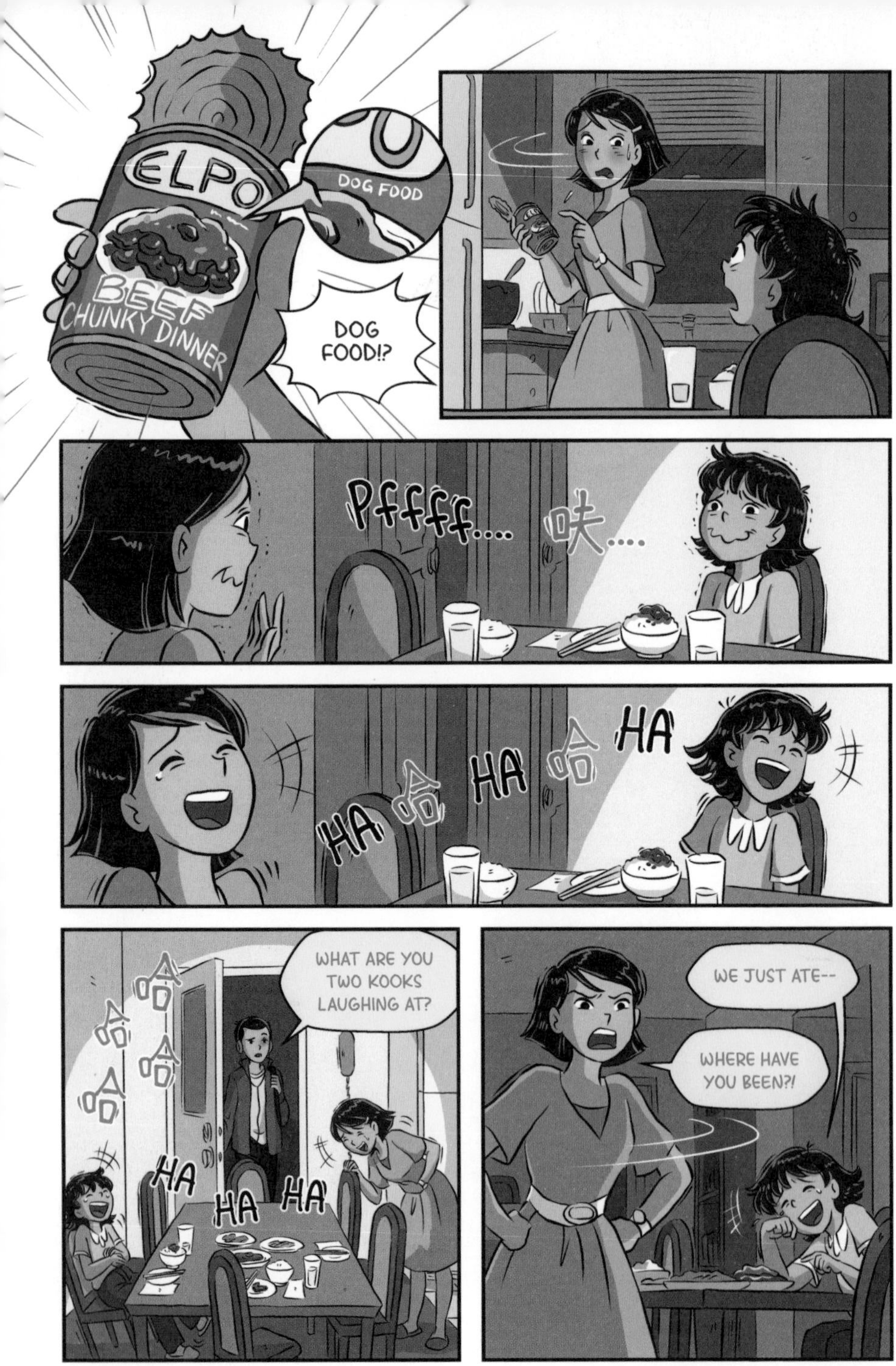
ELPO
BEEF
CHUNKY DINNER
DOG FOOD
DOG FOOD!?
Pffff....
呋....
HA
哈
HA
哈
HA
哈
哈
哈
哈
WHAT ARE YOU TWO KOOKS LAUGHING AT?
HA
HA
HA
WE JUST ATE--
WHERE HAVE YOU BEEN?!

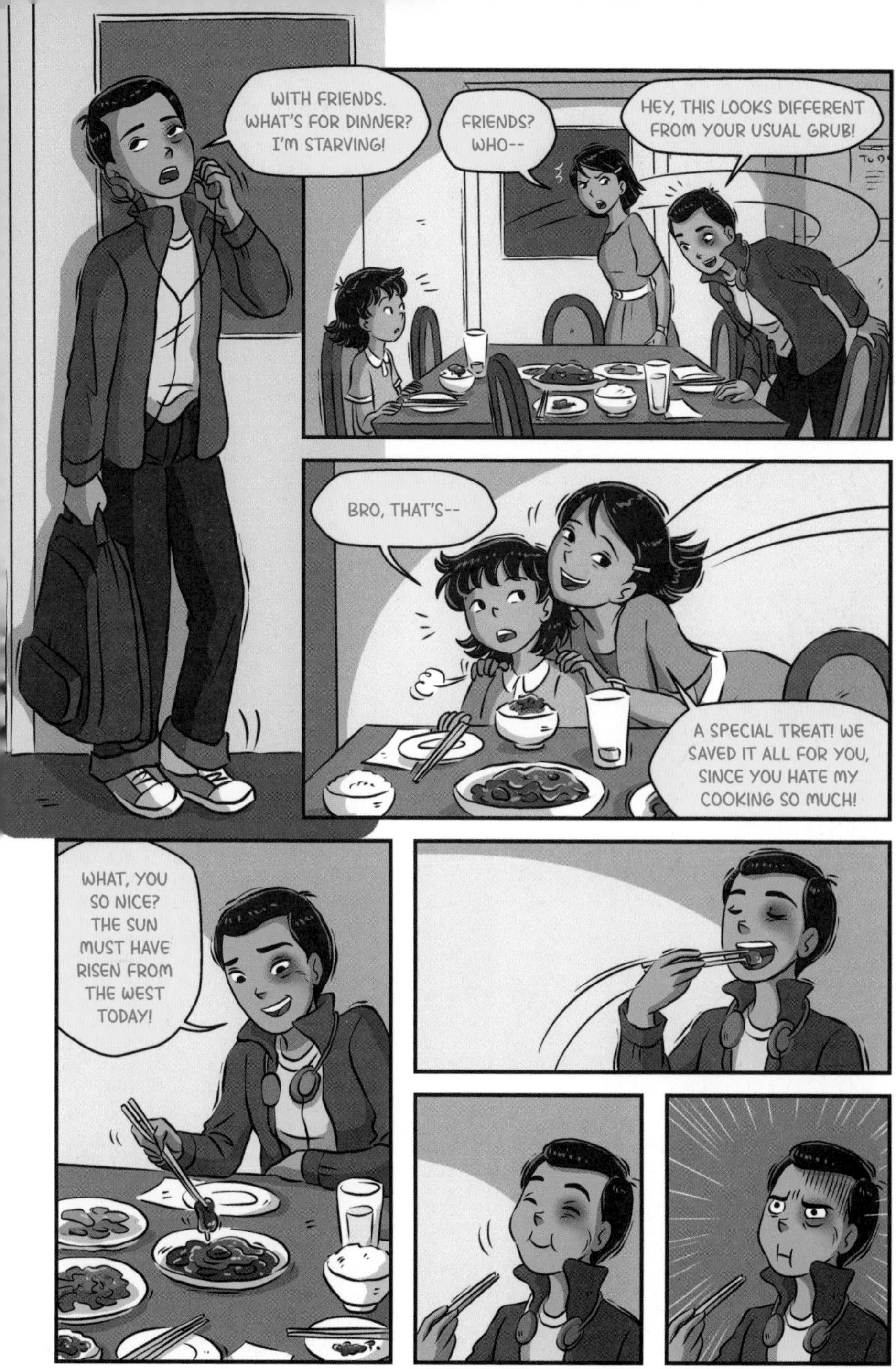
WITH FRIENDS. WHAT'S FOR DINNER? I'M STARVING!
FRIENDS? WHO--
HEY, THIS LOOKS DIFFERENT FROM YOUR USUAL GRUB!
BRO, THAT'S--
A SPECIAL TREAT! WE SAVED IT ALL FOR YOU, SINCE YOU HATE MY COOKING SO MUCH!
WHAT, YOU SO NICE? THE SUN MUST HAVE RISEN FROM THE WEST TODAY!

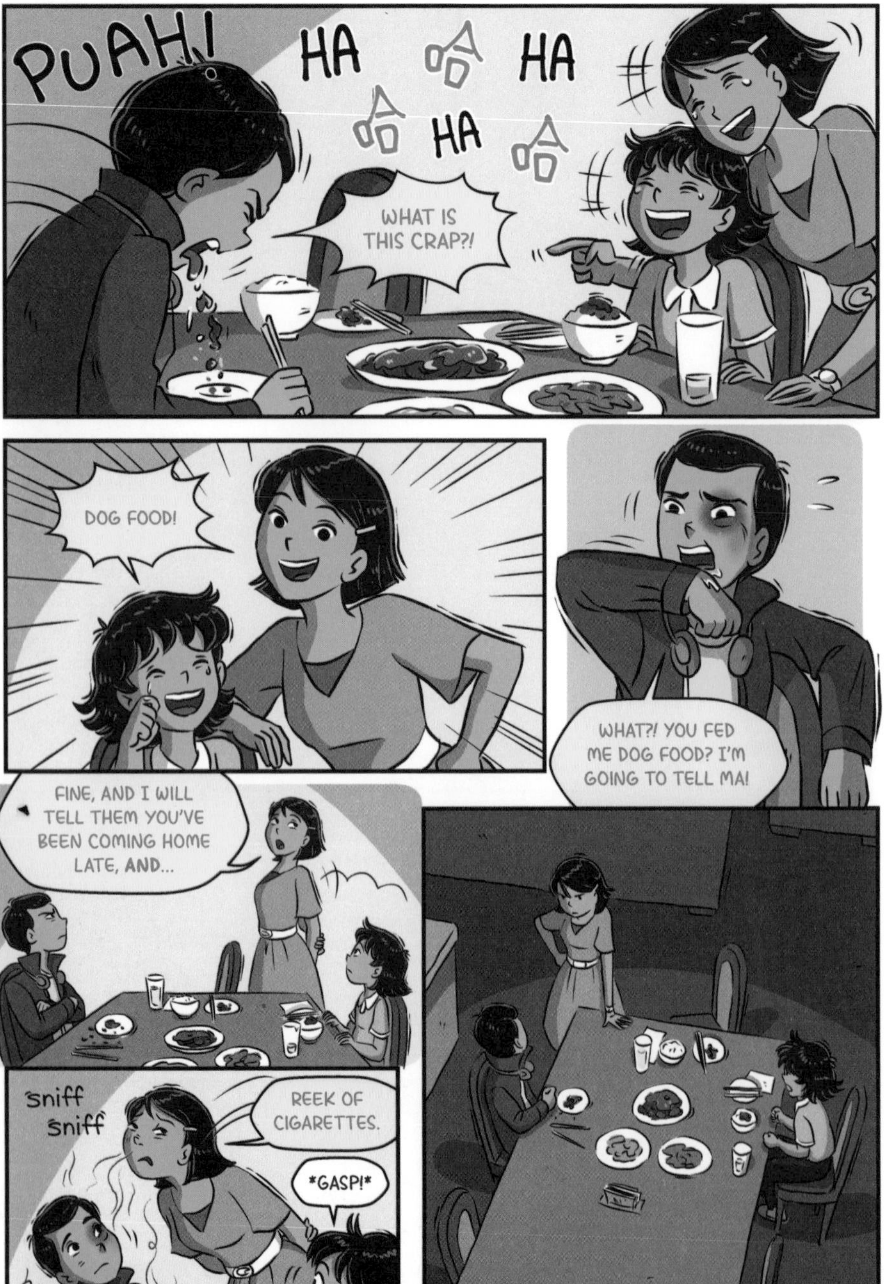
PUAH!
HA
HA
HA
WHAT IS THIS CRAP?!
DOG FOOD!
WHAT?! YOU FED ME DOG FOOD? I'M GOING TO TELL MA!
FINE, AND I WILL TELL THEM YOU'VE BEEN COMING HOME LATE, AND...
sniff sniff
REEK OF CIGARETTES.
GASP!

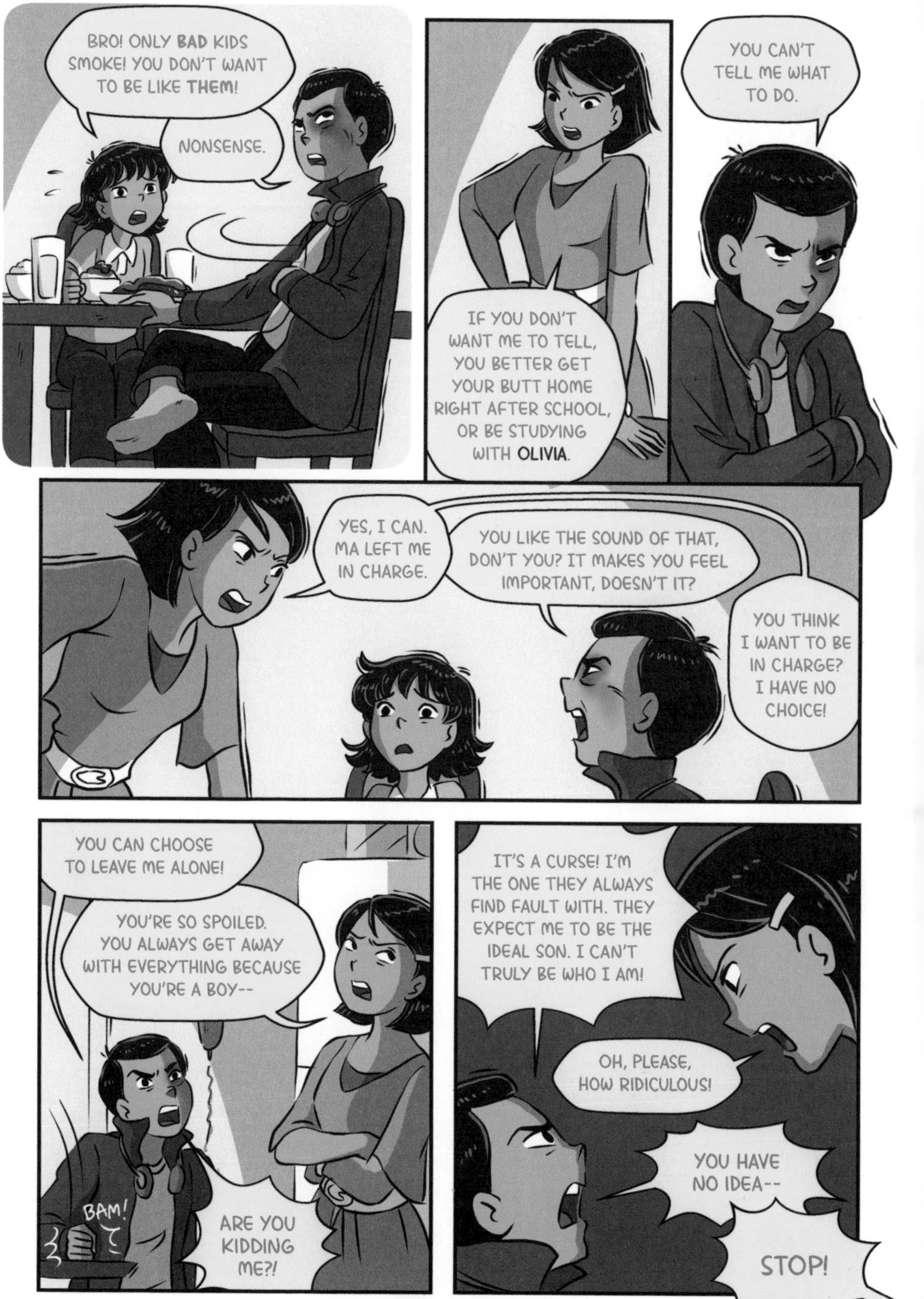
BRO! ONLY BAD KIDS SMOKE! YOU DON'T WANT TO BE LIKE THEM!
NONSENSE.
IF YOU DON'T WANT ME TO TELL, YOU BETTER GET YOUR BUTT HOME RIGHT AFTER SCHOOL, OR BE STUDYING WITH OLIVIA.
YOU CAN'T TELL ME WHAT TO DO.
YES, I CAN. MA LEFT ME IN CHARGE.
YOU LIKE THE SOUND OF THAT, DON'T YOU? IT MAKES YOU FEEL IMPORTANT, DOESN'T IT?
YOU THINK I WANT TO BE IN CHARGE? I HAVE NO CHOICE!
YOU CAN CHOOSE TO LEAVE ME ALONE!
YOU'RE SO SPOILED. YOU ALWAYS GET AWAY WITH EVERYTHING BECAUSE YOU'RE A BOY--
BAM!
ARE YOU KIDDING ME?!
IT'S A CURSE! I'M THE ONE THEY ALWAYS FIND FAULT WITH. THEY EXPECT ME TO BE THE IDEAL SON. I CAN'T TRULY BE WHO I AM!
OH, PLEASE, HOW RIDICULOUS!
YOU HAVE NO IDEA--
STOP!

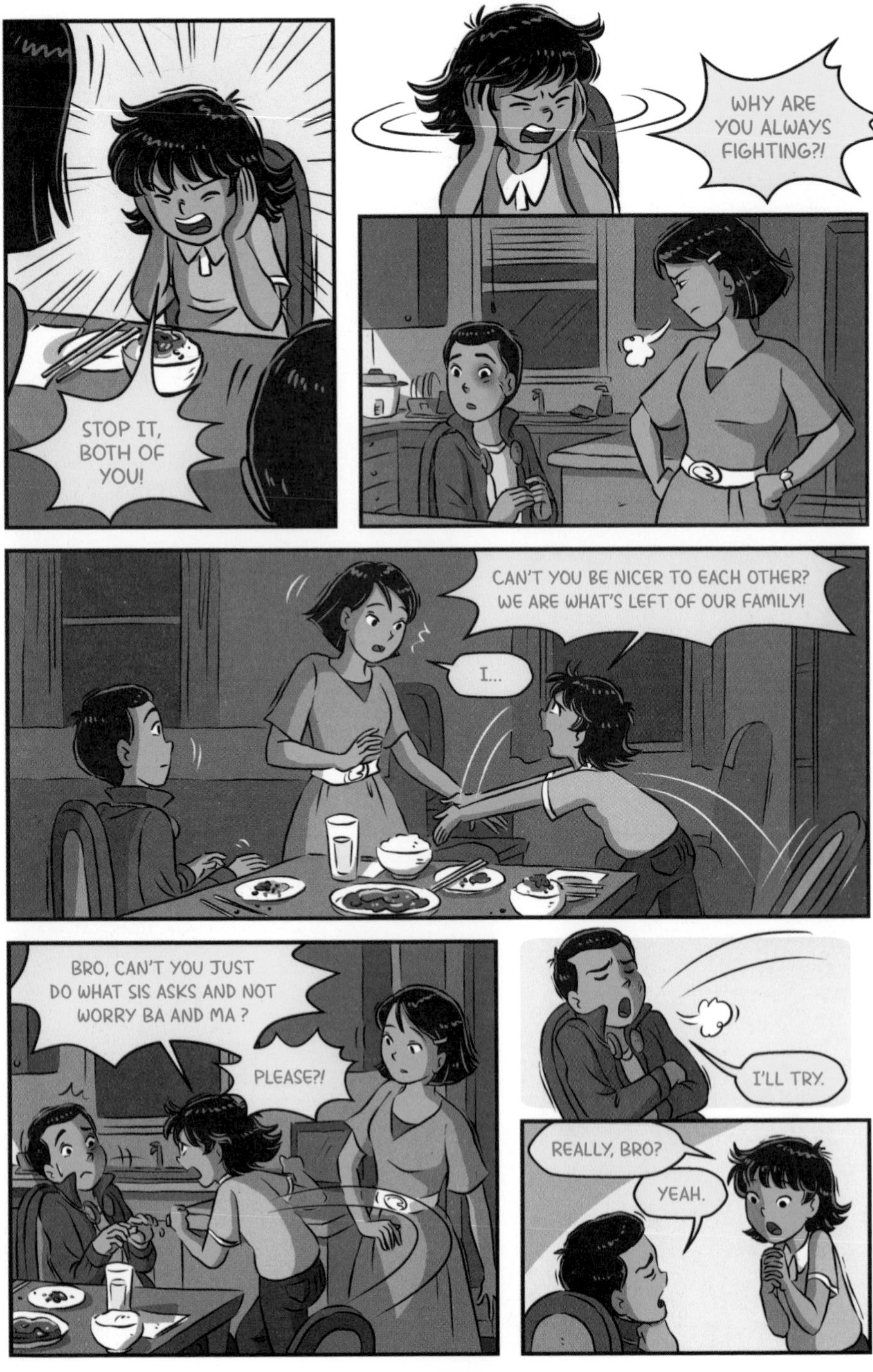
STOP IT, BOTH OF YOU!
WHY ARE YOU ALWAYS FIGHTING?!
CAN'T YOU BE NICER TO EACH OTHER? WE ARE WHAT'S LEFT OF OUR FAMILY!
I...
BRO, CAN'T YOU JUST DO WHAT SIS ASKS AND NOT WORRY BA AND MA ?
PLEASE?!
I'LL TRY.
REALLY, BRO?
YEAH.

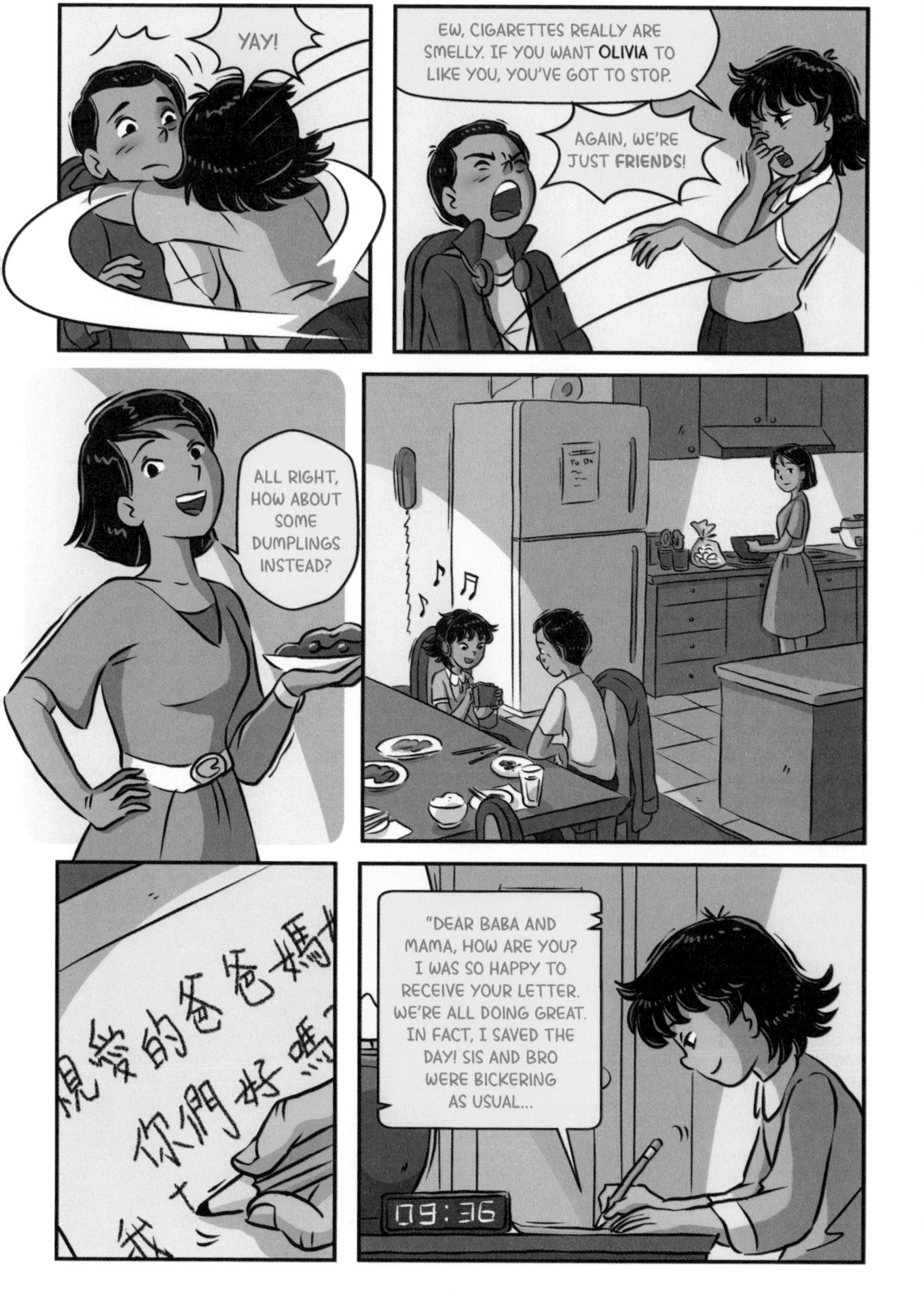
YAY!
EW, CIGARETTES REALLY ARE SMELLY. IF YOU WANT **OLIVIA** TO LIKE YOU, YOU'VE GOT TO STOP.
AGAIN, WE'RE JUST **FRIENDS**!
ALL RIGHT, HOW ABOUT SOME DUMPLINGS INSTEAD?
TO DO
愛的爸爸
你們好
"DEAR BABA AND MAMA, HOW ARE YOU? I WAS SO HAPPY TO RECEIVE YOUR LETTER. WE'RE ALL DOING GREAT. IN FACT, I SAVED THE DAY! SIS AND BRO WERE BICKERING AS USUAL...
09:36

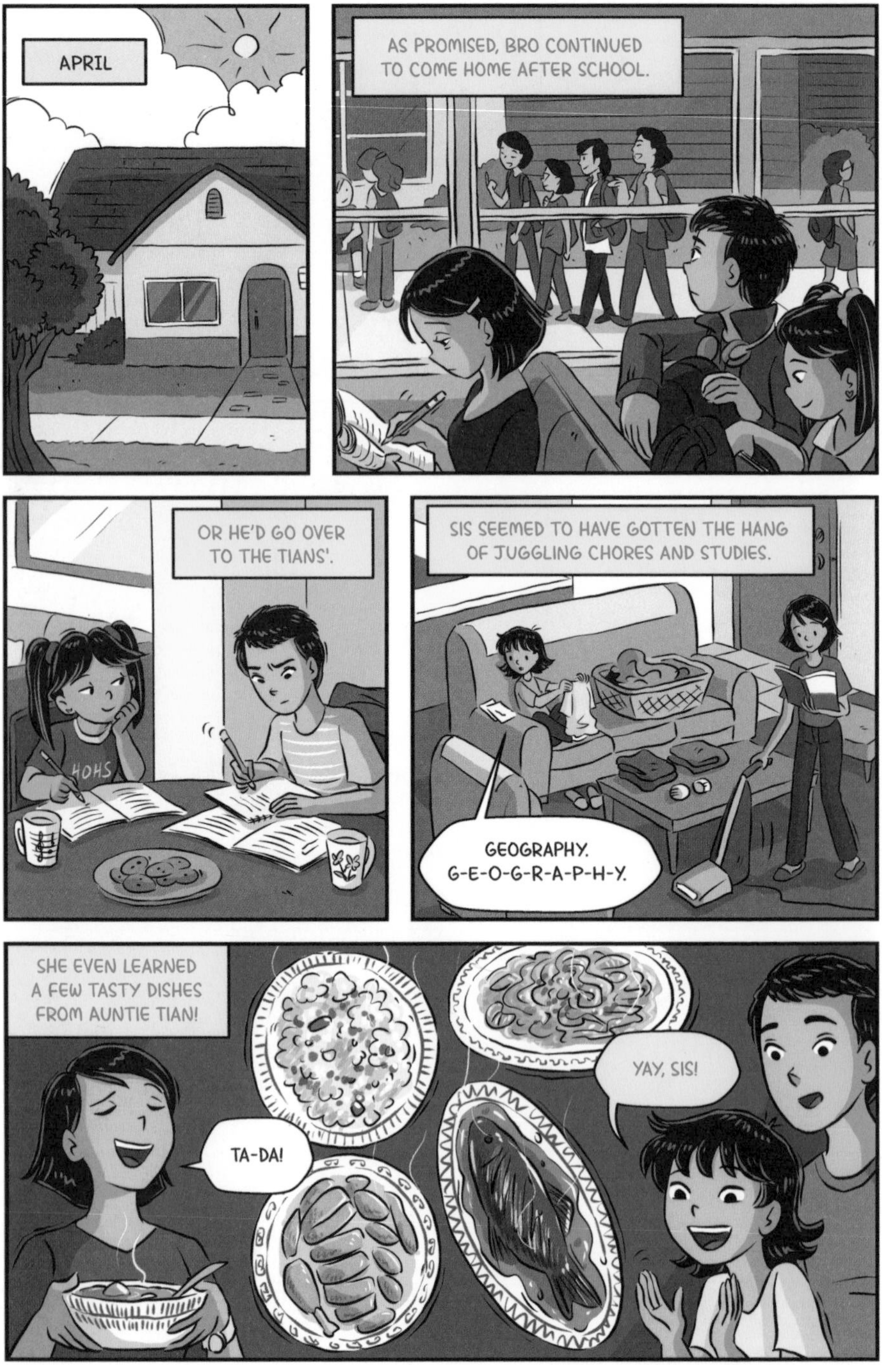
APRIL
AS PROMISED, BRO CONTINUED TO COME HOME AFTER SCHOOL.
OR HE'D GO OVER TO THE TIANS'.
HOHS
SIS SEEMED TO HAVE GOTTEN THE HANG OF JUGGLING CHORES AND STUDIES.
GEOGRAPHY. G-E-O-G-R-A-P-H-Y.
SHE EVEN LEARNED A FEW TASTY DISHES FROM AUNTIE TIAN!
TA-DA!
YAY, SIS!

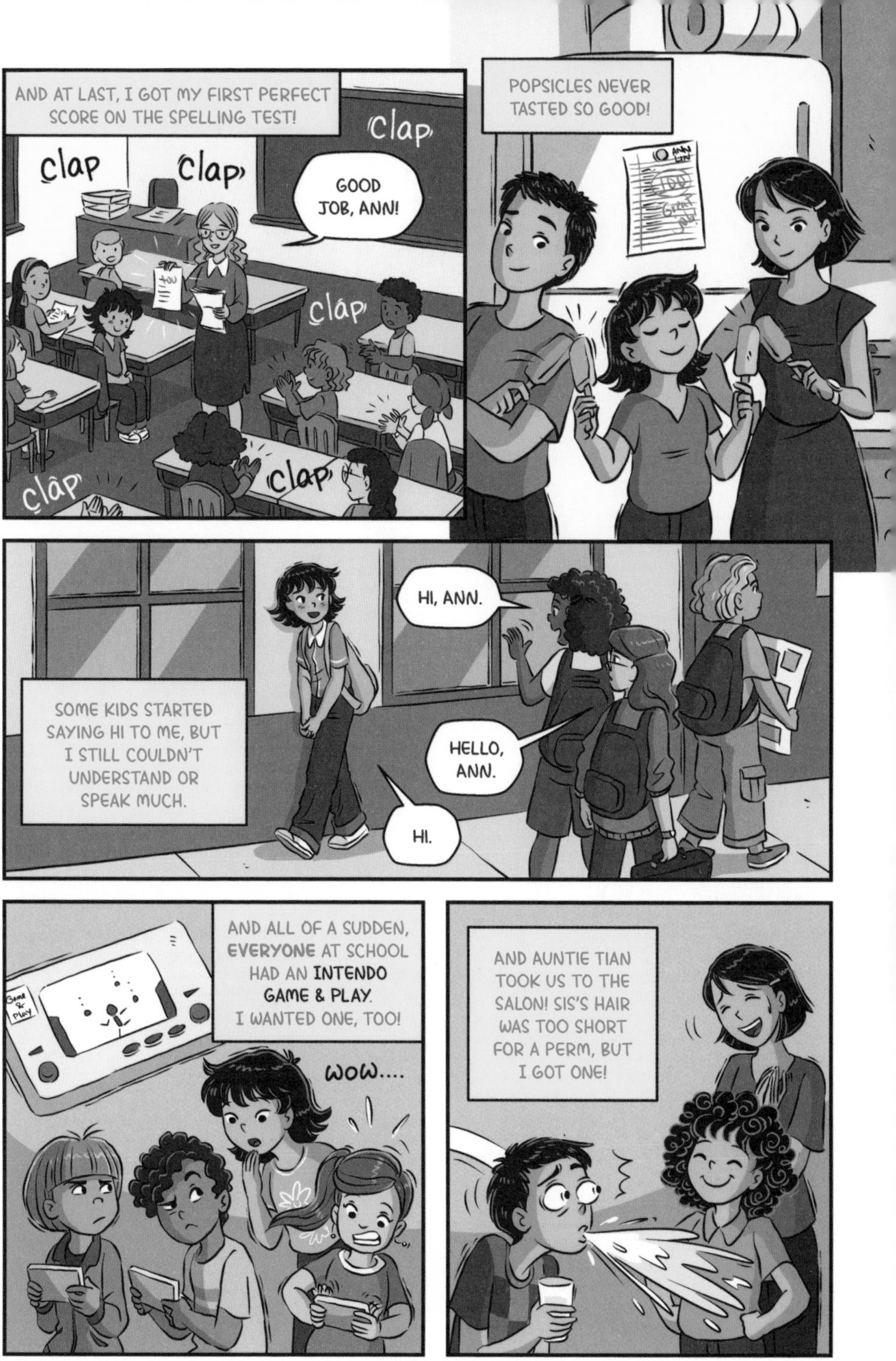
AND AT LAST, I GOT MY FIRST PERFECT SCORE ON THE SPELLING TEST!
CLAP
CLAP
CLAP
GOOD JOB, ANN!
CLAP
CLAP
CLAP
POPSICLES NEVER TASTED SO GOOD!
SOME KIDS STARTED SAYING HI TO ME, BUT I STILL COULDN'T UNDERSTAND OR SPEAK MUCH.
HI, ANN.
HELLO, ANN.
HI.
AND ALL OF A SUDDEN, EVERYONE AT SCHOOL HAD AN INTENDO GAME & PLAY. I WANTED ONE, TOO!
WOW....
AND AUNTIE TIAN TOOK US TO THE SALON! SIS'S HAIR WAS TOO SHORT FOR A PERM, BUT I GOT ONE!

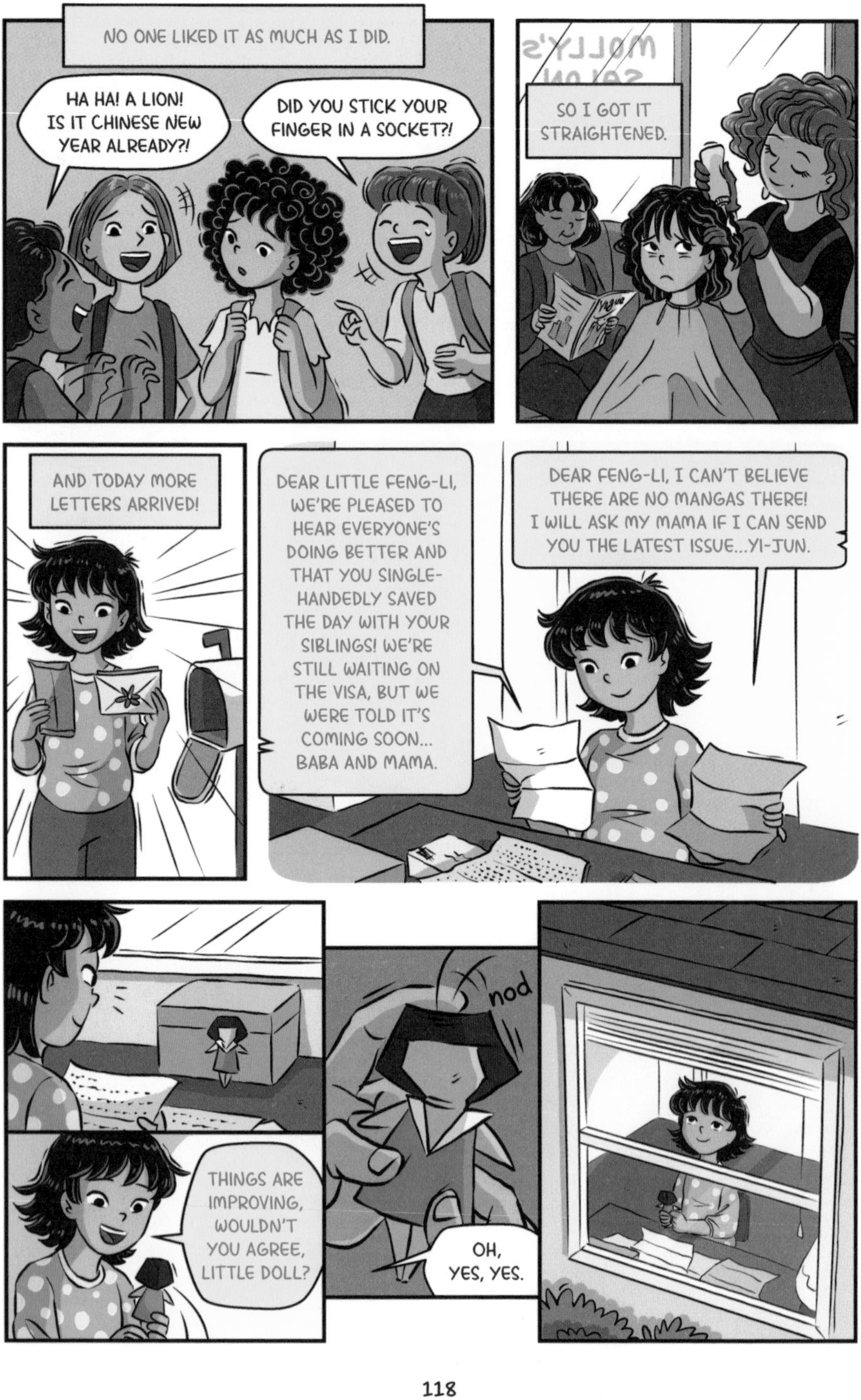

NO ONE LIKED IT AS MUCH AS I DID.
HA HA! A LION! IS IT CHINESE NEW YEAR ALREADY?!
DID YOU STICK YOUR FINGER IN A SOCKET?!
MOLLY'S SALON
SO I GOT IT STRAIGHTENED.
AND TODAY MORE LETTERS ARRIVED!
DEAR LITTLE FENG-LI, WE'RE PLEASED TO HEAR EVERYONE'S DOING BETTER AND THAT YOU SINGLE-HANDEDLY SAVED THE DAY WITH YOUR SIBLINGS! WE'RE STILL WAITING ON THE VISA, BUT WE WERE TOLD IT'S COMING SOON... BABA AND MAMA.
DEAR FENG-LI, I CAN'T BELIEVE THERE ARE NO MANGAS THERE! I WILL ASK MY MAMA IF I CAN SEND YOU THE LATEST ISSUE...YI-JUN.
THINGS ARE IMPROVING, WOULDN'T YOU AGREE, LITTLE DOLL?
nod
OH, YES, YES.

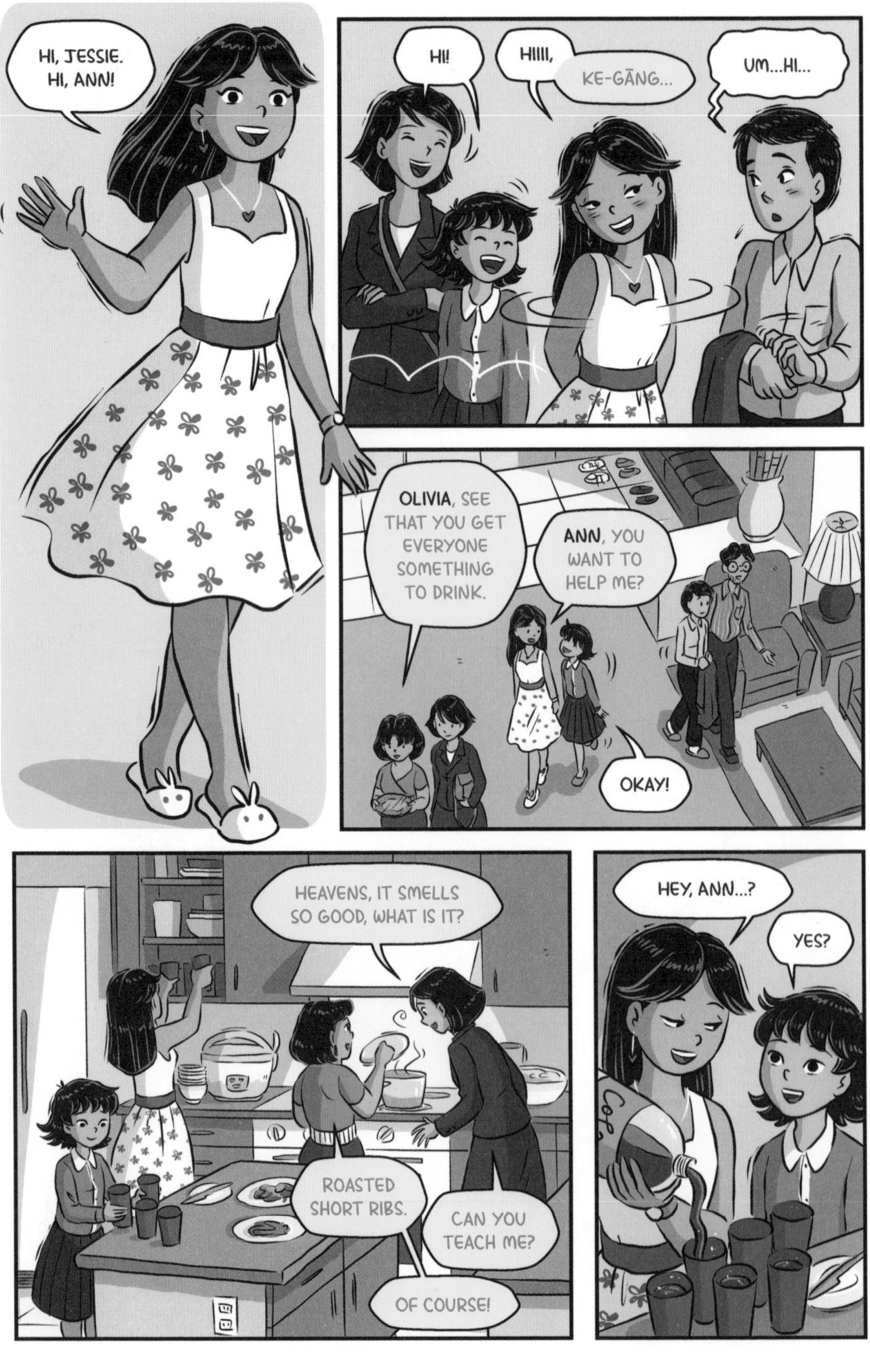
HI, JESSIE.
HI, ANN!
HI!
HIIII,
KE-GĀNG...
UM...HI...
OLIVIA, SEE THAT YOU GET EVERYONE SOMETHING TO DRINK.
ANN, YOU WANT TO HELP ME?
OKAY!
HEAVENS, IT SMELLS SO GOOD, WHAT IS IT?
ROASTED SHORT RIBS.
CAN YOU TEACH ME?
OF COURSE!
HEY, ANN...?
YES?

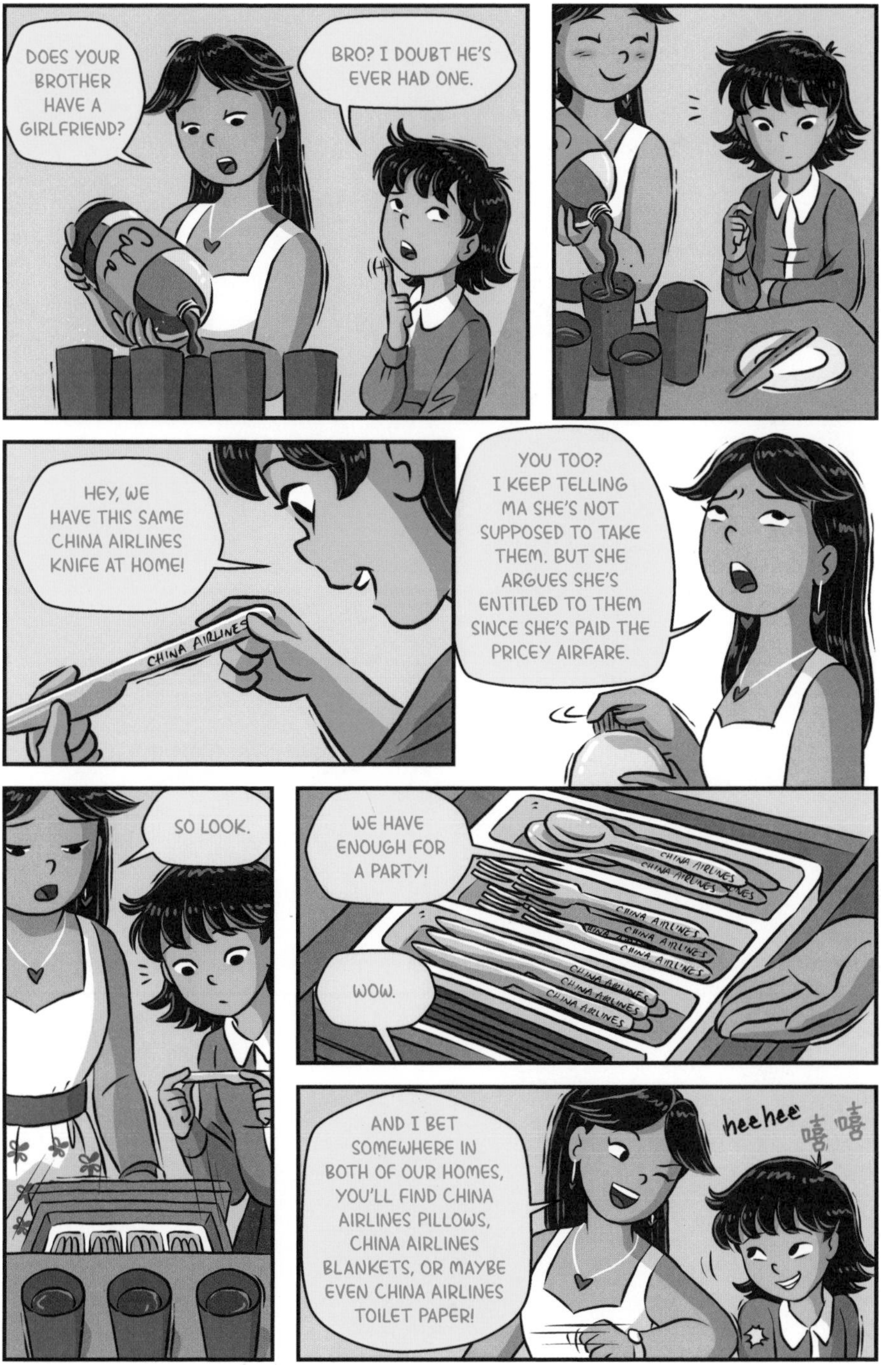
DOES YOUR BROTHER HAVE A GIRLFRIEND?
BRO? I DOUBT HE'S EVER HAD ONE.
HEY, WE HAVE THIS SAME CHINA AIRLINES KNIFE AT HOME!
CHINA AIRLINES
YOU TOO? I KEEP TELLING MA SHE'S NOT SUPPOSED TO TAKE THEM. BUT SHE ARGUES SHE'S ENTITLED TO THEM SINCE SHE'S PAID THE PRICEY AIRFARE.
SO LOOK.
WE HAVE ENOUGH FOR A PARTY!
WOW.
AND I BET SOMEWHERE IN BOTH OF OUR HOMES, YOU'LL FIND CHINA AIRLINES PILLOWS, CHINA AIRLINES BLANKETS, OR MAYBE EVEN CHINA AIRLINES TOILET PAPER!
heehee 嘻嘻

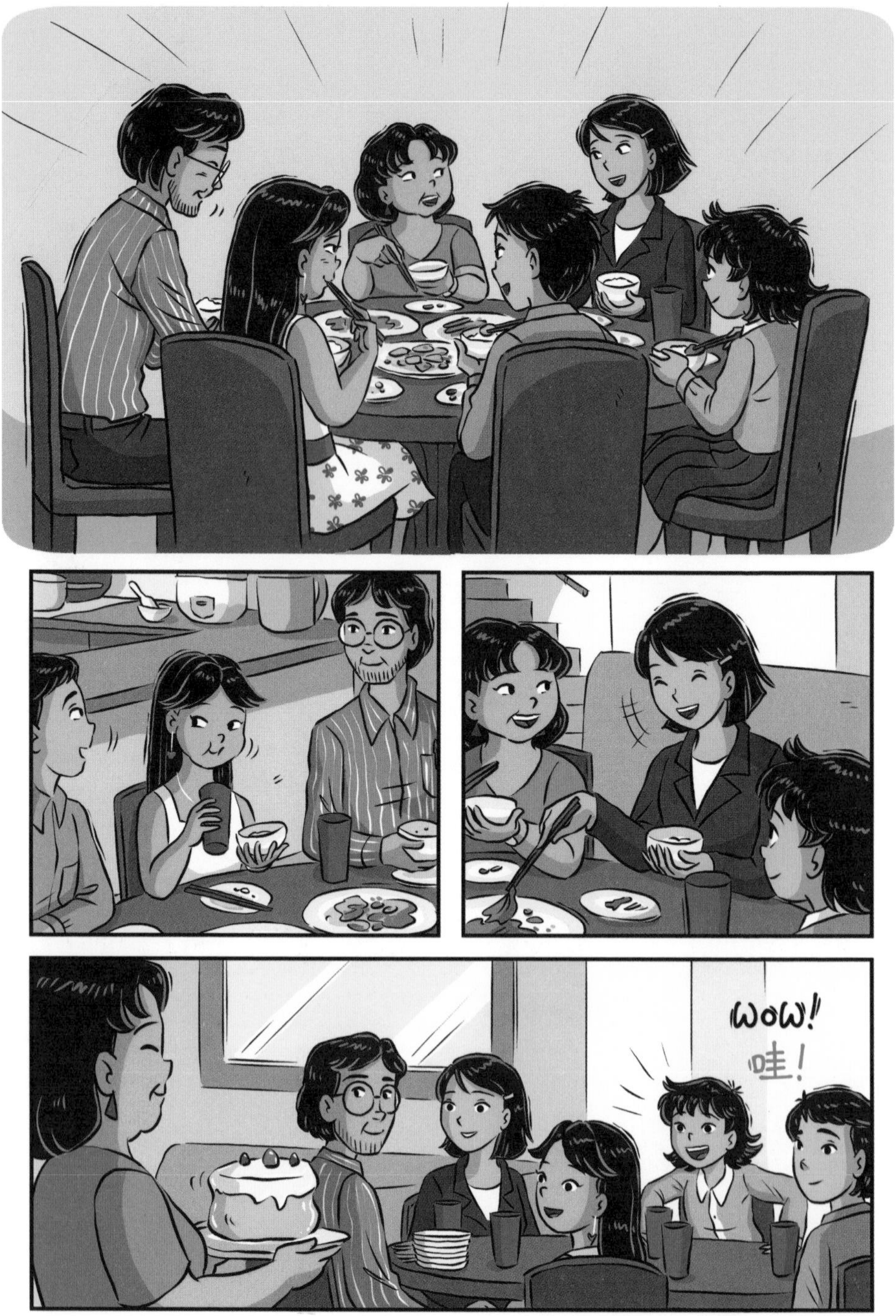
WOW!
哇!

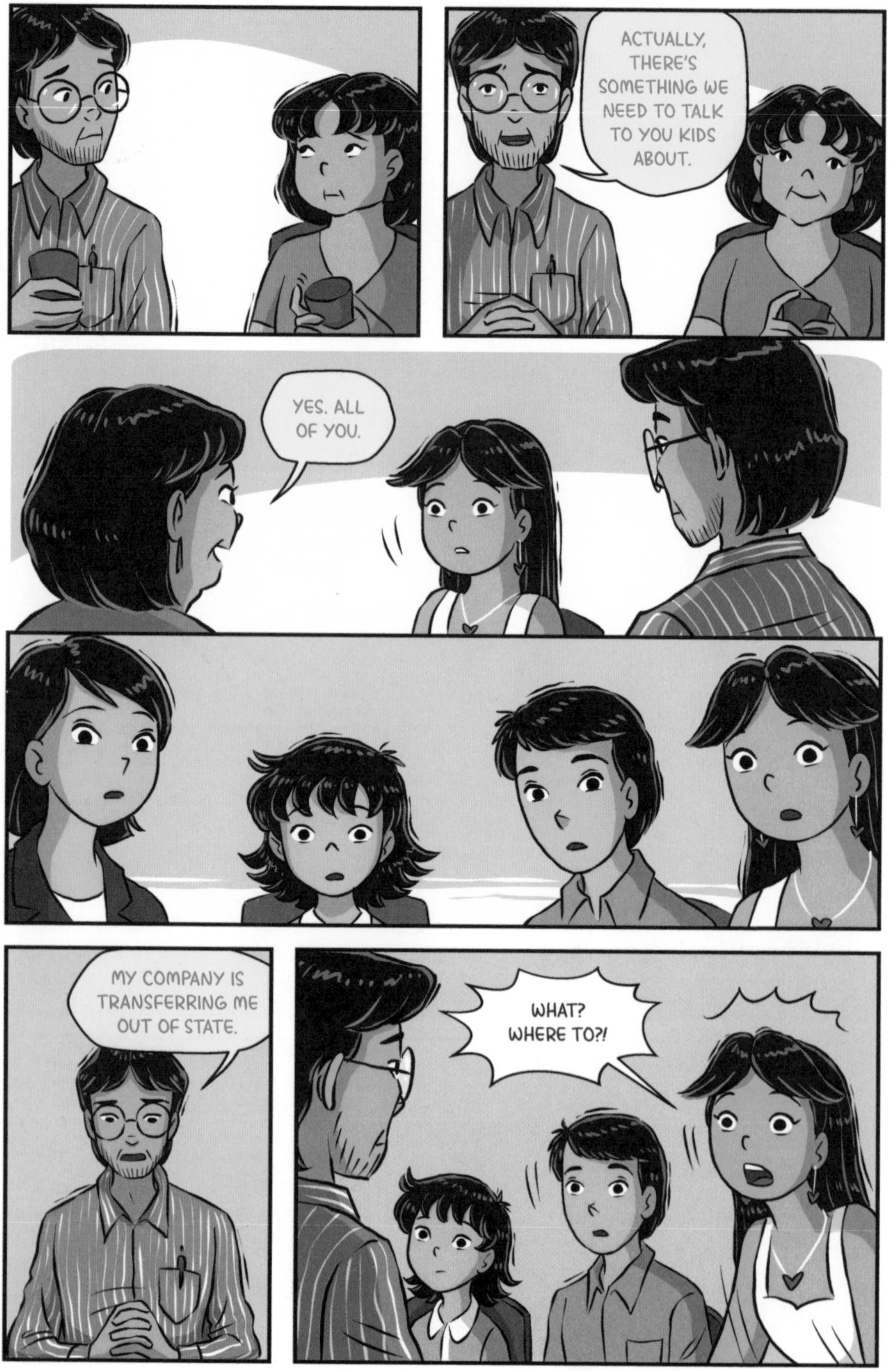
ACTUALLY, THERE'S SOMETHING WE NEED TO TALK TO YOU KIDS ABOUT.
YES. ALL OF YOU.
MY COMPANY IS TRANSFERRING ME OUT OF STATE.
WHAT? WHERE TO?!

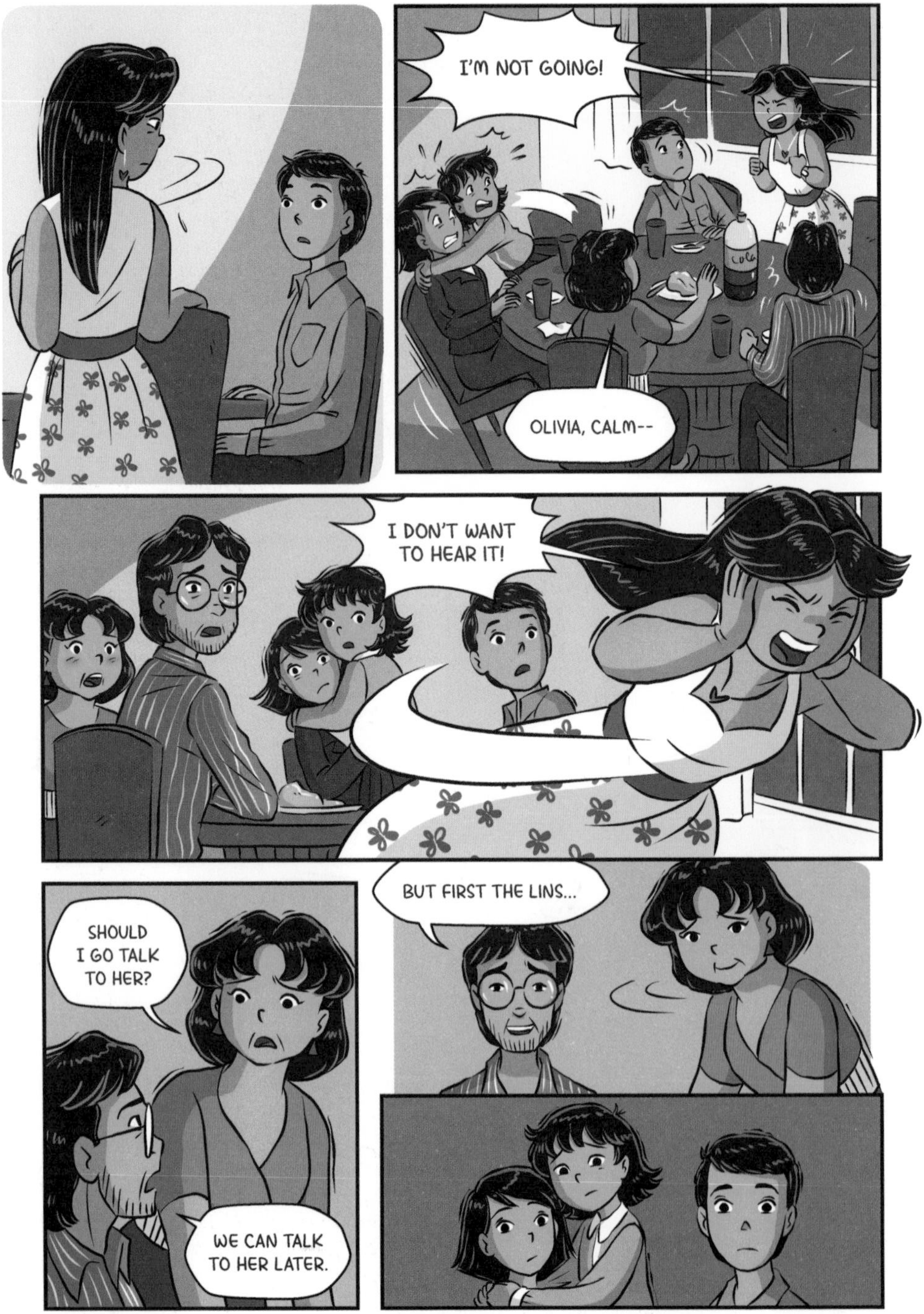
I'M NOT GOING!
OLIVIA, CALM--
I DON'T WANT TO HEAR IT!
SHOULD I GO TALK TO HER?
WE CAN TALK TO HER LATER.
BUT FIRST THE LINS...

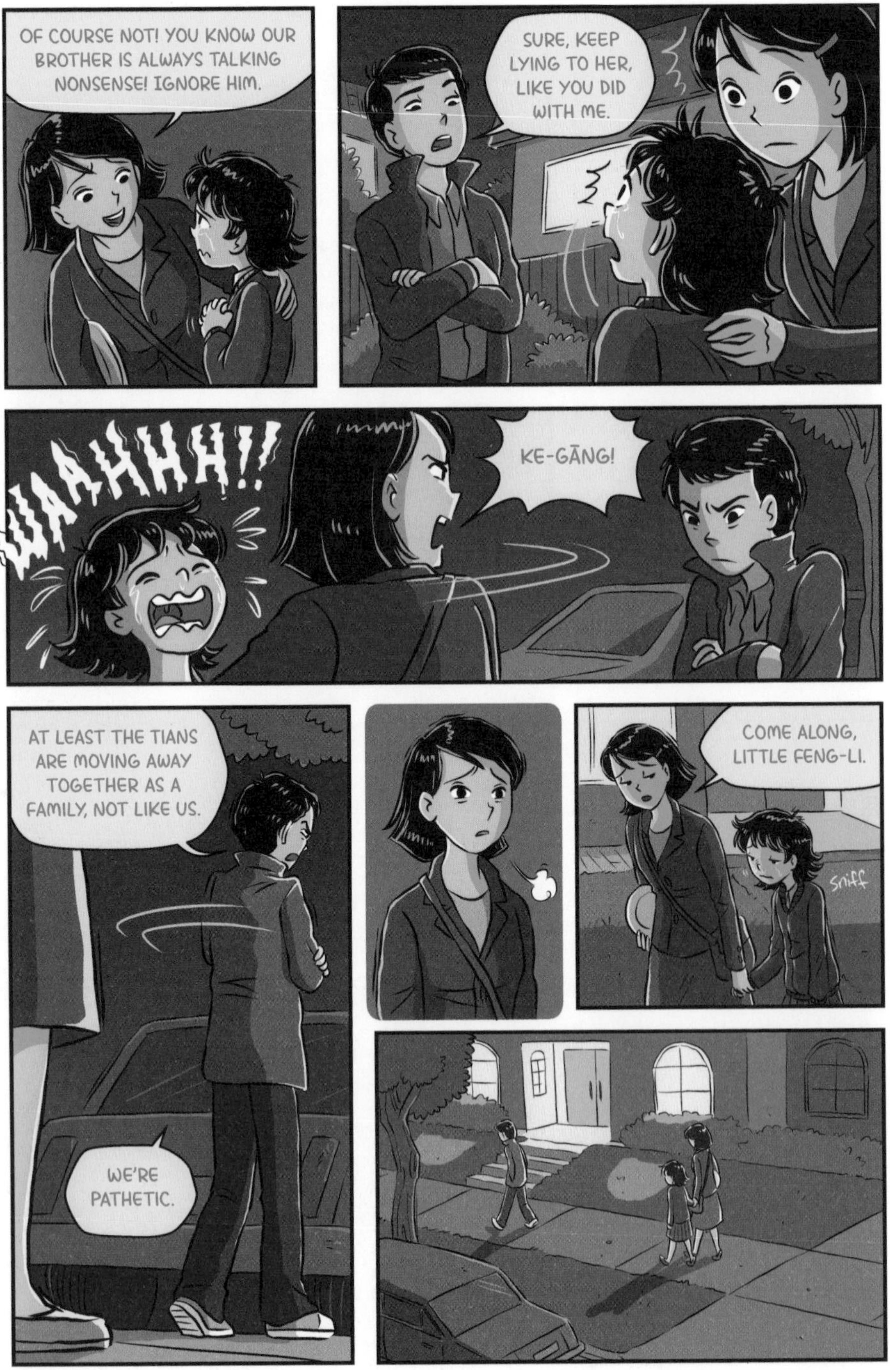
OF COURSE NOT! YOU KNOW OUR BROTHER IS ALWAYS TALKING NONSENSE! IGNORE HIM.
SURE, KEEP LYING TO HER, LIKE YOU DID WITH ME.
WAHHH!!
KE-GĀNG!
AT LEAST THE TIANS ARE MOVING AWAY TOGETHER AS A FAMILY, NOT LIKE US.
WE'RE PATHETIC.
COME ALONG, LITTLE FENG-LI.
Sniff

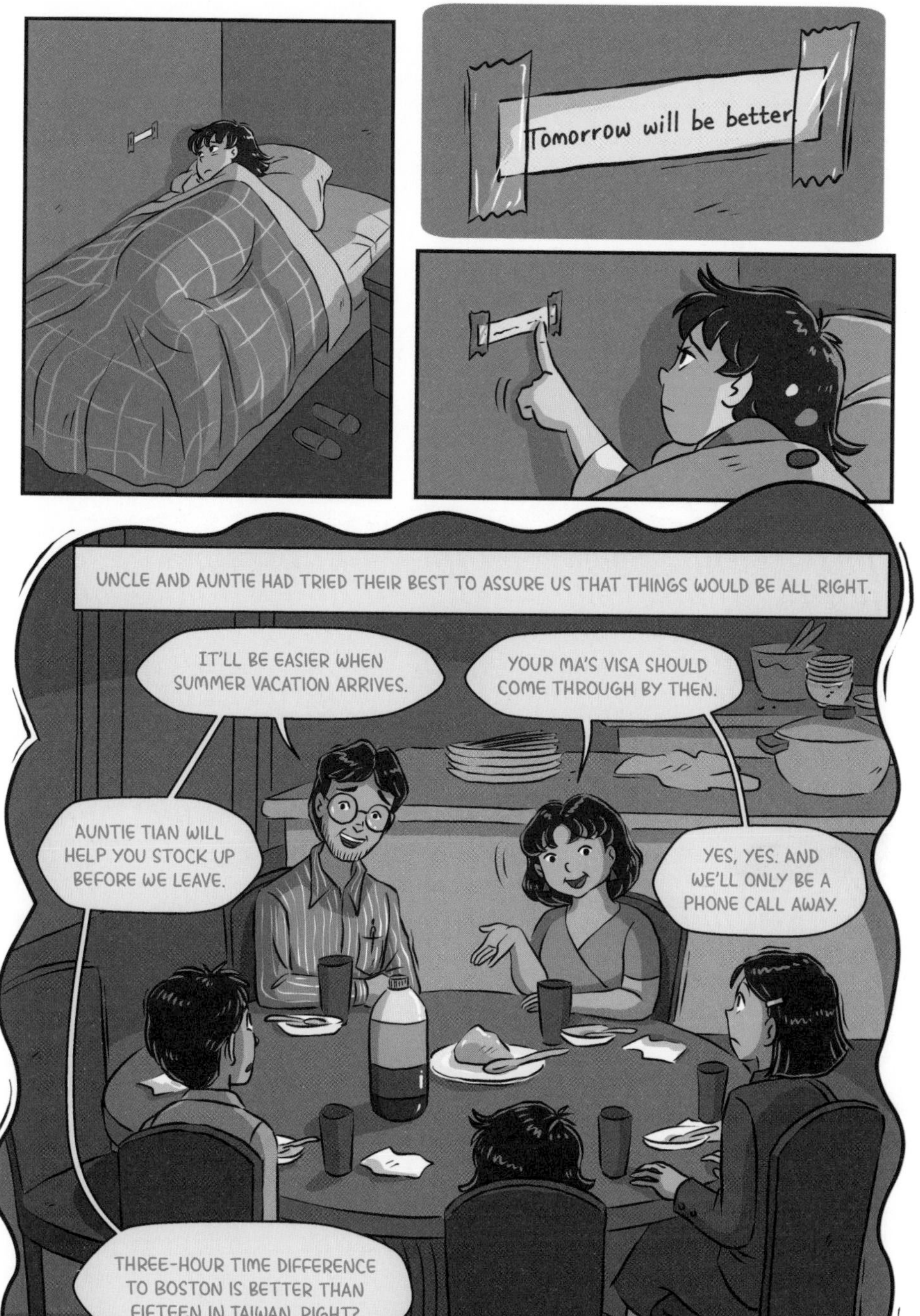
Tomorrow will be better.
UNCLE AND AUNTIE HAD TRIED THEIR BEST TO ASSURE US THAT THINGS WOULD BE ALL RIGHT.
IT'LL BE EASIER WHEN SUMMER VACATION ARRIVES.
YOUR MA'S VISA SHOULD COME THROUGH BY THEN.
AUNTIE TIAN WILL HELP YOU STOCK UP BEFORE WE LEAVE.
YES, YES. AND WE'LL ONLY BE A PHONE CALL AWAY.
THREE-HOUR TIME DIFFERENCE TO BOSTON IS BETTER THAN FIFTEEN IN TAIWAN, RIGHT?

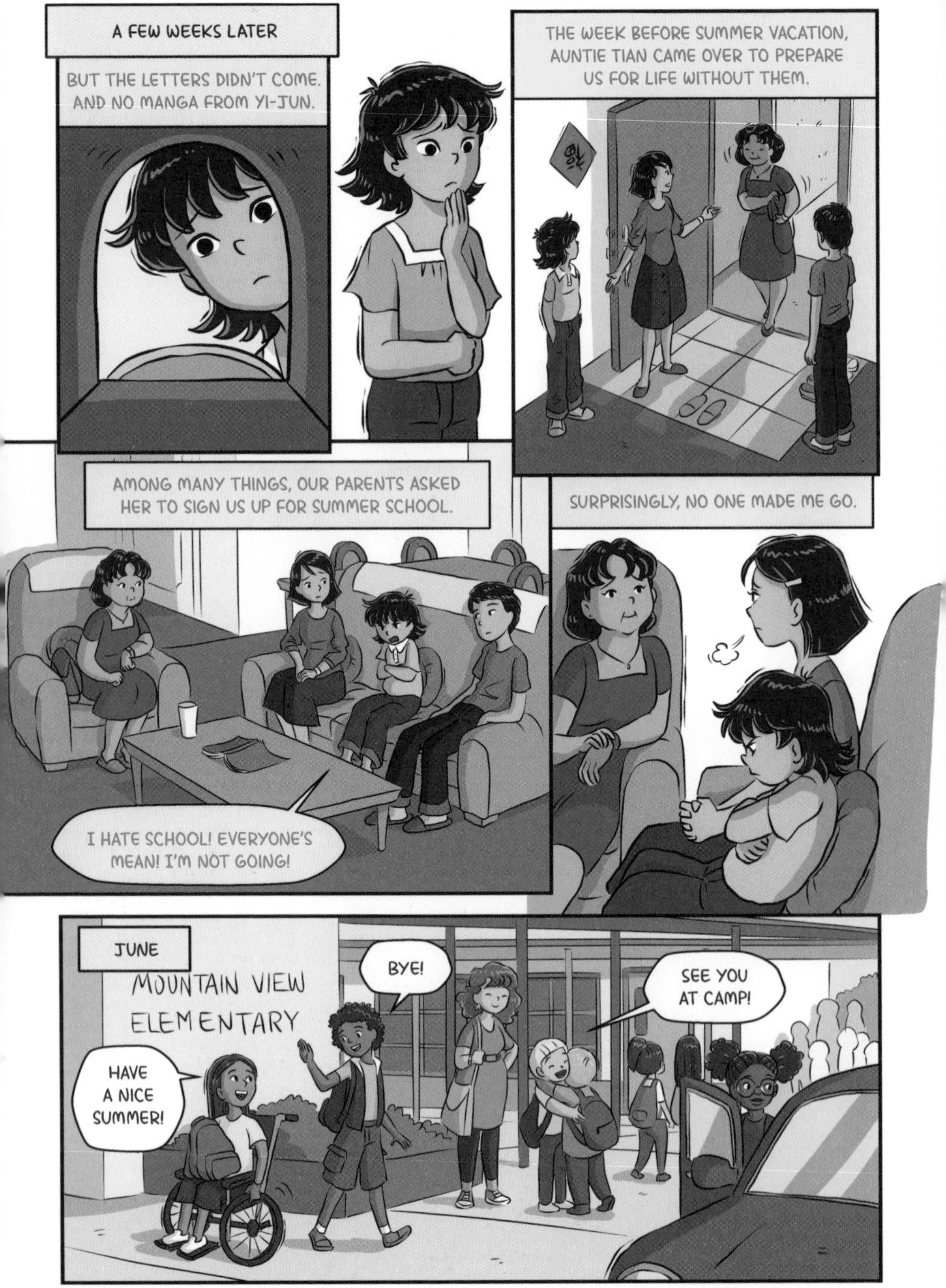
A FEW WEEKS LATER
BUT THE LETTERS DIDN'T COME. AND NO MANGA FROM YI-JUN.
THE WEEK BEFORE SUMMER VACATION, AUNTIE TIAN CAME OVER TO PREPARE US FOR LIFE WITHOUT THEM.
AMONG MANY THINGS, OUR PARENTS ASKED HER TO SIGN US UP FOR SUMMER SCHOOL.
I HATE SCHOOL! EVERYONE'S MEAN! I'M NOT GOING!
SURPRISINGLY, NO ONE MADE ME GO.
JUNE
MOUNTAIN VIEW ELEMENTARY
HAVE A NICE SUMMER!
BYE!
SEE YOU AT CAMP!

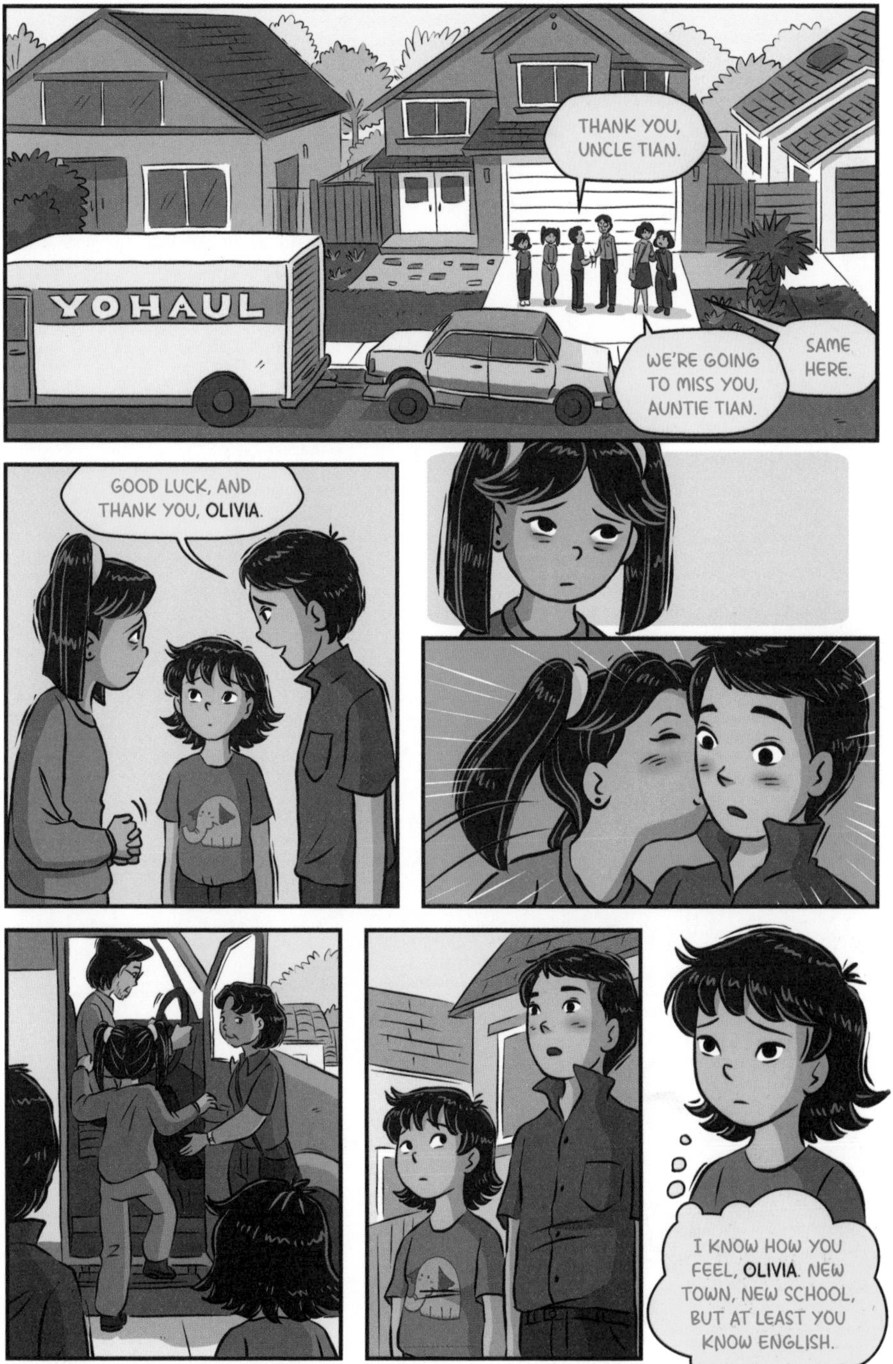
YOHAUL
THANK YOU, UNCLE TIAN.
WE'RE GOING TO MISS YOU, AUNTIE TIAN.
SAME HERE.
GOOD LUCK, AND THANK YOU, OLIVIA.
I KNOW HOW YOU FEEL, OLIVIA. NEW TOWN, NEW SCHOOL, BUT AT LEAST YOU KNOW ENGLISH.

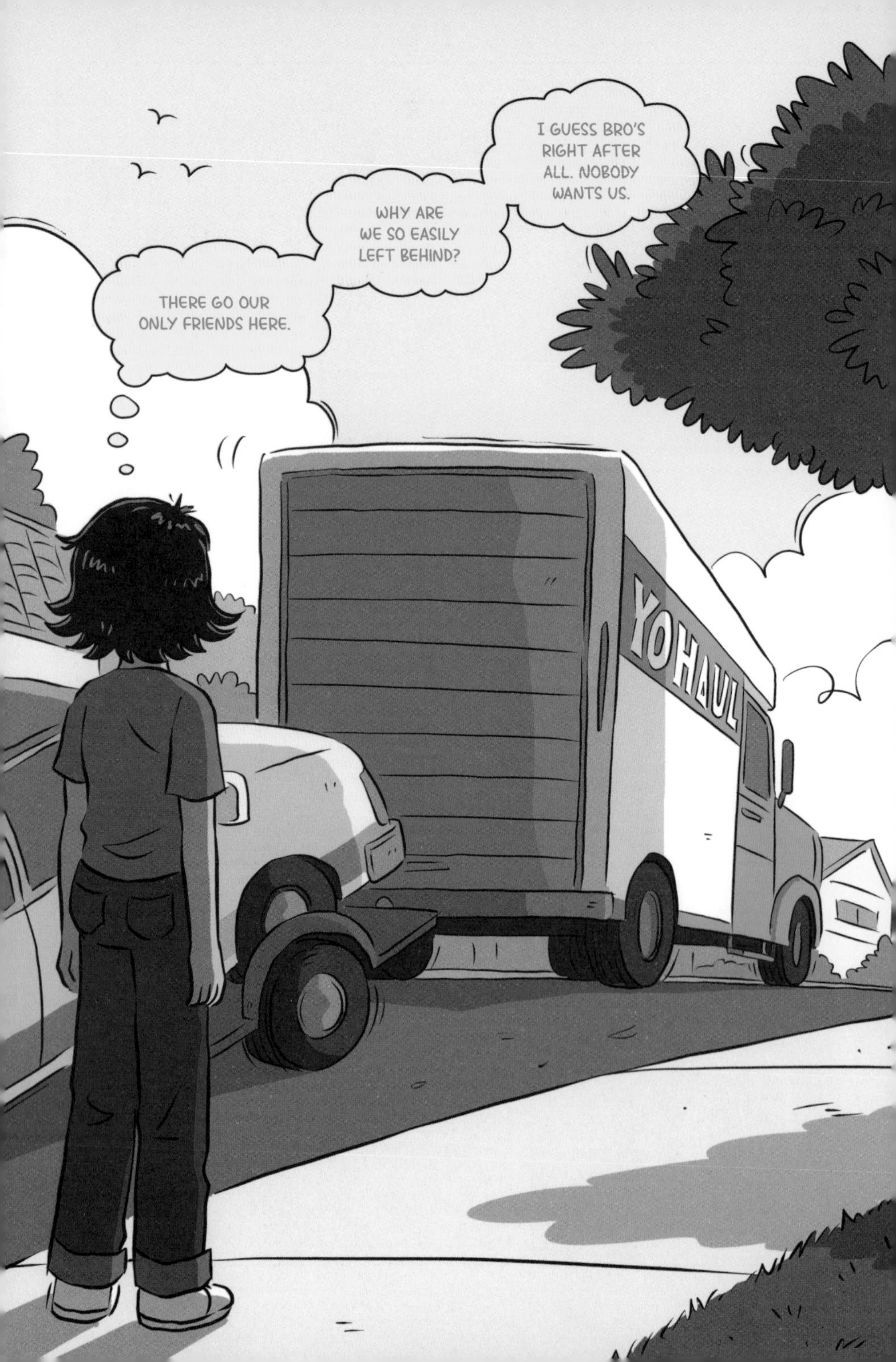
THERE GO OUR ONLY FRIENDS HERE.
WHY ARE WE SO EASILY LEFT BEHIND?
I GUESS BRO'S RIGHT AFTER ALL. NOBODY WANTS US.
YOHAUL

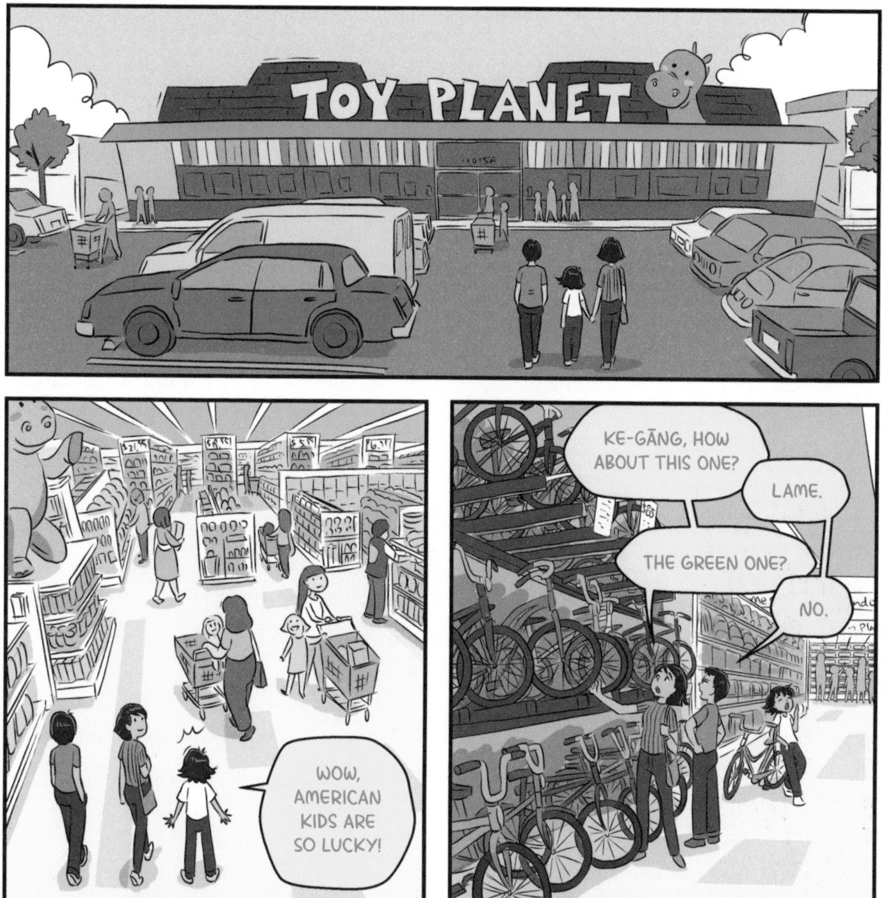
TOY PLANET
WOW, AMERICAN KIDS ARE SO LUCKY!
KE-GĀNG, HOW ABOUT THIS ONE?
LAME.
THE GREEN ONE?
NO.
I LIKE THIS BLUE ONE.
BUT THE GREEN ONE IS ON SALE.
Intendo
Game & Play

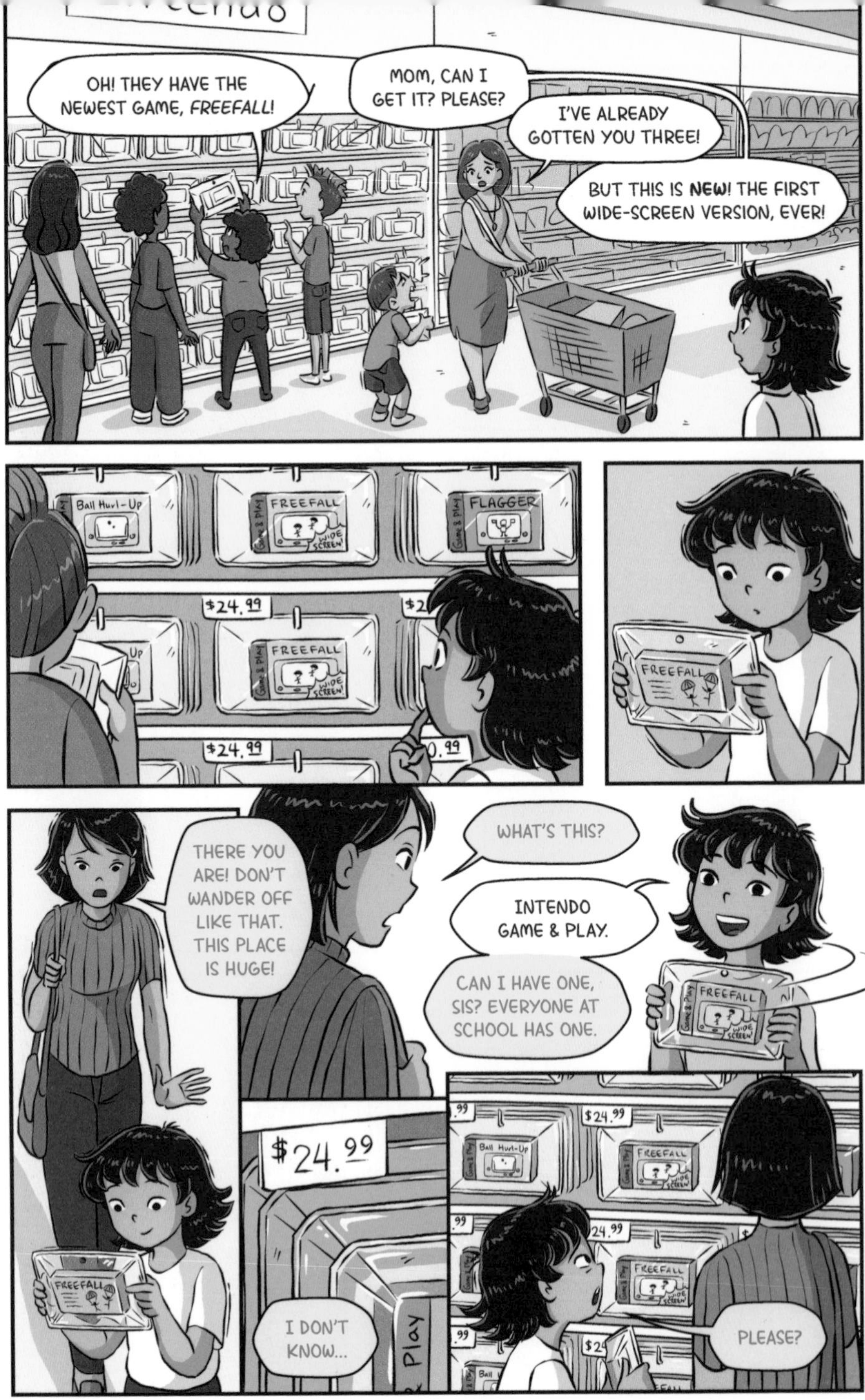
OH! THEY HAVE THE NEWEST GAME, FREEFALL!
MOM, CAN I GET IT? PLEASE?
I'VE ALREADY GOTTEN YOU THREE!
BUT THIS IS NEW! THE FIRST WIDE-SCREEN VERSION, EVER!
Ball Hurl-Up
FREEFALL
WIDE SCREEN!
FLAGGER
$24.99
$24.99
FREEFALL
THERE YOU ARE! DON'T WANDER OFF LIKE THAT. THIS PLACE IS HUGE!
WHAT'S THIS?
INTENDO GAME & PLAY.
CAN I HAVE ONE, SIS? EVERYONE AT SCHOOL HAS ONE.
FREEFALL
$24.99
I DON'T KNOW...
PLEASE?

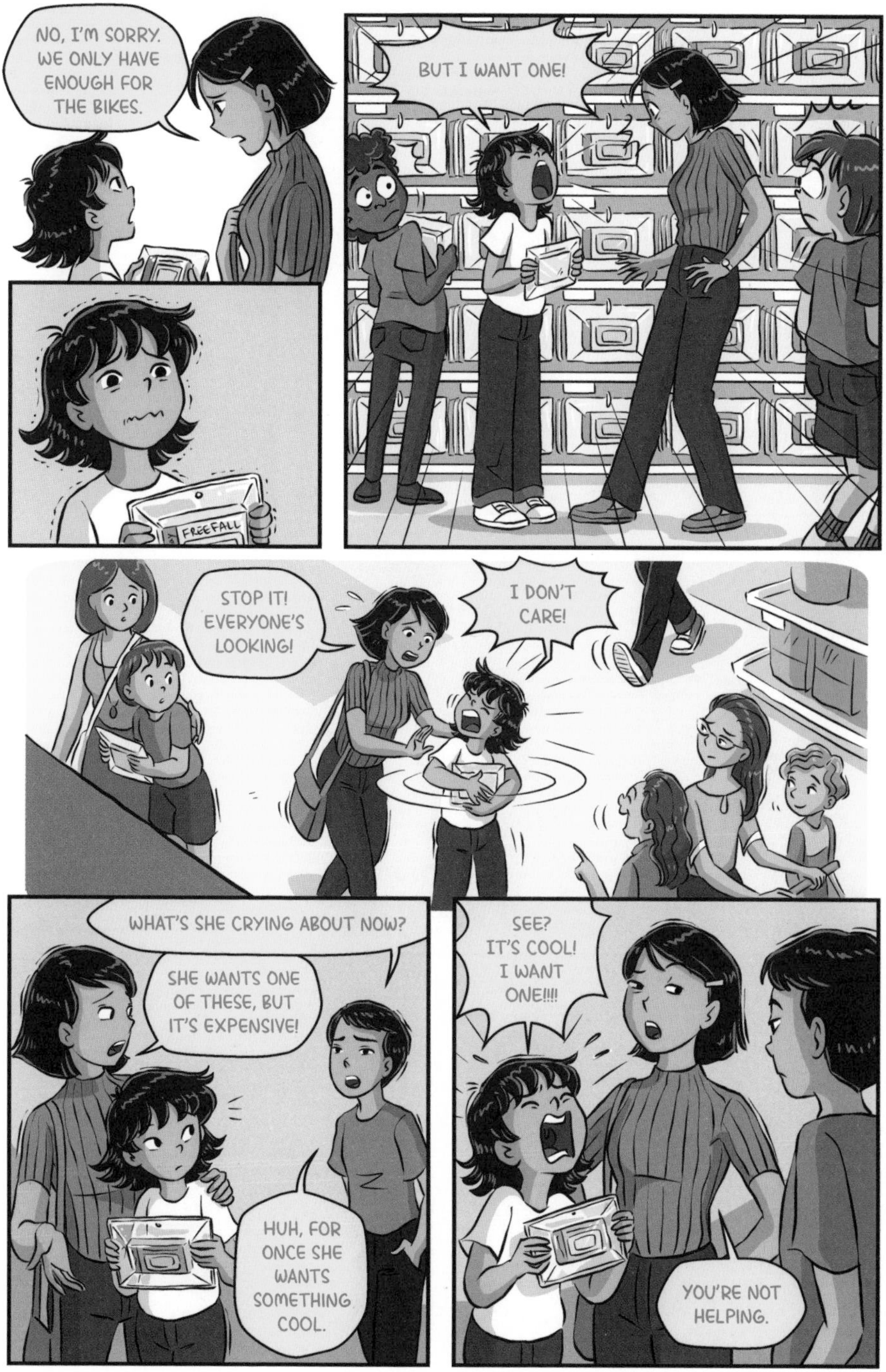
NO, I'M SORRY. WE ONLY HAVE ENOUGH FOR THE BIKES.
BUT I WANT ONE!
FREEFALL
STOP IT! EVERYONE'S LOOKING!
I DON'T CARE!
WHAT'S SHE CRYING ABOUT NOW?
SHE WANTS ONE OF THESE, BUT IT'S EXPENSIVE!
HUH, FOR ONCE SHE WANTS SOMETHING COOL.
SEE? IT'S COOL! I WANT ONE!!!!
YOU'RE NOT HELPING.

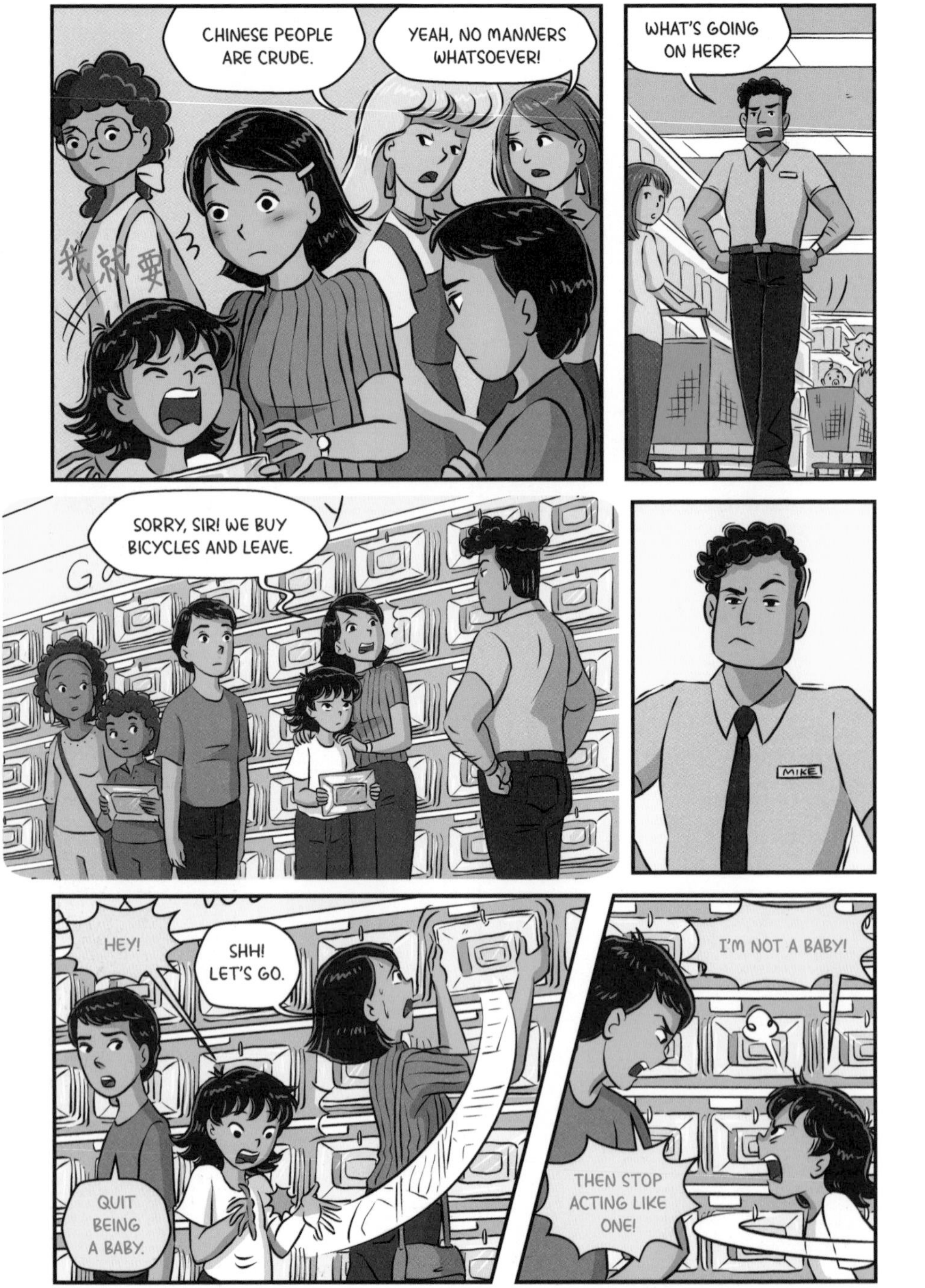
CHINESE PEOPLE ARE CRUDE.
YEAH, NO MANNERS WHATSOEVER!
我就要!
WHAT'S GOING ON HERE?
SORRY, SIR! WE BUY BICYCLES AND LEAVE.
MIKE
HEY!
SHH! LET'S GO.
QUIT BEING A BABY.
I'M NOT A BABY!
THEN STOP ACTING LIKE ONE!

MID-JUNE

Shuffle
Shuffle

Shuffle
Shuffle

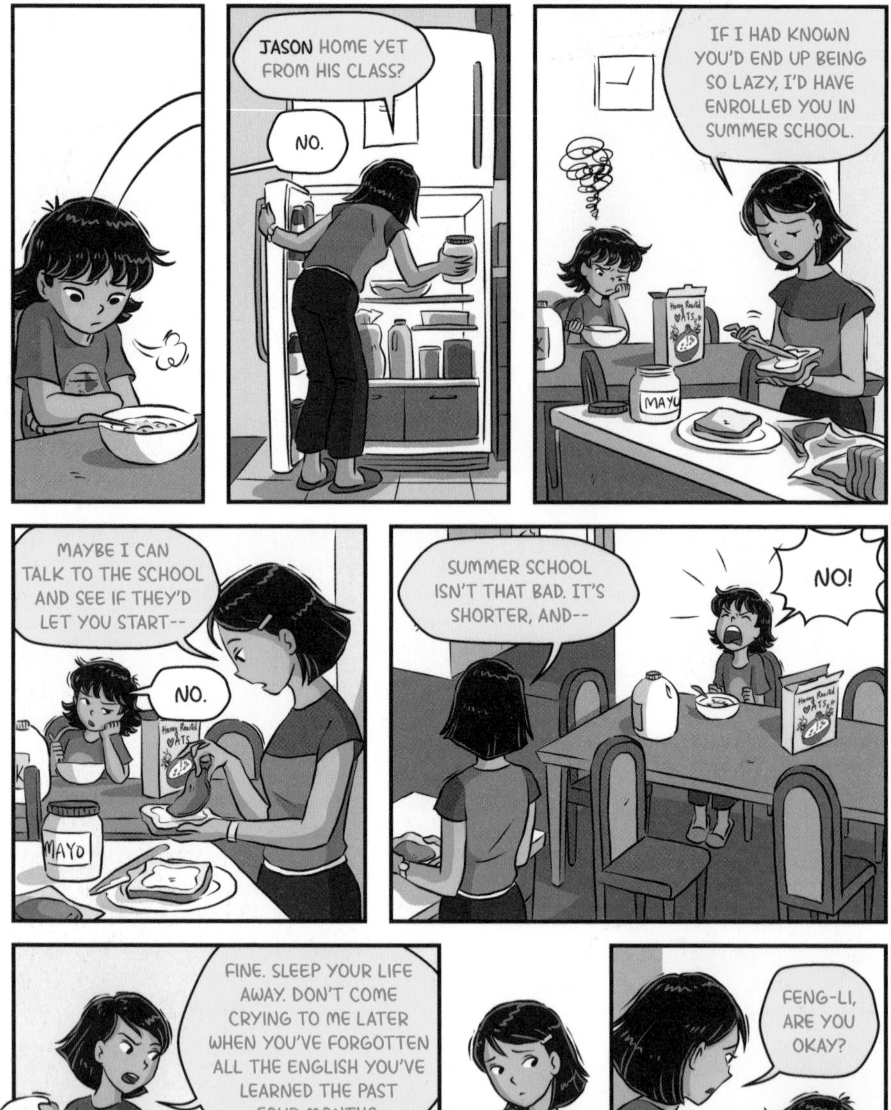
JASON HOME YET FROM HIS CLASS?
NO.
IF I HAD KNOWN YOU'D END UP BEING SO LAZY, I'D HAVE ENROLLED YOU IN SUMMER SCHOOL.
MAYO
MAYBE I CAN TALK TO THE SCHOOL AND SEE IF THEY'D LET YOU START--
NO.
MAYO
SUMMER SCHOOL ISN'T THAT BAD. IT'S SHORTER, AND--
NO!
FINE. SLEEP YOUR LIFE AWAY. DON'T COME CRYING TO ME LATER WHEN YOU'VE FORGOTTEN ALL THE ENGLISH YOU'VE LEARNED THE PAST FOUR MONTHS.
pffft
Honey Roasted OATS
FENG-LI, ARE YOU OKAY?

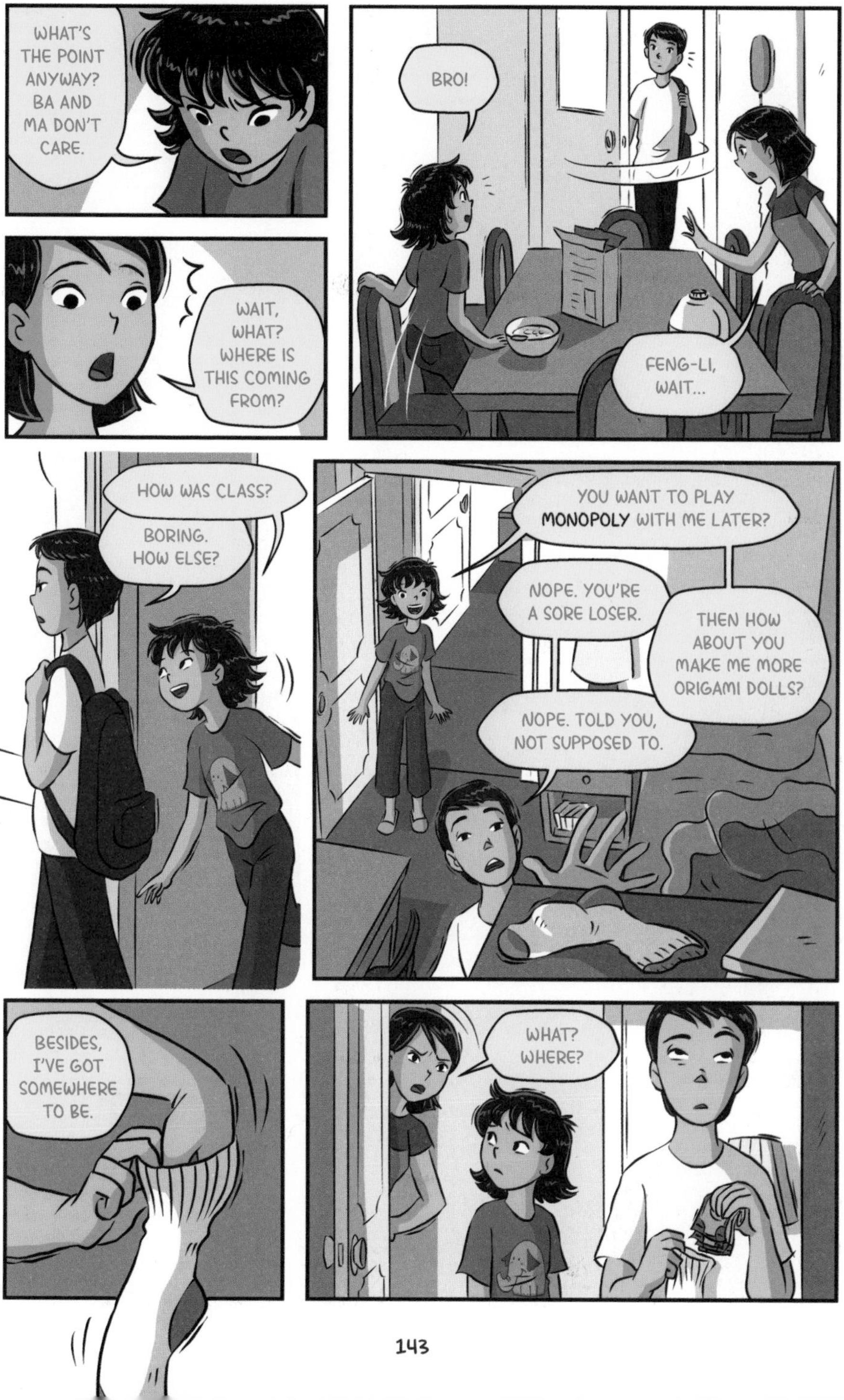
WHAT'S THE POINT ANYWAY? BA AND MA DON'T CARE.
BRO!
WAIT, WHAT? WHERE IS THIS COMING FROM?
FENG-LI, WAIT...
HOW WAS CLASS?
BORING. HOW ELSE?
YOU WANT TO PLAY MONOPOLY WITH ME LATER?
NOPE. YOU'RE A SORE LOSER.
THEN HOW ABOUT YOU MAKE ME MORE ORIGAMI DOLLS?
NOPE. TOLD YOU, NOT SUPPOSED TO.
BESIDES, I'VE GOT SOMEWHERE TO BE.
WHAT? WHERE?

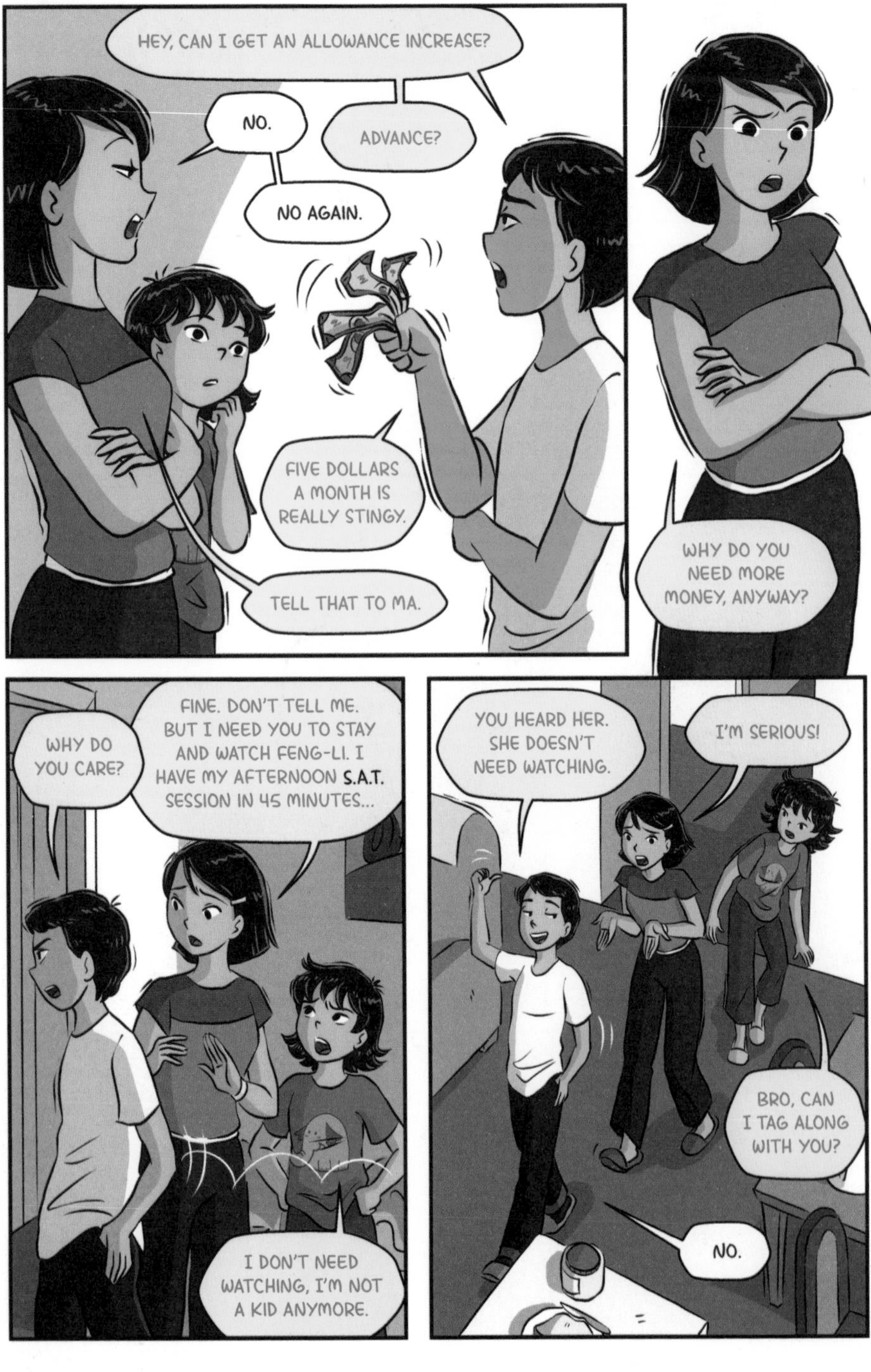
HEY, CAN I GET AN ALLOWANCE INCREASE?
NO.
ADVANCE?
NO AGAIN.
FIVE DOLLARS A MONTH IS REALLY STINGY.
TELL THAT TO MA.
WHY DO YOU NEED MORE MONEY, ANYWAY?
WHY DO YOU CARE?
FINE. DON'T TELL ME. BUT I NEED YOU TO STAY AND WATCH FENG-LI. I HAVE MY AFTERNOON S.A.T. SESSION IN 45 MINUTES...
I DON'T NEED WATCHING, I'M NOT A KID ANYMORE.
YOU HEARD HER. SHE DOESN'T NEED WATCHING.
I'M SERIOUS!
BRO, CAN I TAG ALONG WITH YOU?
NO.

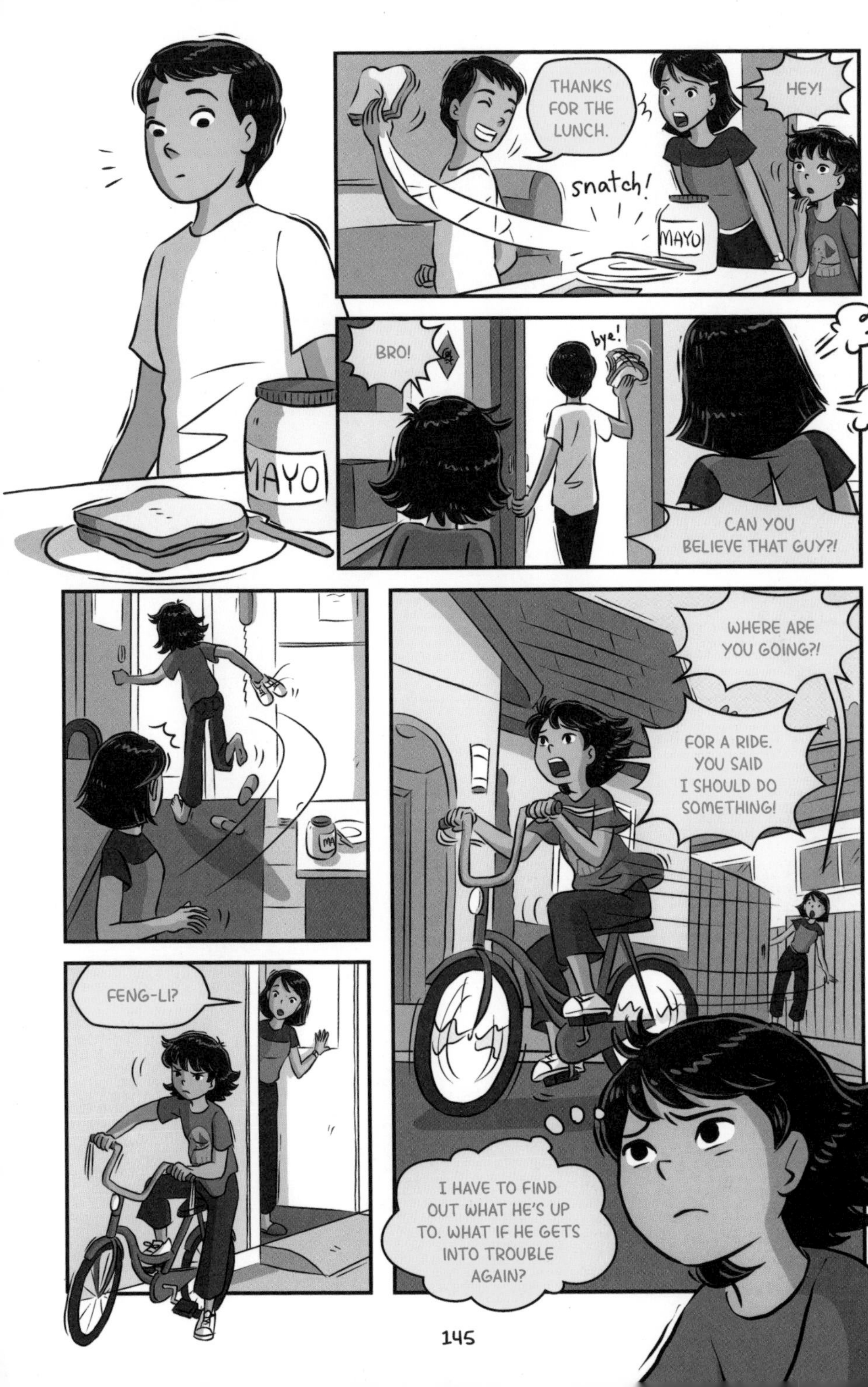
THANKS FOR THE LUNCH.
HEY!
snatch!
MAYO
BRO!
bye!
CAN YOU BELIEVE THAT GUY?!
WHERE ARE YOU GOING?!
FOR A RIDE. YOU SAID I SHOULD DO SOMETHING!
FENG-LI?
I HAVE TO FIND OUT WHAT HE'S UP TO. WHAT IF HE GETS INTO TROUBLE AGAIN?

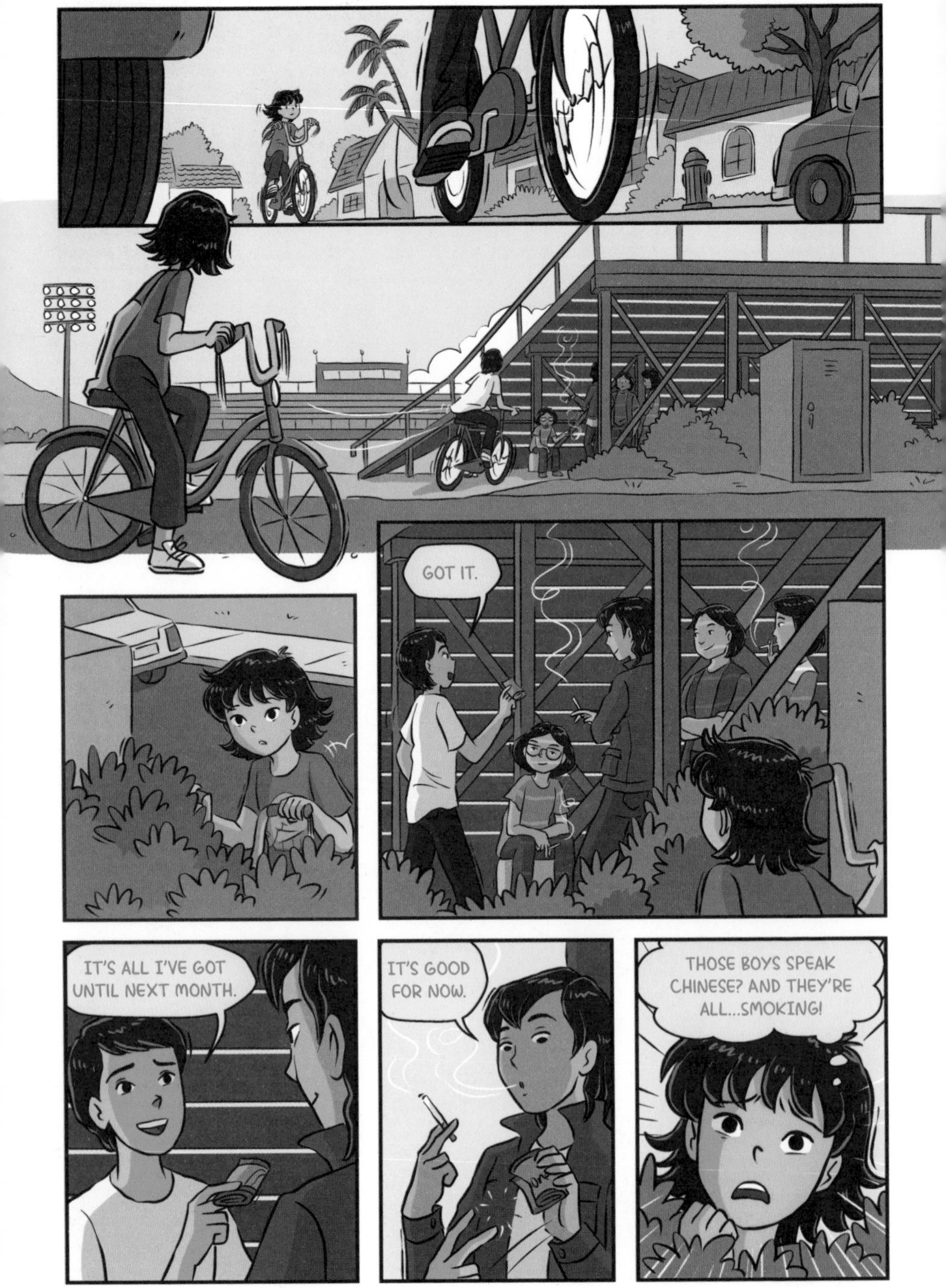
GOT IT.
IT'S ALL I'VE GOT UNTIL NEXT MONTH.
IT'S GOOD FOR NOW.
THOSE BOYS SPEAK CHINESE? AND THEY'RE ALL...SMOKING!

148

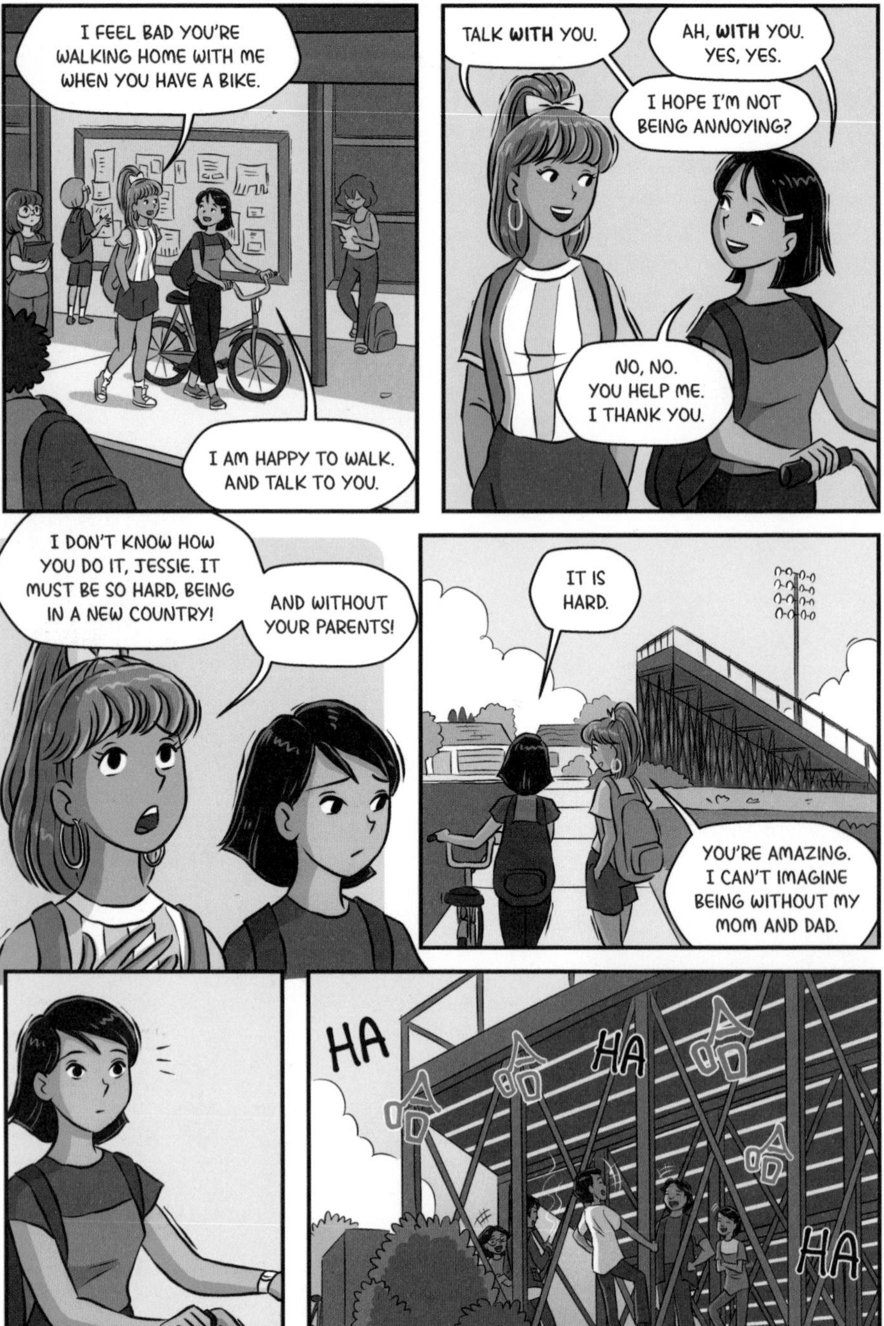
I FEEL BAD YOU'RE WALKING HOME WITH ME WHEN YOU HAVE A BIKE.
I AM HAPPY TO WALK. AND TALK TO YOU.
TALK **WITH** YOU.
AH, **WITH** YOU. YES, YES.
I HOPE I'M NOT BEING ANNOYING?
NO, NO. YOU HELP ME. I THANK YOU.
I DON'T KNOW HOW YOU DO IT, JESSIE. IT MUST BE SO HARD, BEING IN A NEW COUNTRY!
AND WITHOUT YOUR PARENTS!
IT IS HARD.
YOU'RE AMAZING. I CAN'T IMAGINE BEING WITHOUT MY MOM AND DAD.
HA
哈
哈
HA
哈
哈
HA

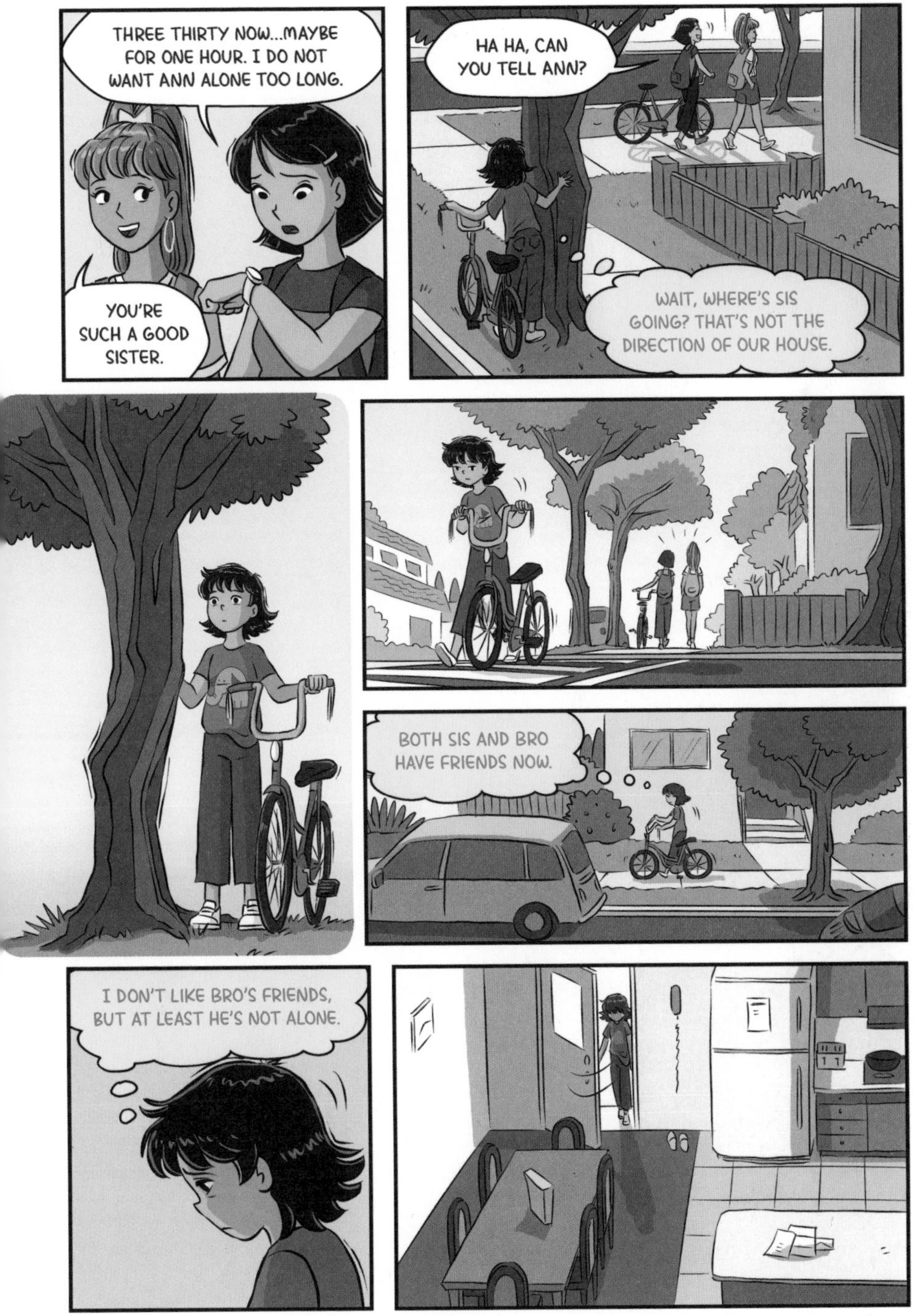
THREE THIRTY NOW...MAYBE FOR ONE HOUR. I DO NOT WANT ANN ALONE TOO LONG.
YOU'RE SUCH A GOOD SISTER.
HA HA, CAN YOU TELL ANN?
WAIT, WHERE'S SIS GOING? THAT'S NOT THE DIRECTION OF OUR HOUSE.
BOTH SIS AND BRO HAVE FRIENDS NOW.
I DON'T LIKE BRO'S FRIENDS, BUT AT LEAST HE'S NOT ALONE.

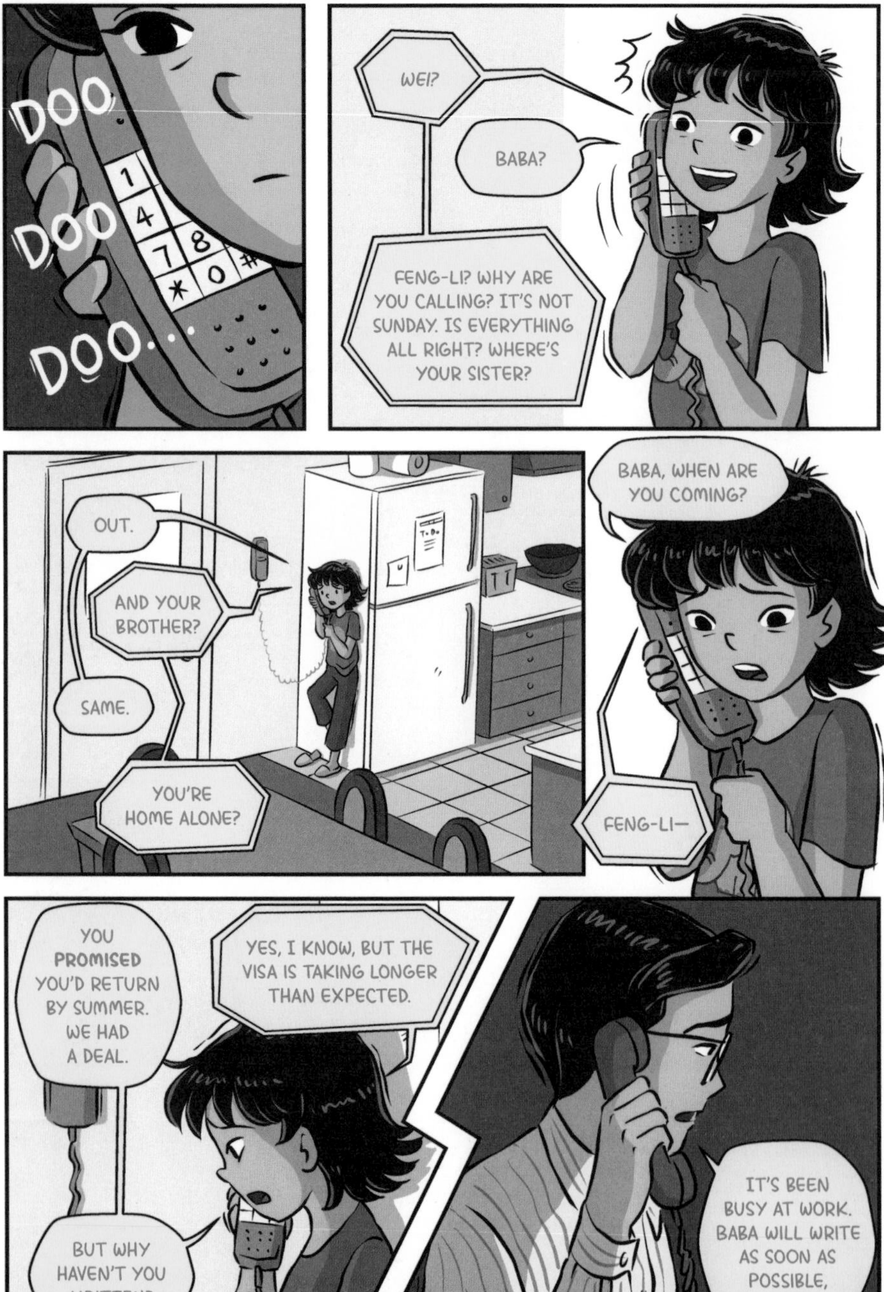
DOO
DOO
DOO...
WEI?
BABA?
FENG-LI? WHY ARE YOU CALLING? IT'S NOT SUNDAY. IS EVERYTHING ALL RIGHT? WHERE'S YOUR SISTER?
OUT.
AND YOUR BROTHER?
SAME.
YOU'RE HOME ALONE?
BABA, WHEN ARE YOU COMING?
FENG-LI—
YOU **PROMISED** YOU'D RETURN BY SUMMER. WE HAD A DEAL.
YES, I KNOW, BUT THE VISA IS TAKING LONGER THAN EXPECTED.
BUT WHY HAVEN'T YOU WRITTEN?
IT'S BEEN BUSY AT WORK. BABA WILL WRITE AS SOON AS POSSIBLE, OKAY?

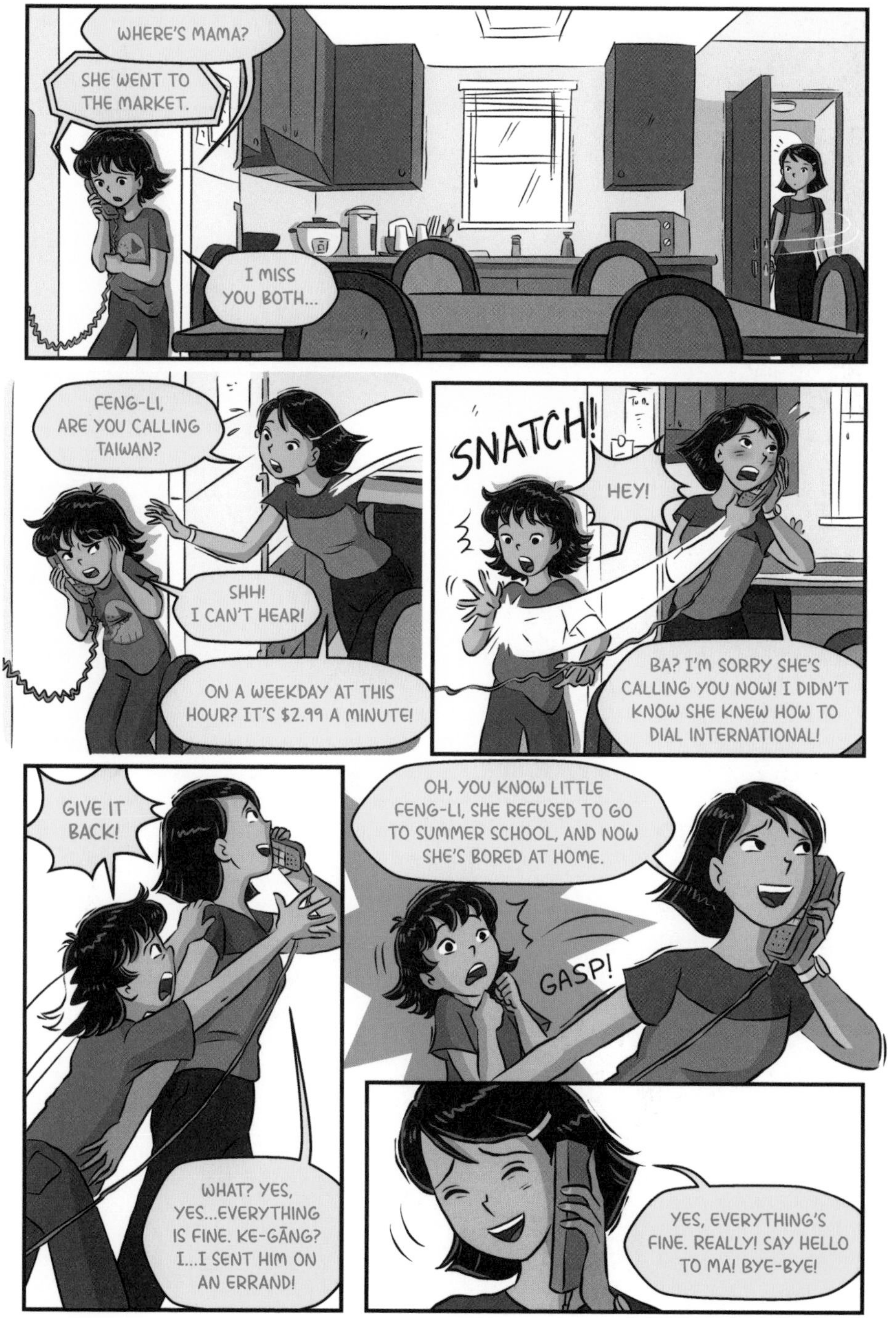
WHERE'S MAMA?
SHE WENT TO THE MARKET.
I MISS YOU BOTH...
FENG-LI, ARE YOU CALLING TAIWAN?
SHH! I CAN'T HEAR!
ON A WEEKDAY AT THIS HOUR? IT'S $2.99 A MINUTE!
SNATCH!
HEY!
BA? I'M SORRY SHE'S CALLING YOU NOW! I DIDN'T KNOW SHE KNEW HOW TO DIAL INTERNATIONAL!
GIVE IT BACK!
WHAT? YES, YES...EVERYTHING IS FINE. KE-GĀNG? I...I SENT HIM ON AN ERRAND!
OH, YOU KNOW LITTLE FENG-LI, SHE REFUSED TO GO TO SUMMER SCHOOL, AND NOW SHE'S BORED AT HOME.
GASP!
YES, EVERYTHING'S FINE. REALLY! SAY HELLO TO MA! BYE-BYE!

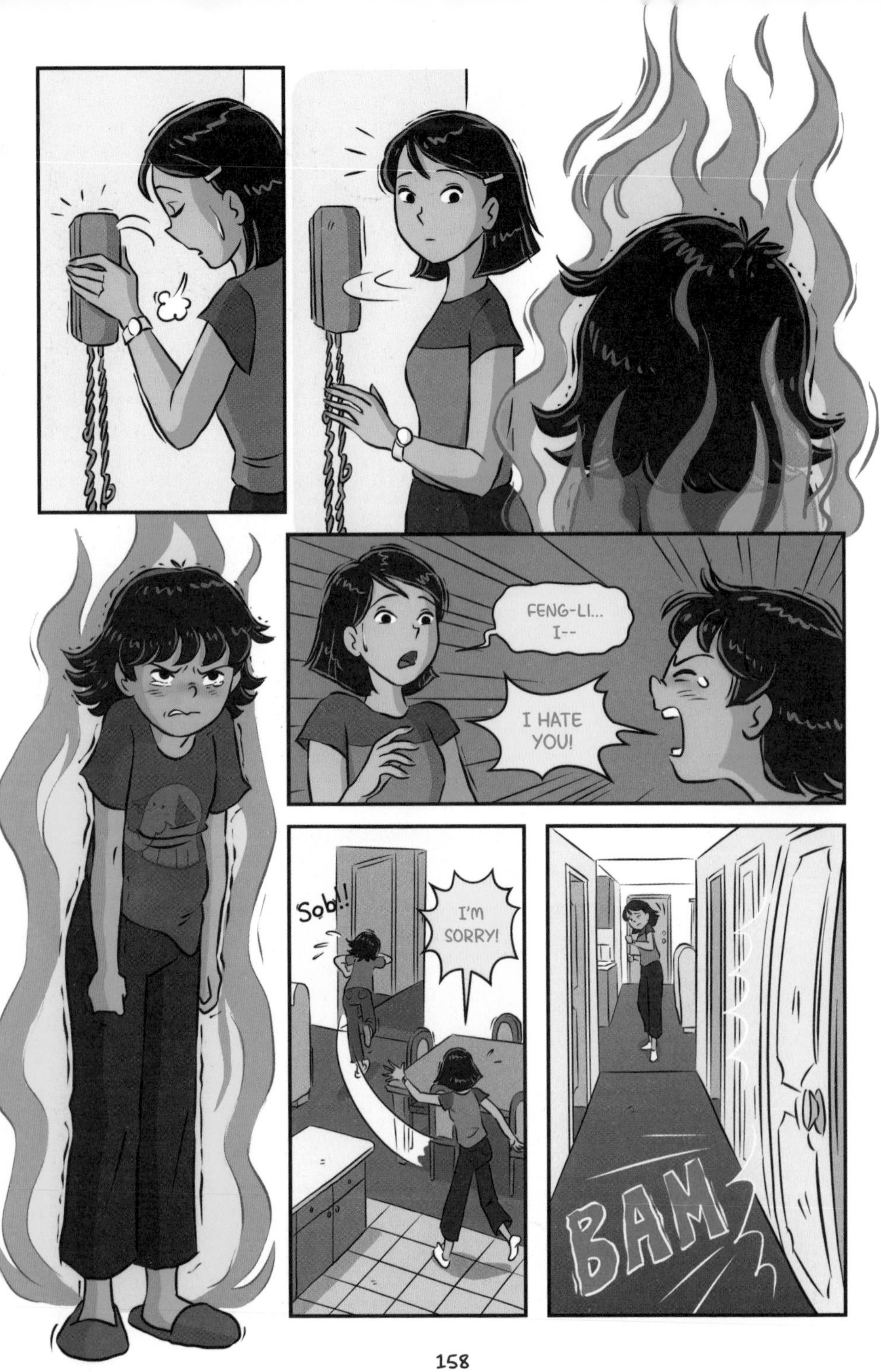
FENG-LI...
I--
I HATE YOU!
Sob!!
I'M SORRY!
BAM

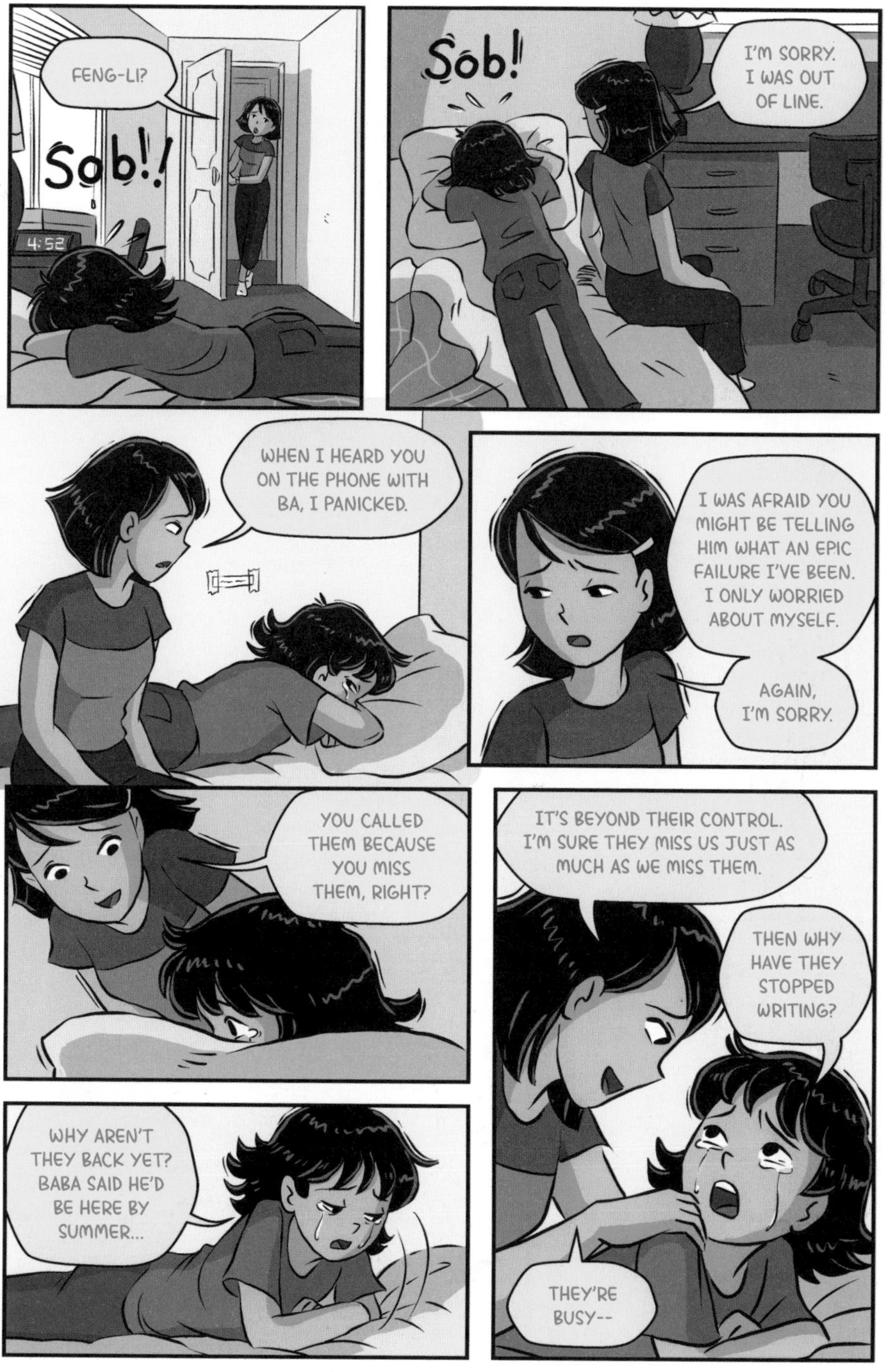
FENG-LI?
SOB!!
4:52
SOB!
I'M SORRY. I WAS OUT OF LINE.
WHEN I HEARD YOU ON THE PHONE WITH BA, I PANICKED.
I WAS AFRAID YOU MIGHT BE TELLING HIM WHAT AN EPIC FAILURE I'VE BEEN. I ONLY WORRIED ABOUT MYSELF.
AGAIN, I'M SORRY.
YOU CALLED THEM BECAUSE YOU MISS THEM, RIGHT?
WHY AREN'T THEY BACK YET? BABA SAID HE'D BE HERE BY SUMMER...
THEY'RE BUSY--
IT'S BEYOND THEIR CONTROL. I'M SURE THEY MISS US JUST AS MUCH AS WE MISS THEM.
THEN WHY HAVE THEY STOPPED WRITING?

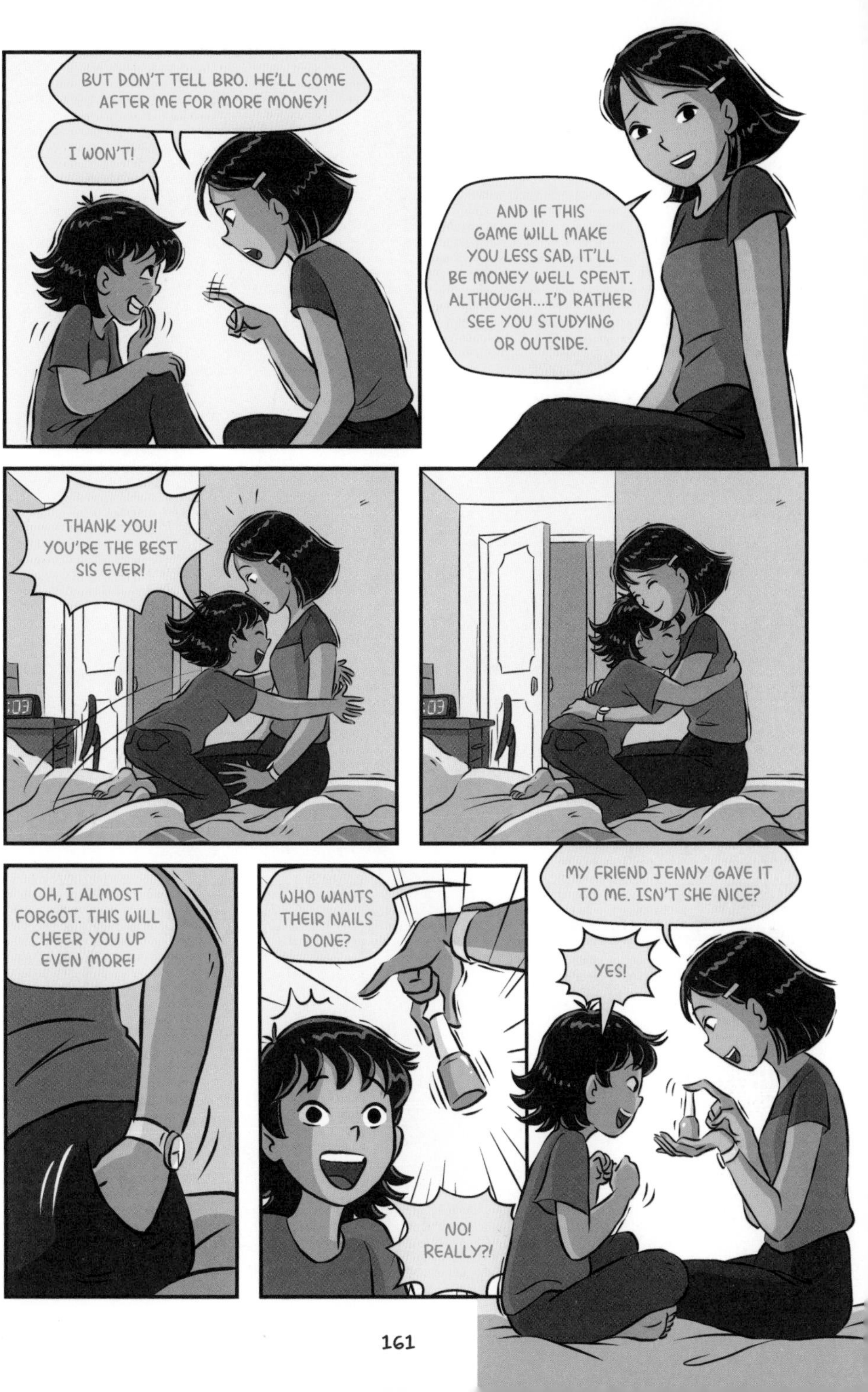
BUT DON'T TELL BRO. HE'LL COME AFTER ME FOR MORE MONEY!
I WON'T!
AND IF THIS GAME WILL MAKE YOU LESS SAD, IT'LL BE MONEY WELL SPENT. ALTHOUGH...I'D RATHER SEE YOU STUDYING OR OUTSIDE.
THANK YOU! YOU'RE THE BEST SIS EVER!
OH, I ALMOST FORGOT. THIS WILL CHEER YOU UP EVEN MORE!
WHO WANTS THEIR NAILS DONE?
NO! REALLY?!
MY FRIEND JENNY GAVE IT TO ME. ISN'T SHE NICE?
YES!

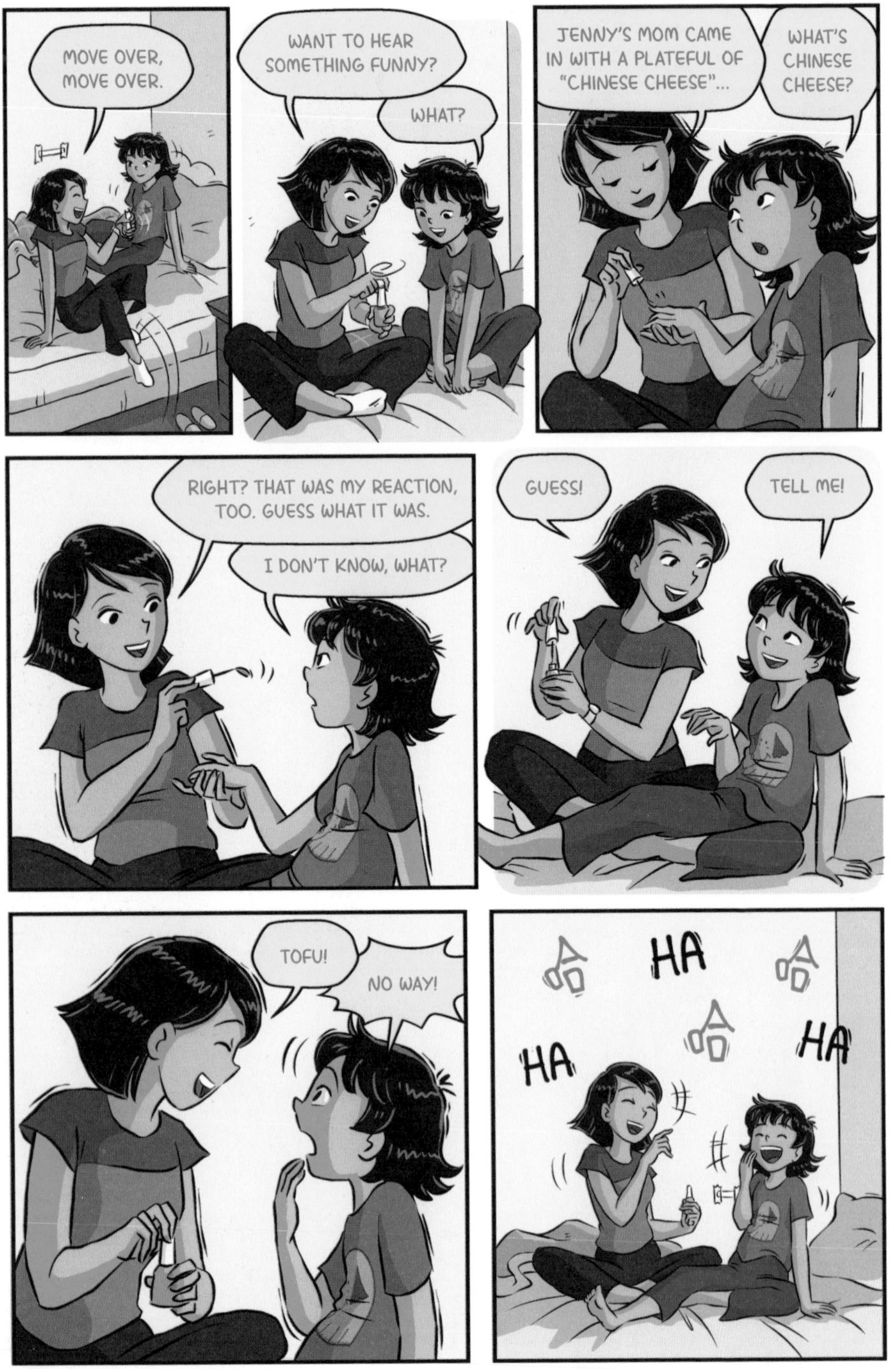
MOVE OVER, MOVE OVER.
WANT TO HEAR SOMETHING FUNNY?
WHAT?
JENNY'S MOM CAME IN WITH A PLATEFUL OF "CHINESE CHEESE"...
WHAT'S CHINESE CHEESE?
RIGHT? THAT WAS MY REACTION, TOO. GUESS WHAT IT WAS.
I DON'T KNOW, WHAT?
GUESS!
TELL ME!
TOFU!
NO WAY!
HA
HA
HA

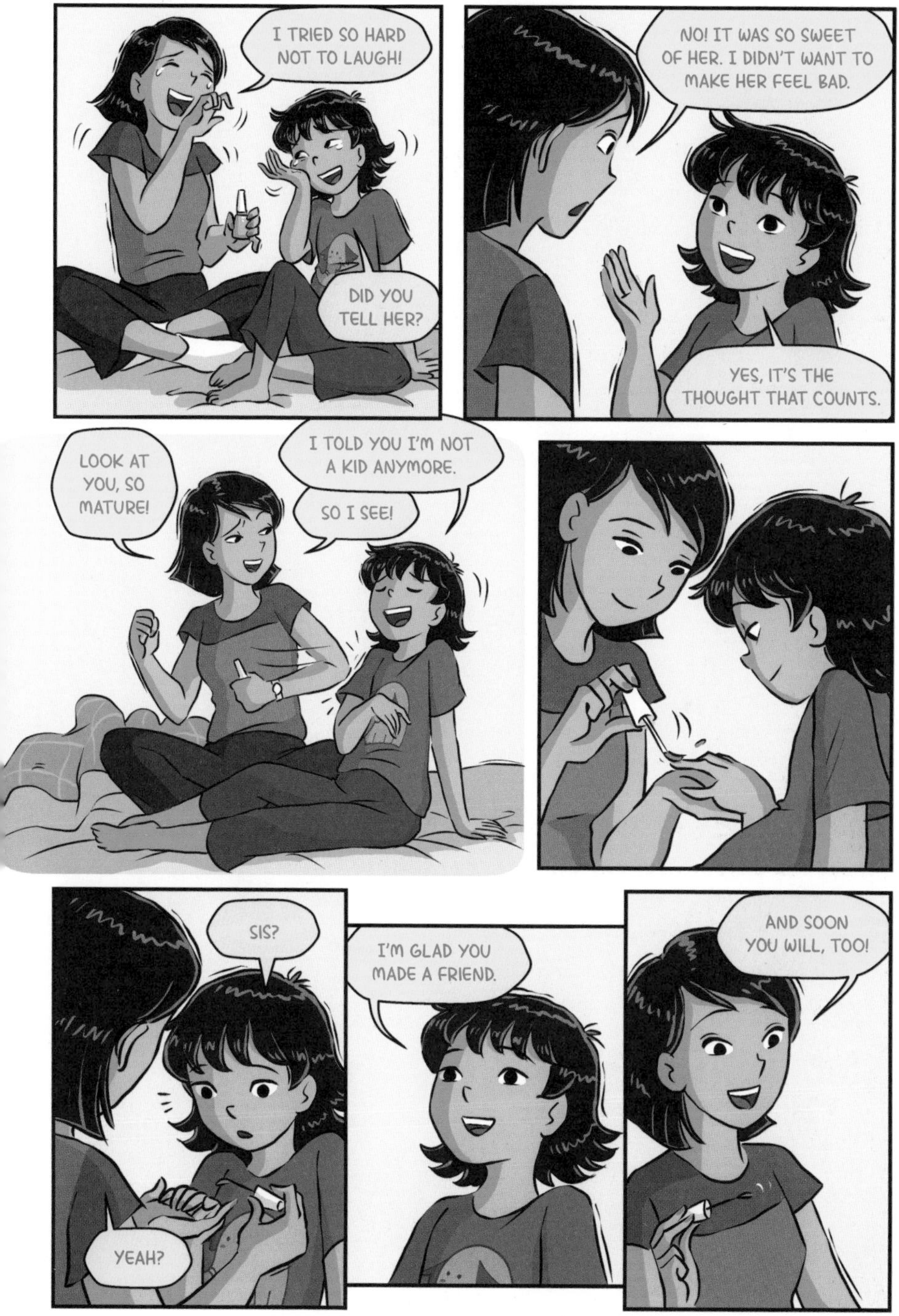
I TRIED SO HARD NOT TO LAUGH!
DID YOU TELL HER?
NO! IT WAS SO SWEET OF HER. I DIDN'T WANT TO MAKE HER FEEL BAD.
YES, IT'S THE THOUGHT THAT COUNTS.
LOOK AT YOU, SO MATURE!
I TOLD YOU I'M NOT A KID ANYMORE.
SO I SEE!
SIS?
YEAH?
I'M GLAD YOU MADE A FRIEND.
AND SOON YOU WILL, TOO!

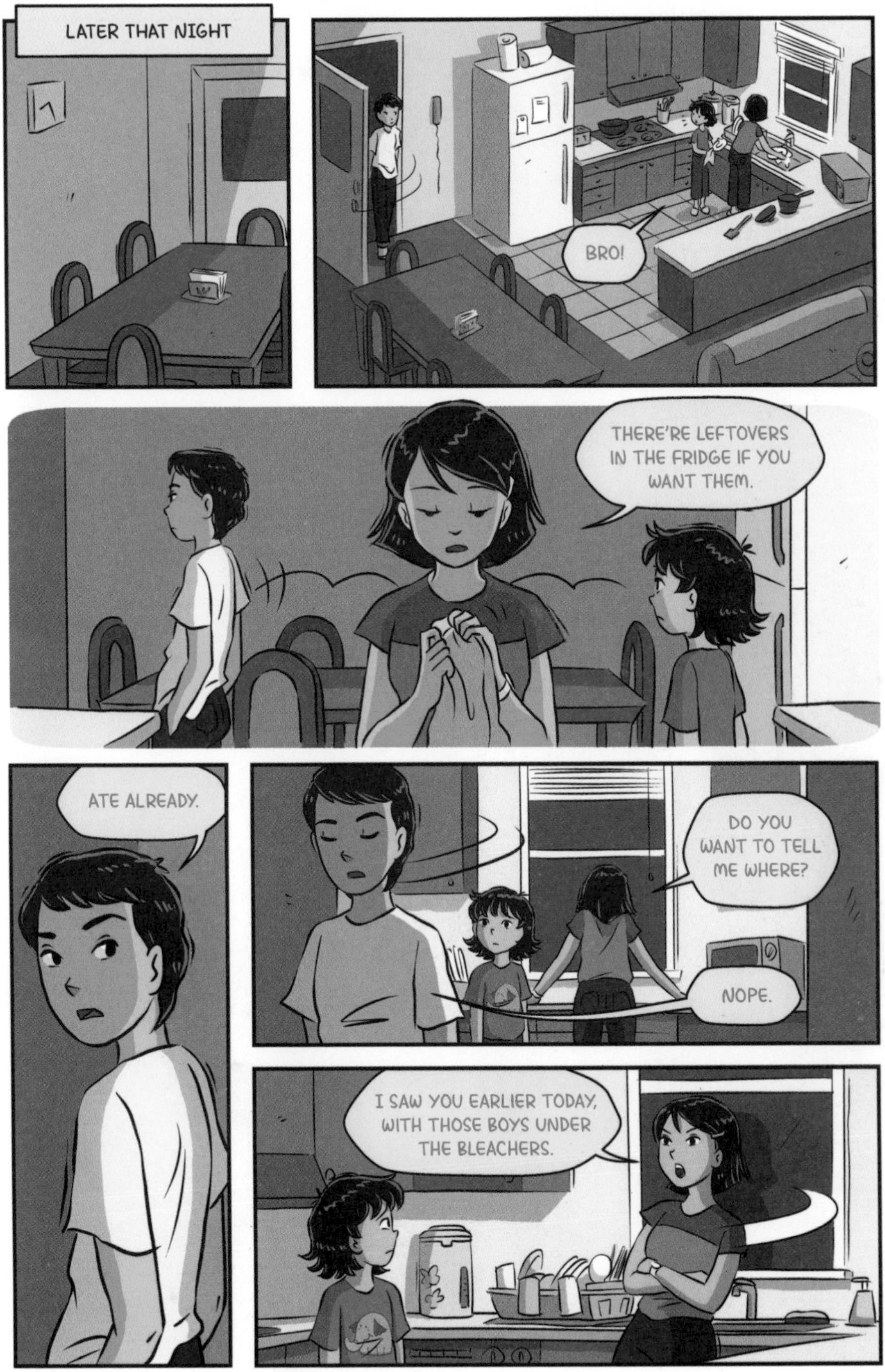
LATER THAT NIGHT
BRO!
THERE'RE LEFTOVERS IN THE FRIDGE IF YOU WANT THEM.
ATE ALREADY.
DO YOU WANT TO TELL ME WHERE?
NOPE.
I SAW YOU EARLIER TODAY, WITH THOSE BOYS UNDER THE BLEACHERS.

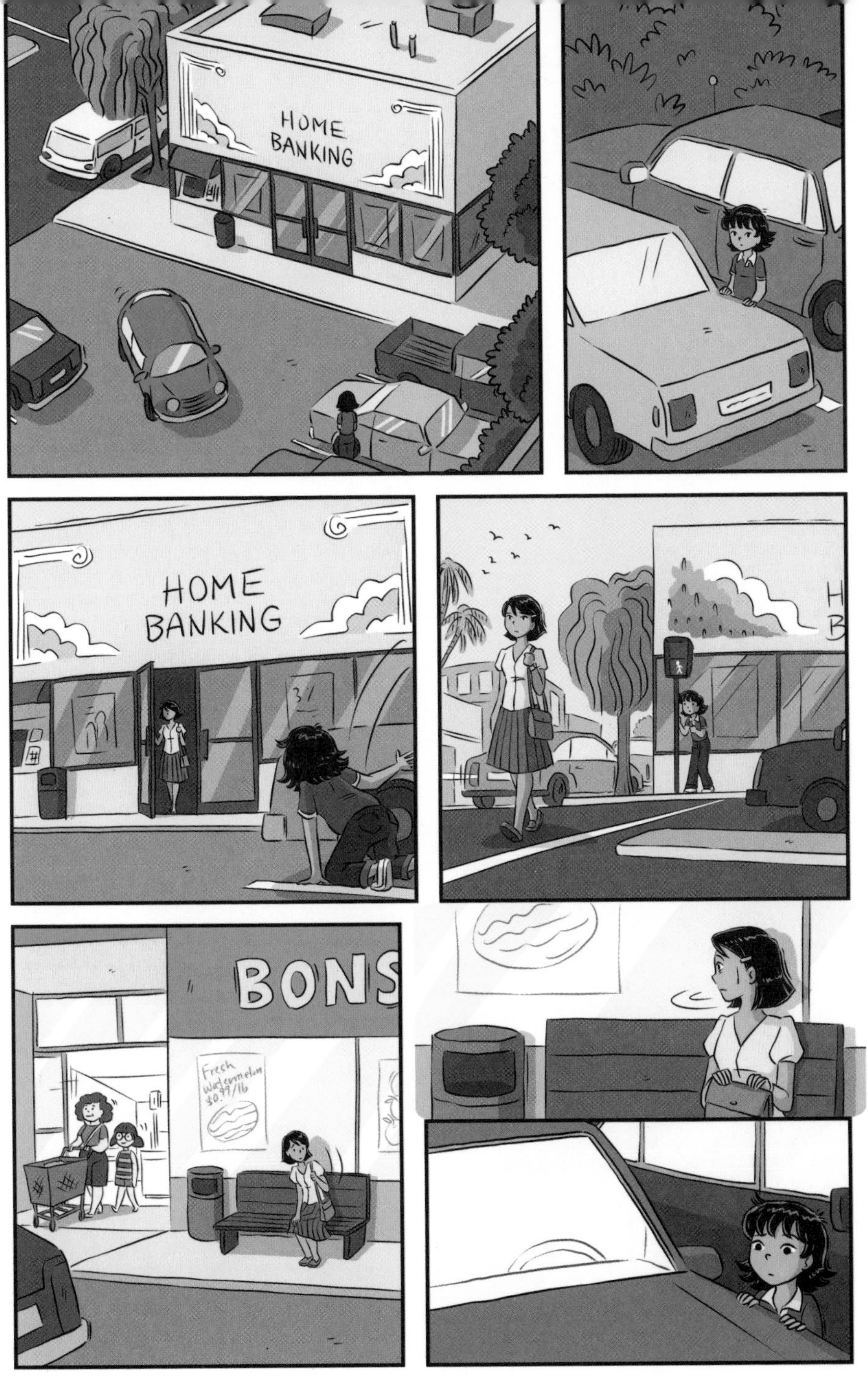
HOME
BANKING
HOME
BANKING
BONS
Fresh
Watermelon
$0.99/lb

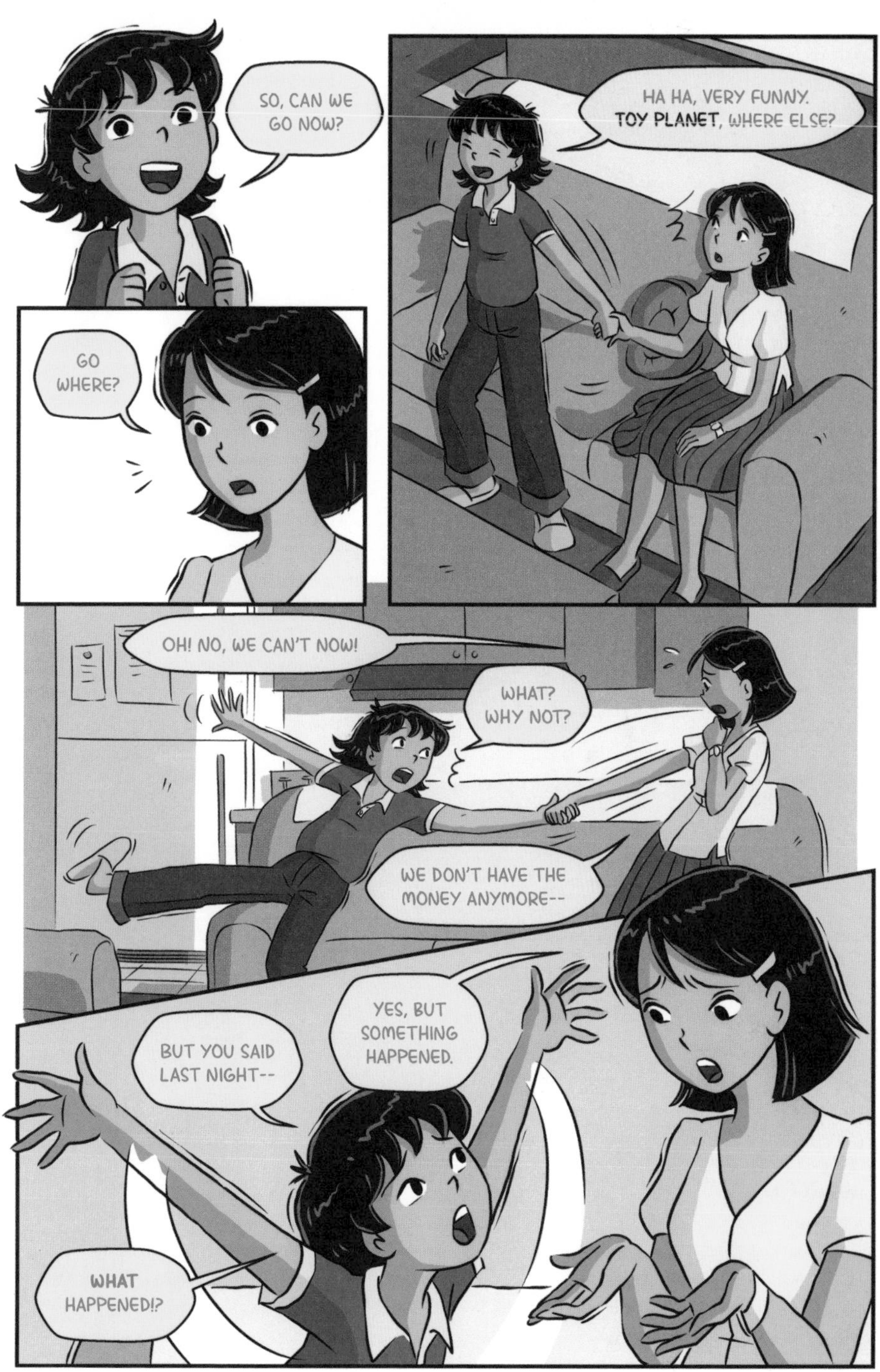
SO, CAN WE GO NOW?
HA HA, VERY FUNNY. TOY PLANET, WHERE ELSE?
GO WHERE?
OH! NO, WE CAN'T NOW!
WHAT? WHY NOT?
WE DON'T HAVE THE MONEY ANYMORE--
BUT YOU SAID LAST NIGHT--
YES, BUT SOMETHING HAPPENED.
WHAT HAPPENED!?

FOR THE NEXT WEEK, SIS KEPT BEATING ME TO THE MAILBOX.

HEY, LOOK, BA AND MA **FINALLY** WROTE US!

YAY...

THE FOLLOWING WEEK, SIS CALLED AUNTIE TIAN.

JIA-XI!! HOW ARE YOU?

GOOD, YOU? EVERYONE SETTLED IN?

A WEEK AGO I GOT A CALL FROM AN **I.N.S.** OFFICIAL, SAYING HE COULD GET US PERMITS TO STAY IN THE COUNTRY--

AIYA, JIA-XI, NO!

185

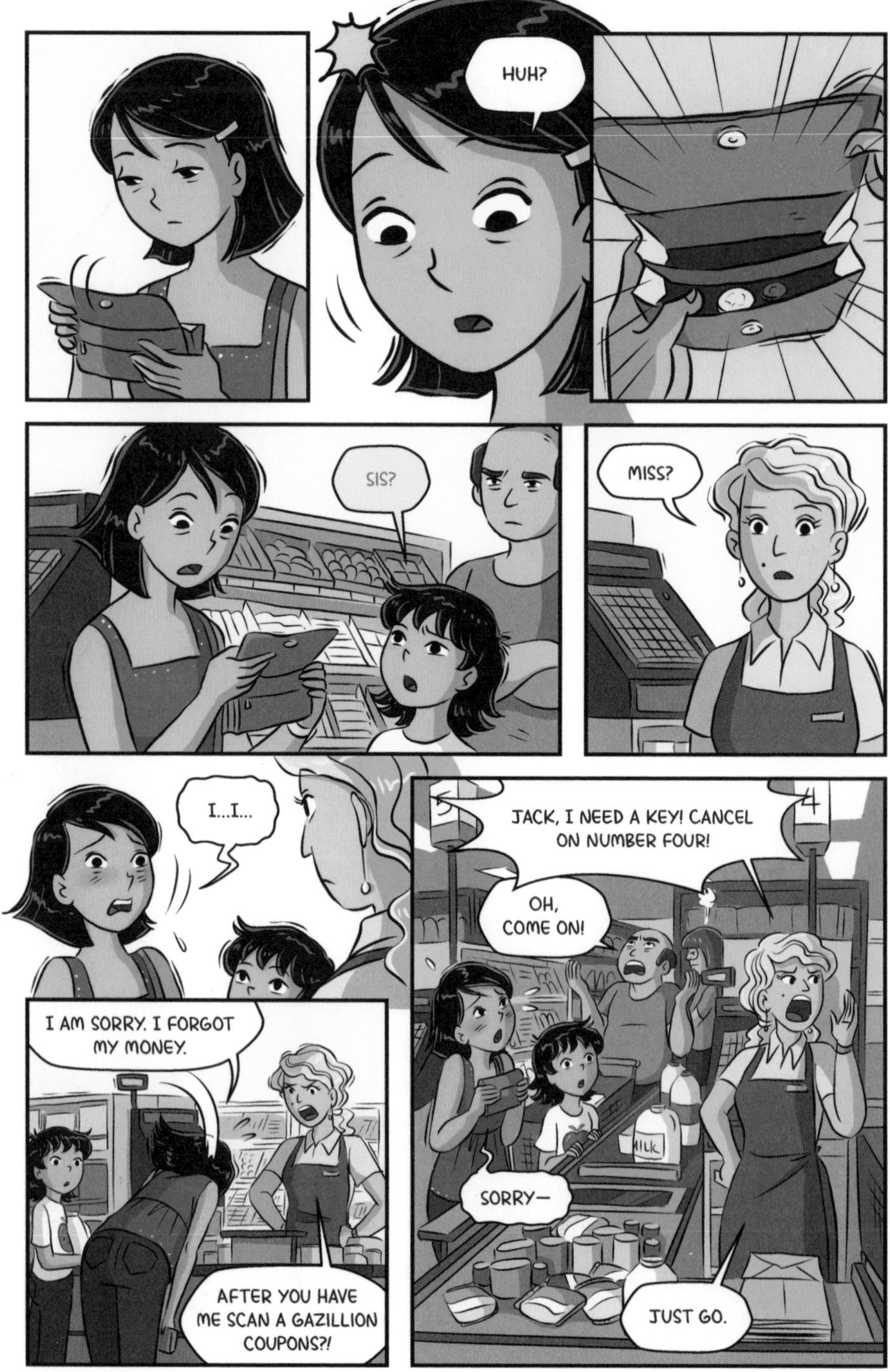
HUH?
SIS?
MISS?
I...I...
JACK, I NEED A KEY! CANCEL ON NUMBER FOUR!
OH, COME ON!
I AM SORRY. I FORGOT MY MONEY.
AFTER YOU HAVE ME SCAN A GAZILLION COUPONS?!
SORRY—
JUST GO.

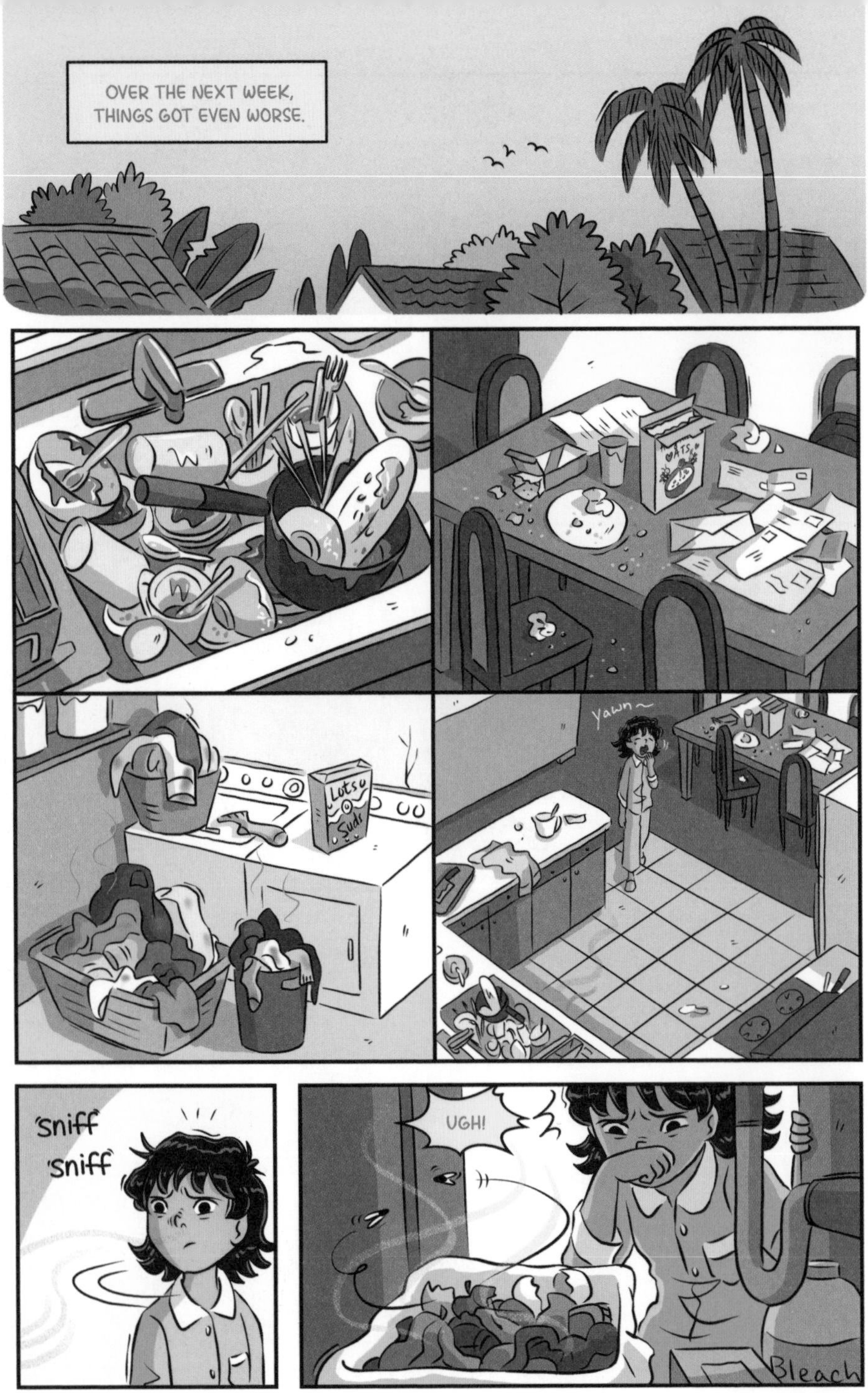
OVER THE NEXT WEEK, THINGS GOT EVEN WORSE.
OATS
Lotsa Suds
yawn~
'sniff 'sniff
UGH!
Bleach

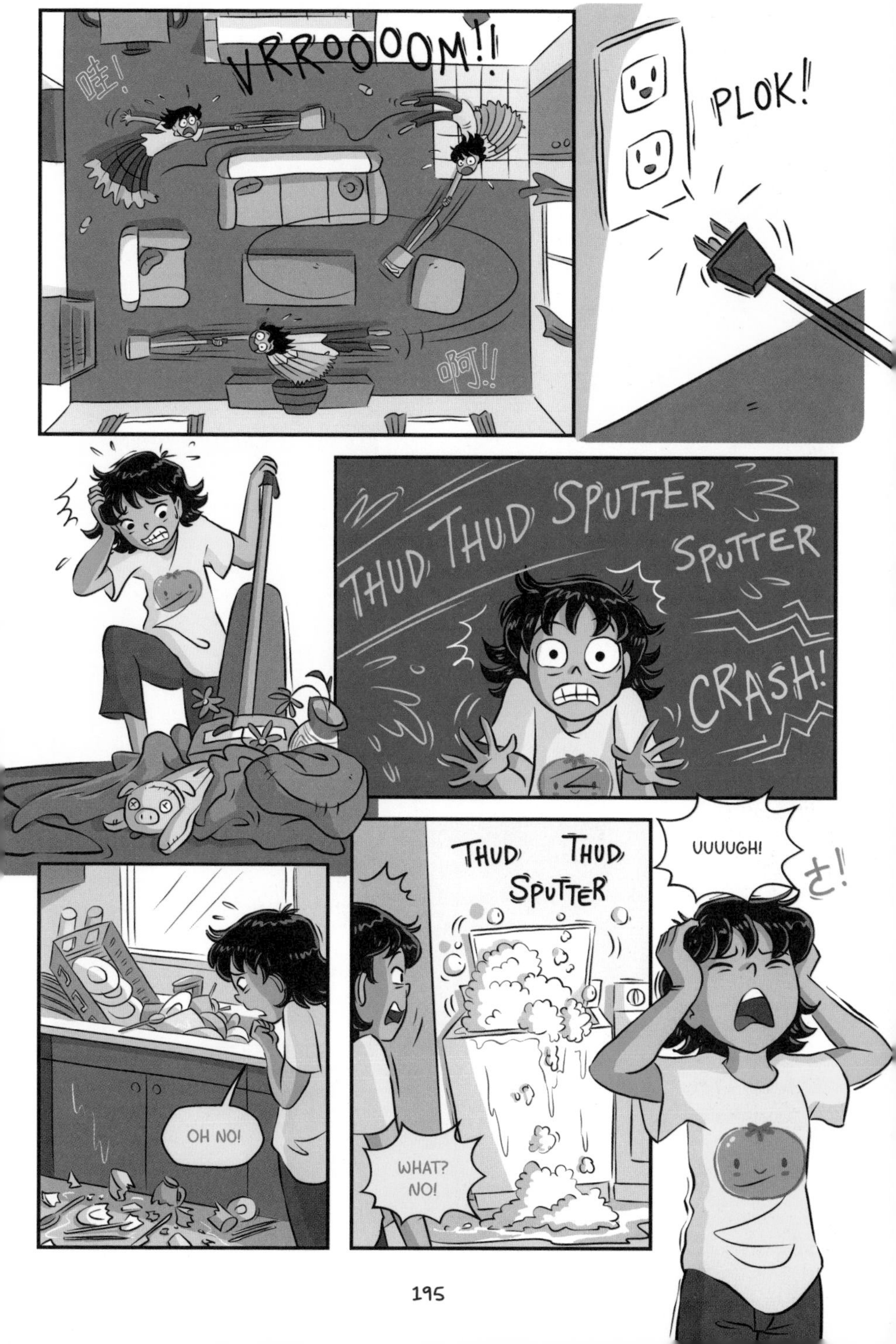

VRROOOOM!!
哇!
啊!!
PLOK!
THUD THUD SPUTTER
SPUTTER
CRASH!
OH NO!
THUD THUD
SPUTTER
WHAT? NO!
UUUUGH!
さ!

MANAGER

STILL NO ANSWER.

ANN, IS THERE ANYONE ELSE WE CAN CALL?

SIS, WHERE ARE YOU?

I...NO... UNDERSTAND...

I SUPPOSE I CAN SEE IF I CAN FIND A TRANSLATOR...

BUT WE DON'T KNOW WHAT LANGUAGE SHE SPEAKS.

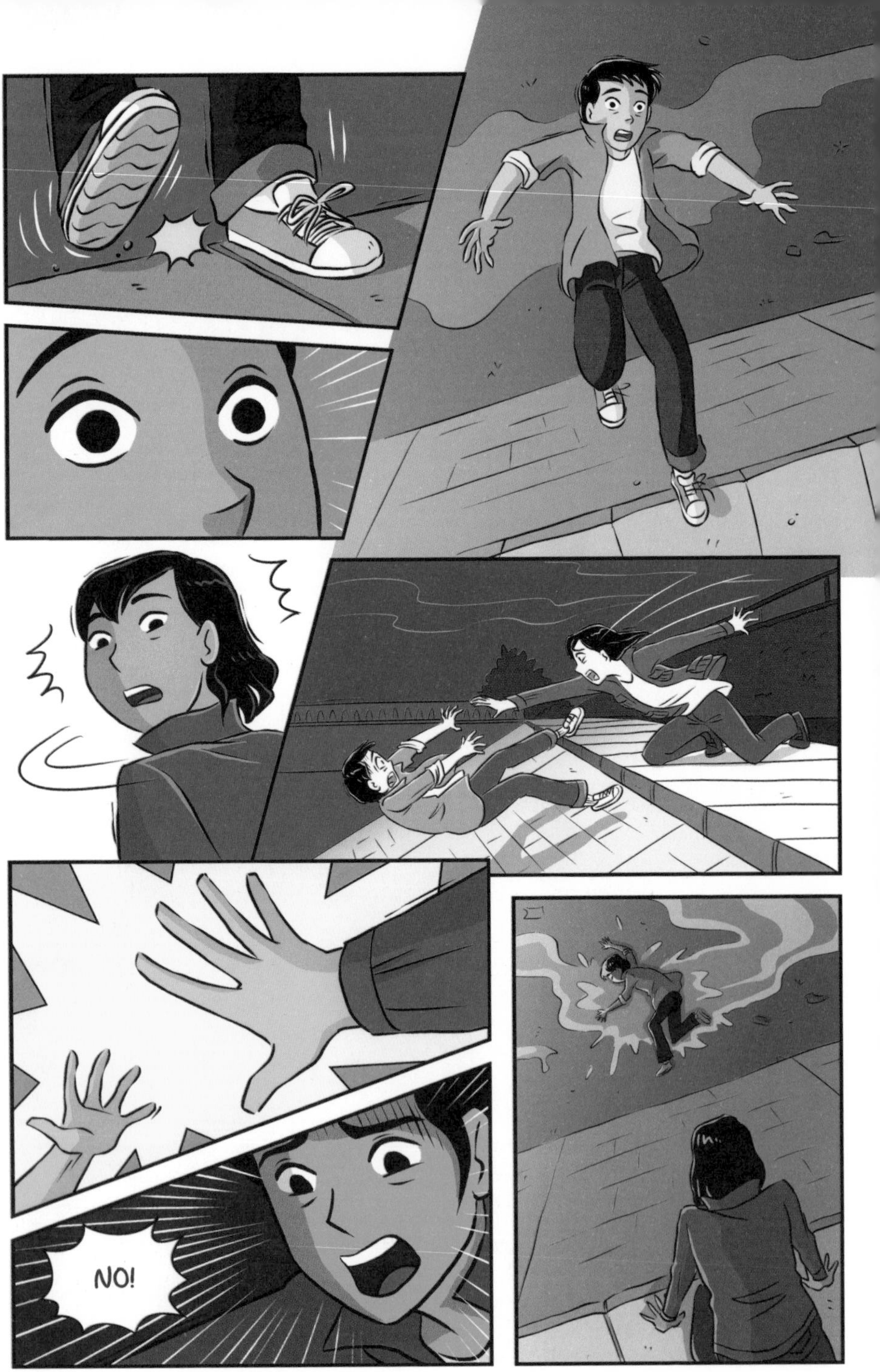
NO!

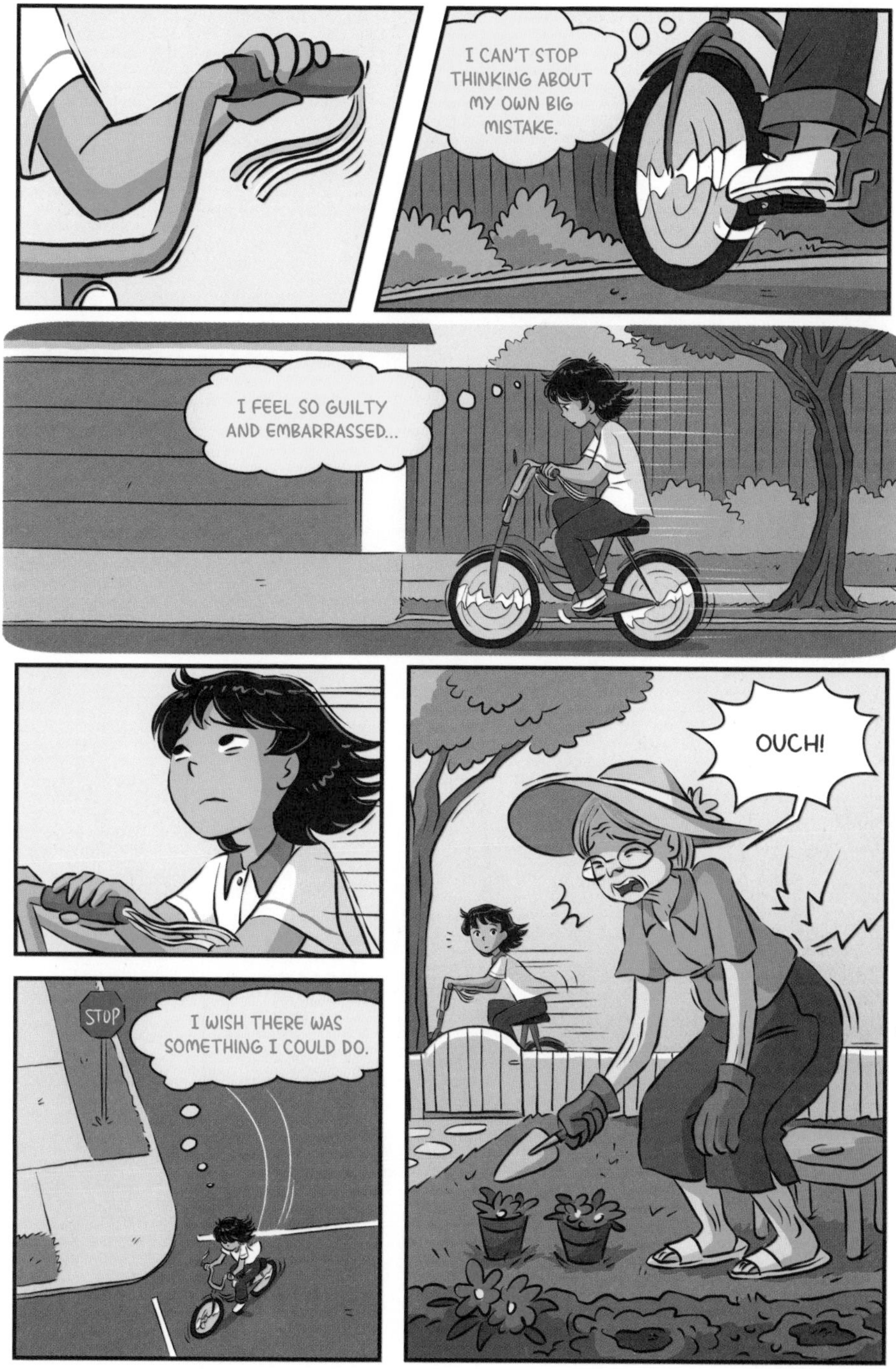
I CAN'T STOP THINKING ABOUT MY OWN BIG MISTAKE.
I FEEL SO GUILTY AND EMBARRASSED...
STOP
I WISH THERE WAS SOMETHING I COULD DO.
OUCH!

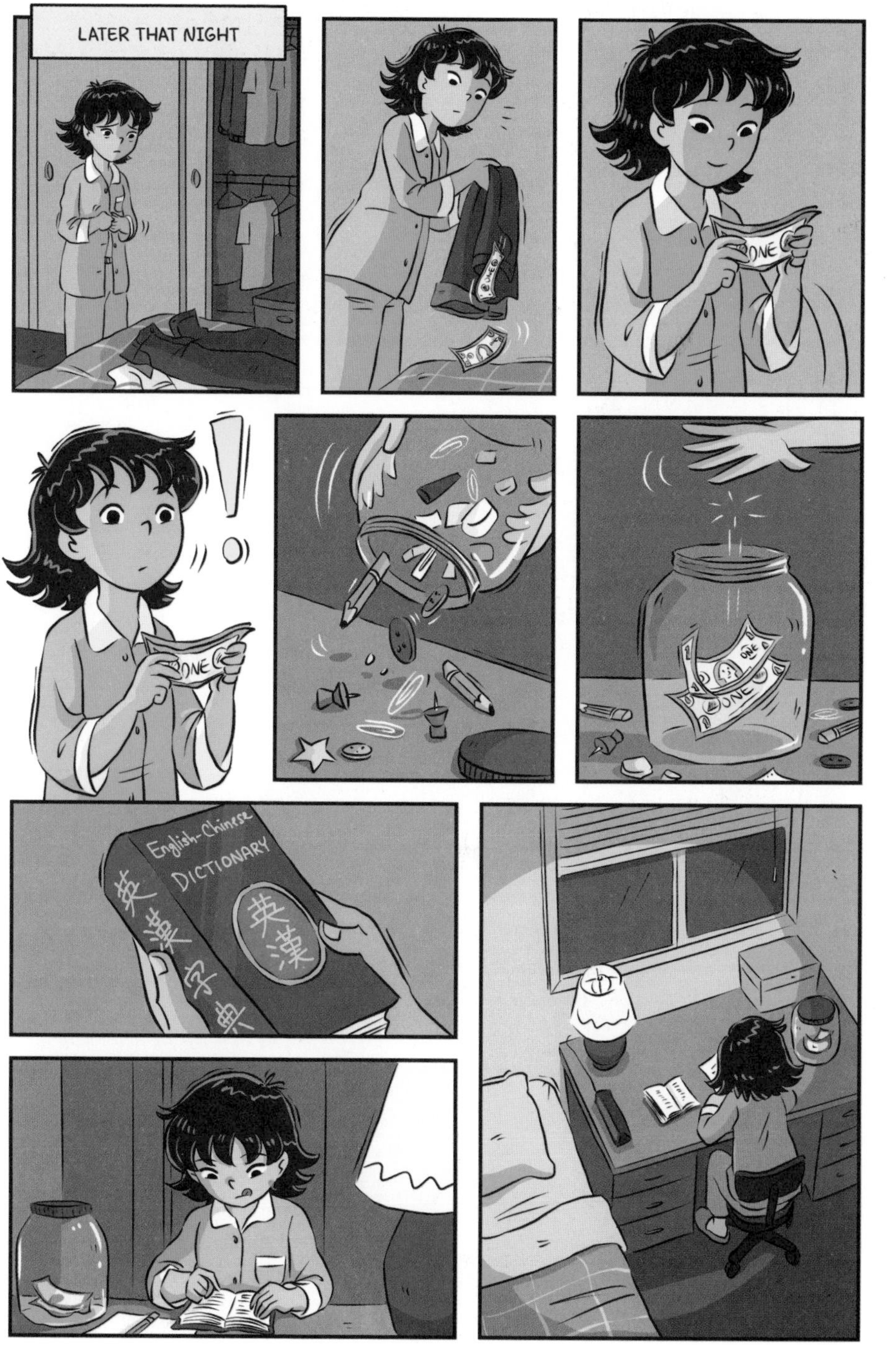
LATER THAT NIGHT
ONE
ONE
ONE
ONE
English-Chinese
DICTIONARY
英漢
英漢字典

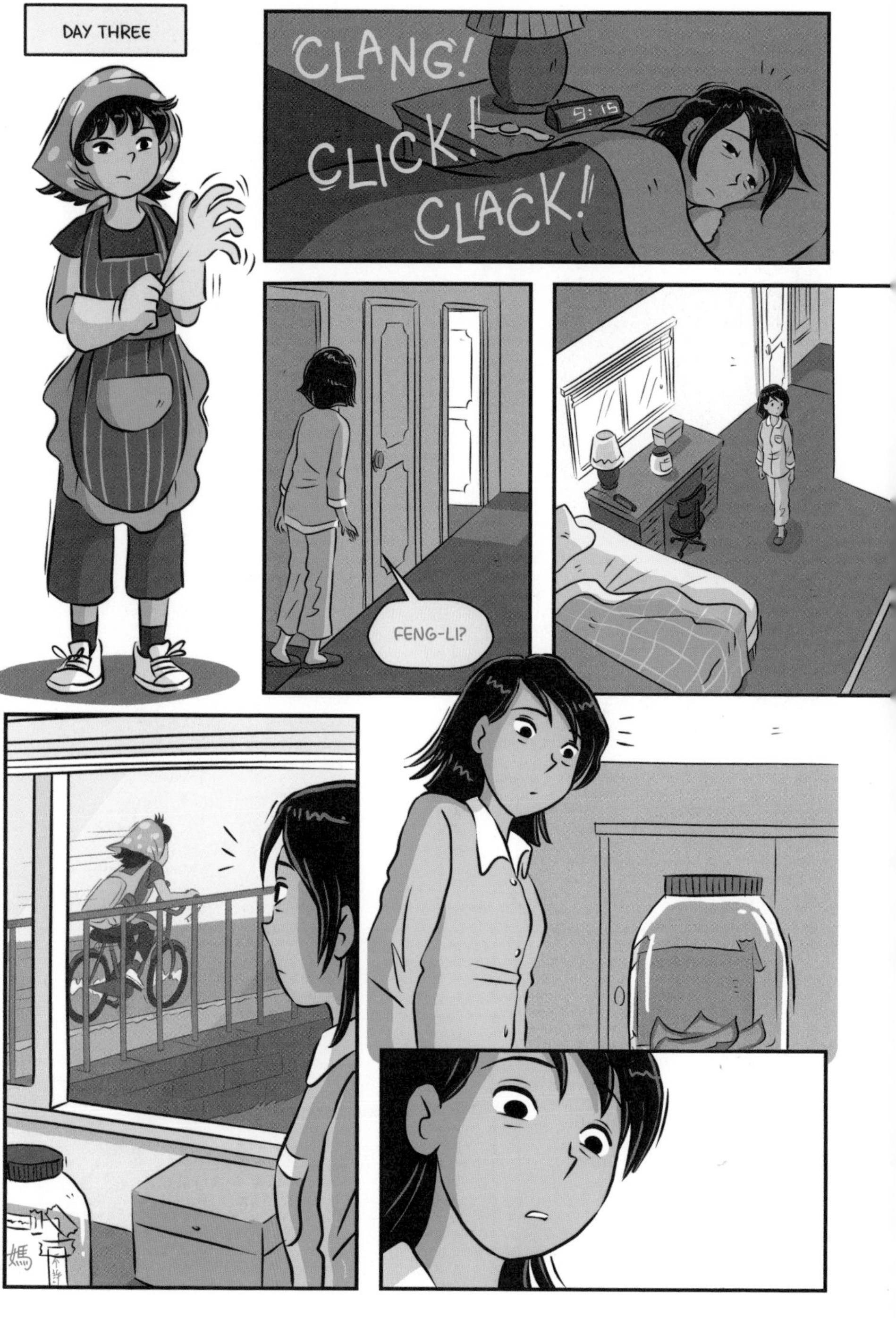
DAY THREE
CLANG!
CLICK!
CLACK!
9:15
FENG-LI?
媽

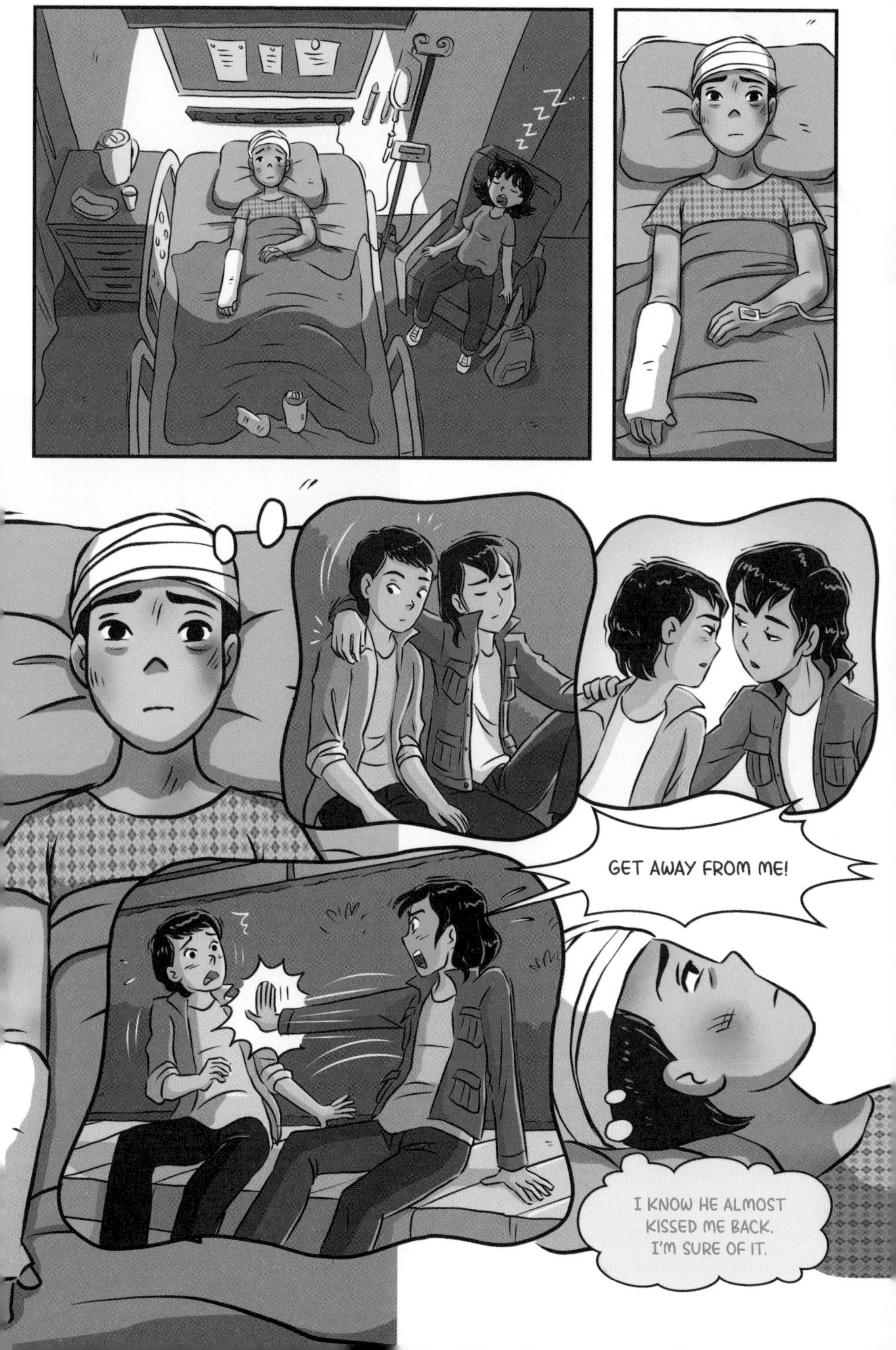
Z Z Z Z Z…
GET AWAY FROM ME!
I KNOW HE ALMOST
KISSED ME BACK.
I'M SURE OF IT.

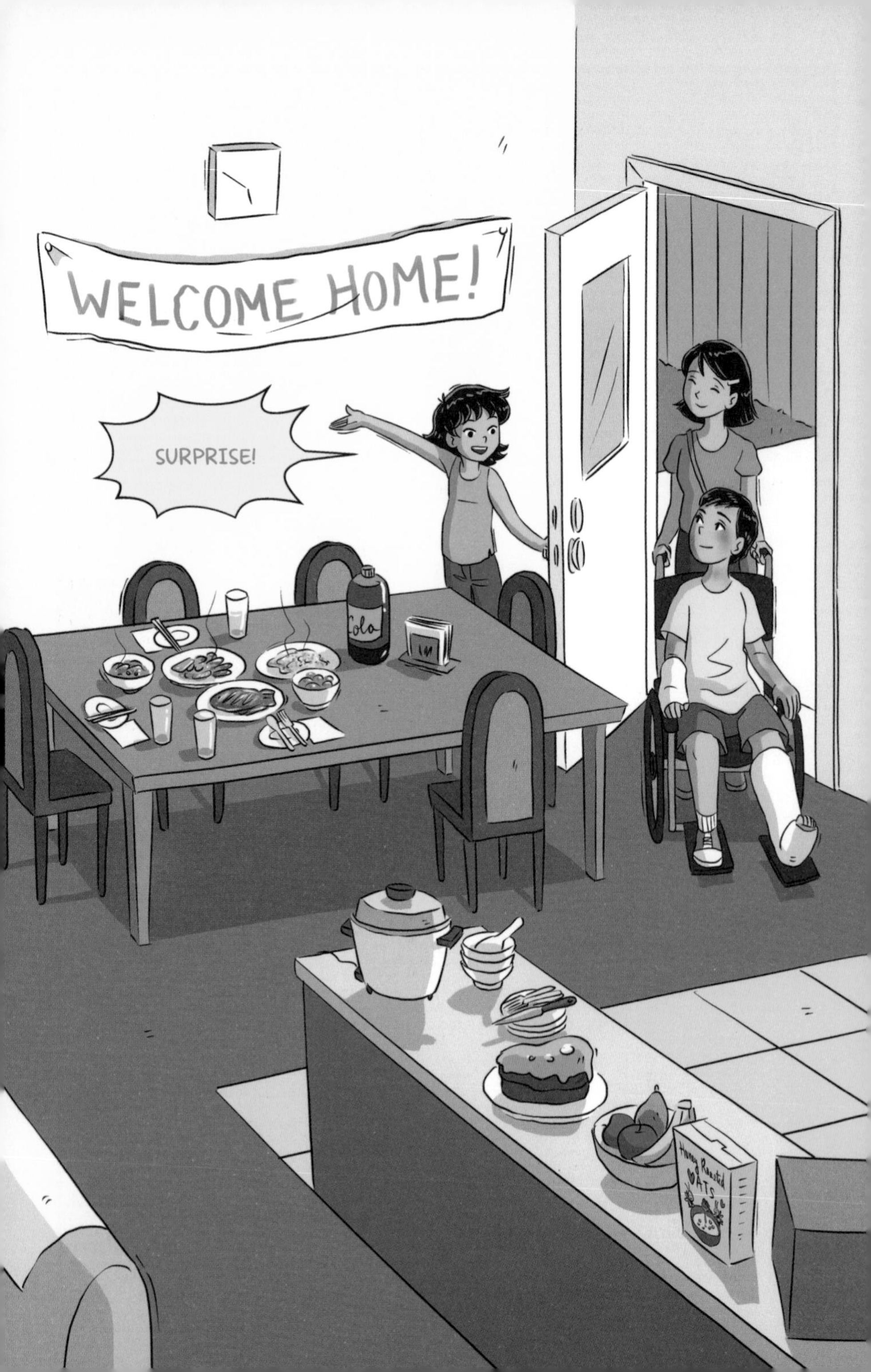
WELCOME HOME!
SURPRISE!
Cola
Honey Roasted OATS

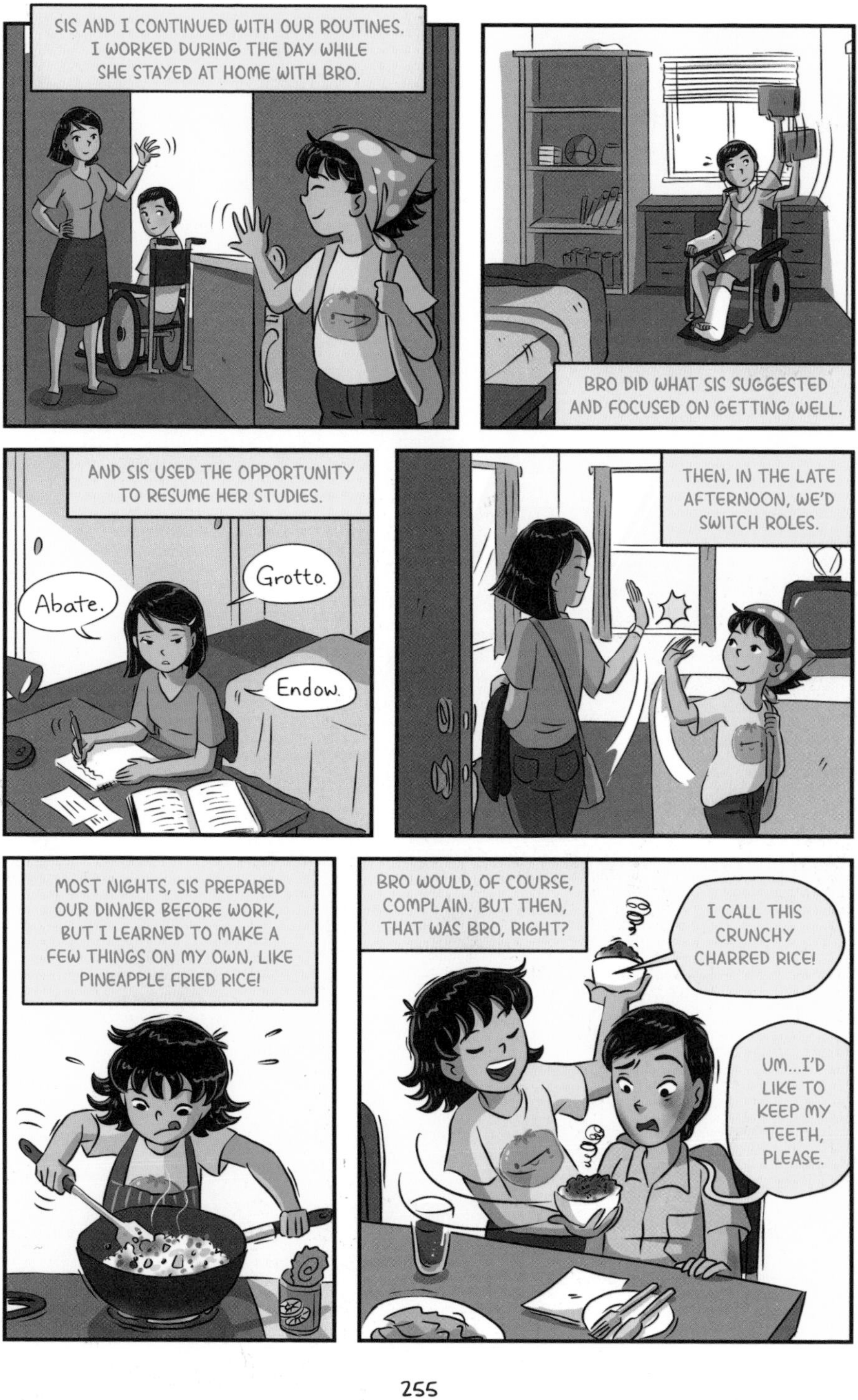
SIS AND I CONTINUED WITH OUR ROUTINES. I WORKED DURING THE DAY WHILE SHE STAYED AT HOME WITH BRO.
BRO DID WHAT SIS SUGGESTED AND FOCUSED ON GETTING WELL.
AND SIS USED THE OPPORTUNITY TO RESUME HER STUDIES.
Abate.
Grotto.
Endow.
THEN, IN THE LATE AFTERNOON, WE'D SWITCH ROLES.
MOST NIGHTS, SIS PREPARED OUR DINNER BEFORE WORK, BUT I LEARNED TO MAKE A FEW THINGS ON MY OWN, LIKE PINEAPPLE FRIED RICE!
BRO WOULD, OF COURSE, COMPLAIN. BUT THEN, THAT WAS BRO, RIGHT?
I CALL THIS CRUNCHY CHARRED RICE!
UM...I'D LIKE TO KEEP MY TEETH, PLEASE.

THEN, SURPRISE!

BABA AND I ARE COMING NEXT WEEK!

WE WORKED TOGETHER TO GET THE HOUSE READY.

IT WAS REALLY NICE TO SEE THEM NOT BICKER FOR ONCE.

AND AT LAST, A LETTER FROM JING-LING! SIS WAS RIGHT!

SORRY FOR NOT WRITING SOONER. WE WENT ON VACATION, AND I LEFT MY ADDRESS BOOK AT HOME.

BUT THE HORRENDOUS HOSPITAL BILL ALSO CAME.

RVICES .... $ 500.35
BORATORY .... $
OOM .... $ 5,250.50
CU .... $ 4,000.00
PHARMACY .... $ 750.25
EMERGENCY .... $ 2,500.00
INSURANCE PAID ... $ 0.00

$ 15,350.56   DUE: 08/15/81

WE TRIED NOT TO LET IT GET US DOWN.

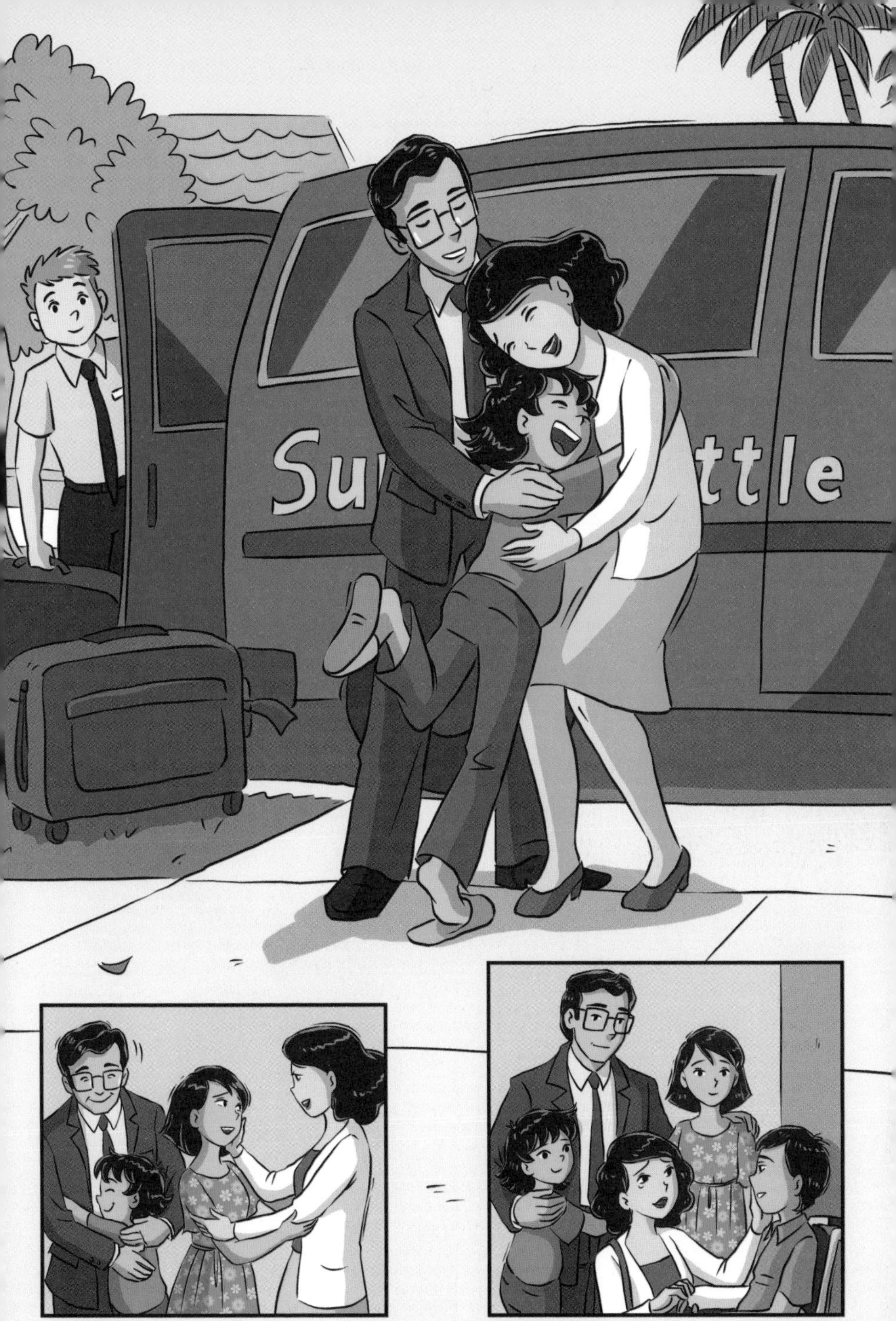
Su
ttle

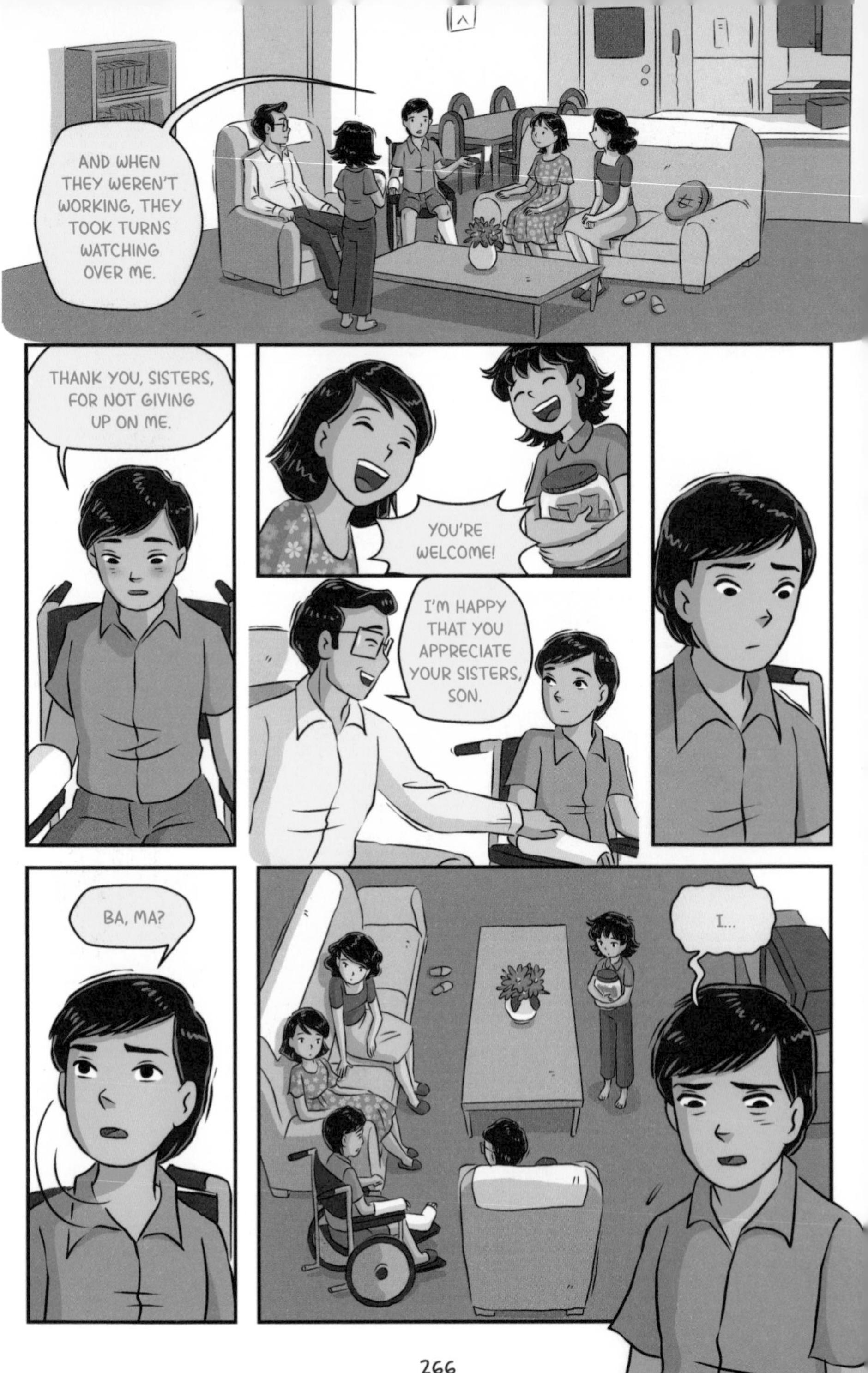
AND WHEN THEY WEREN'T WORKING, THEY TOOK TURNS WATCHING OVER ME.
THANK YOU, SISTERS, FOR NOT GIVING UP ON ME.
YOU'RE WELCOME!
I'M HAPPY THAT YOU APPRECIATE YOUR SISTERS, SON.
BA, MA?
I...

WE MOVED FORWARD WITH OUR LIVES.

SIS CONTINUED HER **S.A.T.** STUDIES.

BUT SHE ALSO HAD FUN.

giggle

SHE CONTINUED HER RESTAURANT JOB AND NOW KEPT HALF THE PAY FOR HERSELF.

BRO KEPT UP WITH HIS EXERCISES, BUT HE DIDN'T HIDE IN HIS ROOM ALL DAY LIKE BEFORE.

HE AND BABA EVEN TRIED PLAYING PLUMBER. **DIY** FOR THEM WAS ANOTHER AMERICAN FIRST.

EASY DIY PLUMBING

MY SCHOOL DIDN'T START YET. I GOT MAMA ALL TO MYSELF.

I DIDN'T CARE WHERE WE WENT...

WE HAD THE NICEST TIME TOGETHER.

50% off

SALE

OR WHAT WE DID.

I DIDN'T CHOOSE TO COME HERE. AMERICA ISN'T MY HOME, BUT IT'S STARTING TO GROW ON ME.
THERE WILL BE CHALLENGES AHEAD, BUT I FEEL CONFIDENT I WILL BE OKAY AS LONG AS I FACE THEM TOGETHER WITH MY FAMILY.

To all the parachute kids out there:
When the going gets tough,
remember, you can get through this.
You are never alone. This book is for you.

AUTHOR'S NOTE

The term *parachute kids* refers to children from Asia who have been "dropped off" with friends or relatives in foreign countries while their parents stayed behind. This practice has been ongoing for decades and continues today. Parachute kids face the challenges of a new country, culture, and language without their parents. My siblings and I were among these children.

In 1979, when the United States changed its diplomatic recognition of Taiwan to China, my parents—fearing war—made the decision to send us to the United States, while my dad stayed in Taiwan to earn money to support us and my mom visited us whenever she could. Like Feng-Li, I was an excited ten-year-old upon arrival, but soon found myself lonely and friendless. My siblings were around, but they had their own issues and were in no mood to hear about mine. I became unforgiving toward my parents, once even accusing my mother of abandoning me, which caused her much grief. Then, slowly, my English improved, which made all the difference in the world, as I could finally communicate and make friends. Eventually, the foreign turned familiar, and America became my new home. Now I fully appreciate the sacrifice my parents made to give us a more promising future. It could not have been an easy decision, for what parents would willingly break up the family and live apart from their children?

Parachute Kids is not a memoir, but a mixture of fiction, my family's first experiences in America, and anecdotes of immigrant friends I met along the way. I felt compelled to write it because I think it is important for more people to know about these children and their parents.

Asians in general are not very vocal. We are taught to work hard, mind our own business, and as the Chinese saying goes, "eat bitterness." So, to outsiders, it might appear that our achievements were easily attained, that we all come from money, or that we are all naturally smart. But what remains unsaid are the efforts, failures, and sacrifices. Through Feng-Li Lin and her siblings, I hope to show this struggle and share a small but important part of who we are.

I do feel a huge sense of responsibility in writing this book. I am aware that each parachute kid will have had their own unique experiences, different from the ones portrayed in the story. In no way am I trying to say that the Lin family's experiences are representative of all parachute kids. For how can any one book possibly represent an entire group of people or subject matter? Perhaps the answer is that we need more diverse books, so eventually, everyone can find a piece of themselves reflected and their voices heard. I hope *Parachute Kids* will encourage others to share their own unique stories.

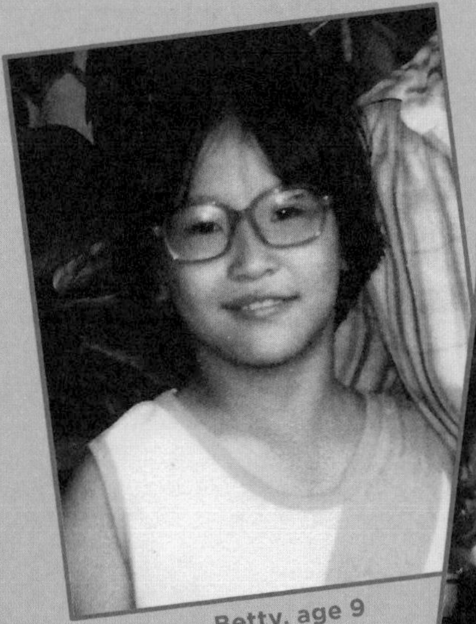

Betty, age 9

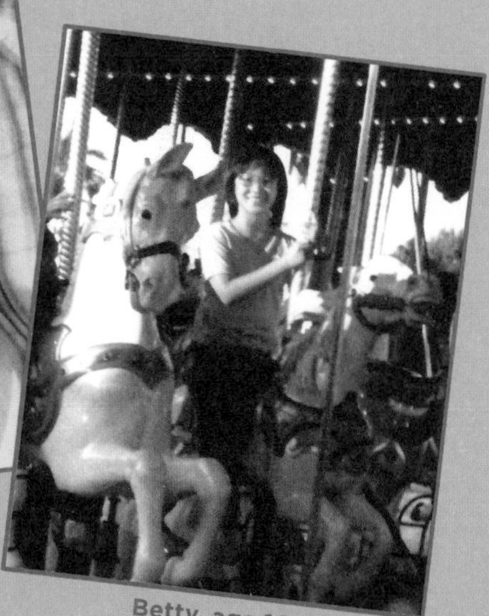

Betty, age 10

BETTY C. TANG is the *New York Times* bestselling illustrator of the Jacky Ha-Ha series of graphic novels by James Patterson and Chris Grabenstein. She has worked for various animation studios in Hollywood, including Disney TV and Dreamworks Animation, and codirected an animated feature called *Where's the Dragon?* Betty is also a fourth-degree black belt in aikido, a Japanese martial art. Born in Taiwan, Betty immigrated to California as a parachute kid when she was ten. She lives in Los Angeles. Learn more about her work at bettyctang.com.

ACKNOWLEDGMENTS

I want to express my gratitude to those who made this book possible: first and foremost, my parents, without whom I would not be who I am today; my siblings and friends, who generously shared their own experiences; my agent, Christy Ewers, who helped my career take flight; my editor, Tracy Mack, whose keen eye for detail helped me polish the story until it shined; my creative director and senior designer, Phil Falco and Carina Taylor, who came to my rescue and made everything work out; Leslie Owusu, the mighty editorial assistant who kept things flowing; everyone else at Scholastic and Graphix who contributed to this book; and last but not least, Andy Molisch, who supported me every step of the way. You are all the wind beneath my wings!